Abby I. B. Bulkley, Henry T. Beckwith

The Chad Browne Memorial

consisting of genealogical memoirs of a portion of the descendants of Chad and

Elizabeth Browne; with an appendix, containing sketches of other early Rhode

Island settlers, 1638-1888

Abby I. B. Bulkley, Henry T. Beckwith

The Chad Browne Memorial
*consisting of genealogical memoirs of a portion of the descendants of Chad and Elizabeth
Browne; with an appendix, containing sketches of other early Rhode Island settlers,
1638-1888*

ISBN/EAN: 9783337378806

Printed in Europe, USA, Canada, Australia, Japan

Cover: Foto ©Andreas Hilbeck / pixelio.de

More available books at **www.hansebooks.com**

THE

CHAD BROWNE MEMORIAL

'CONSISTING OF

GENEALOGICAL MEMOIRS

OF A

PORTION OF THE DESCENDANTS

OF

CHAD AND ELIZABETH BROWNE

WITH AN APPENDIX

CONTAINING SKETCHES OF OTHER EARLY RHODE ISLAND
SETTLERS,

1638=1888.

COMPILED BY A DESCENDANT.

PRINTED FOR THE FAMILY.

EDITION OF THREE HUNDRED ILLUSTRATED COPIES, OF WHICH THIS BOOK IS NO.-

BROOKLYN, N. Y.

Press of
Brooklyn Daily Eagle
Book Printing Department,
Brooklyn, N. Y.

1888.

PREFACE.

The Chad Browne Memorial is intended to supplement the "Genealogy of a Portion of the Brown Family," a pamphlet of sixteen pages, compiled by Henry Truman Beckwith, and printed in Providence, R. I., by Hugh H. Brown, in 1851. The title page states that it was derived "principally from the Moses Brown papers and from other authentic sources." Like its predecessor, this book follows chiefly the line of the eldest son John. No preference has here been given to the descendants of sons over that of daughters, as the aim has been to preserve the records of the Chad Browne posterity, irrespective of the name. This volume, though incomplete and imperfect, is the result of four years of laborious investigation and extensive correspondence. It is to be hoped that the publication of these memoirs may stimulate research, and that some future compiler may prepare a more extended work which shall include the lines of the younger sons, concerning which, at present, comparatively little is known.

Until nearly the close of the last century marriages were confined chiefly to Rhode Island families, about thirty of whom are closely connected with the Browns by frequent alliances. It has been deemed desirable to present sketches of the founders of these families, and, as far as possible, trace the line of descent. Much more could have been done in this direction, but research having been restricted in most instances to published records, the results are often incomplete. These sketches, with a few others of families outside of the State, form the Appendix.*

It will be observed that the Chad Browne Memorial is not strictly genealogical in its character. The design has been not only to preserve to coming generations an unbroken account of descent from the emigrant ancestor, but also to trace the influence of this family during the two hundred and fifty years that have elapsed since its founders, Chad and Elizabeth Browne, sailed from the Old World to found a home in New England. It is believed that few similar works contain an equal number of names illustrious for the service their possessors rendered to the times in which they lived, and for the provision they made with reference to the

---

* "The annals of Rhode Island are unique. The heroic steps by which a few exiles, banished from Massachusetts Bay for political and religious heresies, founded a permanent colony on the shores of the Narragansett Bay, based on new and untried theories of religion and politics, will never cease to interest the historian and the philosopher. The influence and example of this little colony of freemen have not yet ceased to affect the interests of mankind."—*New England Hist. and Genealogical Register*, Oct., 1877. C. W. T.

welfare of future generations. Example is often more powerful for good than precept, and many of the lives here recorded are well worthy of emulation.

The genealogical arrangement requires little explanation. The names at the right of heads of families, enclosed in parenthesis, indicate the line of descent. The figures attached to these names are for reference, by means of which each preceding generation can be distinctly identified. Every name bearing a number (No. 1 excepted) appears twice : first, in connection with the parents, and later, when the subsequent history is traced. Names which bear no number do not reappear. In other instances where the line of descent is indicated by names included in parenthesis, the accompanying figures simply point out the number of the generation.

Acknowledgments are gratefully tendered to the many individuals of the family, as well as to those not connected with it by ties of kindred, without whose friendly aid and zealous co-operation this volume could have had no existence. The information has been derived from many sources, both public and private, and only that deemed trustworthy has been admitted. Should errors be detected, the finder will confer a favor by communicating the correction to the author, in order that a list of the same may be inserted in the copy to be placed in the Library of the Rhode Island Historical Society.

ABBY ISABEL (BROWN) BULKLEY.

BROOKLYN, N. Y., March 14, 1888.
No. 167 South Elliott Place.

CONTENTS.

LIST OF ILLUSTRATIONS.

The Chad Brown Memorial.

FIRST GENERATION.

1. Of the parentage, birthplace and early history of Chad Brown nothing is now known. Accompanied by his wife Elizabeth and son John, then eight years of age, and perhaps his younger sons, he emigrated from England in the ship Martin, which arrived in Boston, Mass., July, 1638. A fellow passenger, Sylvester Baldwin, of Aston Clinton, Bucks Co., Eng., died during the voyage, and Chad Brown, soon after his arrival, witnessed the nuncupative will. Of this Savage gives the following account :
"On the main ocean, bound for N. E., his nuncupative will was made 21 June, and proved 13 July of that year, before Dep. Gov. Dudley, by oaths of Chad Brown, Francis Bolt, James Weeden and John Baldwin."

It is probable that his religious views were not in harmony with those of the Massachussetts settlers, as he soon removed to Providence, where he became at once a leader in the colony and one of its most valued citizens. According to tradition, he was an exile from Salem "for conscience' sake." His coming to Providence was the same year of his arrival, and there, with twelve others, he signed the following compact : "We whose names are hereunder, desirous to inhabit in the town of Providence, do promise to subject ourselves in active or passive obedience to all such orders or agreements as shall be made for the public good of the body, in an orderly way, by the major assent of the present inhabitants, masters of families, incorporated together into a town fellowship, and such others as they shall admit into them, only in civil things."

In his capacity as surveyor, he was soon after appointed on a committee to compile a list of the Home Lots of the first settlers on the "Towne Streete" and the meadows allotted to them. It is to this important work that we are indebted for our knowledge of these properties. His Home Lot fronted on the "Towne Streete," now South Main and Market Square, with the southern boundary to the southward of College and South Main Streets. It was about one hundred and twelve feet wide, and extended eastwardly to the "Highway," now Hope Street. The College Grounds of Brown University comprise a large portion of this lot.

In 1640 he served on a committee with three others regarding the disputed boundary line between Providence and Pawtuxet. They reported in July that they had given the matter serious and careful consideration. "We have gone the fairest and equallest way to produce our peace."

The same year, Robert Cole, Chad Brown, William Harris and John Warner, were the committee of Providence Colony who reported to them their first written form of government, which was adopted and continued in force until 1644, when Roger Williams returned from England with the first Charter. Of the thirty-nine signatures to this agreement, Chad Brown's is the first. This instrument contains the arbitration decision to which in later years Roger Williams, in speaking of the dissensions which so disturbed the peace of the early colonists referred on this wise : "'The truth is that Chad Brown, that Holy man, now with God, and myself, brought the remaining after-comers and the first twelve to a one-ness by arbitration."

In 1642 he was ordained as the first settled Pastor of the Baptist Church and is thus mentioned by Hague in his Historical Discourse : "Contemporary with Roger Williams, he possessed a cooler temperament, and was happily adapted to sustain the interests of religion just where that great man failed. Not being affected by the arguments of the Seekers, he maintained his standing firmly in a church which he believed to be founded on the Rock of eternal truth 'even the Word of God which abideth forever.' We know only enough of his character to excite the wish to know more : but from that little it is clear that he was highly esteemed as a man of sound judgment and of a Christian spirit. Often referred to as the arbitrator of existing differences, in a state of society where individual influence was needed as a substitute for well digested laws, he won that commendation which the Savior pronounced when he said, 'blessed are the peace-makers, for they shall be called the children of God.'"

In 1643 he was on a committee to negotiate peace between the Warwick settlers and Massachusetts Bay. Their efforts, however, proved ineffectual, and it was not until 1665 that the claims of Massachusetts Bay Colony in regard to Warwick were set aside by the Royal Commissioners, and a decision rendered in favor of the Rhode Island and Providence Plantations.

It is evident that he died some years earlier than has been supposed, as the name of his widow occurs in a tax list of Sept. 2, 1650. His sons allude in deeds to the will of their father. Chad and Elizabeth Browne were buried in an orchard on his Home Lot, College Street, corner of Benefit, where the County Court House now stands. Their remains were removed in 1792 to the Nicholas Brown lot in the North Burial Ground where a stone with this inscription marks the spot :

" In Memory of
CHAD BROWN,
Elder of the Baptist Church in
this Town.
He was one of the original Proprietors of
the Providence Purchase,
Having been exiled from Massachusetts
for conscience' sake.
He had five sons,
JOHN, JAMES, JEREMIAH, CHAD AND DANIEL,
Who have left a numerous Posterity.
He died about A. D. 1665.
This Monument
Was erected by the Town of Providence."

Other early settlers bore the name of Browne and may have been related to Chad, but of this no evidence exists. The final E has been dropped by nearly all the descendants of Chad Browne, and occurs at the present time only in the Glocester, R. I. branch.

The children of Chad and Elizabeth Browne were:

2. i. JOHN, b. 1630.
   ii. JAMES, } removed to Newport, R. I.
   iii. JEREMIAH, }
   iv. JUDAH, or CHAD, d. May 10, 1663, unmarried.
   v. DANIEL.

SECOND GENERATION.

2. JOHN BROWN (*Chad*¹), b. 1630, d. about 1706, m. Mary, daughter of Rev. Obadiah and Catharine Holmes of Newport, R. I. He resided in Providence at the North End, in the house afterwards occupied by his son, Elder James, near the junction of North Main and Randall Streets. We learn from the town records that he frequently served as Juryman, was commissioner on union of towns in 1654, and Freeman in 1665. Like his father he was a surveyor as well as Baptist Elder, and in 1659 was appointed Surveyor of Highways. He served on various committees, was moderator, member of the Town Council, deputy in legislature, assistant, and took the oath of allegiance, May 31, 1666. In 1661 the town allowed a way that had been laid out across his land and other lots to be fenced under certain restrictions. It was afterwards laid out as Camp Street.

In 1672, after the death of his mother, he sold the home lot of his father to his brother James of Newport, who re-sold it the same day to Daniel Abbot. The burial place of his parents, twenty feet square with free egress, was reserved. Nearly one hundred years later, his great grandsons, John and Moses Brown, repurchased a part of this land, and presented it to the College of Rhode Island, at the time of its removal from Warren to Providence. On the 14th of May, 1770, the corner-stone of University Hall, the first and for many years the only building, was laid by John Brown. In 1804, the name of the institution was changed to Brown University.

In 1701 he and Pardon Tillinghast, elders of the church, ordained James Clarke as pastor of the Second Baptist Church in Newport.

CHILDREN.

i. SARAH, m. Nov. 14, 1678, John Pray, of Richard and Mary Pray. He d. Oct. 9, 1730. She d. after 1733. They had eight children :—*John, Hugh, Richard, Mary, Catharine, Sarah, Penelope, Martha.* Of these, *Catharine* m. Hazadiah[4] Comstock (*Samuel,*[3] *Samuel,*[2] *William*[1]), and had ten children. She d. Nov. 27, 1728. He was born April 16, 1682, and died Feb 21, 1764 He had a mare worth £2, taken from him for not training, he being a Quaker. The mare was afterwards returned. They had 10 children.

Sarah m Capt. Joseph Brown, son of Henry and Waite (Waterman) Brown, and had 10 children, among whom were three sons, Stephen, Benjamin and Joseph. They lived in Smithfield, R. I *Penelope* m John Aldrich, of Jacob and Huldah (Thayer) Aldrich, and had 10 children.

Martha m. Joseph Wilkinson, of Samuel and Plain (Wickenden) Wilkinson, and had 15 children.

3. ii. JOHN, b. March 18, 1662 (Ensign).
4. iii. JAMES, b. 1666.
5. iv. OBADIAH.
6. v.   MARTHA.
7. vi. MARY.
   vii. DEBORAH.

BROWN UNIVERSITY.

THIRD GENERATION.

3. JOHN⁴ BROWN (*John,²* *Chad¹*), b. March 18, 1662, d.
Sept. 19, 1719, held the title of Ensign, and lived in Johnston,
R. I. May 20, 1706, he deeded to his brother Obadiah, certain
lands inherited from his father. The inventory of his personal
estate amounted to £253, 1s. 8d. His real estate consisted of the
homestead, farm, &c., £500 ; lands and meadows at Wanscott,
£100 ; land west of the Seven Mile Line, &c. He married June
9, 1696, Isabel, dau. of James and Hannah (Field) Matthewson,
and gr. dau. of John Field. She d. after 1719.

CHILDREN.

  i. JOHN, b. March 26, 1697. d at Newport, R. I., in 1764. Is said
      to have been a successful shipping merchant.
  ii MARY, b. July 30, 1699.
  iii. LYDIA, b. Dec. 21, 1701.
  iv. ISABEL, b. April 17, 1705, was m. June 10, 1722, to Joseph Smith,
      Jr. (*Joseph,³* *John,²* *John Smith¹ Miller*). One of her
      descendants, *Naomi A. Angell*, b. March 7, 1788, became
      the third wife of Judge Samuel Eddy. (See No. 11)
  v. NATHAN, b. Aug. 24, 1707, d. Sept. 17, 1783.
  vi. OBADIAH, b. Aug. 17, 1710, d. April 27, 1753. He m. Martha*
      ——, who may have been dau. of Benjamin Waterman, gr.
      dau. of Nathaniel and g. gr. dau. of the first Richard Water-
      man. She d. Dec. 3, 1778, in her 63d year. Of their children,
      Isabel, d. Feb. 5, 1753, in her 16th year. *Obadiah, Jr.*,
      belonged to Sullivan's Life Guards, who particularly distin-
      guished themselves in the repulse of the British forces on
      Rhode Island. "He fell bravely fighting for the liberties of
      his country, Aug. 29, 1778, in his 36th year." His remains
      were interred in the North Ground, Providence, where a stone
      marks the spot. *Nathan* d. May 11, 1750, aged 3 years and
      six months.

4. JAMES BROWN (*John,²* *Chad¹*), b. 1666, d. Oct. 28,
1732. He m. Dec. 17, 1691, Mary, dau. of Andrew and Mary
(Tew) Harris, gr. dau. of William and Susannah Harris, and
also gr. dau. of Richard and Mary (Clarke) Tew. She was b.
Dec. 17, 1671, and d. Aug. 18, 1736. From 1705–1725 he served
almost continuously as member of the Town Council, and from
1714–'18 was Town Treasurer. He was pastor or elder of the
First Baptist Church, being associated first with Elder Pardon
Tillinghast, and later with Rev. Ebenezer Jenckes. In 1726 he
succeeded the latter in the ministry, remaining pastor until his
death in 1732. †Edwards says : " He was an example of piety
and meekness worthy of admiration."

His will, made March 3, 1728, indicates that he did not lack
thrift in wordly matters. His older sons, partly provided for in

* Benjamin Waterman mentions in his will of Oct. 9, 1765, his daughter Martha
Brown, and his grand-daughter Amey, wife of Obadiah Brown.
† See Hague's Hist. Discourse and Benedict's History of the Baptists.

his lifetime, were well remembered. His two daughters, Mary and Ann, (the former died before her father) were to receive £200 each, partly paid with a negro woman at £80, and also two lots in town each. To his grandson, James Greene, then in the fourth year of his age, he gave 150 acres of land, a lot in Town, and adds, "And I give him one Cow and a Calfe." His two younger sons, Jeremiah and Elisha, minors, were made residuary legatees in equal portions. They were to care for their mother, receiving the homestead at her death, and to provide suitable things for her, "as firewood, vittles and drink for her comfort." The inventory of his personal estate amounted to £915, 6d. The items, "2 Hogsheads of sider and 4 Hogsheads of apple beere," give assurance that good cheer was not wanting. Of tobacco there were 133 pounds in store. A negro woman and child, Quassie and Cuffie, are valued at £100.

It is evident that Elder James was a dutiful son, as his father, July 6, 1690, deeded to him "for his well being and settlement, and also in consideration of his good obedience and pains, care and diligence which he constantly hath taken in providing for my family, my three house lots or home shares of land lying all together, with my dwelling house, etc. and other land." The conditions were, use of the house and comfortable maintainance for life of his parents.

CHILDREN.

   i. JOHN, b. Oct. 8, 1695 ; d. unm. aged about 21.
8. ii. JAMES, b. March 22, 1698.
9. iii. JOSEPH, b. May 5, 1701.
   iv. MARTHA, b. Oct. 12, 1703. m. Sept. 26, 1723, Rev. Elisha[4] Greene of Warwick, R. I. (James,[3] James,[2] John Greene[1], surgeon). She d. July 27, 1725, leaving a son James, b. Sept. 15, 1724, who m. Dec. 12, 1745, Freelove Burlingame. She d. March 6, 1761, in the 34th year of her age. Had issue.
10. v. ANDREW, b. Sept. 20, 1706.
   vi. MARY, b. April 29, 1708 ; d Feb. 20, 1729.
11. vii. ANNA, b. 1710.
12. viii. OBADIAH, b. Oct. 2, 1712.
13. ix. JEREMIAH, b. Nov. 25, 1715.
14. x. ELISHA, b. May 25, 1717.

5. OBADIAH BROWN (*John,*[2] *Chad*[1]), d. Aug. 24, 1716. The name of his wife was Mary. In 1688 his name occurs in the list of taxable persons over sixteen years of age. The inventory of his personal property amounted to £377, 1d.

CHILDREN.

   i. JOHN, JR. March 23, 1728, he deeded to Chad Browne, his brother, 200 acres of land on Chepachet Hill, "Being laid out the most part in or upon the original right of Mr. Chad Browne deceased, and part being land my honored father, the above named Obadiah Browne, bought of the purchasers." (See Providence Deeds, Book 6, p. 52. Also, Book 8, pages 364 and 366).

15. ii. CHAD, b. Oct. 13, 1705.

6. MARTHA BROWN (*John*,[2] *Chad*[1]). m. Joseph[3] Jenckes, who was b. 1656 (*Joseph*[2], *Joseph*[1]). He was grandson of the first Joseph Jenckes of Buckinghamshire, Eng., who emigrated with the Winthrop company in 1630, and settled in Lynn, Mass., where he erected a brass and iron foundry, the first on this continent. His eldest son, Joseph, who accompanied his father, afterwards established himself in the same business at Pawtucket, R. I., where Joseph Jenckes[3] was born.

Gov. Jenckes early entered public life. He was Freeman in 1681, then Deputy; Speaker of House of Deputies, Major for the Main,* and Assistant. He held the office of Deputy Governor from 1715-1727. During this time he was appointed Agent in England to settle the boundary dispute between Rhode Island and the neighboring colonies, Massachusetts and Connecticut. He served as Governor from 1727 to 1732, residing during most of his term at Newport. Benedict says of him that he was "distinguished not only by the urbanity of his manners and intellectual endowments, but by the graces of religion." It is recorded that he was the tallest man of his time in Rhode Island, being two inches over seven feet in height.

The inscription on his tomb in the North Burial Ground is as follows: "In memory of Hon. Joseph Jencks, Esq., late Governor of the Colony of Rhode Island, deceased the 15th day of June, A D. 1740, in the eighty-fourth year of his age. He was much Honored and Beloved in Life and Lamented in Death. He was a bright example of Virtue in every Stage of Life. He was a zealous Christian, a Wise and Prudent Governor, a Kind Husband and a Tender Father, a good Neighbor and a Faithful Friend, Grave, Sober, Pleasant in Behavior, Beautiful in Person with a soul truly Great, Heroic and Sweetly Tempered."

CHILDREN.

i. JOSEPH, d. young.
16. ii. OBADIAH.
17. iii. CATHARINE
iv. NATHANIEL (Captain), m. Catharine Scott[4] (*Sylvanus*,[3] *John*,[2] *Richard*[1]).
v. MARTHA d. after 1719. She m. James Andrew, son of John, who d. July 10, 1716. He was a mariner. The widow Martha, Oct. 8, 1719, deeded to her only child *John*, for love, etc., a half part of 128 acres in Coweset, and half part of a right in undivided lands there, and said son being in minority, she appointed her brother, John Jenckes, of Providence "Studiant in Physic and Chirurgery, feoffe in trust for said son." She m. 2d, Peleg Cook.

* Highest military title of the period.

vi. LYDIA.
18. vii. JOHN.
19. viii. MARY.
    ix. ESTHER.

7. MARY BROWN (*John,* *Chad*[1]), m. Arthur Aylworth, who came to America from either England or Wales, previous to July, 1679, and settled at Quidnesset, North Kingstown, R. I., where he died about 1726. It is supposed that she died some years earlier.

CHILDREN. (Order not positively known).

i. ROBERT. d. 1760; m. May 20, 1708, Anna Davis, and had 6 children.

ii. ARTHUR, b. 1685, d. July, 1761 ; m. Mary Franklin, and had 9 children. A descendant in the eighth generation, Cora Elizabeth Aylsworth (*Hiram B.,*[7] *Eli,*[6] *Arthur.*[5] *James,*[4] *Philip,*[3] *Arthur,*[2] *Arthur,*[1]) m. Feb. 12, 1885, Arthur Lewis Brown, in the eighth generation from Chad.

iii. JOHN, d. 1771, m. Dorcas, dau. of Josiah and Elizabeth Jones, and had 8 children.

iv. PHILIP, b. 1692, m. Rachel, b. May 6. 1698, dau. of Daniel and Rebecca (Barrow) Greene, and gr. dau. of John and Joan Greene of North Kingstown. (Not John Greene Surgeon). They had 12 children. the last 5 of whom died young.

v. CHAD, OR JEDIAH, b. 1686. d. March 23, 1773 ; m. Nov. 15, 1725, Elizabeth, dau. of David Major of the island of Guernsey. She died in Foster, R. I., leaving six children, the eldest of whom, *Capt. Thomas,* b. Aug. 21, 1736, m. for his second wife, Martha, dau. of Amos and Mary (Bates) Harrington, and was the great grandfather of Dr. Homer[6] E. Aylsworth, the compiler of "Arthur Aylworth and his Descendants in America," Providence, R. I., 1887. (*Perry,*[5] *Elhanan,*[4] *Capt. Thomas.*[3] *Chad.*[2] *Arthur;*[1]).

Homer E. Aylsworth was born Sept. 8, 1838, in Burlington, Otsego Co., N. Y., and died at his residence, Roseville, Warren Co., Ill., Jan. 30, 1885. In his youth he was a student of music, for which he possessed talents of a high order, and subsequently taught music, and in the schools of Michigan and Illinois. In 1861 he entered Union College, Schenectady, N Y., for the scientific course, where he graduated in 1863 with the degree of A. M. After a year's interval spent in teaching, he returned to Illinois and commenced the study of medicine at Roseville. Later he attended medical lectures at Ann Arbor, and graduated at the University of Michigan in 1867. He engaged in the active practice of his profession at Roseville for a year, and then founded the Pioneer Drug Store, successfully conducting the business until his death. He was an upright business man, a pronounced advocate of temperance, and an exemplary Christian in the Methodist Church with which he had been connected from the age of thirteen. His death was deeply lamented in the community in which he lived. He married, June 26, 1867, Flora A. Jones (adopted name, Eldridge, foster daughter of Truman Eldridge). She is a descendant in the eighth generation from Arthur and Mary (Brown) Aylworth. Their three children are Murray

Delong, b. May 9, 1870; Mabel Whitford, b. July 20, 1876;
Ivan Stewart, b. March 2, 1878. The grandmother of Dr.
H. E. Aylsworth was Mary (Harrington) Aylsworth, a great
grand-daughter of Gov. Joseph and Martha (Brown)
Jenckes. Thus the present generation of this family have
a three-fold descent from Chad Browne.

vi. MARY, m. John Greene, son of Benjamin* and Humility
(Coggeshall) Greene, and grandson of John and Joan Greene
of North Kingstown They had 12 children, of whom
Benjamin, the second, married Mercy Rogers. From this
line descends Flora A. Eldridge, who married Dr. H E.
Aylsworth.

vii. ELIZABETH, m. —— Dolliver, or Dolover. She m. 2d Peleg
Card, and had seven children.

viii. CATHARINE, m. —— Greene.

ix. MARTHA, m. before Dec. 1, 1727, John Davis of East Greenwich, who died before Feb. 25, 1738.

The *Aylsworth Register*, published in Utica in 1840, by
Sylvester Aylsworth, mentions another son of Arthur and
Mary (Brown) Aylsworth, Thomas, deaf and dumb. No
issue.

* Daniel Greene who m. Rebecca Barrow, and Benjamin were brothers.

FOURTH GENERATION.

8. JAMES BROWN (*James,*[4] *John,*[2] *Chad*[1]), b. March 22,
1698, d. April 27, 1739. The house which he owned and occupied on South Main Street, was afterwards removed to the south
side of Wickenden Street, between Hope and East Streets, and
Mallet's Building erected on the site. It has since been demolished. The following item is from the will of his father, Elder
James : "I give unto my Eldest sonne, James Browne, he having Received part of his Portion already, one Lot of Land in the
Stated Common as it fell on the Frances Wickes Right as will
appear by Record, and my severall Rights in the Ceedar Swamp
at Wanscutt, and one quarter of my several Rights in the
Thatch beds. And I give to him my Greate Bible and my Book
called Roberd's Key. I also give him my gun which was my
father's."

He m. Hope. dau. of Nicholas[3] and Mercy (Tillinghast)
Power, and gr.-dau. of Elder Pardon & Lydia (Tabor) Tillinghast. He entered into business shortly after his marriage, and
later his younger brother Obadiah, became a partner. These
brothers were the founders of the commercial house of the Browns.
His widow, Hope Brown, survived him more than fifty years.
She was born January 4, 1702, and died June 8, 1792, in her 91st
year. It is recorded upon her tomb-stone that she was the
mother of *Nicholas*, *Joseph*, *John* and *Moses Brown*.

CHILDREN.

    i.   James, b. Feb. 12, 1724, d. unmarried at York, Va. in 1750.
         Was master of a vessel.
20. ii.   Nicholas, b. July 28, 1729.
         Mary, b. 1731, d. May 26 1795, She m. Dr. John Van-
         derlight, son of John, and grandson of Cornelius Van-
         derlight of Steenwyk.* Holland. He was a graduate of
         Leyden University, and the first to give practical instruction
         in anatomy in Providence. He was the principal druggist
         of the town, and lived on South Main Street, between Col-
         lege and Hopkins, where his house, a wooden structure
         erected in 1745 (Young's Hotel), is still standing, in good
         preservation and but little changed in appearance In con-
         nection with his brothers in-law, he engaged in the manu-
         facture of candles, having brought with him from Europe
         a knowledge of the Dutch process of separating spermaceti
         from its oil. He d. Feb. 14, 1755. Their only child, *John*,
         d. Feb. 9, 1755, aged ten months. After the death of her
         husband, the widow resided with her brother Moses, at
         whose house she died.
21. iv.   Joseph, b. Dec. 3, 1733.
22. v.   John, b. Jan. 27, 1736.
23. vi.   Moses, b. Sept. 12, 1728.
         The names of these sons will be recognized as those of
         "the four brothers," whose history is intimately connected
         with that of the times in which they lived.

* A town near the eastern shore of Zuider Zee.

9. JOSEPH BROWN (*James*,[4] *John*,[2] *Chad*[1]), b. May 5, 1701, d. May 8, 1778. He lived in North Providence. The following item is from the will of his father, Elder James, of which he and his brother James were the executors. "I give to my son Joseph Browne, he having received part of his Portion already, Two Lotts which I bought of Edward Manton on the north, Joyneing to the Land now in possession of Job Harris, and on the south side with my own Land : and also the highway that I bought of the Towne, so far as across the two Lotts ; and I give him also three quarters of John Joneses Right in that part Called the stated Common, as it fell by devise which may appear by Record, And I give him half a Lott in the same Right which Lies neare Waterman's meadow, south westerly of Waybanset, neare the Lime House as may appeare by Record. I also give him one quarter of my severall Rights in the Thatch beds." He received £40 from the will of his mother, who died in 1736.

He m. Jan. 7, 1727. Martha, dau. of William and Martha Field, and gr.-dau. of Thomas and Martha (Harris) Field. The latter was dau. of the first Thomas and Elizabeth Harris. She d. April 19, 1736, in her 26th year, leaving a son *Gideon*, mentioned in the will of his grandfather William Field, who also alludes to an elder brother of *Gideon*, name unknown. He m. 2d, Abigail Waterman, who d. May 23, 1784, aged 73.

CHILDREN.

    JOSEPH, b. 1739, d. March 1802 ; m. ———. Had two sons.
        Obadiah, b. 1762, d. Feb. 14, 1815, and Joseph, Jr., d. 1791, at the age of 16.
24.   ELISHA, b April 1, 1748
25.   ANDREW, b. July 30, 1750.

10. ANDREW BROWN (*James*,[4] *John*,[2] *Chad*[1]), b. Sept. 20, 1706, d. Feb. 12, 1783. He removed about 1730 to Glocester, where he purchased a large tract of land on the east side of Chepachet river, in the south part of the town. Somewhat later his cousin Chad (*Obadiah*,[3] *John*,[2] *Chad*[1]), bought adjoining land on the west side of the river, two miles southeast of the present village. Two other cousins, Othniel Brown (*Hosanna*,[3] *Daniel*,[2] *Chad*[1]), and Obadiah Jenckes (*Martha*,[3] *John*,[2] *Chad*[1]), also settled in Glocester. He was admitted Freeman in May, 1732, and was the first town clerk. Backus says of him : "He was a Justice of Peace in the State, and long an exemplary Christian in the Baptist Church."

The following is from the will of his father, Elder James : "Item.—I give to my son, Andrew, my house at Chapatsett, and one-half of all my Land that is Laid out to me there, the one-half beside six acres in the Pine Swamp which I give to him, and one-half of all the Rest of my Land at Chapatsett, for him to have the northermost part so as to divide Equal by quantity :

only Andrew to have that six Acres by Reason of sum waste
Land in that Part : I also Give to my son, Andrew, one Lott
of Land in Towne of fifty foot wide north and south, and eighty
foot long east and west to be against William Turpins, joyneing
on the south to the Seator house Lott. I also Give to my son,
Andrew, one-half of my Right of the Seven Mile line, that right
which did belong to Chad Browne, the devisions that are already
agreed upon only excepted." He m. Mary Knowlton, dau. of
Elisha.

CHILDREN.

i. ANNE, b. July 7,1734, m. Oct. 14. 1756, Knight[5] Dexter
   (Stephen,[4]John,[3] Stephen,[2] Gregory[1]). She d. Feb. 4, 1759,
   without issue.
ii. RHOBY, b. Aug. 6, 1741. d young.
iii. ELISHA, b. May 11, 1744, m. Huldah Arnold of Smithfield.
   and had 8 children. (1.) Mary, b. Oct, 29, 1768, m. Joseph
   Steere of Glocester. She is spoken of by the late Col.
   George H. Browne as a woman of intelligence, to whom and
   his grandfather Esek, he was indebted for information regarding Andrew Brown and his descendants. The records
   of the Glocester Browns have been derived largely from the
   papers of Col. Browne compiled in 1850 to '52 supplemented
   by recent letters of Alexander Eddy, Esq., of Chepachet,
   and the History of Glocester, R. I., by Elizabeth A. Perry,
   published in 1885. (2.) Rhoby, b. Oct. 12, 1771, m. John
   Hawkins, and had Ara and Allen Hawkins. She m. 2d.
   Richard Burlingame, and had Brown Burlingame. Ara
   Hawkins, who owned and lived on the farm of his great-
   grandfather, Andrew Brown, died recently at the age of 95.
   Allen Hawkins aged 90 is still living (1887). The house occupied by Elisha[5] Brown was built for him by his father,
   Andrew, who also settled upon him a part of his lands. (3.)
   Phebe, b. Dec. 19, 1773, m. Dr. Ezra Winsor, and removed
   to Laurens, N. Y. Had issue. (4.) Andrew, b. May 24,
   1778, m. ——— and removed to Sutton, Vt. Had issue.
   (5.) Thomas, b. May 24, 1778, m. Abby, dau. of Capt.
   Solomon Owen. (6.) Anna, b. Aug. 15, 1780, m. her
   second cousin, James Fenner, son of John and Phebe
   (Brown) Fenner. Removed to Ohio. Had issue. (7.) Sarah,
   b. Oct, 8, 1782, m. Daniel Medbury, and had 2 sons and 4
   daus. Removed to Pomfret, Ct. (8.) Arnold, b. March
   13, 1786, m. Feb. 21, 1808, Betsey, dau. of Capt. Solomon
   Owen. He and his brother Thomas, each with large families
   removed about 1830, to Ohio, where there descendants still
   live. Andrew Brown, son of Thomas, resides in Oxford,
   Ohio, and Elizabeth, dau. of Arnold, in Troy, Ohio
   Joseph, son of Arnold, removed to La Fayette, Indiana.
   The wives of Thomas and Arnold Brown were sisters, daus.
   of Capt. Solomon Owen,* who, after sailing many years between Providence and the East Indies, returned to his
   native village, Chepachet, where he was " proprietor and
   Keeper of an excellent public house previous to the year
   1800."†

* Solomon,[4] Thomas,[3] Josiah,[2] Samuel[1].
† See Hist. of Glocester.

iv. KEZIAH, b. June 3, 1745, m. Enos Smith, and removed to Norwich, Chenango Co., N. Y., where their descendants still live.
v. DEBORAH, b June 24, 1747, m. Benjamin Colwell, and removed to Whitestone, N. Y.
vi. LYDIA, b. Jan. 24, 1751, m. Benjamin Smith, and removed to Norwich, N. Y.

11. ANNA BROWN (*James,*[4] *John,*[2] *Chad*[1]), b. 1710, d. Nov. 6, 1776, is thus mentioned in the will of her mother, July 20, 1736 : " To my daughter Ann Brown, wearing apparel, £100 due from Brother Toleration Harris, &c." She was m. Jan. 1, 1738, to Samuel[5] Comstock, who d. Jan. 16, 1755, in his 41st year. (*John,*[4] *Samuel,*[3] *Samuel,*[2] *William*[1] *of England*). The records available of her family are fragmentary, but the following account, though imperfect, is believed to be correct in its particulars.

CHILDREN.

i. CAPT. JESSE, b. 1740, d. March 8, 1776.
ii. JOSEPH.
iii. SAMUEL.
iv. BENJAMIN. He was the father of *Jesse, Joseph, William, Samuel* and *Benjamin* Comstock, the first three of whom for many years commanded packets between Providence and New York. He had also two daughters, *Ann B.* and *Sally B. Ann B.* was m. Nov. 20, 1808, to Samuel[6] Thurber, Jr. (*Samuel,*[5] *Samuel,*[4] *Samuel,*[3] *James,*[2] *John*[1]), and had (1) Mary, m. Ira Winsor ; (2) Benjamin C., d. Sept. 7, 1840 ; (3) Samuel, d. March 19, 1835 ; (4) George I., d. Jan. 6, 1856 ; (5) Joseph, d. Nov. 5, 1820. *Sally B.*, b. June 27, 1780, d. Feb. 16, 1878, was m. to her cousin Samuel Comstock, and had two daughters, Maria Ann, b. in Lansingburgh, N. Y., April 5, 1805, d. in Providence, April 25, 1871, and Martha, b. 1807. Maria A. Comstock was m. to Capt. William H. Townsend, b. in Newport, Dec. 31, 1802, d. in Providence, July 23, 1880. One of their sons, Capt. Benjamin C. Townsend, b. Nov. 15, 1827, perished by shipwreck of British bark " Guardian Angel," off the coast of Wales, Dec. 2, 1867. His remains were recovered and interred in the Cemetery at Pensarn, Abergele, Wales. Martha Comstock, b. 1807, died of cholera in Roxbury, Mass., Aug. 29, 1849. She was m. to Col. Almon Danforth Hodges, b. in Norton, Mass., Jan. 25, 1801, d. in Portsmouth, R I., his summer residence, Sept. 27, 1878. He was President of the New England Hist. Genealogical Society from 1859 to 1861. They had 8 children.
v. MARTHA, b. Feb. 24, 1744, d. Dec. 8, 1802, was m. July 10, 1765, to Richard[6] Eddy, b. Dec. 11, 1736, d. Oct. 20, 1784. (*Jonathan,*[5] *Joshua,*[4] *Zachariah,*[3] *Samuel*[2] *Rev. William Eddye.*[1]) After the birth of his children, he removed from Johnston to Providence, where he was Steward of the College. His widow was m. second, Feb. 15, 1786, to David Bucklin. No issue by second marriage.

CHILDREN (by first husband).

(1.) MOSES, b. March 26, 1766, d. May 29, 1823 ; m. Oct. 17, 1794,
Hannah Carpenter, who d. May 14, 1838. Of their six
children, *Anna*, b. July 5. 1796, was m. Oct. 5, 1820, to
Reuben Torrey and had children, one of whom, Moses E.
Torrey, is Cashier of the Roger Williams Bank, Providence.
Hannah, b. Oct. 16, 1799, m. Richard Evans.
(2.) SAMUEL, b. March 31, 1769, d. Feb 3, 1839.
(3.) JONATHAN, b. Jan. 21, 1772, d. Aug. 25, 1800.
The second son, Hon. Samuel Eddy, LL. D * graduated at
Brown University in 1787, and later studied law, but did not
long practice it. He was clerk of the Supreme Judicial
Court for the county of Providence from 1790–93; Secretary
of State from 1798–1819; Member of Congress from 1819–25,
and Chief Justice of the Superior Court of R. I. from 1827
until June, 1835, when ill-health compelled him to retire
from public life. He performed the duties of these various
offices with great credit to himself and satisfaction to the
people of his native State. "Throughout his long and
useful life he was diligent in the cultivation of his intellectual powers. At one time he gave his attention almost
exclusively to studies connected with the evidences, doctrines
and duties of religion At a subsequent period, he devoted
much of his leisure to the physical sciences, such as geology,
mineralogy, and especially conchology, to illustrate which
he made very creditable collections. The Transactions of
the Massachusetts Historical Society are enriched with
several contributions from his pen." His portrait is in possession of the R. I. Historical Society.
Judge Eddy had four wives. He m. first. Nov. 11, 1792,
Elizabeth, dau. of Samuel and Eliza (Carpenter) Bucklin,
b. Sept. 20, 1768, d. Oct. 27, 1799. Of their three children,
Martha,[†] the eldest. b. Sept. 2, 1793 m. Dec. 10, 1814, Oroo-
dates Mauran, son of Joseph Carlo Mauran, a native of
Villa Franca, Italy. He m. 2d., Dec. 2, 1801, Martha, dau.
of James and Ann (Angell) Wheaton, b. Oct. 22, 1780, d.
Feb. 1, 1818. They had six children, five of whom died
young. *Mary*,[†] the second child, b. April 16, 1804, m. William Chase. He m. 3d., April 25, 1809, Naomi Annt, dau.
of Elisha and Anna (Fenner) Angell, b. March 7, 1788, d.
Feb. 13, 1817. She was in the eighth generation from Chad
Brown, the seventh from John Smith, the Miller, and the
sixth from Thomas Angell .
Of their four children, only *Anna*,[†] the eldest, survived
infancy. She was b. Dec. 15, 1810, d. Jan. 25, 1881 ; was
m. Aug 15, 1831, to George M. Richmond. They had five
children, a daughter and four sons. Two of the latter died
young.
Judge Eddy m. 4th, Oct. 7, 1824, Sarah Howell, widow of
Gamaliel Lyman Dwight, and dau. of David and Mary
(Brown) Howell. She was b. Feb. 1, 1781, d. Feb. 23, 1860,
surviving her husband twenty years. They were second
cousins, both being in the sixth generation from Chad
Browne, and in the fourth from Elder James Brown. No
issue by last marriage.
But a small portion of the posterity of Anna (Brown) Comstock is represented in the above account. One of her descend -

* See Eddy Genealogy and Writings of William G. Goddard.
† A descendant of Isabel (Brown) Smith. See No. 3.

ants, Capt. Jesse, son of Jesse and Ann Comstock, perished
in Long Island Sound on the evening of Jan. 13, 1840, by
the burning of the Steamboat Lexington, aged 20 years
and 7 months. Capt. Joseph Comstock, long a popular
commander of the Collins Line of Steamers, died in New
York, Aug. 16, 1838. He was well known as a faithful,
vigilant and competent seaman, and was selected by Mr.
Webb to take the Ram Dunderburg to France.

12. OBADIAH BROWN (*James*,⁴ *John*,² *Chad*¹), b. Oct.
12, 1712, m. June 15, 1737, his first cousin, Mary Harris, dau.
of his uncle Toleration Harris, whose wife was Sarah Foster. She
was b. Dec. 18, 1718. They lived on North Main St. at the
foot of Waterman, the site now occupied by the Arnold Block,
which was erected by his grandson, James Arnold, in 1853.
James, an older brother, and Obadiah were the founders of the
commercial house of the Browns. After the death of James, as
his sons attained manhood they became partners with their
uncle Obadiah, and at the death of the latter, Nicholas, Joseph
and John were associated with him in business. Their success
in after years bore testimony to the excellence of the training received from his example and instructions.

The following item is from the will of his father, Elder
James : "I give to my Sonne Obadiah one half of my Land at
Chepatsett, only that six acres which I gave to Andrew, but my
will is that he shall have the one half of all the rest of my Land
at Chepatsett, and that Obadiah shall have his halfe on the
south part adjoyneing to Samuel Winsors Land : to be equally
divided to him by quantity. And I give him one Lott of Land
in Towne joyneing to that which I gave to Andrew against
William Turpins of fifty foot wide north and south, and eighty
foot long east and west, Joyneing to the Towne Streets and I
give unto him one half of frances Wickes Right on the west side
of the seven mile Line, the divisions Already agreed upon only
excepted."

Obadiah Brown was a public spirited citizen, and, though his
time was largely given to business, took a deep interest in all
matters pertaining to the welfare of the town and colony. He
was especially active in the contest against paper money. He
died in the 50th year of his age, and was buried in the North
Ground. The inscription on his tombstone is as follows : "In
Memory of Obadiah Brown, Esquire, Who departed this Life
the seventeenth of June, MDCCLXII, Aged forty-nine years,
eight months and four days. Descended of a Good Family. He
had strong natural Powers, Guided with exquisite Judgment ;
was honest, industrious, frugal, Temperate, affable, benevolent ;
A grave Magistrate, a Kind Husband, Tender Parent, A perfect
Pattern for Masters, And all useful Men.
　　As our country suffers when the useful die,
　　Heal up the Breach by following their Example."

They had 4 sons and 4 daus., but the sons all died young. The daughters lived to maturity. Of these children. *Phebe* was the eldest. *Sarah*, the third, *Anna*, the fourth, and *Mary*, the eighth child.

 i. PHEBE,[5] b. April 21, 1738, m. July 11, 1758, John Fenner, son of Hon. Arthur and Mary (Olney) Fenner, gr. son of Major Thomas. and g. gr. son of Capt. Arthur Fenner. He was b Oct. 2, 1739, and was an elder brother of Gov. Arthur Fenner. His maternal grandmother, Hallelujah Brown, wife of Capt. James Olney, was dau. of Daniel Brown and gr. dau of Chad.[1] They lived on a large farm in Glocester. some three miles south of Chepachet, the property of her father. The name of John Fenner occurs in a record of the families in the town of Glocester, taken in June, 1774, by order of the General Assembly He was a slaveholder, as is evident from the following advertisement which appeared in the *Providence Gazette*, Oct. 18, 1777:

"Run away from John Fenner, of Glocester, a negro man named Yockwhy, about 28 years of age, 5 ft. 8 inches high, marked on both cheeks; had on and took with him a light cloth-colored homespun coat, with wooden buttons, breeches of the same color, blue serge jacket, pair of good leather breeches, a fine Holland shirt, a fine tow shirt, a new pair of thread stockings, one pair of new dark worsted stockings, one pair of white ribbed yarn do., one dark silk handkerchief, one linen do., one good castor hat without loops, one felt do., one pair of shoes with strings, one pair of silver sleeve buttons. Whoever will take up and secure said negro, and return him to his master, shall have six dollars reward All masters of vessels are forbidden to carry off said negro at their peril."

  (Signed)   JOHN FENNER.

They had four children : (1). Obadiah, of Foster, settled in his youth on the farm where he spent his life, attaining the age of 90 or over. The trees which he planted in front of the house, attained their full size during his life time, notwithstanding the prophecy of some one who spoke disparagingly of his labor, telling him that he would not live to reap the reward He often told the story, adding "I have lived to see them grow up.' His name occurs in the list of freemen who voted against the new constitution in 1788. (2.) James m. his second cousin Anna Brown, (*Elisha, Andrew, James, John, Chad*). (See No. 10.) They removed to Nelson Township, Miami Co. Ohio. (3.) William, kept a tavern on Sterling Hill. (4). Mary, m. Charles Harris, of Scituate, R. I.

26. iii. SARAH,[5] b. Sept. 24, 1742.
 iv. ANNA,[5] b. Nov. 28, 1744, m. Jan. 1, 1764, her cousin Moses Brown. (*James, James, John, Chad*). (See No. 23.) She d. Feb. 5, 1773, leaving two children, *Sarah* and *Obadiah*.
27. viii. MARY,[5] b. Nov. 25, 1753.

13. CAPT. JEREMIAH BROWN (*James,[4] John,[2] Chad[1]*), b. Nov. 25, 1715, was lost at sea in the winter of 1740–41. He m. Waitstill, dau. of William and Mary (Sheldon) Rhodes, gr.-dau. of John and Waite (Waterman) Rhodes and gr. gr.-dau. of

Zachary and Joanna (Arnold) Rhodes. She was a descendant of Roger Williams in the fifth generation through her grandmother, Waite Waterman, who was dau. of Resolved and Mercy (Williams) Waterman, and gr.-dau. of both Roger Williams and Richard Waterman, She was b. Feb. 8, 1722, and d. Oct. 21, 1783. She m. 2d Jan. 20, 1745, Captain George Corlis, who d. June 16, 1790, in his 73d year. Several generations later, two of the descendants of their daughter Sarah Corlis, intermarried in the Ives and Goddard families, of the posterity of Nicholas Brown. (See Nos. 72 and 74).

CHILD.

28. i. Mary, b. July 28, 1740.

14. ELISHA BROWN, (James,[4] John,[2] Chad[1]), b. May 25, 1717, was a man of great ability and enterprise, and possessed at one time a large property, but was afterwards unfortunate in business, and lost the greater part of it. He was a prominent politician, and for some years a member of the General Assembly. During the Ward-Hopkins controversy he supported Gov. Ward, and served as Deputy Governor of the Colony of Rhode Island from 1765-67.

The following item is from the will of his father, Elder James : " I give to Jeremiah and Elisha, my two sons, my homestead where my house stands, my meadow Paster, Orchard, woodland, all my land lying between the Towne Street and that highway in the neck by Justice Brown's. All that I have not disposed of in this way, I give to them to be divided between them, and that Land which I bought of Israel Harding and all my Land ajoyneing thereabout to the West River on both sides of the River, and my meadow at Wainscutt, norwest from the Pine hill, and also my new field in that part Called the Stated Common, I give unto them; also one half of all my rights in the Thatch bed, each of them one quarter : all to be equally Devided between them. And my will is that my two youngest sons, Jeremiah and Elisha, shall take care of their mother."

From the will of their mother, widow Mary, dated July 20, 1736, Jeremiah and Elisha received 33½ acres in Smithfield, given her by her brother, Andrew Harris. To Jeremiah she left the apprentice boy, Othniel Hearnden, and to Elisha, the negro boy Cuffey. The homestead of Elisha Brown was on North Main, north of Olney Street. It stood in an orchard, with its gable end to the street, and the door to the South. The Church of the Redeemer was built upon the site in 1859, the house having been moved a little to the N. E. and a basement added. It is now approached through Riley street. The stone bearing the inscription E. B. 1749, which formerly formed a part of the wall in front of the house, has been placed in the underpinning of the church, near the robing room. He afterwards removed to

Wenscutt, N. Providence, some distance to the west of the locality now bearing that name. The house which he occupied has been demolished and a new one built on the site. He d. April 20, 1802, and according to the testimony of Moses Brown, in the Quaker records, was "buried in public burying ground by his wife Martha." Late in life, he became a Friend, and his grave was unmarked by a head stone.

He m. Martha, dau. of John and Deborah (Angell) Smith, b. April 3, 1719, the only child of her parents. Her father, John Smith, the Fuller, d. May 24, 1719, shortly after her birth. She was gr.-dau. of James and Abigail (Dexter) Angell, and g. gr.-dau. of the first Thomas Angell and Gregory Dexter. In consequence of the failure of male heirs in the direct line, the grist mill and adjoining territory reverted to Martha (Smith) Brown, and was recovered by her as heir-at-law to Charles Smith, (son of her uncle Philip Smith, Miller) at a Superior Court held at Providence in March, 1754. This subdivision of the Home Seat of John Smith, Miller, comprised the land now known as Smith's Hill, between Smith Street on the south and Orms Street on the north, and extended to the Moshassuck River. It was called Charlestown, and after the building of the first Mill Street Bridge, in 1733, was the most populous part of the town. The first plat of house lots in Providence was made at this time for the John Smith heirs by Stephen Jackson, and bears date of May 15, 1754. This map was copied Dec. 12, 1797, by Jeremiah B. Howell, and subsequently, Henry T. Beckwith in Aug. 1, 1859, made a copy of the Howell Map. Recent copies of the Beckwith Map by Charles. F. Wilcox in March, 1886, have preserved to the descendants of Martha (Smith) Brown a correct knowledge of the landed estate of their ancestors. Portions of this land still remain in possession of the family. In the will of Martha Brown. July, 1760, lot no. 19 near the junction of Orms and Charles Streets, is mentioned as the burial place of the Smiths.

Martha, d. Sept. 1, 1760, in the 42d year of her age, leaving six sons. Elisha Brown m. 2d., Feb. 22, 1761, Hannah, widow of Elijah Cushing,* and dau. of James Barker, of Newport. She was b. May —, 1721. Her children are thus enumerated in the will of Nehemiah Cushing, as "children of my late son, Elijah : Mary Brown, Deborah, Lydia Howland, Elijah, Elizabeth, Isaac and Sarah." The eldest of these, Mary Cushing, m. Jeremiah Brown, third son of Elisha. Elizabeth Cushing m. Benjamin Taylor, who in 1809 bought and occupied the south part of the brick house on North Main Street, near Olney, built about 1760 by Elisha Brown. (See illustration). The only child of Elisha and Hannah Brown was a dau. Martha, who died at the age of nine months.

---

* Matthew Cushing, the emigrant ancestor of the Cushings in New England, came from Hingham, Norfolk Co., Eng., in 1638, and founded the town of Hingham, Mass. For coat of arms see America Heraldica, New York, 1887.

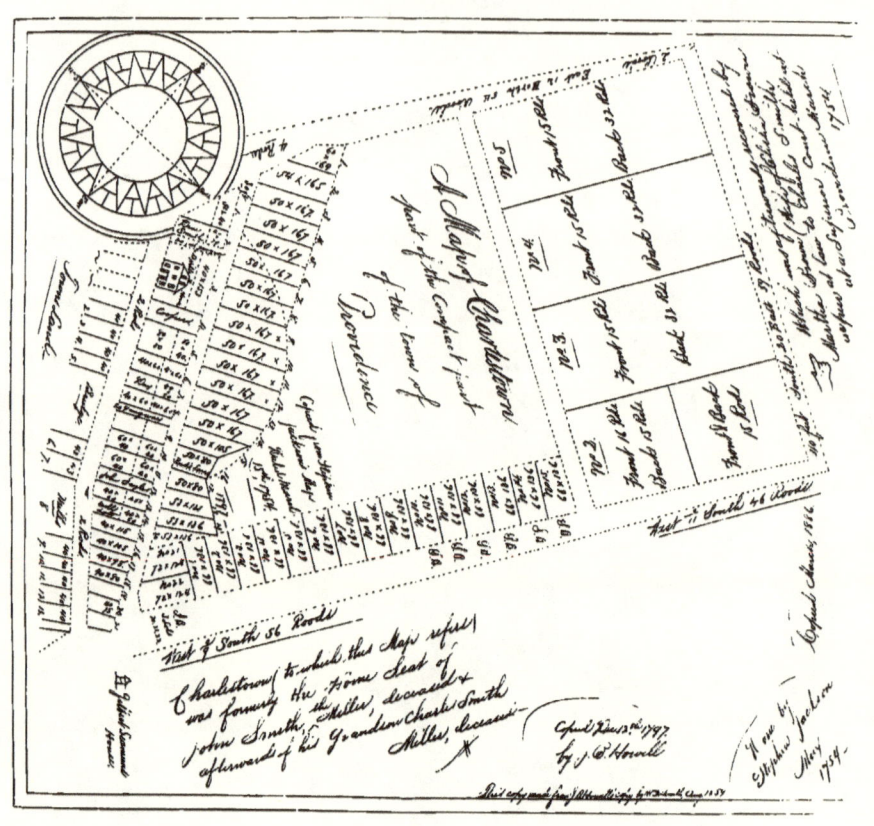

CHILDREN OF ELISHA AND MARTHA (SMITH) BROWN.

 i.   DEBORAH, b. ——, 1740 ; d. July 7, 1745. The inscription
   on her stone in the North Burial ground reads thus :
   On y^e Sixth, this infant with pleasant smiles did play,
   And on ye Seventh, the Lord took her away.
29. ii.   JOHN, b. Jan. 28, 1742.
30. iii.   JAMES, b. April 27, 1744.
31. iv.   JEREMIAH, b Dec 28, 1746.
32. v   ELISHA, b. June 1, 1749.
33. vi.   ISAAC, b. May 23, 1751.
 vii.   MARTHA, b April 17, 1754 ; d. June 27, 1755.
34. viii.   SMITH, b. April 12, 1756.
 ix.   A daughter, d. June 26, 1760, aged seven days.

THE ELISHA BROWN HOUSE.

The old brick house built by Deputy Governor Elisha Brown, about the
year 1760, on North Main Street, north of Olney, Providence. Original
dimensions, 72 x 28 feet. The perpendicular line shown on the front
represents the line of separation between the part yet standing and the
northern half part, which was demolished between 1809 and 1817, on
account of an insecure foundation which threatened a collapse.

EXPLANATORY NOTES *

Recent investigations prove that the part of the brick building yet standing is a counterpart of the portion demolished. Hence the published
statement, based upon conjecture (that seemed reasonable in the absence of

* This account was furnished by Mr. Albert Holbrook, of Providence, whose investigations settled a dispute relative to the original size of the building, and who presented
the accompanying illustration.

CHILDREN OF ELISHA AND MARTHA (SMITH) BROWN.

  i. DEBORAH, b. ——, 1740; d. July 7, 1745. The inscription
    on her stone in the North Burial ground reads thus :
    On y^r Sixth, this infant with pleasant smiles did play,
    And on ye Seventh, the Lord took her away.
29. ii. JOHN, b. Jan. 28, 1742.
30. iii. JAMES, b. April 27, 1744.
31. iv. JEREMIAH, b Dec 28, 1746.
32. v. ELISHA, b. June 1, 1749.
33. vi. ISAAC, b. May 23, 1751.
  vii. MARTHA, b April 17, 1754 ; d. June 27, 1755.
34. viii. SMITH, b. April 12, 1756.
  ix. A daughter, d. June 26, 1760, aged seven days.

THE ELISHA BROWN HOUSE.

The old brick house built by Deputy Governor Elisha Brown, about the
year 1760, on North Main Street, north of Olney, Providence. Original
dimensions, 72 x 28 feet. The perpendicular line shown on the front
represents the line of separation between the part yet standing and the
northern half part, which was demolished between 1809 and 1817, on
account of an insecure foundation which threatened a collapse.

EXPLANATORY NOTES *

Recent investigations prove that the part of the brick building yet standing is a counterpart of the portion demolished. Hence the published
statement, based upon conjecture (that seemed reasonable in the absence of

* This account was furnished by Mr. Albert Holbrook, of Providence, whose investigations settled a dispute relative to the original size of the building, and who presented
the accompanying illustration.

positive information) that the centre of the three north windows was the centre of the street line of the building, is erroneous. Mr. Brown sold the estate to Paul Bunker, of Nantucket, Aug. 21, 1770. The next owner was Thomas Jenkins, also of Nantucket, who bought it April 12, 1776. He removed to Providence about that time, and probably, at first, occupied it as a home, though he subsequently lived at the south end of the town. Under his ownership the estate was divided, the south part which yet remains standing, being sold to Samuel Hamlin, Pewterer, of Providence, Nov. 12, 1782. It was next owned by Esek Aldrich, innkeeper, who sold it Jan. 3, 1787, to Capt. James Westcott. He sold it, Sept. 10, 1809, to Benjamin Taylor, whose wife, Elizabeth Cushing, was a stepdaughter of Elisha Brown. The present owner is Lewis Taylor Hubbard, a grandson of Benjamin Taylor.

The north part was sold by Thomas Jenkins, Sept 22, 1784, to Deborah Jenkins, widow of his brother Benjamin. After her removal to Hudson, N. Y., she sold it June 4, 1791, to James Graves, whose wife Hope, owned adjoining property. When next sold to Earl D. Pearce, April 5, 1817, the northern part had been taken down. For many years a small frame cottage has occupied the site.

15. CHAD BROWNE, (*Obadiah*,[5] *John*,[2] *Chad*[1]), b. Oct. 13, 1705, removed about 1730 to Glocester, R. I. and settled upon a large tract of land on the west side of Chepachet river, about two miles southeast of the present village. This was probably the land deeded to him by his brother, John Browne, Jr., and adjoined that of his cousin Andrew on the east side of the river. At the present time it remains largely in possession of his descendants. His house is not now standing. He m. Sarah Smith, who may have been dau. of Elisha and Experience (Mowry) Smith, and had 3 sons and 2 daus.

CHILDREN.

i. OBADIAH, lived in the homestead of his father Chad, where he died, Dec. 19, 1789. He was a schoolmaster, and possessed considerable learning for that time, though he never attended school a day. He had three wives, the last of whom was Anna Lovell. A marriage contract between himself and one of his intended wives is remarkable for the plainness and beauty of the chirography. He had three children, *Martha*, *Nancy* and *Mary*. Of these *Martha* m. Peter Coombs, 2d. —— Tripp, and 3d, Abraham Clarke. By 2d husband, she had a dau. Irene, and by 3d husband, four children, one of whom named Chad, lived, in 1851, near Buffalo, N. Y. Abraham and *Martha* occupied the homestead of her grandfather Chad. The name of Abraham Clark appears in the list of freemen who voted against the adoption of the constitution in 1788. *Nancy* m. —— Fiske and removed to Cooperstown, N. Y. They had children, one of whom was Chad. *Mary* m. Benjamin Jencks and removed to Ludlow, Mass. Had issue.

35. ii. ELISHA, m. Sarah Olney.

36. iii. JESSE, b. in 1739.

iv. DORCAS, was m. Jan., 1753, to Lawrence[5] Southwick, b Jan. 11, 1731, d. 1810. (*Daniel*,[4] *Lawrence*,[3] *Daniel*,[2] *Lawrence*[1]) She d. in 1758, leaving three children. (1) *Sarah*, b. April 27, 1754, d. Feb. 14, 1836 ; was m. Nov. 4, 1774, to Benedict Arnold, of Burrillville, and had William and Benedict Arnold, and other children. (2) *Elisha*, b. Feb. 17, 1757, m. Aug. 16, 1777, Margaret Moshier, and settled in Danby, Vt., where he kept a tavern. He removed in 1811 to Scipio, Cayuga Co., N. Y., and died there in 1841, at the age of 84. They had five children : Waity, Daniel. Cynthia, Sophronia, Phebe. (3) *Ruth*, b. 1758, d. young. Daniel Southwick, father of Lawrence, was a distinguished preacher of the Society of Friends in Uxbridge, Mass., where he carried on the business of tanning. Lawrence[1] Southwick and his wife Cassandra emigrated in 1696 from Lancashire. Eng., to Salem, Mass.

v. MARY. m. Stephen Aldrich, of Northbridge, Mass., and removed to Long Island, where their descendants still live.

16. OBADIAH JENCKES (*Martha*,[6] *John*,[2] *Chad*[1]), second son of Gov. Joseph Jenckes. lived in Glocester, where he m. May 21, 1713. Alice, dau. of Zachariah and Mercy (Baker) Eddy, b. Jan. 5, 1694. (*Zachariah*,[4] *Zachariah*,[3] *Samuel, the Pilgrim*,[2] *Rev. William Eddye*[1])   At a town meeting called March 16, 1731, to organize the town of Glocester, Obadiah Jenckes was chosen one of the town councilmen. In 1736 the name of *Obadiah Jenckes, Jr.*, occurs among the Freemen of Glocester : that of *John Jenckes* in 1739, and of *Zachariah Jenckes* in 1746. They were probably sons of Obadiah. John Jenckes, Jr., was a member of the Smithfield Grenadiers in 1791, and may have been grandson of Obadiah.

In the Sayles Pedigree it is stated that *Martha Jenckes*,[5] dau. of Obadiah, m. Daniel Hopkins[5] (*Ezekiel*,[4] *Thomas*,[3] *William*, and *Joanna* (*Arnold*) *Hopkins*[1].)

Amey Hopkins,[6] dau. of Daniel and Martha. b. 1742, d. 1782, m. 1760, Emor[5] Olney (*James*,[4] *Epenetus*,[3] *Epenetus*,[2] *Thomas*[1]).

Paris Olney,[7] son of Emor and Amey, b. 1770. d. 1850, m. Mercy Winsor[6] (*Jeremiah*,[5] *Joshua*,[4] *Joshua*,[3] *Samuel*,[2] *Joshua*[1]). She was b. Aug. 31, 1769. Mary Ann Olney,[8] dau. of Paris and Mercy, b. June 21, 1803, d. Sept. 11, 1878. m. Dec. 25, 1822, Clark Sayles[6] (*Ahab*,[5] *Israel*,[4] *Richard*,[3] *John*,[2] *John*,[1]). Of the five children of the latter. two only survived infancy—William Francis and Frederick Clark.

i. WILLIAM FRANCIS SAYLES,[9] b. Sept. 20, 1824, m. Oct. 30, 1849, Mary Wilkinson, dau. of Benjamin and Mary (Wilkinson) Fessenden, of Valley Falls, R. I. She was b. Oct. 24, 1827, and d. Sept. 20, 1886. They had six children. (1.) *Mary Fessenden*,[10] b. Sept. 29, 1850, was m. May 21, 1872 to Roscoe Stetson Washburn, b. July 11, 1847. son of Oliver A. Washburn, Jr.. and his wife Matilda (King) Washburn. They have had four children, viz. : Morris King,[11] b. Oct. 3, 1872 ; William Francis Sayles,[11] b. Sept. 3, 1874, d. Aug. 19. 1879 ; Roscoe Clifton,[11] b. June, 1887; John Fessenden,[11] b. March 8, 1879, d. Aug. 27, 1882.

(2.) *Louise*,[10] b. April 24, 1853, d. Aug. 16, 1859. (3.)

William Clark,[10] b. Oct. 12, 1855, d. Feb. 13, 1876. (4.)
Martha Fessenden,[10] b. July 27, 1864. (5.) *Frank Arthur,*[10]
b. Dec. 14, 1866. (6.) *Nannie Nye,*[10] b. Dec. 14, 1866, d.
June 2, 1873.

    ii. FREDERICK CLARK SAYLES,[9] b. July 17, 1835. m. Oct.
16, 1851, Deborah Cook Wilcox, dau. of Robert and Deborah
(Cook) Wilcox. They have had six children. (1.) *A son,*[10]
b. Jan. 14, 1865, d. in infancy. (2.) *Carrie Minerva,*[10] b.
Jan. 15, 1866. (3.) *Frederick Clark,*[10] b. Aug. 21, 1868.
(4.) *Benjamin Paris,*[10] b. Oct. 31, 1871, d. May 30, 1873.
(5.) *Robert Wilcox,*[10] b. Jan. 28, 1878. (6.) *Deborah
Wilcox,*[10] b. Nov. 17, 1880.

    The Sayles Brothers comprise the firm of W. F. and F. C.
Sayles, proprietors of the Moshassuck Bleachery, dye works and
woolen mills near Pawtucket. R. I. The Bleachery commenced
in 1848, has rapidly increased in extent and facilities, until now
it is the most extensive and completely equipped establishment of
the kind in the country. It occupies substantial buildings, surrounded by dwellings erected for the employes, some of whom
have become owners of their residences and sufficient land for
garden purposes. Encouragement and pecuniary aid are extended
by the proprietors for the promotion of social order, temperance,
education and religious welfare.

    Sayles' Memorial Hall, the last of the Brown University group
of buildings, was erected at the expense of the Hon. William F.
Sayles in memory of his son, William Clark Sayles, who died in
1876, while a student at that institution. It was dedicated in
June, 1881.

    Frederick C. Sayles is the first Mayor of Pawtucket, incor-
porated as a city Jan. 4, 1886. The Sayles Brothers were influential in securing the success of the reunion of the Roger
Williams descendants, which took place at Sayles' Memorial
Hall, June 22, 1886. The Hon. Frederick C. Sayles was one of
the committee of arrangements, and presided at the meeting.
They trace their descent from Roger Williams through three of
his children, Mary, Mercy and Daniel Williams.

    17. CATHARINE JENCKES (*Martha,*[6] *John,*[2] *Chad*[1]),
eldest dau. of Gov. Joseph Jenckes, b. 1694, d. 1782 ; m. William Turpin. son of William. He was an innkeeper and Town
Treasurer from 1737-44. He was b. 1690, and d. March, 15,
1744. Of their ten children. *Catharine Turpin*[5] m. Capt. John
Hopkins, son of William and Ruth (Wilkinson) Hopkins, and
brother of Gov. Stephen Hopkins.* Capt. John died at sea,
Feb. 1, 1745, and left his widow with three young daughters.
Ruth, b. ——, d. ———— : Sarah, d. Oct. 14, 1818, and Anna d.
Dec. 26, 1823. She m. 2d, Dr. Job Hawkins and d. Dec. 30,
1749, in her 31st year. Her second dau., Sarah Hopkins,[6] m.

Capt. John.[5] *William.*[4] *Major William.*[3] *Thomas.*[2] *William.*[1]

Aug. 2, 1761, Abraham Whipple, b. Sept. 26, 1733. He commanded the expedition that burned the British schooner *Gaspee*, on the evening of June 9, 1772. (See No. 22.) He was afterwards a Commodore in the Continental Navy. After a distinguished career in the service of his country, he removed in 1796 to Marietta, Ohio, where he died May 29, 1819. His wife d. Oct. 14, 1818, aged 78 years. They had two children, Katy,[7] who m. April, 1781, Lieut.-Colonel Sproat, of the Massachusetts line, and Polly,[7] who m. July, 1789, Dr. Ezekiel Comstock, of Smithfield.

Anna Hopkins,[6] sister of Sarah, m. Dec. 13, 1761, William Metcalf, who died in early manhood. She m. second, Esek Esten. A daughter by the first husband m. Alfred Mann, and had among other children, William Metcalf Mann,[8] one of the editors of the *Providence American*. By the second husband she had nine children, one of whom, Esek Esten, b. Dec. 14, 1779, d. May 21, 1842 ; m. Sept. 14, 1800, Sarah, dau. of Benjamin Jenckes. They had 12 children. (See Genealogy of One Line of the Hopkins Family, by Albert Holbrook.)

18. DR. JOHN JENCKES, (*Martha,[6] John,[2] Chad[1]*), son of Gov. Joseph Jenckes, m. March 22, 1721, Sarah, dau. of Major Thomas and Dinah (Burden) Fenner, and gr.-dau. of Capt. Arthur and Mehitable (Waterman) Fenner. She was b. 1698, and d. April 17, 1736. He died in 1730, probably on ship board, returning from England, where he had been on a visit with his father.

CHILDREN.

  i.   MARY, b. 1721, d. Nov. 14, 1723. Buried in Major Thomas Fenner's burying ground.
 ii.   LYDIA, m. Jonathan Jenckes.
iii   JOSEPH.
 iv.   BENJAMIN.

19. MARY JENCKES, (*Martha,[6] James,[2] Chad[1]*), eighth child of Gov. Joseph Jenckes, was m. May 20, 1722, to John Herndon, Jr., and second, to. Capt. John Harrington, son of John, of Scituate, R. I. Her oldest child *Nathaniel*, b. probably, May 15, 1727, bore the surname of Harrington, though he is supposed to be a son of the first husband. The children of the second husband were *Obadiah, John, Amey, Catharine, Jemima. Nathaniel* Harrington m. Nov. 6, 1748, Mary Bates, b. Oct. 17, 1729, dau. of James, and lived in Foster, R. 1. They had five children : Waty, Caleb, John, Nathaniel, Mary or Polly. The latter, b. June 12, 1769, was m Jan. 21, 1793, to her third cousin, Elhanan Aylsworth,[4] (*Thomas,[3] Chad,[2] Arthur[1]*), b. Aug. 31, 1772. They removed to Hoosick, N. Y., and in the winter of 1766-7 settled perma-

nently in Burlington, Otsego Co., N. Y., where she d. Sept. 9, 1855. He outlived her but a short time and d. Oct. 17, 1857. Of their nine children, Perry, the youngest, b. Nov. 21, 1812, m. March 21, 1836, Luna Norton, dau. of James and Hannah (Stewart) DeLong, of Watertown, N. Y. The latter were the parents of Dr. Homer E Aylsworth, the compiler of the Aylsworth Genealogy. (See No. 7.)

FIFTH GENERATION.

20. NICHOLAS BROWN, (*James*,[8] *James*,[4] *John*,[2] *Chad*[1]), b. July 28. 1729, was the eldest of the four brothers who were associated in business under the name of Nicholas Brown and Company. The first son, Capt. James, died unmarried shortly before Nicholas became of age. Instead of appropriating to himself, as he could have done under existing colonial laws, a double portion of his father's estate, Nicholas promptly divided the inheritance equally with his brothers and sister. The commercial business founded by his father and uncle Obadiah, was greatly extended by the brothers, and under their judicious management yielded large returns. Of the ample fortunes thus acquired they gave judiciously and liberally to every worthy enterprise of their times, in which they were usually leaders or active co-operators.

He m. May 2, 1762, Rhoda, fifth dau. of Daniel and Joanna (Scott) Jenckes, b. —— and d. Dec. 16, 1783. (*Daniel*,[4] *Rev. Ebenezer*,[3] *Joseph*,[2] *Joseph Jenckes*[1]). She was granddaughter of Sylvanus and Joanna (Jenckes) Scott, and gr. gr. dau. of John and Rebecca Scott. John was son of the first Richard and Catharine (Marbury) Scott. Daniel Jenckes was a wealthy merchant of Providence, and an active member of the First Baptist Church, of which his father, Rev. Ebenezer Jenckes, was pastor from 1719–26. He was for forty years a member of the General Assembly, and for nearly thirty years Chief Justice of the Providence County Court.

The residence of Nicholas Brown on South Main Street (present number 27) is still standing, but has long since been devoted to business purposes. Of the ten children of Nicholas and Rhoda Brown, but two lived to maturity, a son and daughter, *Nicholas and Hope*. He married second, Sept. 9, 1785, Avis, daughter of Capt. Barnabas Binney, of Boston, who survived him. The following inscription from the tablet erected over his grave in the North Burial Ground, shows the esteem in which he was held by his contemporaries:

"In Memory of Nicholas Brown, Esq., who died May 29, A. D. 1791, aet. 62. He descended from respectable ancestors, who were some of the first settlers in this State. His stature was large ; his personal appearance manly and noble ; his genius penetrating ; his memory tenacious ; his judgment strong ; his affections lively and warm. He was an early, persevering and liberal patron of the College in this town ; and a member and great benefactor of the Baptist Society. His donations in support of learning and religion were generous and abundant. His occupation was merchandise, in which by industry, punctuality and success, he accumulated a large fortune. He was plain and sincere in his manners, a faithful friend, a good neighbor and entertaining companion. His knowledge of books, of men, of

business and of the world was great and of the most useful kind.
He loved his country, and had an equal esteem of liberty and
good government. He had deeply studied the Holy Scriptures
and was convinced of the great truths of revelation. He was a
religious observer of the Sabbath, and of public worship,
and trained up his household after him. He was a lover
of all men, especially good men, the ministers and disciples
of Christ, who always received a friendly welcome under his
hospitable roof. As in life he was universally esteemed, so in
death he was universally lamented. The conjugal affection of a
mourning widow, and the filial affection of an orphan son and
daughter have erected this monument."

CHILDREN (by first wife).

i   HOPE, b. Aug. 1, 1763, d. July 30, 1767.
ii.   JOANNA, b. Jan. 13, 1766, d. Jan. 8, 1785.
iii. HOPE, b. ―――― 1767, d. July 29, 1768.
27. iv. NICHOLAS, b. April 4, 1769.
v   CHAD, b. May 27, 1771, d. Oct. 7, 1778.
38. vi   HOPE, b. Feb 22, 1773
vii. MOSES, b. Feb. 3, 1775, d. Feb. 28, 1791.
viii RHODA, b. March 20, 1777, d. April 8, 1787.
ix.   JENCKES, b. Nov. 7, 1778, d. April 22, 1783.
x.   NANCY, b. July 9, 1783, d. Aug. 3, 1783.

CHILD (by second wife).

xi. JOHN, b. Dec. 26, 1786, d. Jan. 10, 1787.

21. JOSEPH BROWN (*James*,[8] *James*,[4] *John*,[2] *Chad*[1]), b.
Dec. 3, 1733, N. S., was the second of " the Four Brothers." He
early gave proofs of a superior genius, and was inclined to philosophical study, especially in the higher natural sciences. After
acquiring a competence he withdrew from the firm in order to
devote himself to his favorite studies. The closing years of his
life were spent in the service of Brown University, where he
became a Professor of Experimental Philosophy. He was also
one of the Trustees of the college, and its liberal patron. He
was an adept in electricity, and his researches in astronomy
attracted the notice of the *Literati*. His favorite study, however, was mechanics. In testimony of his merits the degree of
A. M. was conferred upon him, and he was elected a member of
the American Academy of Arts and Sciences. Joseph and
Moses took an active part in the observation of the transit of
Venus in 1769, importing the instruments used at their own
expense. Joseph, John and Moses were Freemasons, being
among the first initiated at St. John's Lodge, the charter of
which was issued Jan. 18, 1757. Joseph was an active member,
the second master, and presided at every meeting from 1762–'69.
He was associated with Stephen Hopkins in building the Town
Market House, and Nicholas Brown laid the first stone June 11,

1773. Joseph Brown and James Sumner were the architects of the First Baptist Church erected in 1774–'75. The residence which he built on South Main Street in 1774, and in which he lived until his death, is still standing. The Old Providence Bank moved into this building in 1801, and occupies it at the present time. It is somewhat altered in its appearance, the double flight of steps leading to the street door in the centre of the house above the basement story, having been removed. The first floor was handsomely paneled.

He was for several years a Representative in the General Assembly, and Assistant to the Governor in Council, the latter of which offices he filled at the time of his first stroke of apoplexy, Nov. 24, 1784. This rendered him at times incapable of business, and after repeated attacks of the disease he expired Dec. 3, 1785, wanting only eleven days of completing the fifty-second year of his age. He was an exemplary member of the First Baptist Church, and an ornament to the Christian religion, which he embraced in the vigor of his life and maturity of his judgment, on a full conviction of its truth and Divine Origin. He m. Sept. 30, 1759, his cousin Elizabeth, b. 1736, d. Sept. 6, 1806, dau. of the third Nicholas and Anne (Tillinghast) Power. She was gr. dau. of Philip and Martha (Holmes) Tillinghast, and also gr. dau. of Nicholas and Mercy (Tillinghast) Power. Martha Holmes was dau. of Jonathan and gr. dau. of Obadiah Holmes.

CHILDREN.

39. i. MARY, b July 30, 1760.
   ii. OBADIAH, b. May 16, 1762, d. unm. Feb. 14, 1815.
   iii. ELIZABETH, b. June 28, 1769, d. March 1, 1845. She was m. to Richard[5] Ward, a merchant in New York city, b. March 5, 1765, d. Oct, 1808. (*Gov. Samuel,[4] Gov.[8] Richard,[3] Thomas,[2] John Ward*[1]). The emigrant ancestor of the Ward Family came from Gloucester, Eng., after the accession of Charles II. and settled in Newport, R I, where he died, April, 1698, aged 79. He had been an officer in one of Cromwell's Cavalry regiments, and his sword was long preserved in the family. The following extract from an obituary notice of Mrs. Elizabeth Ward is from the pen of the late Prof. William Goddard : "The long probation which it pleased the Giver of Life to allot to this excellent woman was not spent in vain. With all fidelity did she discharge her high trust, always obedient to sympathies the most generous and comprehensive. never weary of the work of benevolence, and never suffering the good she did to exalt her estimate of herself. To the sorrows of others she was most tenderly alive. She never mocked the sufferer with an expression of barren sympathy. Her hand was as open as her heart was warm. To the sharp ills of poverty she administered substantial relief. The solitude of the bereaved she cheered with the voice of Christian consolation. For a long course of years she was the centre of a large circle of relatives and friends, who loved her for her

* The Armorial bearings of Gov. Richard Ward were engraved upon his tombstone in Newport. (See America Heraldica.)

many virtues. Mrs. Ward had no children, but she watched
with rare fidelity and with maternal tenderness over those
who stood to her in the relation of children. Protracted
was her sickness. Her Heavenly Father, however, in the
midst of His corrective discipline, remembered her in mercy.
He spared to the last her unusually clear, inquisitive and
vigorous intellect, and confirmed her faith in Christ as the
Saviour of all those who put their trust in him."

   iv.   JOSEPH, b. 1768, d. 1771.
   v.   JOSEPH, b. 1775, d 1791.

22. JOHN BROWN, (*James*,[3] *James*,[4] *John*,[2] *Chad*,[1])
b. Jan. 27, 1736, d. Sept. 20, 1803, was the third of the Four
Brothers, and associated with them in business until 1782, when
he withdrew from the firm, and established himself at India
Point, where he entered upon the bold but successful venture
of direct trade with the East Indies and China. He is said to
have been "a man of magnificent projects and extraordinary
enterprise." Though a wealthy merchant and having larger interests at stake than most men, he was a patriotic leader in the
struggle for American Independence, and contributed substantial aid to the cause. At the Hope Furnace in Cranston, built
largely by the Browns, was manufactured cannon for use in the
Continental army.

He was the leader of the party which destroyed the British
armed schooner the *Gaspee*, in Narragansett Bay in June 1772.

NEW SONG CALLED THE GASPEE.*

Author Unknown.

'Twas in the reign of George the Third,
The public peace was much disturbed
By ships of war that came and laid,
Within our ports to stop our trade,
In seventeen hundred and seventy-two,
In Newport harbor lay a crew
That played the part of pirates there,
The sons of Freedom could not bear.
Sometimes they'd weigh and give them
   chase,
Such actions, sure were very base !
No honest coasters could pass by,
But what they would let some shot fly.

Which did provoke to high degree,
Those true-born sons of Liberty,—
So that they could no longer bear
Those sons of Belial staying there,

It was not long 'ere it fell out
That William Duddingston so stout
Commander of the Gaspee tender,
Which he has reason to remember—
Because, as people do assert,
He almost met his just desert :
Here on the twelfth † day of June,
Between the hours of twelve and one,

Did chase the sloop called the Hannah,
Of which one Lindsay was commander :—
They dogged her up Providence Sound,
And there the rascals got aground.

The news of it flew that very day,
That they on Namquit Point did lay :—
That night, about half-past ten,
Some Narragansett Indian-men,

Being sixty-four if I remember,
Soon made this stout coxcomb surrender—
And what was best of all their tricks,
In him a ball too they did fix—

Then set the men upon the land,
And burnt her up, we understand—
Which thing provoked the King so high
He said these men should surely die.

So if he can but find them out,
King George has offered very stout
One thousand pounds to find out one
That wounded William Duddingston.

One thousand more he says he'll spare
To those who say they sheriffs were—
One thousand more there doth remain
For to find out the *leader's* name.

Likewise one hundred pounds per man,
For any one of all the clan :
But let him try his utmost skill,
I'm apt to think he never will
Find out one of those hearts of gold,
Though he should offer fifty fold.

* From Sketches of Newport and its Vicinity, John S. Taylor, New York, 1842.
† Historians say the ninth of June.

This passage of history is thus related by Bancroft. "On the ninth of June the Providence Packet was returning to Providence, and proud of its speed went gayly on, heedless of the *Gaspee.* Dudingston gave chase. The tide being at flood the Packet ventured near shore ; the *Gaspee* confidently followed, and drawing more water ran aground on * Namquit Point. The following night a party of men in six or seven boats led by John Brown and Joseph Brown of Providence, and Simeon Potter, of Bristol,† boarded the stranded schooner, after a scuffle in which Dudingston was wounded, took and landed its crew, and then set it on fire." The rendezvous of the party was the Sabin Tavern, at the north east corner of Planet and South Main Streets, afterwards the residence of Welcome Arnold. John Brown was sent in irons to Boston on suspicion of being concerned in the *Gaspee* affair, but released through the efforts of his brother Moses. To lessen the probabilities of arrest, it is said that until the formal declaration of war, he avoided sleeping two nights in succession under the same roof, by making the rounds of his country seats, of which he possessed several,‡ not far removed from Providence. He instructed his captains to freight their vessels with powder on the return voyages, and furnished the army at Cambridge with a supply when it had not four rounds to a man.

The first attempt to introduce free schools in Providence was made in 1767, and John and Moses Brown served on the committees appointed by the town to prepare for this new system of instruction. The project, however, was unsuccessful, and it was not until 1800 that a law was passed to establish free schools throughout the State. In three years this law was repealed, but the schools of Providence were maintained, and have been continuously in operation since the beginning of the century. In 1828 the passage of a new law secured free instruction for the entire State.

The Brown brothers were influential in the removal of the College of Rhode Island from Warren to Providence, and were its constant benefactors. John Brown was one of the largest contributors to this institution, of which he was for twenty years the treasurer. May 14, 1770, he laid the corner-stone of its first building, now known as *University Hall,* which was erected on the Home Lot of his ancestor, Chad Browne. This land at an early date went out of the possession of the family, but was repurchased by John and Moses Brown, and a deed of the same presented to the Corporation. The interests of the Baptist Church of which Chad and James Brown had been elders, were well sustained by John Brown who gave to it liber-

*On Spring Green Farm, Warwick.
† Another account states that "after discussion the participants in the meeting went to the wharf and embarked in eight long boats under command of Abraham Whipple, afterwards a captain in the Continental Navy." (See "The Providence Plantations." J. A. & R. A. Reid, Providence, 1886).
‡ These were located at Cranston, Glocester, North Providence, Point Pleasant in Bristol, and Spring Green in Warwick.

ally of his wealth for the support of preaching, and the creation
of a permanent fund for the society.

For thirty years, from 1760–90, the brothers were, one or
more of them, in the General Assembly, and prominent in local
matters

The building of the Washington Bridge across the Seekonk at
the lower ferry was secured by John Brown, and that of the Red
or Central Bridge, by Moses, at the upper ferry. These bridges
were carried away by the disastrous flood of 1807, but soon
rebuilt. In 1789, the Assembly, to encourage home manufacture,
increased the import duty on many foreign goods, and citizens of
wealth often wore homespun woolen clothing. It is recorded
that John Brown appeared in the Assembly in Jan., 1789, dressed
in a suit the cloth of which was made from the wool of his
own sheep kept on his Glocester farm ; the yarn was spun by
a woman 88 years of age. His town residence was on South
Main street, next south of that of his brother Nicholas. The
house, which he built on land from his father's estate, was afterwards torn down, and the Mechanics' Bank building, No. 37,
erected on the site. It is not now occupied by the bank. It
was here that he gave his famous dinner party in honor of Gen.
Nathanael Greene—the largest, it is said, that had ever been
given in Rhode Island. His commencement dinners to the
graduates and their friends were occasions long remembered with
pleasure.

Apropos of his dinner parties, it is related that on one occasion,
when the clerical element was well represented, "Nephew
Obadiah," son of Joseph, was called on for a toast. It was
known that he was somewhat of a free-thinker, but all were
startled by the response : "Here's a short respite to the
damned in hell." A moment of embarrassing silence ensued.
Who could refuse assent to so charitable a wish, but how at vari-
ance with their orthodox proclivities ! John, the host, however,
was equal to the occasion. Raising his glass, he exclaimed :
"Truly, a most admirable sentiment, gentlemen, and one in
which I am sure we can all heartily join." Glad to be relieved
from so awkward a dilemma, the company followed his example,
and, without a dissenting voice, drained their glasses : and the
"feast of reason and flow of soul" continued, unmarred by the
incident.

In 1787 he built his Power street mansion, at that time the
finest in the city, from plans made by his brother Joseph. It is
now occupied by Prof. William Gammell. John Brown was a
member of the society formed in June, 1790, for promoting the
abolition of slavery in the United States, and for improving the
condition of the African race. In 1799 he was elected a member
of Congress and served two years. He was a man of large
physical proportions, and accustomed to riding about in a sulkey,
a two-seated open chaise, which he so completely filled that his

MOSES BROWN

Born 9th Mo. 23d, 1738.
Died 9th Mo. 6th, 1836.
From a steel engraving by T. Pollock, 1856.
Original drawing by W. J. Harris, 5th Mo. 4th, 1836.

little grandson, John B. Frances, rode on a stool between his
knees because there was no room for him on the seat. He m.,
Nov. 27, 1760, Sarah, dau. of Daniel[4] and Dorcas (Harris)
Smith, b. May 13, 1738, d. Feb. 25, 1825. (Benjamin,[3] John,[2]
John Smith[1] Miller). She was a gr. dau. of Benjamin and
Mercy (Angell) Smith, and also of William and Abigail Harris.

CHILDREN.

i. JAMES, b. Sept. 22, 1761, d. unm. Dec. 12, 1834. He was a
graduate of Harvard in 1780, and in 1789 was elected a member of the Board of Fellows of Brown University. Enjoying an ample patrimony, and having no taste for active
pursuits, he did not enter a business life or seek public
distinction. He was a gentleman of the old school, upright
and pure minded in all the relations of private life.

ii BENJAMIN, b. Feb. 13, 1763, d. July 7, 1773.

iii. ABIGAIL, b. Nov. 26, 1754, d. Oct. 16, 1766.

40. iv. ABIGAIL or ABBY, b. Nov. 20, 1766.

41. v. SALLY or SARAH, b. Sept. 5, 1773.

42. vi. ALICE, b. Jan. 1, 1777.

MOSES BROWN (James,[5] James,[4] John,[2] Chad[1]), the
youngest of "the Four Brothers," was b. Sept. 23, 1738. His
father died the next April, but his mother, Hope, attained an
advanced age, dying in 1792 in her 91st year. He long survived
his three elder brothers, Nicholas having died in 1791, Joseph
in 1784, and John in 1803. Moses was spared until he had
nearly completed 98 years. He died Sept. 6, 1836, at his residence, near the banks of the Seekonk, where he had lived for
more than 60 years. He left school at the age of thirteen and
passed his early years in the family of his paternal uncle,
Obadiah, who from the first had regarded him in the light of a
son. In 1763 he entered the firm of Nicholas Brown & Co.,
and the four brothers combined, largely extended the business
of the commercial house founded by their father and uncle
Obadiah. The following year he married his cousin, Anna
Brown, dau. of Obadiah, a portion of whose large estate he subsequently inherited by will.

His health was not robust and after ten years he withdrew
from the firm and retired to his farm, then quite in the country,
but now within the city limits. His mansion house, formerly
the property of Mr. Merritt, an English gentleman of fortune,
stood on the north side of Angell street, some distance back
from the road. The former entrance to the grounds is now occupied by the large house on Angell street, built by the late
Estus Lamb. Some years since, his house, at that time, unin-
habited, was burned to the ground. It was bequeathed by Mr.
Brown in his will to the only son of his grand-daughter, Moses
Brown Jenkins.

After his retirement from business he devoted his time to the
care of his estate, and the society and service of his friends,

indulging his tastes for intellectual pursuits, especially experimental illustration in the line of Chemistry and Natural
Philosophy of which he was particularly fond. In 1774 he
joined the Society of Friends, and from that time was closely
identified with their interests. He manumitted all his slaves in
1773, continuing, however, a benevolent interest in their welfare.
He was a liberal supporter of the Rhode Island Peace Society,
which he assisted in founding in 1818. His elder brother, Nicholas, was one of its officers, and he and his son Obadiah were
treasurers. He was an active member of the Abolition Society
of Rhode Island, and an earnest and unceasing advocate of
universal emancipation. Consistently with his principles, he
kept aloof from the Revolutionary struggle in which his brothers
were conspicuous participants ; but his motives were understood
and his patriotism unquestioned.

His name will long be known to posterity in connection with
the Yearly Meeting Boarding School, of which he was a munificent patron and founder. The school was removed from Portsmouth, R. I., where it was commenced in 1784, and opened at
its present location, Jan. 1, 1819. The lot of land containing
about forty-three acres on which the school buildings were
erected, was given by him for this purpose, besides a contribution
to the building fund. For more than fifty years he served as
Treasurer, and watched over with unceasing solicitude the various interests of the institution, until the close of his life. His
son Obadiah, and son-in-law, William Almy, were also large
contributors.

Moses Brown was an influential member of the General
Assembly from 1764-1771. He was the leader in the movement
to introduce paved streets in 1763. Other services to his native
city have been alluded to in connection with his elder brothers,
and also his co-operation in establishing the College of Rhode
Island at Providence. In 1790 he initiated his son and son-in-
law in the business of cotton manufacture at Pawtucket, R. I.,
under the firm name of Almy, Brown & Slater. He was instrumental in inducing the late Samuel Slater, an English mechanic
and inventor, to employ his skill in working the first *water
frames* in America. Up to this time no carding or spinning
machinery had been successfully operated, and none at all by
water. All obstacles were at length overcome, and the great
industry of cotton spinning by water power was successfully
inaugurated.

He executed his last will and testament at the great age of
ninety-six. Time had spared his intellectual faculties, and during his final illness of two weeks, he awaited with Christian
composure the summons that was to unite him with the family
and friends from whom he had so long been separated. He
married, Jan. 1, 1764, Anna Brown, who died Feb. 5, 1773, in
her 29th year. Of their three children one died in infancy.

FRIENDS' NEW ENGLAND BOARDING SCHOOL, PROVIDENCE, R. I.

His daughter, Sarah (Brown) Almy, an estimable woman, died in her 30th year. Obadiah, "my beloved son, in my old age, on whom I was looking to lean," died in his 52d year. He married, second, March 4, 1779, Mary Olney, who died Jan. 10, 1798, at the age of 54. He married, third, May 2, 1799, Phebe Lockwood. She died Oct. 19, 1808, in her 61st year. There was no issue except by the first marriage.

These successive bereavements, in the language of the late Prof. William Goddard, "took away from the aged pilgrim his staff and the companions of his journey, but they taught him to lean with more confidence upon an Almighty arm and to look forward with a more sustaining hope, to a communion with the society of Heaven. Around his fireside he could, it is true, summon neither wife nor children, nor early friend, but there were not wanting those, who, year after year, watched over him with unwearied and affectionate assiduity, and who, in some sort, compensated him for the loss of friends, whom, 'though he less deplored, he ne'er forgot.'"

His portrait, painted by Mr. Heade from an original sketch by William J. Harris, has been placed in Sayles' Memorial Hall. He was buried in his family lot in the North Ground, in the Quaker inclosure.

CHILDREN.

43. i. SARAH, b. Oct. 16, 1764.
    ii. A daughter died in infancy.
    iii. OBADIAH, b. July 15, 1770, d. Oct. 15, 1822. He was a member of the Society of Friends, and in his lifetime a generous supporter of the school which his father had been instrumental in founding. In his last will he bequeathed to the institution $100,000, besides his library of books, maps, &c. This money is said to have been largely acquired in the manufacture of cotton goods.
    He m. March 1, 1798, Dorcas, dau. of John and Elizabeth Hadwen, of Newport. R I., b. April 8, 1765, d. May 15, 1826. They had no children. His residence on Thomas Street, No. 11, next to the corner of Benefit, is now occupied by the Providence Art Club. To distinguish himself from Obadiah Brown,[6] son of Joseph,[5] he added Moses to his name, writing it Obadiah M. Brown. He died in the vigor of manhood in his 52d year.

24. ELISHA BROWN (*Joseph*,[3] *James*,[4] *John*,[2] *Chad*[1]), b. April 1, 1748, d. Feb. 13, 1832, lived in N. Providence on a part of the generous paternal estate. He m. Waite Waterman, who d. Oct. 2, 1840, aged 87.

CHILDREN.

44. i. WELCOME, b. May 12, 1777.
    ii. WATERMAN m. Hannah, dau. of Joseph and Hannah Farnum.
    iii. ELIZABETH m. Peleg Fuller.
    iv. LYDIA m. Jabez Latham.

v. PHILANEY m. Andrew Angell.
vi. SUSAN, b. 1788 m. Jason Young ; d. Sept. 20, 1875. They
     lived on the homestead farm. No issue.
vii. WAITSTILL, b. 1789, d. May 3, 1859, unmarried.
viii. CATHARINE, b. 1793, m. Freeman Fisher ; d. March 3, 1847.

25. ANDREW BROWN (*Joseph*,[9] *James*,[4] *John*,[2] *Chad*[1]),
b. Jan. 1751, d. June 8, 1832, lived in N. Providence, where all
his children were born. He had three wives, but there was issue
only by the first. He m. June 27, 1773, Dorcas Knight, b. Jan.
20, 1750, d. Jan. 12, 1791. He m. second, Lydia Dyer, widow
of Stukely Westcott, who d. April 9, 1804, He m. third, April
14, 1805, Sarah Humphrey, widow of Miles Shory, who d. Sept.
27, 1840, and was buried on her 81st birthday.

CHILDREN.

i.   ABIGAIL, b. Sept. 30, 1773, m. Emor Whipple.
ii.   WAITE, b. Sept 10, 1775, m. Asel Waterman.
iii.   MARY, b May 10, 1778, m. John Manton, and lived and died
     in Kinderhook, N Y.
iv.   SARAH, b. May 20, 1780, m. William Manton, brother of John,
     also lived in Kinderhook, and died in Johnston, R. I.
v.   JEREMIAH, b June 14, 1782, m. Esther Whipple. Had a son
     Richard, who lived, in 1885, at Central Falls, R. I.
vi.   JOSEPH, b. May 10, 1784, d. May 10, 1803.
vii.   ETHAN, b Oct. 20, 1785.
45. viii RICHARD, b. June 17, 1789.

26. SARAH BROWN (*Obadiah*,[12] *James*,[4] *John*,[2] *Chad*[1]).
b. Sept. 24, 1742, d. March 17, 1800. She m. Dec. 19, 1762,
Jabez Bowen, son of Dr. Ephraim and Mary (Fenner) Bowen.
He was in the fifth generation from Dr. Richard Bowen of England, who settled in Dorchester. Mass. in 1642. Dr. Ephraim
Bowen was a well-known practitioner of medicine in Providence,
where he died Oct. 21, 1812, at the age of 96. His father,
grandfather, and the first Richard were all physicians. Of his
fourteen children, Jabez, the eldest, was b. June 13, 1739, and
d. May 8, 1815. Maternally, he was in the fifth generation
from Arthur Fenner (*Mary*,[4] *Thomas*,[3] *Major Thomas*,[2] *Capt.
Arthur*[1]). He graduated at Yale in 1757, received the honorary
degree of A. M. from the College of R. I. at its first commencement in Warren, 1769, and the degree of LL.D. from Dartmouth College. N. H., in 1800. He was a member of the Town
Council from 1773-75, a Representative in the General Assembly
from 1777-90, and Deputy Governor in 1788. An active patriot
in the war for American Independence, he commanded a R. I.
regiment in the winter of 1777, was an influential member of
the Board of War, and also of the Convention that adopted the
Constitution of the United States, May 29, 1790. He was on
the first school committee appointed by the town in 1800, President of the Bible Society, a member of the Board of Fellows of

Brown University from 1768–85, and Chancellor from 1785–1815. He was a prominent Free Mason in St. John's Lodge, and from 1794–99 served as Grand Master.

In all these various relations, his eminent executive ability and unquestioned integrity were wholly devoted to the generation which he served so wisely and so well. His religious affiliations were with the First Congregational Church, of which he was a devout and consistent member. He died at his residence, George Street, corner of Prospect, and was buried in the West ground from which his remains were afterwards removed to Swan Point Cemetery. The portraits of Jabez and Sarah Bowen, painted by Copley, are the property of their grandson, William H. Bowen, of Providence.

CHILDREN.

i. OBADIAH, b. Oct. 5, 1763, d. July 25, 1793.
ii. OLIVER, b. April 21, 1767. He married and left two daus. neither of whom is now living,
iii. MARY, b. June 28, 1772, d. July 15, 1792.
iv. JABEZ, b. Jan. 29, 1774, d. unm. Aug. 8, 1816. Graduated at Brown University, in 1788.
v. HENRY, b. Feb. 8, 1776, d. Aug. 31, 1777.
vi. HORATIO GATES, b. June 18, 1779, d. March 21, 1848. Graduated at Brown University in 1797 ; was for 17 years its librarian, and Professor of Natural History in 1828. He married, but left no children.
vii. An infant son, b. Sept. 10, d. Oct. 1, 1782.
46. viii. HENRY 2d. b. Jan 5, 1785.

27. MARY BROWN (*Obadiah,*[12] *James,*[4] *John,*[2] *Chad*[1]), b. Nov. 25, 1753, m. Jan. 14, 1779, Thomas, son of Jonathan and Abigail (Smith) Arnold. (*Jonathan,*[4] *Thomas,*[3] *Richard,*[2] *Thomas*[1]). The first Thomas of England was half brother of William Arnold, one of the 13 original proprietors of Providence, and of Joanna (Arnold) Hopkins, the ancestress of Gov. Stephen Hopkins. Abigail Smith was dau. of Benjamin, gr. dau. of John, and g. gr. dau. of John Smith, Miller. Thomas Arnold was b. Oct. 10, 1751, and d. Nov. 8, 1826. Thomas and Mary Arnold lived on the Neck Road, opposite Swan Point Cemetery. A large elm tree stands in front of the house, since called the Perry place.

They had two children : *Anna,*[6] b. Nov. 5, 1779, d. in New Bedford, Mass., May 28, 1865, unmarried. *James Arnold,*[6] b. Sept. 9, 1781, d. Dec. 3, 1868. He m. Oct. 27, 1807, Sarah Rodman, dau. of William Rotch. Their only child, Elizabeth Rotch, b. Jan. 17, 1809, was m. March 17, 1859, to Dr. Charles M. Tuttle. She d. Oct. 26, 1860, childless, and the line is extinct. *James Arnold* removed to New Bedford, and engaged extensively in the shipping business with his father-in-law, Mr. William Rotch, a prominent merchant of Nantucket and New Bedford. They had many vessels employed in the whale fishery. His house was surrounded by extensive and beautiful grounds, which were freely open to strangers and residents.

He left a large estate, and by his will bequeathed $100,000 to Harvard University for the founding of the Arnold Arboretum, on the Bussey estate in West Roxbury, to be in charge of a professor, called the Arnold Professor. Of this sum the greater part of the income was to be accumulated until the fund amounted to at least $150,000, and the Bussey estate passed completely into the hands of the President and Fellows. It will include about one hundred and thirty-seven acres, and is to be laid out as an open park with suitable walks and roadways, containing, as far as practicable, all the trees, shrubs and herbaceous plants, either indigenous or exotic, which can be raised in the open air. All the specimens are to be distinctly labelled, as it is intended to educate the public, as well as the special students who resort to it.

At a recent meeting of the Massachusetts Horticultural and American Pomological Societies in Boston, Sept. 1887. there was an interesting exhibition of shrubs in fruit from the Arnold Aboretum. The selection comprised branches from sixty-eight shrubs, hardy in this latitude, and all in fruit, and as a single collection, probably, could not have been matched in the world. The fruit was of all sizes and colors, and the mass of crab apples, buckthorns, euonymus, wild roses. dogwoods. sumachs and viburnums, made a striking display.

28. MARY BROWN (*Jeremiah.*[13] *James,*[4] *John,*[2] *Chad*[1]), b. July 28, 1740, d. July 6, 1801, was m. Sept. 30, 1770, to David Howell,* son of Aaron and Sarah Howell. Their residence, on the east side of Benefit, near Angell street, is still standing. The following sketch is from the "Biographical Cyclopedia of Representative Men of Rhode Island."

"David Howell, LL. D., was born in Morristown, New Jersey, Jan. 1, 1747. (O. S.) and was a graduate of the College of New Jersey, in the class of 1766. Soon after leaving college, at the urgent request of President Manning, he became his associate in the College of Rhode Island, now Brown University, which had commenced its existence in Warren in 1764. He was a tutor in the institution three years, and then in 1769 was appointed Professor of Mathematics and Natural Philosophy, holding that office until the suspension of college exercises in consequence of the Revolutionary War. Besides giving instruction in the studies which belonged to his special department, he also taught the French, German and Hebrew languages. He was Professor of Law for

---

* He was probably a descendant of Edward Howell, Gentleman, of Marsh Gibbon, Buckinghamshire. Eng., who was one of the original settlers of Southampton, L. I., in 1640. Before the close of the century, New Jersey received many settlers from Long Island families, among whom the Howells were represented.

thirty-four years, although it does not appear that he gave lectures in that department. He was for many years the Secretary of the Corporation of Brown University, and for fifty-two years a member of the Board of Fellows. Upon the decease of President Manning, July 24, 1791, he was requested to preside at the approaching commencement in September and also at the commencement following, on which occasions, says Professor Goddard, 'he delivered to the graduating classes Baccalaureate Addresses, which, as specimens of undefiled English and excellent counsel, were deservedly admired.'"

"For many years he practiced law in Providence, and held a high rank among the members of the Rhode Island bar. He was a Member of Congress under the Confederation, from Rhode Island, and subsequently was called to fill offices of trust and responsibility of the highest character in the State. He was appointed United States Judge for the District of Rhode Island in 1812, and filled that important position until his death."

"Judge Howell," says Professor Goddard, "was endowed with extraordinary talents, and he superadded to his endowments extensive and accurate learning. As an able jurist he established for himself a solid reputation. He was, however, yet more distinguished as a keen and brilliant wit, and as a scholar extensively acquainted not only with the ancient, but with several of the modern languages. As a pungent and effective public writer, he was almost unrivalled ; and in conversation, whatever chanced to be the theme, whether politics or law, literature or theology, grammar or criticism, a Greek tragedy or a difficult problem in mathematics, Judge Howell was never found wanting. Upon all occasions which made any demands upon him, he gave the most convincing evidence of the vigor of his powers, and of the variety and extent of his erudition."

He died in Providence, July 21, 1824. The accompanying portrait of David Howell is copied from Trumbull's great painting of Washington resigning his Commission to Congress, in the Rotunda at Washington, D. C. The original sketch was taken by the artist, from life, in Providence in 1793.

CHILDREN.

47. i. JEREMIAH BROWN, b. Aug. 28, 1771.
 ii. ROGER WILLIAMS, b. Aug. 11, 1773, d. Oct. 7, 1792. A member of the Senior class of Brown University.
 iii. SARAH COOKE, b. June 27, d. July 25, 1775, aged four weeks.
48. iv WAITSTILL, b. June 27, 1776.
49. v. MARIA B., b. Feb. 5, 1779.
50. vi. SARAH, b. Feb. 1, 1781.

29. JOHN BROWN (*Dep.-Gov. Elisha,*[14] *James,*[4] *John,*[2] *Chad*[1]), b. Jan. 28, 1742, d. May 24, 1775. He m. Wait, dau. of Charles and Wait (Dexter) Field. The ceremony was performed on Sunday evening, Jan. 25, 1772, by Rev. James Man-

ning, D. D. She was grand dau. of William and Mary Field,
and g. gr.-dau. of Thomas and Martha (Harris) Field. Martha
was dau. of the first Thomas Harris. On the maternal side she
was grand-dau. of Stephen and Susannah (Whipple) Dexter and
g. gr.-dau. of John and Alice (Smith) Dexter. John Dexter was
the third son of Rev. Gregory and Abigail (Fullerton) Dexter.
Alice Smith was dau. of John and Sarah (Whipple) Smith. The
mother of Susannah Whipple was also an Alice Smith, but she
was of another line, dau. of Edward[2] and gr.-dau. of the first
Christopher Smith. Edward Smith[2] m. Amphillis Angell[2]
(Thomas[1]), and had a dau. Alice, who became the wife of
Joseph[2] Whipple, son of the first John. Joseph and Alice
Whipple were the parents of Susannah.* Wait Field was b.
May 24, 1744, and d. July 19, 1819. She was left a widow at
the age of thirty-one with an infant dau. Martha Brown. She
m. second, John Smith, Jr., born Oct. 7, 1742, who d. in
Smithfield, Feb. 1807. It is said that her second husband, then a
widower, offered himself in marriage during the early years of
her widowhood, but she, fearing that a second marriage might
imperil the interests of her young daughter, who had inherited
from her father the grist mill property and a large portion of the
estate of John Smith, Miller, declined the offer. Her dau.
Martha married soon after coming of age, Oct. 17, 1793, and the
long-deferred union of the widow Brown and John Smith, Jr.,
was consummated the following winter, Feb. 13, 1794. The
second husband was a worthy man, and proved in every way so
acceptable, that Mrs. Smith always regretted that she had put his
love to so severe a test. Such devotion is worthy of record, and
an attempt has been made to rescue from oblivion the genealogical line of John Smith, Jr. It is probable that he was a descendant in the fifth generation of John Smith, the Mason (*John
Smith, Jr.,[5] John,[4] Joseph,[3] of Smithfield, John,[2] John[1]*).
By the second marriage there was no issue. The only child of
John and Wait (Field) Brown was

51.   MARTHA, b. Sept. 5, 1772.

30. JAMES BROWN (*Dep.-Gov. Elisha,[14] James,[4] John,[2]
Chad[1]*), b. April 27, 1744, m. July 19, 1764, Freelove, b. April
17, 1742, dau. of Colonel William and Susannah (Dexter)
Brown, grand dau. of Colonel Richard and great gr. dau. of the
first Henry and Waite (Waterman) Brown. No connection has
been traced between Chad and Henry Brown, but their descendants intermarried as early as the third generation. Her grandfather, Col. Richard Brown, built the brick house on the Swan
Point Road, now in the Butler Hospital grounds, which is supposed to antedate the Elisha Brown house by several years.

* The intermarriages in the ancestory of Wait Field are easily understood by means
of an admirably arranged chart designed by one of her great grandsons, Charles Field
Wilcox.

The bricks used in the construction of these buildings, the first of the kind in town, were probably the product of the brick yard on the Neck, established at an early date. Col. William and Elisha Brown were at one time partners in business. Richard Brown, brother of Col. William, died in 1812, aged 100 years and 12 days. He celebrated the hundredth anniversary of his birth by inviting his friends to a dance, and, it is said, played on a violin for their amusement. James Brown d. at St. Croix, Jan. 6, 1766, leaving one son. *James*, who married, but left no children, and this line is extinct.*

31. CAPT. JEREMIAH BROWN (*Dep.-Gov. Elisha,*[14] *James,*[4] *John,*[2] *Chad*[1]), b. Dec. 28, 1746, m. first, April 21, 1765, Mary, dau. of Elijah and Hannah (Barker) Cushing, b. at Hanover, Mass. (now Scituate), Dec. 27, 1737. She was the eldest dau. of his step-mother, Hannah, the second wife of Elisha Brown. He m. second, in Boston, Oct. 1791, Susannah, widow of Thomas Bowen, of Seekonk, and dau. of John Welch, of Boston. She was b. April 29, 1756, and d. Dec. 16, 1821. Her father is thus mentioned in the Report of Record Commissioners of Boston, Mass., book No. 13, page 236.

May 2, 1733, "The Selectmen leased to John Welch of Boston, *Carver*, a wooden Shop or building now in his Possession, called No. 9, fronting Dock Square, for 4 years and 3 months at Twenty Pounds Pr. annum." In April, 1736, John was chosen one of the Clerks in the Market, and in March, 1737, scavenger. May 25, 1735, John subscribed £15 towards a Workhouse. The measurement of his land, in 1802, is found in No. 3, page 249. From John Welch's land over to Mr. Gill's is 20 feet. Length of Gill street is 214 feet. From Ezra Welch's house over to Dr. Morse's fence is 43 feet 6 inches. In book No. 1, June 6, 1687, John Welch is on the tax list for 1 head—2 housings, and wharf and trucks. His name also appears in several succeeding years. The partial records given of his family indicate that the latter John Welch was the g. gr. father of Susannah.

The residence of Jeremiah Brown was on Smith street, on land bequeathed to him by his mother, Martha (Smith) Brown. It was a two story frame house, with a row of Lombardy poplars in front. Many years since it was burned, and the land is now used for railroad purposes. The following inscription is from his gravestone in the North Ground. "Sacred to the Memory of Capt. Jeremiah Brown, who was born Dec. 28, 1746, (O. S.) And after many trying misfortunes and vicissitudes in life which he sustained with fortitude and resignation, calmly exchanged this, in full hope of a happier state of existence, Jan. 4, 1817, (N. S.)

CHILDREN (by first wife).

52. i.   ABIGAIL, b. June 2, 1766.
53. ii. CATHARINE, b. April 11, 1768.

*James Brown, of James, deceased, and Elizabeth Appleby, of James, Jr., were married by John Sayles, Nov. 25, 1792. He was probably son of James and Freelove Brown. (See Marriage Records of Old Smithfield.)

54. iii. MARY, b. May 19, 1770.
55. iv.   CUSHING, b. Jan. 5, 1777.
56. v.   JEREMIAH, b. Nov. 10, 1778.

CHILDREN (by second wife),

57. vi.   HUGH HALL, b. May 16, 1792.
     vii. OBADIAH, b. 1793 ; d. in infancy.
58. viii. EBENEZER PERKINS, b. April 10, 1797.
59. ix.   JOHN SMITH, b. Oct. 4, 1799.

32. ELISHA BROWN (*Dep.-Gov. Elisha*,[1][4] *James*,[4] *John*,[2] *Chad*[1]), b. June 1, 1749, d. March, 1827 : m. April 24, 1774, Elizabeth Bowen, of Rehoboth.   She d. 181—.

CHILDREN.

60. i.   LYDIA, b. Jan. 2, 1775.
     ii.   DEBORAH, b. Dec. 27, 1776; d. April 26, 1800.
61. iii. ELIZABETH, b. Sept. 24, 1779.
     iv.   LUCY, b. Nov. 1, 1781; d. Jan. 25, 1784.
     v.   ELISHA,) b. Jan. 20, 1784; d. at Batavia, Oct. 6, 1802.
62. vi.   JOHN,   ) .
     vii. LUCY, b. May 24, 1785 ; d. May 15, 1787.
     viii. ALONZO, b. Dec 24, 1787 ; d. Jan. 16, 1866.   Buried in North Ground, Providence.
     ix.   JAMES, b. Oct. 4, 1790; d. May 12, 1791.

33. ISAAC BROWN (*Dep.-Gov. Elisha*,[1][4] *James*,[4] *John*,[2] *Chad*[1]), b. May 23, 1751, was a sea captain, and at the time of his death was in command of the sloop *Hannah*.   Nov. 20, 1793, he was knocked overboard by the swinging of the boom of his vessel, and drowned. He was probably stunned by the blow, as he did not rise. *The Providence Gazette* of Saturday, Dec. 7, 1793, thus refers to the event.   "On Sunday last arrived from Charleston the sloop *Hannah*, late commanded by Capt. Isaac Brown, of this place. Near Charleston Bar, Capt. Brown accidentally fell overboard and was unfortunately drowned, notwithstanding every exertion of the mate and crew to save him. He was a worthy man, an industrious and useful citizen, and his loss is justly regretted."

In the Custom House Book of Manifest, there is frequent mention of Capt. Isaac Brown. June 6, 1785, he entered port from Hispaniola, in the brigantine *New Weuscutt*, with a miscellaneous cargo of 374 bbls. of salt, molasses, anise-seed, limes, cordials, 8 tierces of Taflier rum, coffee, &c.   Feb. 18, 1788, he returned from Cape Francois, in the sloop *Providence*. His cargo consisted of molasses, salt, claret, brandy, spirits, turpentine, old iron, &c.   May 2, 1788, he entered from Charleston, in the same sloop with corn, deerskins, red cedar, rice, indigo, potatoes, brooms, &c.   There is no mention of him after Aug. 12, 1793, when he was licensed as commander of the sloop *Han-*

nah. He m. Jan. 21, 1776, Amey, eldest dau. of Christopher and Priscilla (Carpenter*) Dexter, of North Providence. She was the gr.-dau. of Stephen and Susannah (Whipple) Dexter, and the g. gr.-dau. of John and Alice (Smith) Dexter.† John Dexter was the third son of Gregory and Abigail (Fullerton) Dexter. Capt. Brown lived on North Main street, near the present Doyle avenue. An engine-house, has, within recent years, been erected nearly on the site of the old house. Of their nine children only three survived infancy, viz. :

   63. i. AMEY, b. July 7, 1784.
   64. ii. ISAAC, b. Oct. 4, 1787.
   65. iii. ALICE DEXTER. b. Jan. 2, 1790.
        Epitaph, North Ground, Providence : " Mrs. Amey Brown died March 28. 1844, aged 94 years, widow of Capt. Isaac Brown, who was lost at sea Nov. 20, 1793, aged 42. Erected by her son, Isaac Brown. as a testimonial of her watchful care over and unceasing kindness to her children and grandchildren during her long and useful life."

34. SMITH BROWN (*Dep.-Gov. Elisha,* [14] *James,* [4] *John,* [2] *Chad* [1]), b. April 12, 1756, d. Nov. 20, 1826. He m. Oct. 12, 1785, Lydia, dau. of Samuel and Elizabeth (Barker) Gould, of Pembroke, Mass. She was the gr.-dau. of Isaac Barker, and probably related to Hannah, the stepmother of Smith, who was the dau. of James Barker, of Newport. He resided the latter part of his life at Pembroke, Mass., on what is now known as Oak Dale Farm.

CHILDREN.

   66. i. SAMUEL, b. Feb. 12, 1787.
      ii ANNA, b. Oct. 4, 1788; d. June 16, 1813.
      iii. GOOLD, b. March 7, 1791; d. in Lynn, Mass.. March 31. 1857. He m. Nov. 8, 1842, Mary, dau. of Nathaniel Starbuck. They had no children, but adopted two daughters, whose history is omitted, as they were not descendants of Chad Brown. "The profession of a teacher, which he pursued during many years, and an inclination for philological studies, not only taught him an existing deficiency in educational books, but enabled him to supply it by his *Institutes of English Grammar.* This work soon superseded the school grammars formerly in use, and by its pecuniary success, with that of other enterprises, enabled him to fulfill the design he had long before formed, of presenting to the world something like a complete grammar of the English language. This work, entitled *The Grammar of English Grammars,* is not more a monument of industry and exact and systematic method, than of thorough comprehension and masterly analysis. It contains a ' condensed mass of special criticism such as is not elsewhere to be found in any language,' and, while it is specially characterized by an almost microscopic minuteness of grammatical investigation, it often ascends into the region of general principles. His labors, always stimulated and sustained by a severe and reverential sense

* Probably a descendant of William and Elizabeth (Arnold) Carpenter.
† See No. 29.

of duty, were not remitted even after his great object had
been attained, and are supposed to have hastened his death."
(See Grammar of English Grammars.)

67. iv. WILLIAM B., b. March 21, 1793.
68. v. ELIZABETH, b. May 10, 1795.
    vi. LYDIA, b. Jan. 14, 1798, d. in Pembroke, Mass., Nov. 22, 1883,
        in her 86th year. Of the 35 grandchildren of Elisha and
        Martha (Smith) Brown, 11 of whom died young, she was the
        youngest but one, and the last survivor. She attained the
        greatest age of them all. Two others died at past four score
        ——, her brother Samuel, in his 82d year, and her cousin,
        Isaac Brown, in his 85th year. The history of these grand-
        children covers a period of 118 years, from the birth of
        James in 1765, to the death of Lydia in 1883.
        The following sketch of her life, abridged from the
        Woman's Journal of Dec. 22, 1883, was contributed by her
        nephew, William A. Brown : "She was the youngest of
        six children, and received what was, for those days, a
        fair education, both at home and at the Friends' School at
        Nine Partners, N. Y., where her eldest brother Samuel was
        a teacher, and her second brother, Goold Brown, afterwards
        so well known as the author of Brown's Grammar, and a
        younger brother, the late Dr. William B. Brown, of Lynn,
        were scholars. From her early years she manifested an
        active interest in literary and educational matters. Born
        and living a member of the Society of Friends, her attention
        was naturally drawn to the great subjects of anti-slavery,
        peace, temperance, woman's rights and all moral reforms.
        She was one of the early members of the Anti-Slavery
        Society, and a constant reader of the *Liberator*, from its start
        until, when its work was done, it ceased from its labors.
        Her voice and purse were always ready to counsel and assist
        every worker in the anti-slavery ranks. When slavery
        ceased to exist in America, her heart prompted her to lend
        all her strength in aid of the Freemen, and in 1865 she went
        South as a teacher of the race she had so long worked to
        emancipate. Owing to failing health she was obliged to
        return North, but she never lost her interest in the good
        work. She was an early subscriber to the *Woman's Journal*,
        and a frequent contributor to its columns. She was one of
        the most advanced believers in the right of woman to take
        her part in the management of human affairs, and devoted
        much time, money and thought, to the elevation of woman.
        Every benevolent, charitable and elevating object found in
        her an ardent supporter and firm friend, and no appeal to
        her kind heart was ever unheeded. Naturally possessed of
        a strong, retentive memory, which she retained unto the
        last, her personal reminiscences were highly instructive.
        By her death we lose almost the last of the band of pioneers
        in the anti-slavery, temperance, peace and woman suffrage
        reforms of the country."

35. ELISHA BROWN (*Chad,*[15] *Obadiah,*[5] *John,*[2] *Chad*[1])
lived and died in Glocester, R. I., and was buried on the Esek
Brown farm. As before stated, information regarding this
branch of the Browns, the posterity of Andrew and Chad, who
settled in Glocester, on land separated by the Chepachet river,
has been derived mainly from the papers of the late Col. George
H. Browne, compiled more than thirty-five years since. In a few

LYDIA BROWN.

Born 1st mo., 14th, 1798.

Died 11th mo., 22d, 1883.

instances errors have been corrected, but in the main the records have been copied *verbatim*. They are incomplete, but afford in many cases the only information obtainable. and without them this branch would have had no representation. Elisha m. Sarah Olney, of North Providence.

CHILDREN

    i. CHAD d. in infancy.
69. ii. ESEK.
   iii. OLNEY. He lived on the southwestern part of his father's estate, married and had a large family. He is said to have been a passionate lover of the chase. Of his children (1) *Chad*[7] m. Nancy Wade and had Nancy[8] (who m Lorenzo Carpenter), Chad[8] and others. (2) *Marcelous*[7] d. unm. (3) *Olney*[7] was twice m. and had children. (4) *Amey*[7] d. unm. (5) *Jesse*[7] m. and had children. (6) *William*[7] m. —— Burnham and had children. (7) *Haney*[7] m. Donnoud Burrill and had Charles[8] and Lafayette.[8] (8) *A daughter*[7] m. Jonathan Wade and had children. (9) *Deborah*[7] m. Anthony Clemence. of Glocester, and removed to Connecticut.
   iv. DORKIS m. Esek Sayles, of Burrillville, and had *Rebecca*,[7] *Chad*[7] and others.
   v. SARAH m. —— Handy. No issue.
   vi. MERCY m. Abram Belknap, of Johnston, and had numerous descendants.

36. JESSE BROWN (*Chad*,[15] *Obadiah*,[5] *John*,[2] *Chad*[1]), b. 1739, d. Sept. 11, 1815 ; m. ——.

CHILDREN.

    i. ANN PHILLIS, b. July 15, 1759, m. Philip Sweet ; she d. Oct. 1836, leaving a large family among whom were *Ethan Sweet*,[7] *Jesse B. Sweet*,[7] of Providence. *Betsy Sweet*,[7] m. Ethan Olney, of N. Providence, and *Sarah Sweet*,[7] m. —— Harris and removed to Ohio.
   ii. ABIGAIL, b. Sept. 8, 1761, m. Thomas Owen, a merchant and farmer, in Chepachet. Their children were *Ann Phillis*,[7] b. Aug. 1787, (?) *Sabin*,[7] b. July 19, 1792, *Brown*,[7] and *Ruth*,[7] b. June 30, 1800. Of these, *Brown*,[7] a seafaring man, d. young ; *Sabin*,[7] a farmer in Glocester, m. Susan Wilbur and had one child Mary Frances.[8] The sisters married brothers and reared large families. *Ann Phillis*[7] m. Hon. Ira P. Evans, of Glocester, and had (1) Mary,[8] m. Silas Kimball, of Blackstone ; (2) Rebecca,[8] m. Elisha M. Aldrich, of Glocester ; (3) Thomas O.[8] m. Emily Farr, of Vermont (4) George C.[8] m. Mary Ann Reynolds, dau. of Jacob, and removed to Grand Rapids, Mich.; (5) Daniel W[8] m. Elizabeth ——, of Cleveland, Ohio ; (6) Ira P. Jr.[8] m. —— and had several daughters He died at Buda. Bureau Co. Ill., where his widow now resides. *Ruth Owen*,[7] sister of *Ann Phillis*, m. Duty Evans, of Glocester, and lived in Providence. They had seven children :—Abby O.,[8] Caroline,[8] Gilbert,[8] William,[8] Mary,[8] Anna,[8] Frances.[8] Of these, Abby O. m. Dr. George Angell, son of Nedebiah.
   iii. AMEY, b. Oct. 17, 1763, m. Nicholas Smith. son of Capt. John, and lived in Thompson, Ct. They had four daughters besides other children The daughters were *Hannah*[7] m. —— Eddy ; *Elizabeth*[7] m —— ; *Asenath*[7] m. —— ; *Rhoda*[7] m. —— Torrey.

SIXTH GENERATION.

37. NICHOLAS BROWN (*Nicholas*,[20] *James*,[8] *James*,[4] *John*,[2] *Chad*[1]), b. April 4, 1769, was educated at the College of Rhode Island, where he graduated in 1786 in his eighteenth year. Upon coming of age he was admitted to a share in his father's business and the firm became Browns & Benson. In 1792, Thomas P. Ives, who had married Hope Brown, sister of Nicholas, was received as partner. Four years later, after the withdrawal of Mr. Benson, the house assumed the name of Brown & Ives and soon achieved a world-wide reputation. Extending its operations to every part of the commercial world, it was beset by more than ordinary perils arising from the troubled state of Europe during the French Revolution, the wars of Napoleon, the war of 1812 between the United States and England, and the restrictive policy of our own government. But this hazardous business of foreign commerce was steadily and successfully prosecuted, and the credit of the house unimpaired during its long career of fifty years. After the death of Mr. Ives in 1835, Mr. Brown's interest in mercantile affairs declined somewhat, but his business activities continued almost to the close of his life. The attention of the house had early been attracted to manufacturing, and in 1804 Brown & Ives became interested in the cotton mill at Blackstone, Mass. Manufactures gradually superseded commerce, and after the formation of the Lonsdale Company, the change in the business of the firm was marked. The mercantile career of Brown & Ives was practically closed in 1838, by the sale of their last ship, the *Hanover*. Since that time the chief concern of the house has been manufacturing, which has developed into such proportions that their establishments are now among the largest in the State.

In politics Nicholas Brown was a Federalist, and from 1807–'21 was in the General Assembly either as Senator or Representative. In the Presidential canvass of 1840 he was chosen one of the electors of Rhode Island, and gave his vote for William H. Harrison, his last political service.

His official relations with the University which bears his name, were intimate and protracted during a term of fifty years. He was a Trustee in 1791, Treasurer from 1796–1825, and a member of the Board of Fellows from 1825 until his death in 1841. In 1804 he presented to the College a good law library, and gave five thousand dollars to found a Professorship of Oratory and *Belles Lettres*. In grateful acknowledgment of his benefactions, the name of the institution was changed the same year from Rhode Island College to Brown University. In 1823 and 1834 he erected, at his sole expense, Hope College and Manning Hall, and presented them to the corporation. Brown & Ives purchased and gave to the University in 1829, a set of philosophical apparatus adequate for any purpose of scientific illustration. In 1832

Mr. Brown subscribed ten thousand dollars towards the fund for the Library and the Chemical and Philosophical Departments. He also contributed ten thousand dollars to the sum required in 1839 for the erection of Rhode Island Hall and the President's Mansion. The sum total of his benefactions to his Alma Mater is estimated at one hundred and sixty thousand dollars.

He was one of the founders of the Providence Athenæum to which he contributed liberally. For the building of churches and the endowment of colleges in different parts of the country, he gave large sums annually, and no appeal to his generosity for a worthy cause was unheeded. Although he made no public profession of his faith, he was a life-long worshiper in the First Baptist Church, and warmly attached to the principles of that denomination. In 1792 he presented to the Charitable Baptist Society the property at 38 Angell Street, as a Parsonage for the First Baptist Church.* In his will he bequeathed the sum of thirty thousand dollars toward the erection or endowment of an Insane Asylum. The Butler Hospital for the Insane had its origin in this gift.

He died Sept. 27, 1841, after a long illness, which he bore with Christian composure in the assured hope of a better life. The following inscription marks his last resting place in the North Burial Ground : "The grave of Nicholas Brown, An eminent merchant, the friend of the friendless, the patron of learning, the benefactor of the insane and the liberal promoter of every good design."

He married, Nov. 3, 1791, Ann, daughter of Ann and Amey (Crawford) Carter, and gr.-dau. of John and Amey (Whipple) Crawford. John Crawford, b. Aug. 1693, was son of Gideon and Freelove (Fenner) Crawford, and gr. son of Capt. Arthur Fenner. John Carter was an early printer of Providence. Ann (Carter) Brown died June 16, 1798, in her 29th year, leaving two sons and a daughter. Nicholas Brown married second, July 22, 1801, Mary Bowen Stelle, daughter of Benjamin and Huldah (Crawford) Stelle, who died without issue, Dec. 12, 1836, in her 67th year. Benjamin Stelle, son of Rev. Isaac, established a Latin school in Providence, in 1776.

CHILDREN.

70. i. NICHOLAS, b. Oct. 2, 1792.
    ii. MOSES, b. Sept. 2, 1793, d. July 17, 1794.
    iii. ANN CARTER, b Oct. 11, 1795, d May 1, 1828 ; was m. June 18, 1822, to John Brown Francis. (See No. 75.)
71. iv. JOHN CARTER, b. Aug. 28, 1797.

38. HOPE BROWN (See No. 37), dau. of Nicholas and Rhoda (Jenckes) Brown, b. Feb. 22, 1773, d. Aug. 21, 1855, was m. March 5, 1792, to Thomas Poynton Ives, b. in Beverly, Mass.,

* A new parsonage was erected in 1884 upon the old site.

April 9, 1769, d. in Providence, April 30, 1835. He was the
second son of Robert Hale and Sarah (Bray) Ives, gr. son of
Benjamin and Sarah (Driver) Bray, and g. gr. son of Capt.
Michael and Sarah (Gray) Driver. He was in the fifth generation from Thomas Ives, of Beverly, Mass. (*Robert II.,⁴ Capt.
Benja.nin,³ Capt. Benjamin,² Thomas¹*). His parents dying
in early life, he was committed to the care of relatives in Boston.
At the age of thirteen he was taken from school and placed as a
clerk in the house of Brown & Benson, Providence. After his
marriage with Hope Brown he became a partner in the business,
which, in 1796, in consequence of the retirement of Mr. Benson,
assumed the name of Brown & Ives. His executive talent was
remarkable and contributed largely to the success of the firm.
He was a liberal benefactor of Brown University, and for forty-
three years a member of its Board of Trustees. During twenty-
four years he was President of the Providence Bank, and was the
first President of the Providence Institution for Savings, which
owes much of its present prosperity and usefulness to the wisdom
of his early supervision. His benevolence was active but unostentatious, and no worthy applicant, however humble, was
repulsed. In his attendance upon public worship he was constant and devout, and his daily life bore testimony to the sin-
cerity of his Christian principles. His integrity was unquestioned, his honor without a blemish. He died in the fulness of
his intellectual powers, before he had attained the Scriptural
limit of three score years and ten, leaving to the community of
his adopted city an example worthy of imitation as a man and a
Christian merchant.

CHILDREN.

72. i   CHARLOTTE RHODA, b. Dec. 18, 1792.
73. ii. MOSES BROWN, b. July 21, 1794.
     iii. ELIZABETH, b Aug. 6, 1796, d. March 12, 1813.
74. iv. ROBERT HALE, b. Sept. 16, 1798.
     v. HOPE BROWN, b. May 14, 1802, d. April 15, 1837. "She was
         an invalid for many years, but possessed a gentle and lovable
         character, and bore her long seclusion with patience and
         Christian fortitude. Premature disease blighted the bril-
         liant promises of her youth, and she passed through a pro-
         tracted period of suffering to the rest which awaited her—
         from the trials of human virtue to the scene of its everlast-
         ing triumphs " *
     vi. THOMAS POYNTON, b. March 25, 1804, d. Aug. 15, 1804.

39. MARY BROWN (*Joseph,²¹ James,⁸ James,⁴ John,²
Chad¹*), b. July 30, 1760, d. Dec. 8, 1800. She is said to have
been a woman of great worth, possessing many and rare accom-
plishments. She was married July 18, 1799, to Dr. Stephen
Gano, the honored pastor of the First Baptist Church in Providence. His ministry extended over a period of thirty-six years

* See Writings of William G. Goddard.

Thomas P. Ives

Eliza B. Rogers

from 1792-1828. He was the son of Rev. John and Sarah (Stites) Gano, and was a descendant of Francis Gerneaux, a Huguenot refugee from the island of Guernsey, after the revocation of the Edict of Nantes, who settled in New Rochelle, where he died at the age of one hundred and three years. The only child of Dr. Stephen and Mary (Brown) Gano, and the only grand-child of Joseph and Elizabeth (Power) Brown, was *Eliza Brown Gano*, b. Nov. 6, 1800, d. Dec. 23, 1877. She was married Nov. 7, 1821, to Joseph Rogers, b. March 21, 1794, son of John and Elizabeth (Rodman) Rogers, of Providence. He died May 14, 1873. (By this marriage there was no issue.)

"The predominant traits of her character—her deep piety, large benevolence, wide sympathy and warm affections, showed themselves early in life and were inherited in a large degree from her father, Dr. Gano, who was so long and devotedly loved in the city of her birth. She helped to found many of the benevolent organizations of her day, and to every worthy cause was a liberal contributor. Her labors in behalf of Sunday Schools, and in missionary, church and prayer meetings, were unceasing and ended only with her life. But to the wide circle of her relatives and friends whose reverence for her memory is deep and abiding, it is the thought of what she was, rather than what she did, that is oftenest recalled. Her wonderfully sympathetic nature alleviated the afflictions, lightened the burdens, relieved the perplexities, and restored the courage of all that came within her influence, or sought her loving counsels and prayerful intercession. Her many natural gifts had been consecrated to the service of her Master, and no sacrifice for the good of others—saints or sinners, was deemed too great an offering for the glory of His cause. Perhaps her crowning grace was that of power in prayer. Her strong faith bore to the throne of mercy the penitent, imploring supplication of many a sin-stricken soul, till forgiveness seemed assured and despair gave place to joy and peace. She was a woman of strong convictions, but tolerant of the opinions of others, and wherever she recognized the spirit of the Master, the flow of her sympathies was too broad to be hindered by the barriers of creed or faith. She passed in perfect peace to the higher life, grateful for the many mercies that surrounded her, and sustained by an unfaltering trust in the merits of her Redeemer."

40. ABBY BROWN (*John,*[22] *James,*[5] *James,*[4] *John,*[2] *Chad*[1]), b. Nov. 20, 1766, d. March 5, 1821, was the eldest dau. of John and Sarah (Smith) Brown. She was married Jan. 1, 1788, to John Francis, a merchant of Philadelphia. b. May 30, 1763, d. in Providence, Oct. 8, 1796. He was the son of Tench and Anne (Willing) Francis, and gr.-son of Tench and Elizabeth (Turbutt) Francis. Mrs. Francis was early left a widow, and devoted herself with maternal care and solicitude to

the welfare of her only surviving child, John Brown Francis, afterwards Governor of Rhode Island. He was the special charge of his grandfather, John Brown, the third of the four brothers, who directed his education, and in his will indicated the course he wished him to pursue in succeeding years.

The following lines are quoted from an obituary of Mrs. Francis by the late Prof. William G. Goddard : "In an extensive acquaintance with the world, and in the various relations of domestic life, the character of this amiable woman exemplified, in harmonious combination, many of the finest virtues of our nature. Her unaffected courtesy and genuine hospitality were the natural fruit of that law of kindness which dwelt in her heart and which indicated itself in a watchful regard to the happiness of those around her, and in the exemplary discharge of those unobserved and less prominent offices of benevolence which help to smooth the rugged corners of life."

CHILDREN.

    i. ANNE WILLING, b. Feb. 24, 1790, d. May 20, 1798
75. ii. JOHN BROWN, b. May 31, 1791.

41. SARAH BROWN* (See No. 40), b. in Providence, Sept. 5, 1773, d. in Bristol, Aug. 2, 1846, was the fifth child of John and Sarah (Smith) Brown. She was m. July 2, 1801, to Charles Frederick Herreshoff, a native of Minden, Prussia, then of the city of New York. "A few months after their marriage they removed to Rhode Island, their home being alternately in Providence and Bristol. Her father gave her the best education obtainable, and she was especially proficient in music and mathematics, deriving consolation and giving pleasure to others by her skill on the piano, which she played in a remarkably correct and brilliant manner. Her knowledge of astronomy also afforded her pleasure during many periods of quiet life spent in the country, in the years of her long widowhood. She was delicate in constitution, austere in presence and exact and methodical in all her daily vocations. She read much and led a life of ease, indulging her love of music and literary pursuits to her last days."

"CARL FRIEDERICH HERRSCHHOFF (original spelling), b. Dec. 27, 1763, was the only child of Carl Friederich and Agnes (Müller) Herrschhoff. His mother dying when he was but three years of age, his father entrusted him to the care of a friend living near Berlin, and went to Italy, where he soon after died. The son continued during his youth with his father's friend, an author and professor. In 1799, April 1, he entered the *Philanthropin*, an educational institution, then recently founded at Dessau. Here he remained eight years until 1787, when he emigrated to America, and settling in New York, became associated

---

* These two biographical sketches were contributed by the family.

in business with a Mr. Goch. The affairs of the firm led him about 1792 to Rhode Island on a visit to John Brown, the merchant, who introduced him to his family. In 1801 he married Sarah Brown, dau. of John, and after that time was more or less connected in business with his father-in-law, particularly in the development of a part of the John Brown tract in Herkimer Co., N. Y., where he died Dec. 19, 1819. He was a man of polished address, highly educated, an accomplished linguist in seven languages, and a good musician. His education and tastes were illy adapted to frontier life, and were not conducive to success in the pursuits in which he was engaged."

CHILDREN. (All born in Providence.)

  i. ANNA FRANCIS, b. April 2, 1802, d. in Bristol, Sept. 4, 1887, unm.
  ii. SARAH, b. April 27, 1803, d. in Bristol, June 2, 1882, unm.
  iii. JOHN BROWN, b. March 27, 1805, d. in Bristol, June 11, 1861, unm. Graduated at Brown University in 1825.
  iv. AGNES, b. July 6, 1807, d. in Providence, March 3, 1849, unm.
76. v. CHARLES FREDERICK, b. July 26, 1809.
  vi. JAMES BROWN, b. Dec. 20, 1811, d. Jan. 4, 1812.

42. ALICE BROWN (*See No.* 40), b. Jan. 1, 1777, d. Oct. 23, 1823, youngest child of John and Sarah (Smith) Brown, was married to James Brown Mason, son of John and Rose Anna (Brown) Mason. He was a graduate of Brown University in 1791, Trustee of the institution, Speaker of the Gen. Assembly, Major General of the State of Rhode Island, and Representative in the Congress of the United States. He died Aug. 31, 1819, in his 45th year.

CHILDREN.

  i. ABBY, b. July 17, 1800, was m. July 5, 1820, to her cousin Nicholas Brown, son of Nicholas and Ann (Carter) Brown. She d. Nov. 7, 1822, without issue. (See No. 70).
  ii. ZERVIAH, b. Jan. 22, 1801, d. Oct. 28, 1802.
  iii. ZERVIAH (2), b. April 6, 1803, d. July 18, 1812.
77. iv. SARAH BROWN, b. July 25, 1804.
78. v. ROSA ANNE, b. Nov. 10, 1817.

43. SARAH BROWN (*Moses,*[23] *James,*[8] *James,*[4] *John,*[2] *Chad*[1]), b. Oct. 16, 1764, d. June 26, 1794, eldest child of Moses and Anna Brown, was m. to William Almy, who d. Feb. 5, 1836, in his 75th year. He was of the firm of Almy and Brown, pioneers with Samuel Slater in the cotton manufacture at Pawtucket, R. I. He was a devout and worthy member of the Society of Friends, and a liberal benefactor of the Friends Boarding School, to whose welfare he was devotedly attached.

CHILDREN.

79. i. ANNA, b. Sept. 1, 1790.
  ii. MARY, b. July 6, 1793, d. March 1, 1794.

44. WELCOME BROWN (*Elisha*,[24] *Joseph*,[9] *James*,[4] *John*,[2] *Chad*[1]), b. May 12, 1777, m. Feb. 6, 1800, Phebe, dau. of Joseph and Hannah Farnum, and removed to Barton, Vt., where he d. March 5, 1850. He m. second, Nov. 10, 1812, Freelove, dau. of Hon. Daniel and Hannah* (Angell) † Owen, gr. dau. of Thomas and Ruth ‡ (Angell) Owen, and also gr. dau. of John and Lydia § (Winsor) Angell. Daniel Owen was Dep. Gov. from 1786-1800 and one of the earliest Chief Justices of the Supreme Court of Rhode Island. He was a large land holder in Northern Vermont, where many of his descendants are now living. Oct. 20, 1781, he and William Barton received the grant of the town of Barton, Vt.

CHILDREN (by first wife).

80. i. ELISHA, b. June 26, 1802.
81. ii. JOSEPH FARNUM, b. June 24, 1804.
iii. AMEY, b. June 22, 1806, m. Ebenezer Allen; d. Jan 17, 1851.
iv. CLARISSA, b. Nov. 20, 1807, m. Norman Nye.

CHILDREN (by second wife).

v. PHEBE F. O., b. Nov. 10, 1813, m. Barnabas Balch; d. Aug. 15, 1847.
vi. WAITSTILL, b. May 12, 1815, d. Nov. 10, 1815.
82. vii. DANIEL O , b. Oct. 10, 1816.
viii WAITSTILL W., b. Jan. 14, 1819, d. Aug. 17, 1842; unmarried.
ix. WELCOME OWEN, b. March 27, 1822. A graduate of the Medical University of Pennsylvania in 1852, and a practising physician in Providence, residing, at present (1888) in Barton, Vt. Was President of the Providence Franklin Society from 1869-1880. This branch of the family belongs to the Society of Friends.

45. RICHARD BROWN (*Andrew*,[23] *Joseph*,[9] *James*,[4] *John*,[2] *Chad*[1]), b. June 17, 1789, son of Andrew and Dorcas (Knight) Brown, m. Feb. 23, 1812, Penelope, dau. of Joseph and Hannah Farnum, sister of Phebe. (See No. 44.) She was b. April 12, 1793, and d. July 24, 1869.

CHILDREN.

i. SARAH ANN, b. Feb. 11, 1813, d. March 4, 1815.
ii. MARTHA ANN, b. Feb. 16, 1815, d. of consumption July 15, 1832.
iii. DORCAS K., b. March 29, 1818, m. Benjamin G. Teel; d. Sept. 13, 1861. Had issue.
83. iv. MARY JANE, b. April 6, 1821.
84. v. OBADIAH, b Nov. 30, 1823.
vi. JOSEPH FARNUM, b. May 16, 1835, m. Adelaide Victoria Ballou. He d. Jan. 31, 1886. This family are also Friends, and lived in North Providence.

* Hannah Angell,[5] John,[4] Daniel,[3] John,[2] Thomas[1].
† Daniel Owen,[4] Thomas,[3] Josiah,[2] Samuel[1].
‡ Ruth Angell,[2] John,[2] Thomas[1].
§ Lydia Winsor,[2] Samuel,[2] Samuel[1].

Jeremiah R. Powell

46. HENRY BOWEN (*Sarah*,[26] *Obadiah*,[12] *James*,[4] *John*,[2] *Chad*[1]), youngest child of Jabez and Sarah (Brown) Bowen, b. Jan. 5, 1785, d. April 16, 1867, was a graduate of Brown University in 1802, and thirty years Secretary of State in Rhode Island. He m. Feb. 11, 1808, Amanda, dau. of James and Rebecca (Snow) Monroe.

CHILDREN.

    i.   HENRY LEONARD, b. July 5, 1810, d. Jan. 29, 1865.
    ii. HARRIET AMANDA, b. Nov. 28, 1811, d. Jan. 12, 1860.
    iii. HORATIO, b. May 17, 1814, d. Jan. 16, 1822.
    iv. WILLIAM, b. June 16, 1816, d. Dec. 16, 1821.
    v.   CAROLINE, b July 9, 1819, d. Sept 5, 1838.
    vi. WILLIAM H., b. Oct. 22, 1822, d. Jan. 25, 1823.
85. vii. WILLIAM H. (2d), b. Jan. 7, 1824.
    viii. CHARLES J., b. May 20, 1827, d. April 7, 1869.

47. JEREMIAH BROWN HOWELL (*Mary*,[28] *Jeremiah*,[13] *James*,[4] *John*,[2] *Chad*[1]), eldest child of David and Mary (Brown) Howell, b. Aug. 28, 1771, d. Feb. 6, 1822.

*" He was a graduate of Brown University in the class of 1789, and afterwards studied law and was admitted to the bar and practiced in Providence. He was elected United States Senator from Rhode Island, serving from Nov. 4, 1811, to March 3, 1817. He engaged much of public confidence through life, and held several important offices in the gift of the people, in the discharge of which he was ever found faithful. As Senator in the State Legislature, and afterwards as a member of the United States Senate, he was a vigilant watchman of the rights of the people, and always supported those great Republican principles which he considered best promoted their good and the honor and welfare of his country." He married, Oct. 17, 1793, his second cousin, Martha, only child of John and Wait (Field) Brown. (See No. 29.)

CHILDREN.

    i.   MARY BROWN, b. Aug. 11, 1794, d. Jan. 10, 1795.
86. ii. ELIZABETH BROWN, b. Feb. 9, 1796.
87. iii. MARTHA BROWN, b. Aug. 5, 1798.
    iv. MARY BROWN, b. Sept. 2, 1800, d. March 3, 1801.
88. v.   WAITY FIELD, b. Dec. 28, 1801.
89. vi. JOHN BROWN, b. Dec. 6, 1803.
    vii. MEHETABLE DEXTER, b. Feb. 17, 1806, d. Dec. 19, 1806.
90. viii. CHARLES FIELD, b. March 23, 1807.
91. ix. SALLY BROWN, b. May 14, 1808.
    x.   DAVID, b. Sept. 19, 1809, d. Feb. 28, 1814.

48. WAITSTILL HOWELL (*See No.* 47), dau. of Hon. David and Mary (Brown) Howell, b. June 27, 1776, d. May 15,

* See Major Boris' Biography of Members of Congress.

1819, was married Jan. 1, 1801, to Ebenezer Knight Dexter, b.
in Providence, April 26, 1773, d. Aug. 10, 1824. Their only
child, *Mary*, died in infancy. "By his last will he bequeathed
a large and valuable estate to his native town in perpetual trust
for the benefit of the unfortunate poor. Of his munificence,
the Dexter Asylum and the Dexter Donation Fund are the
enduring memorials. In grateful commemoration of this most
useful benefaction the city of Providence erected a monument in
the North Burial Ground, on the spot to which his remains were
removed." He also gave to the city the Dexter Training Ground.
He was a descendant in the sixth generation of Rev. Gregory
and Abigail (Fullerton) Dexter. (*Ebenezer K.*,[6] *Knight*,[5]
Stephen,[4] *John*,[3] *Stephen*,[2] *Gregory*.[1])

49. MARIA OR MARY B. HOWELL (*See No. 47*), b. Feb.
5, 1779, d. April 27, 1811, was married to Mason Shaw, of
Castine, Maine. She is said to have been "a remarkably gifted
woman, full of *esprit* and apparently much admired by her associates." She left a large collection of interesting letters and
journals, all written in her youth, and giving an entertaining
picture of her times. The following incident of her life is here
reproduced, as it is believed to be worthy of preservation, and,
outside of the family, will be new to the present generation.

Shortly after the death of Gen. Washington, Mary B. Howell
in connection with three other young ladies of Providence, the
Misses Julia Bowen,* Sarah Halsey and Abby Chase, wrote to
Martha Washington expressing their sympathy with her in the
great loss she had suffered, and asking for a lock of Washington's
hair, to be made into mourning rings for each of them. The
promise was made to wear the rings during their lives and be-
queath them to their descendants as mementoes of the departed
President. She granted their request and sent an accompanying
letter, which is here copied *verbatim* :

MOUNT VERNON, March 18th, 1800.

Ladies :

In granting the request contained in your Sympathetic Letter of the
24th of February, I beg you to be assured of the grateful sensibility with
which I received your expressions of condolence and kind wishes for my
happiness——

If innumerable Testimonies of respect and Veneration paid the memory
of my dear departed Husband, or if universal Sympathy in my afflicting
loss could afford consolation, mine would be Compleat. But while I see &
acknowledge those with a grateful heart, I find Consolation only in the
bosom of that being by whose dispensation I have been afflicted.——

That your Virtues may be exemplary, that your passage through life may

* Julia Bowen, dau. of Ephraim, Jr., and Sally Bowen, b. Dec. 1, 1779, was m. Oct. 17,
1803, to John D. Martin ; d. July 30, 1805.
Sarah Halsey, dau. of Thomas L. Halsey, d. Sept. 16, 1864, aged 85, unmarried.
Abby Chase, dau. of Samuel, d. Feb. 13, 1864, aged 84, unmarried.

MRS. SARAH HOWELL EDDY.

be marked with the Blessings of Heaven, and that Happiness hereafter may be your Portion—

Prays your Friend &

Obedient Serv't,

MARTHA WASHINGTON.

MISSES JULIA BOWEN,

MARY B. HOWELL,

SARAH HALSEY,

ABBY CHASE.

This letter was preserved by Mary B. Howell and given by her on her death in 1811 to her sister, Mrs. Sarah H. Dwight, who presented it many years after to her niece, Sally B. (Howell) Wilcox. It is now in possession of one of the daughters of the latter. Mrs. Eddy gave the ring to her executor, the Hon. William S. Patten.

CHILDREN.

    i. SALLY H., b. in Castine, April 28, 1807, d. in Providence, Dec. 1, 1816.

92. ii. WAITSTILL DEXTER, b. Oct. 17, 1809.

50. SARAH HOWELL (See No. 48), b. Feb. 1, 1781, d. Sept. 25, 1859, was m. Feb. 21, 1809, to Gamaliel Lyman Dwight, b. in Belchertown, Mass., March 16, 1777, d. in Louisville, Kentucky, Oct. 8, 1822. She was m. second, Oct. 7, 1824, to her second cousin, Samuel Eddy, b. March 31, 1769, d. Feb. 3, 1839. (See No. 11). By the second marriage there was no issue.

CHILDREN (by first husband).

93. i. GAMALIEL LYMAN, b. Dec. 3, 1809.

    ii. SARAH, b. Aug. 5, 1818, d. Sept. 5. 1815.

    iii. SARAH, b. June 10, 1820, d. Oct. 27, 1821.

    iv. MARY, b. April 5, 1821, d. Jan. 5, 1822.

51. MARTHA BROWN (*John,*[29] *Dep.-Gov. Elisha,*[14] *James,*[4] *John,*[2] *Chad*[1]), only child of John and Wait (Field) Brown, b. Sept. 5, 1772, d. Feb. 14, 1851, was m. Oct. 11, 1793, to Jeremiah B. Howell, her second cousin. (*See No 47*).

52. ABBY BROWN (*Capt. Jeremiah,*[31] *Dep.-Gov. Elisha,*[14] *James,*[4] *John,*[2] *Chad*[1]), b. June 2, 1766, d. Oct. 24, 1839, was dau. of Capt. Jeremiah and Mary (Cushing) Brown. She was m. Sept. 5, 1790, to Nathaniel Smith, son of John, b. July 28, 1763, and d. April 8, 1814. For many years he held the place of Naval Officer in Providence. Their residence was on Benefit street, present number, 86. He was a descendant of Christopher Smith, one of the early settlers of Providence. (*Nathaniel,*[6] *Jehu,*[5] *Edward,*[4] *Edward,*[3] *Edward,*[2] *Christopher*[1]).

CHILDREN.

i.   NATHANIEL, b. Jan. 28, 1793, d. unmarried, Sept. 13, 1863.
He was Cashier of the Roger Williams Bank, Providence,
from 1816-1854.   *"During this protracted period he discharged all the duties devolving upon him with such uniform courtesy and fidelity that he was long considered the
model of a bank officer."   The silver pitcher, alluded to in
the following note, was a testimonial from the Bank, upon
his retirement.

ROGER WILLIAMS BANK, Providence, Aug. 30, 1854.
Nathaniel Smith, Esq.,
Sir :
It gives me great pleasure in behalf of the board of
Directors of this bank, to present for your acceptance the
accompanying pitcher, as a token of their high appreciation
of your long continued and faithful services as cashier, and
for the uniform courtesy and kindness which you have ever
extended to them, and to all persons transacting business
with this institution.   Permit me to express the hope, that
in your retirement from active business, you may find that
happiness and freedom from care which you seek, and
which you so richly merit.
Yours, Very Respectfully,
JABEZ C. KNIGHT,
Pres't.

"Blest beyond most men with vigor of body and exuber-
ance of spirits he seemed always to create about him an
atmosphere of cheerfulness and happiness.   His honor was
without a stain, his integrity without a blemish.   He was
always kind and charitable, doing good by stealth.   Many
recipients of his bounty never knew to whom they were
indebted for succor in the hour of their distress."   Mr.
Smith bequeathed the greater part of his estate by will to his
immediate relatives.

ii.   ABBY ANN, b. June 10, 1796, d. unm. April 16, 1848.   This
line is extinct.   Their place of burial is the Smith lot in the
North Ground.

53.   CATHARINE BROWN (*See No. 52*), b. April 11, 1768,
d. Aug. 28, 1831, was dau. of Capt. Jeremiah and Mary (Cushing) Brown.   She was m. Aug. 25, 1796, to James Yerrinton,
b. in Ashford, Conn., Dec. 31, 1772, d. in Providence, Feb. 24,
1843.   He was a millwright and carpenter, and built the spire
of the First Baptist Church.   The Yarranton family from whom
James Yerrinton was probably descended, resided for many
generations in the parish of Astley, Worcestershire, Eng.
"With that disregard for orthography which prevailed some
three hundred years since, they were indifferently designated as
Yarran, Yarranton and Yarrington.   The name was derived
from two farms, named Great and Little Yarranton or Yarran
(originally Yarhampton), situated in the parish of Astley.
Andrew Yarranton, a distinguished member of the family, a

* Obituary in *Providence Journal.*

Worcester ironmaster and captain in Cromwell's army during the civil wars, was born in Astley in 1616. Bishop Watson said that he ought to have had a statue erected to his memory because of his eminent public services." (See Industrial Biography, Iron-workers and Toolmakers, by Samuel Smiles, Boston, 1871.)

CHILDREN.

94. i. JAMES BROWN, b. Dec. 4, 1800.
95. ii. BARKER TAYLOR, b. April 20, 1803.
    iii. CATHARINE, b. March 22, 1806, d. June 24, 1828, in her 23d year. She m. Eliakim Briggs and left an only child, *Julia A.*, b. Nov. 12, 1827, who m. William H. Randall. Their only child, William H., Jr., b. April 2, 1856, m. Aug. 28, 1882, Betsey A. Whitman, and second, Aug. 27, 1884, Margaret E. Cahoon.
    iv. SARAH, b. Dec. 25, 1807, d. Aug. 20, 1848. She was m. to William Webster, son of Ebenezer, and left an only child *Ebenezer*, who, when last heard from some years since, was living in California.

54. MARY BROWN (*See No.* 52), b. May 19, 1770, d. after 1818, dau. of Jeremiah and Mary (Cushing) Brown, was m. Oct. 28, 1792, to Darius Allen who died in Providence in Aug. 1804. Mrs. Allen resided the latter part of her life in Newbern, N. C.

CHILDREN.

    i. MARY, b Dec 25, 1793.
    ii. ABIGAIL BROWN, b. Sept. 29, 1795, was m. to ——Kendall and removed to Ithaca, N. Y.
96. iii ISAAC BROWN, b. Oct 23, 1800.
97. iv. DARIUS CUSHING, b. March——1802.
    v. JEREMIAH NIGHTINGALE, b. Jan ——1804. He went to Newbern, N. C., between 1815 and 1820, and remained there until 1866, when he removed to Reno, Penn., where he died unm. in 1868.

55. CUSHING BROWN (*See No.* 52), b. Jan. 5, 1777, d. 1834, was eldest son of Jeremiah and Mary (Cushing) Brown. He is said to have been a man of fine physical proportions, command-ing presence and much manly beauty.

The only child of Cushing Brown and Mary Annes, was *Cushing Brown, Jr.*, b. Aug. 14, 1805, d. March 28, 1863. He m. April 7, 1828, Eliza, dau. of Job and Lois Freeman. She was b. April 6, 1807, and d. Jan. 10, 1881. They had four children. (1) James Clark, b. March 22, 1829, d. Dec. 5, 1882. He m. Oct. 15, 1854, Martha Adella Matthews, and has one child, Cushing Francis, b. May 11, 1855. (2) Mary Elizabeth, b. March 6, 1831, was m. Oct. 7, 1868, to Thomas Clifford, and has a son Thomas, b. May 14, 1869. (3) Samuel Freeman, b. April 21, 1833, m. March 31, 1859, Emily Brad-ford Bennet, and has a son, Nathaniel Smith, b. Nov. 15, 1863. (4) Abby Smith, b. March 16, 1835, d. unm. Nov. 29, 1872.

The children of Cushing and Nancy (Arnold) Brown, all born in Providence, were *Eliza, Henry, Amey* and *David. Eliza* m. —————— Slack and removed to Albany, N. Y., where she died, leaving two daughters. *Henry* died in early manhood unm. at Key West, Florida. *Amey* d. unm. at the residence of her sister in Albany. *David* m. Abby Winsor, dau. of Job, and had Josephine, Henry, Mary S., Patience, Frederick and Arthur. Josephine was m. to Capt. John Luther of Somerset, Mass., and with her husband and family removed some years since to the West. Mary S. was m. Nov. 16, 1868, to Henry J. Spooner, a lawyer of Providence, and Representative from R. I. in the U. S. Legislature. They have one son. Patience, m. Charles Rice, and d.—————leaving two children, sons.

56. JEREMIAH BROWN (*See No.* 52), b. Nov. 10, 1778, d. Sept. 30, 1847, son of Jeremiah and Mary (Cushing) Brown, was a merchant of Newbern, N. C., to which place he removed early in life, and where he m. Oct. 15, 1812, Mary Singleton, dau. of Hon. William and Mary (Salter) Blackledge, both of Craven Co., N. C. She d. in 1860.

CHILDREN.   (All born in Newbern.)

i.   MARY ANN, b. Aug. 13, 1813, m. Col. George Whitfield, and removed to Florida, where she d. Oct. 16, 1851. Their two children d. in infancy.
ii.   BENJAMIN WOODS, b. Jan. 31, 1815, d. unm. 1859.
iii. EDWARD SALTER, b. Dec. 9, 1816, d. in Providence, Oct. 20, 1818.
iv.   NATHANIEL SMITH, b. Feb. 2, 1819, d. unm. March, 1857.
v.   RICHARD BLACKLEDGE, b. Dec. 29, 1820, d. unm 1858.
vi.   JOHN, b Aug. 2, 1822, d. June 4, 1837.
vii. WILLIAM SALTER, b. April 12, 1824, d Sept 25, 1824.
viii. PHILIP PHYSICK, b. Aug. 11, 1825, d. unm. 1873.
ix.   THOMAS BLACKLEDGE, b. Oct 16, 1827, removed to St. Louis, Mo., where he m. Isabella, dau. of Arthur Leach, and has a dau. Mary Blackledge.
x.   SAMUEL GREENE, b. Sept. 11. 1829, d. Sept. 27, 1831.
xi.   ISAAC, b. March 17, 1831, d. unm. 1858.
xii   GEORGE HOLLISTER, b. Dec. 7, 1832, d. June 12, 1834.
xiii. HENRY ALLEN, b. Sept. 10, 1835, m. April 10, 1866, Harriette, dau. of John Anderson and Jane (Butler) Brookfield, of Newbern, gr. dau. of Jacob Brookfield, of Rahway, N. J., and also gr. dau. of Raynor and Rachel (Backus) Butler of Conn. They have had six children. (1) Jacob B., b. Jan. 25, 1867. (2) Mary, b. Aug. 10, 1868. (3) Jane, b. March 21, 1870. (4) Henry A., b. July 9, 1872. (5) Rachel E., b. Aug 2, 1874. (6) Isaac, b. June 28, d. Aug. 10, 1878, at the age of six weeks.
xiv. EVELINA CROOM, b. Sept. 2, 1836, d. June 8, 1861.

57. HUGH H. BROWN (*See No.* 52), son of Jeremiah and Susannah (Welch) Brown, b. in Providence, May 16, 1792, d. in Brooklyn, N. Y., Oct 4, 1863. He learned the printer's

trade of John Carter, and after he became of age carried on the
business in Market Square, Providence, until nearly the close of
his life. He was a devoted member of the First Baptist Church,
and for thirty years Clerk of the Warren Baptist Association.
During that long period he was never once absent from its yearly
sessions. He m. May 23, 1815, Eunice E., dau. of Thomas and
Nancy (Eddy) Tabor, b. July 24, 1793, d. in Brooklyn, May 27,
1862.

CHILDREN. (All born in Providence.)

98. i. ELIZABETH E., b. Feb 26, 1816.
99. ii. MARY ALLEN, b. March 5, 1818.
iii. JAMES, b. Aug. 14, 1820, m. Nov., 1841, Virtue Chappell ;
he d. Jan. 16, 1845. No issue.
100. iv. JOSEPH. b. Feb. 19, 1823.
101. v ANN FRANCES, b. Sept 19, 1825.
vi. CHARLES C., b. June 22, 1829, d July 16, 1846.

58. EBENEZER P. BROWN (*See No.* 52), b. in Providence,
April 10, 1797, d. there June 16, 1839, was son of Jeremiah and
Susannah (Welch) Brown. He m. April 3, 1821, Sylvania[5] or
Sally Jillson (*Oliver,*[4] *Daniel,*[3] *James,*[2] *James*[1]). She was b.
May 9, 1800, and d. July 1, 1851.

CHILDREN (born in Providence).

102. i. SAMUEL WELCH, b. Jan. 19, 1824.
ii. EBENEZER PRICE, b. April 14, 1827, m. March 18, 1849,
Mary Briggs, dau. of William Foster, of Newport, R. I.
He d. in Cambridge, Mass , June 28, 1883. They had two
children, *Edward Turner*, b. Nov. 3, 1849, d. March 16,
1866, and *Anna Theresa*, b March 5, 1852, m. Jan., 1880,
Frederick Macdonald of Cambridge, Mass., and has a dau.
Theresa Annie Brown, b. June 10, 1884.

59. JOHN SMITH BROWN (*See No.* 52), b. in Providence,
Oct. 4, 1799, d. at his residence in Central Falls, April 17,
1876, was the youngest child of Jeremiah and Susannah
(Welch) Brown. Of the thirty-five grand-children of Elisha
and Martha (Smith) Brown he was the youngest, and with the
exception of Lydia Brown, the last survivor. She attained the
greatest age of them all, and was the last to depart——Nov.
22, 1883, in her 86th year. He m. Oct. 16, 1829, Ann, eldest
dau. of Richard and Abby (Crandall) Rounds, gr. dau. of
Martin and Wealthy (Briggs) Rounds, and g. gr. dau. of Seth and
Esther (Sooper) Briggs. She was a descendant in the seventh
generation of Elder John Crandall* of Westerly. R. I., born in
Providence, June 14, 1807, and died there, May 6, 1887, in her
eightieth year. The burial place of this family is Swan Point
Cemetery. Elisha Brown and his wife, and nearly all their immediate descendants who lived in Providence, were interred in
the North Ground.

* Abby,[6] Thomas,[5] Samuel,[4] Samuel,[3] Samuel,[2] John Crandall.[1]

CHILDREN. (All born in Providence.)

i.   FERDINAND J., b. Sept. 23, 1831, d. Feb. 23, 1875.
103 ii   ABBY ISABEL, b. Feb. 8, 1834
iii. MARY ADELAIDE, b. Nov. 25, 1836, d Feb. 23, 1841.
iv. ANN ELIZA, b June 8, 1839, d. of consumption, April 9. 1854.
v.   MARY ADELAIDE (2d), d. in infancy.
104 vi. EVA WELCH, b. June 18, 1848.

60. LYDIA BROWN (*Elisha*,[32] *Dep.-Gov. Elisha*,[14]
James,[4] *John*,[2] *Chad*[1]), b. Jan. 2, 1775, d. Sept. 5, 1847, was
the eldest child of Elisha and Elizabeth (Bowen) Brown. She
m. Capt. Colville Dana, of Providence, who was lost at sea, Dec.
1804, aged 35. They' had six children, (1) *Ann Eliza*, (2)
Jonathan, d. unm. (3) *Lucy*, (4) *Deborah*, (5) *Sarah* and (6)
Abby. (1) *Ann Eliza* m. Rev. James Burlingame, of Rice City,
Conn., where he preached nearly 50 years. They had Sophia,
Lydia, James P., Ann Eliza, and John P. (3) *Lucy* became the
second wife of Rev. James Burlingame, and had William and
Mary. (4) *Deborah* m. Samuel Boyd of Providence, and had
twelve children : — Elizabeth, Colville D., Samuel, William,
Henry, Alonzo, Deborah, Helen, William, Alonzo, Frank A.,
and Philip. (5) *Sarah* m. Amasa Stone and had one son,
Walter D. They lived in Philadelphia. (6) *Abby* m. Nelson
Sweetland and removed to New Albany, Ind. They had chil-
dren, among whom were Colville, Nelson, Sarah and Abby.

61. ELIZABETH BROWN (*See No.* 60), b. Sept. 24, 1779,
third dau. of Elisha and Elizabeth (Bowen) Brown, was mar-
ried May 21, 1801, to John Kinnicutt. They had two children,
John Collis, and *Sarah*. She m. 2d, Robert Daggett, (second
wife), and had two children who died young. Her son *John
Collis*, d. Oct. 8, 1821, in his 20th year. Her dau. *Sarah*, m.
Ezra Hubbard, of Providence, and d. March 7, 1878, in her 74th
year. Of their five children two died in infancy. Their dau.
Sarah Elizabeth Hubbard, was m. April 19, 1857, to Samuel A.
Lewis, and died, with her infant son, Charles Edward, Dec. 16,
1857, in the 21st year of her age. Ezra James Hubbard, m.
Oct. 17, 1861, Mary E. Saunders. Their only child, Anna
Cora, d. young. Robert B. Hubbard, m. Oct. 28, 1862, Fannie
Sherman.

62. JOHN BROWN (*See No.* 60), twin son of Elisha and
Elizabeth (Bowen) Brown, b. Jan. 20, 1784, m. Aug. 15, 1808,
Betsey, dau. of Robert Daggett * They had five children :
Elisha, Elinor, Colville, Elizabeth, Abby Ann. Of these,
Elisha, b. April 2, 1810, m. Feb. 1, 1829, Prudence Wilbur of
Taunton, Mass., and had nine children. (1) John, b. Jan. 1,
1830, d. March 13, 1866; m. March 13, 1855, Hannah Wetmore,

* See No. 61.

and had Sophia Ellen, b. Dec. 19, 1856, Annie Alice, b. Feb. 13, 1858, Elisha Ward, b May 24, 1861 and Axie Eva, b. Feb. 11, 1863. (2) *Colville*, b. April 5, 1832, m. Oct. 8, 1859, Ann Brogan, and had Susan, b. Oct. 3, 1860, d. Sept. 30, 1874, Margaret Ann, b. Oct. 19, 1862, Edwin Wilbur, b. Dec. 7, 1864, Mary Esther, b. June 7, 1868. These last all born in Dover, N. H. (The attempt to complete this record was unsuccessful.)

63. AMEY BROWN (*Isaac*,[33] *Dep. Gov. Elisha*,[14] *James*,[4] *John*,[2] *Chad*[1]), b. July 7, 1784, d. Dec. 9, 1822, dau. of Capt. Isaac and Amey (Dexter) Brown, was m. in Providence, Nov. 8, 1807, by the Rev. Dr. Gano, to Capt. Benoni Cooke, son of Christopher and Rebecca Cooke, b. in Scituate, R. I., Aug. 12, 1781, d. in Smithfield, R. I., 1865.

CHILDREN. (All born in Providence.)

i. Isaac Brown, b. Nov. 25, 1809, d. of consumption, Aug. 19, 1836; m. in Newport, R. I., Nov. 25, 1834, Abby Maria Hall. No issue. His widow was married in 1838, to Truman Beckwith.

ii. Rebecca Hill, b. Feb. 26, 1811, d. in Walpole, Mass., Feb. 5, 1835. She was m. Jan. 1, 1834, to the Hon. Francis William Bird, of Walpole, a graduate of Brown University, and had one son, who died in infancy.

105. iii. Charles Dexter, b. Sept 19, 1813.

iv. Elizabeth Sherman, b. Oct. 1, 1815, d. in Savannah, Ga., April 7, 1837, unm.

v. Martha Brown, b. Dec. 12, 1818, d. of consumption, Aug. 19, 1836, unm.

vi. Benoni, b. May 3, 1821, d. in Cincinnati, Ohio, of smallpox, contracted there while on a business trip. Buried in Cincinnati, Dec. 17, 1854. He was unmarried.

64. ISAAC BROWN (*See No.* 63), b. Oct. 4, 1787, d. Sept. 7, 1872, son of Capt. Isaac and Amey (Dexter) Brown, m. April 1, 1810, Lydia, dau. of Nathaniel and Lydia Leonard (Cobb) Williams, of Dighton, Mass. She was a descendant in the sixth generation of Richard Williams of Taunton, Mass. (*Lydia*,[6] *Nathaniel*,[5] *Nathaniel*,[4] *Samuel*,[3] *Samuel*,[2] *Richard*.[1]) She was b. March 3, 1784, and d. May 28, 1848. They had six children. He m. 2d Jan. 30, 1850, Caroline, dau. of Otis Bartlett, of Smithfield, R. I. No issue.

The following is, in part, abridged from an obituary notice in the *Providence Journal:* "With the exception of a brief period in his youth, when he lived in Portsmouth, N. H., and in Boston, Mr. Brown passed his life in the city of his birth. He was long a merchant on South Water street, in the well known house of Cooke and Brown. The firm built for residences two fine mansions on South Main street, which were regarded as very elegant structures in those days, and were some-

times called the ' down town palaces.' The more northern of
these in which Mr. Brown lived for many years and died, is
now (1888) occupied by his widow.

" His partner and brother-in-law, Mr. Cooke, some years before
his death, removed to his farm in Smithfield. R. I., and his
house has passed out of the possession of his descendants.
Throughout his long life of nearly eighty-five years, Mr. Brown
maintained an unstained reputation as a merchant and a citizen.
He was a man of dignified and austere manners, of old-fashioned
integrity, and though of kindly nature, severe in his estimate
of modern innovations upon morals and manners, and exacting
in requiring of others the strict and careful honesty that nature
had implanted, and that habit had strengthened in himself.
He held at different times several municipal trusts ; was in the
Common Council from 1832 to 1835, superintended the first
alterations of the old Market House, when it was fitted up for
the use of the city government, and was chairman of the committee appointed by the town of Providence to superintend the
erection of the Dexter Asylum, in accordance with the will of
Ebenezer Knight Dexter. The work was commenced in 1826
and completed in 1830. His associates on the committee were
Governor Caleb Earle and Truman Beckwith, the latter, his
brother-in-law. He was, for many years, a director in the old
Providence Bank and in the Providence Institution for Savings,
and was the first Treasurer of the Providence and Worcester
Railroad Company.

"An active member of the First Congregational Society (Uni-
tarian), he took a deep and continual interest in its prosperity.
His vigorous constitution and regular and temperate habits maintained him in remarkable health until past the age of four score,
and he died after a short illness with brief suffering, leaving behind him a good name and the record of a useful life. He was
buried in his family plot at the North Burial Ground."

CHILDREN of Isaac and Lydia (Williams) Brown.

106. i.   NATHANIEL WILLIAMS, b Feb. 22, 1811.
     ii. ALICE, b Nov. 8, 1812, d. Aug 31, 1881. She was m May
          9, 1842, to Moses B Lockwood, son of Benoni and Phebe
          (Greene) Lockwood, b. Aug. 25, 1815, d. May 13, 1872.
          No issue.
107. iii. AMEY DEXTER, b. Feb. 22, 1814.
     iv. MARY WILLIAMS. b April 4, 1817, was m. March 29, 1843, to
          Rev. Josiah P. Tustin, D. D., b. April 3, 1817, d. in Phila-
          delphia, Dec. 27, 1887.
     v.   ADELINE. b April 9, 1820.
     vi. ISAAC, b. July 12, 1825, d. July 1, 1865 ; m. May 9, 1854,
          Caroline B Evans. No issue.

65. ALICE D. BROWN (See No. 63), b. Jan. 2, 1790, d. Aug.
19, 1837, dau. of Capt. Isaac and Amey (Dexter) Brown, was
m. Aug. 15, 1814, to Truman Beckwith, son of Rev. Amos and

Truman Beckwith

Susan (Truman) Beckwith, of Lyme, Conn., b. Oct. 15, 1783, d. May 2, 1878, aged ninety-four years, six months and seventeen days. His twin brother Daniel died in 1854. When a lad of nine years Truman Beckwith came to Providence to live with his uncle, Dr. Nathan Truman, in whose apothecary's shop he acquired much knowledge of medicine, and thus gained the familiar appellation of Doctor. In 1806 ill health led him to visit Savannah, Ga., where he entered into business, keeping a general store for some years, and later, buying cotton on commission. After his marriage in 1815 he settled in Providence, where he dealt chiefly in cotton and cotton goods. From 1817 to 1829 he had as partner Luther Pearson, under the firm name of Beckwith and Pearson. In 1838 he married his second wife, Mrs. Abby M. Cooke, of which marriage there was no issue. After fifty-five years of business as a cotton merchant, during a part of which time he was the largest dealer in Providence, he retired in 1861, devoting himself to the care of his estate, which he largely increased by wise management and judicious investments. He was a man of great energy and industry, sagacious and prompt in business, and never disheartened by reverses. He had a good knowledge of law and scientific matters, and was gifted with a keen insight into the true character of men and events. Possessing a vein of humor he uttered many sayings which became proverbial. Though a man of more reflection than words, he was an agreeable companion and fond of relating his reminiscences. Allusion has been made to his services in regard to the Dexter Asylum. He was also on the building committee for the erection of the two What Cheer buildings and for changes in the First Baptist Meeting House. In 1827 he built his brick residence on the corner of College and Benefit streets, where he lived for fifty years. This house contains the first grate that was used for burning anthracite coal in Providence. Although not a church member, Mr. Beckwith was a devout attendant upon religious services during the whole of his long life. His mind remained unimpaired almost to the close of his days.

CHILDREN of Truman and Alice (Brown) Beckwith.

108. i. SUSAN TRUMAN, b. June 13, 1815.
 ii. AMEY BROWN, b. 1817, d. June 23, 1825.
 iii. HENRY TRUMAN, b. Dec. 22, 1818. Compiler of the Brown Genealogy, 1851. Mr. Beckwith is a member of the R. I. Historical Society, and was its Secretary from 1851–1861. He is also a member of the New England Historic Genealogical Society, and Corresponding member of the Pennsylvania Historical Society. He was Treasurer of the Providence Athenaeum from 1850–1860.
 iv. ABBY GREENE, b. Oct. 4, 1820.
109. v. AMOS NEWELL, b. Dec. 4, 1822.
 vi. ISAAC BROWN, b. Jan. 7, d. Aug. 8, 1825.

66. SAMUEL BROWN (Smith,[34] Dep. Gov. Elisha,[14] James,[4] John,[2] Chad[1]), b. Feb. 12, 1787, d. Aug. 19, 1868, son of Smith and Lydia (Goold) Brown, m. March 6, 1816, Maria, dau. of George Gorham and Lydia (Chase) Hussey, of Nantucket, Mass., gr. dau. of George and Deborah (Paddock) Hussey, and also gr. dau. of Francis and Naomi (Chase) Chase. She was born Dec. 1, 1792, and d. Nov. 22, 1868.

CHILDREN.

i. ANN, b. Sept. 28, 1818; was m. Feb. 6, 1844, to Joseph S. Barnard, who d. Jan. 21, 1885. They had two sons, *George Albert*, b. Jan. 11, 1845, and *Edward Goold*, b. Oct. 23, 1847, m. Sept. 4, 1878, Esther F. Haskins. No issue. Mrs. Ann Barnard lives in Pembroke, Mass.

ii. SARAH JOY, b. Nov. 24, 1820. Unmarried, and resides at Pembroke.

iii. LYDIA GOOLD, b. Aug. 27, 1822, was m. Jan. 1, 1843, to Nathaniel K. Randall, who died Dec. 29, 1884. They had three children: (1) *Charles Franklin*, b. Dec. 5, 1843, has lived since 1872 in Brazil, S. A., where he m., Oct. 10, 1874, Mary Ann Sterling Doherty of Louisiana, and has had five children—Nathaniel C., b. Sept. 20, 1875, d. Oct. 23, 1876; Samuel Doherty, b. Nov. 16, 1877; Lydia G., b. June 5, 1879, d. June 1, 1881; Minerva, b Sept. 9, 1880; Guy Hartwell, b. July 17, 1883 (2) *Elizabeth Chase*, b. March 14, 1852, d. March 26, 1874. (3) *Annie Gould*, b. Sept. 4, 1863, d. Sept. 4, 1865.

iv. JOSEPH GOULD BROWN, b. June 19, 1825, m. Dec. 30, 1854, Catharine M. Bostwick. He is a merchant of Lynn, Mass., where they reside. They have five children. (1) *Maria*, b. March 13, 1856, was m. Oct. 29, 1878, to Charles J. H. Woodbury, of Lynn, and has three daughters, viz., Emma Louise, b. Oct. 26, 1879; Laura Brown, b. April 13, 1881; Alice Porter, b. Oct. 26, 1883. (2) *Laura Loring*, b. Dec. 28, 1858, was m. Oct. 26, 1880, to Henry B. Sprague. (3) *Cora E.*, b. July 18, 1863. (4) *Mary Emma*, b. Dec. 9, 1864. (5) *Bethany Smith*, b. Jan. 10, 1871.

v. ELIZABETH, b. Aug. 25, 1827, was m. Oct. 13, 1864, to Jabez Wood of Acushnet, Mass. She d. June 25, 1868.

vi. GEORGE SMITH BROWN, b. Oct. 6, 1829. Is unmarried and resides in Philadelphia, Pa.

vii. WILLIAM AUSTIN BROWN, b. Oct. 11, 1832, m. May 23, 1859, Anna Maria, dau. of Philip Chase, b. Oct. 13, 1830. He is a resident of Lynn, where he is engaged in the manufacture of all kinds of Coffee Machinery. In the prosecution of his business, he has traveled extensively in Central America and South America, and has resided, for long periods, in Brazil. They have had four children. (1) *Samuel Goold*, b. May 16, 1860. (2) *Abby Chase*,* b. Aug. 21, 1861, d. April 26,

* The death of this eldest daughter was an occasion of deep bereavement to her family and a wide circle of relatives and friends, to whom she was endeared by her many excellencies of her character. Her sympathies were enlisted in all things that promised to better humanity, and she gave her whole heart to labors in the temperance cause, the Sabbath School and missionary work. Could her life have been spared, no one would have perused with greater interest these memoirs of her kindred, whose publication she anticipated with so much pleasure. Suddenly, in the bloom of youth, she was called home, but the memory of her virtues lingers like a benediction in the hearts of those who loved her, while they derive sweet consolation from the promise, " Blessed are the pure in heart, for they shall see God."

SAMUEL BROWN.

Born 2d mo., 12th, 1787.

Died 8th mo., 19th, 186?.

Residence of the late Samuel Brown,
PEMBROKE, MASS.

Now owned by his grandsons Samuel Goold Brown,
and William Allerton Brown.

1885. (3) *Alice*, b. July 5, 1863. (4) *William Allerton*, b. Jan. 25, 1865.

viii. MOSES BROWN, b. March 30, 1835, d. Dec. 28, 1861. He was a graduate of the Chandler Scientific School of Dartmouth, N. H., in class of 1858.

67. WILLIAM B. BROWN (*See No.* 66), b. March 21, 1793, d. Feb. 7, 1852, son of Smith and Lydia (Goold) Brown, was a physician of Lynn, Mass., where he m. Nov. 8, 1827, Beulah Purington She d. Dec. 25, 1875.

They had two sons. (1) *William Goold*, b. July 18, 1830, d. Dec. 25, 1887, m. March 3, 1856, Clarinda C. Jillson,* and had James H., b. Aug. 9, 1860, d. Aug. 9, 1861, and George W., b. Jan. 13, 1865. (2) *Charles P.*, b. June 19, 1833, m. Oct. 5, 1861, Vera L. Brackett, and has Martin W., b. Sept. 17, 1862, and Jennie L., b. March 1, 1864.

68. ELIZABETH BROWN (See No. 66), b. May 5, 1795, d. Nov. 20, 1823, dau. of Smith and Lydia (Goold) Brown, was m. May 3, 1821, to James Oliver,† of Lynn, Mass.

They had two daughters. (1) *Lydia Maria*, b. March 18, 1822, d. Nov. 29, 1828. (2) *Elizabeth Brown*, b. Oct. 7, 1823, was m. June 28, 1843, to Pliny Earle Chase, b. at Worcester, Mass., in 1820, d. at Haverford, Penn., Dec. 17, 1886. He graduated at Harvard College in 1839, and soon after settled in Philadelphia, where he engaged in teaching. Later, he turned his attention to mercantile pursuits and devoted his leisure to scientific researches. In 1871 he became Professor of Physics, and afterwards of Languages in Haverford College, with which institution his brother Thomas Chase was long connected, and latterly as President.‡ Professor Chase was one of the most accomplished linguists in the country, and excelled also as a scientist. He wrote many valuable productions which were published in the proceedings of the American Philosophical Society, of which he was Vice-President, and in several scientific journals of London, Dublin and Edinburgh. He received the Magellan medal in 1864 for a paper on the "Numerical Regulations of Gravity and Magnetism," and gave valuable assistance to the company of which he was a member, formed for the purpose of revising the English version of the Old Testament, completed in 1885.

They had six children. (1) *James A.*, b. April 3, 1844, m. Dec. 7, 1870, Mabel Elma Marshall, and had Oscar Marshall, b. Dec. 16, 1871; Warren Abner, b. Aug. 27, 1875, d. July 3, 1876; Ann Eliza, b. June 27, 1881. (2) *Eliza B.*, b. Feb. 11,

* Clarinda,⁷ George,⁶ Abel,⁵ Daniel,⁴ Daniel,³ James,² James¹ Jillson. See " Jillson Genealogy."
† James E. Oliver, a son of the second wife, is Professor of Mathematics at Cornell University.
‡ At the time of his death, Prof. Pliny E. Chase was Acting President of Haverford College.

1846. (3) *Edward O.*, b. Oct. 28, 1850, m. June 27, 1878, Elizabeth Ellen Flanders, and has a dau. Edith Maria, b. Aug. 4, 1879. (4) *William Barker*, b. Jan. 6, 1853, d. May 26, 1872. (5) *Maria B.*, b. Sept. 14, 1856. (6) *Harriet Kennedy*, b. July 4, 1862.

69. ESEK BROWN (*Elisha*,[35] *Chad*,[15] *Obadiah*,[5] *John*,[2] *Chad*[1]), son of Elisha and Sarah (Olney) Brown, lived in Glocester on a part of the estate of his grandfather Chad. His name appears as Ensign of the Third Company of Trained Military Bands of Glocester in 1781 and 1784, and as Lieutenant in the Fourth State Regiment in 1800. In 1788 he voted against the adoption of the new Constitution. He was an officer in the Continental army (see History of Glocester), and in this connection an anecdote has been preserved that seems worth relating.

Though small of stature he was remarkably active and exceedingly quick in his movements. While stationed near Newport, a British officer, a man of large size, was captured and brought into camp. Watching his opportunity when the officers were dismounted or engaged, he started on a full run over fences and across ditches, and soon outstripped all his pursuers except Esek, who kept close at his heels. The Britisher endeavored to leap a ditch, but at that moment Esek caught him by the coat, and jerking him, standing, into the ditch, held on from behind to each ear, until he was secured. Much annoyed at being caught by so little a fellow whom he ought to have taken and put in his pocket, he returned, crestfallen, to camp amid the laughter of his captors.

Esek Brown acquired a considerable estate in Northern Vermont, where some of his descendants now live. He m. Mary, dau. of Israel and Mercy (Whipple) Sayles, gr. dau. of Richard and Mary (Phillips) Sayles, and g. gr. dau. of John Sayles, who was son of John and Mary (Williams) Sayles, and gr. son of Roger Williams. She was born in 1764, and died many years before her husband. They had sixteen children, of whom several died in infancy. The following list is not complete.

> i. JAMES, the third son, b. in Glocester, m. Polly, dau. of Thomas and gr. dau. of Gov. Daniel * Owen, and removed to Westfield, Orleans Co., Vt. They had *Sarah, Matilda, James, Whipple, Arnold, Celia, Ruth, Mary, Loring, Abby, Ellen*—11 children.
>
> 110. ii ELISHA
>
> iii. SAYLES lived in Glocester, and occupied his father's homestead. He is said to have been an industrious and kind hearted man. He m. Freelove, dau. of Sylvanus and Lucy Keech, and had *Almira, Polly, Crana, Lucy, John, Caroline, Miranda, James, Ann, Martin*—10 children.
>
> iv. DORCAS m. John Whipple, of Burrillville, and had *Abby*, m. Alvah Mowry, *Florella, John*—3 children.

* Gov. Daniel,[1] Thomas,[2] Josiah,[2] Samuel[1] of Wales.

v. POLLY m Arnold Owen, grandson of Gov. Daniel Owen. They resided in Glocester and had *Fidelia*, m.——Chace, and had three children ; *Ora*, removed to Boston ; *Brown* m. ——Randall and died on a journey to California, leaving two children, George A. and Laura, (m.——Eaton, of Thompson, Ct. and had one child) ; *Matilda, Daniel, Esek*, and one or two died young, — 7 or 8 children.

vi. SARAH m. James Reynolds of Glocester, and had *Emily*, m. Alexander Bridgham, and had Caroline and Robert ; *Celinda* m. Lewis Day, and had James H., Albert F., George L., and William Edgar ; *James* m. Caroline Winsor, and had Reuben A., William Henry, and Anna ; *Francis*, b. Sept. 9, 1821, m. 1842, Mary Place, and had Henry E., b. Sept. 13, 1847 ; *Albert ; Lafayette* m. Huldah Irons, and had Albert S., and Harriet Frances ; *Mary Eliza*, d. unm. 1842 — 7 children.

111. vii. CELINDA, b. April, 4, 1799.

viii. BETSEY m. Benjamin Owen, son of Solomon of Glocester, removed to Scituate, R. I., and had *Mary, Elisha, Herbert, Sarah*, (m. William Bishop and had one child) *Esten*, and others who died young — 5 children who survived infancy.

ix. MERCY m. Lawton Owen, son of Solomon, and had *George L.*, m. Laura, dau. of Benjamin White of Glocester, and had Mary, Charlotte, Elizabeth, Louisa, Adelaide ; *Mary*, d. young, unm. ; *James ; Job* m. Cordelia Warner, and had Sabin and others ; *Charlotte* m. Andrew F. Harris of Burrilville, and had Emma and Andrew ; *Emeline* m. Philip W. Hawkins of Glocester, and had Philip and Robert ; *Sabin*, d. unmarried ; *Ruth* ; —— 8 children.

SEVENTH GENERATION.

70. NICHOLAS BROWN (Nicholas,[37] Nicholas,[20] James,[8] James,[4] John,[2] Chad[1]), eldest son of Nicholas and Ann (Carter) Brown, was born in Providence Oct. 2, 1792, and died in Troy, N. Y., March 2, 1859.* "At an early age he displayed unusual mental vigor, and entered the College of Rhode Island at the age of fifteen, graduating in 1811. He was distinguished among his classmates for proficiency in all the various branches of learning constituting the usual course of studies at that period. Shortly after graduating he proceeded to Europe on a tour of study and observation. He remained abroad three years, visiting the principal cities of Great Britain and the Continent, and applying himself with energy to the investigation of European politics and institutions. His thorough acquaintance with foreign affairs fitted him for the position of Consul to Rome, to which he was appointed by President Polk in 1846. He was in Italy during the exciting period of the revolution of 1848, and until the summer of 1849. His efforts to remain coldly and diplomatically neutral during these trying times were futile. He possessed a natural and ardent love of liberty that no official position could control, and his sympathy with the cause of Mazzini, Garibaldi and the Roman people, against the vicious rule that had obtained in the States of the Church, was unconcealed and often active. Representations concerning violations of well established rules governing the conduct of diplomatic agents were made to the President of the United States, who superseded Mr. Brown by the appointment of a *Charge d'Affaires*. He remained in Europe until 1854, occupying his time with travel and study, and the superintendence of the education of his children. At the latter date he returned to Rhode Island, and in 1856 was elected by the Democratic party Lieutenant-Governor of the State.†

" From his earliest youth Mr. Brown was an earnest hater of American slavery, and a firm believer in freedom for the whole human race. His denunciations against a wicked and inhuman institution, which he regarded as a great moral stain upon the fame of his country, were uttered without reserve or fear of consequences. When the Free Soil movement was inaugurated he joined it, and became an enthusiastic supporter of its measures for checking the advance of slavery into the new States of Kansas and Nebraska.

" One of the fine traits of his character was his openness of speech and manly frankness ; as his opinions were founded upon honest convictions, he was not ashamed to express them. But the charm experienced by those who enjoyed intimate intercourse with him, came from his perfect simplicity of manners, which

* Communicated by R. C. Hawkins, of New York.
† His residence was in Providence. His country seat, Choppaquansett, was in Warwick, R. I.

were those of a highly cultivated, intelligent and well-bred gentleman. Prince and peasant were alike to him—he regarded the man and not his surroundings. He was neither a toady to the rich and powerful, nor a snob in his demeanor towards the poor and humble, and he had little respect for the super genteel posings and aristocratic longings of those who substitute pretensions for realities. As a conversationalist he had few superiors. His great knowledge of men, things and nations, combined with a retentive memory and a natural, easy flow of refined, lucid expression, made of him a companion never to be forgotten."

This attempt at a brief outline of his character may be appropriately closed by quoting from an obituary notice, written at the time of Mr. Brown's death by an intimate friend who had known him for many years.

" As a man, the deceased was endowed with a genial nature : ardent in his attachments : eminently social among his intimate acquaintances : reserved in the company of strangers : seldom, if ever, subject to passion ; kind and courteous in all his relations ; unobtrusive in the highest degree ; chary of his opinions or advice, but never witholding either when pressed : in fine, a man whom to know was to love,—whose friendship had the ring of the true metal. His domestic life was characterized by the purity which distinguished him elsewhere. He lived after the manner of a gentleman of the old school. His hospitalities were dispensed with unostentatious liberality. Born the heir of wealth (which he did not inherit), he did not thence despise labor, nor view poverty as a crime. He looked upon merit wherever found, in the light of a philosopher, and used his efforts to draw it forth accordingly. Like the good parson described by Goldsmith, he was ' More bent to raise the wretched than to rise.' None who knew him but could fully attest this, and especially prominent among their recollections was the trait which the line quoted so beautifully describes. It may be written of him, that which could be said of but few others, his whole life proved that he was above and beyond the influence of race, nor was he dependent upon condition. For he was in the broadest sense and better acceptation of the term, a true citizen of the world."

Nicholas Brown married July 5, 1820, his second cousin Abby Mason, daughter of James B. and Alice (Brown) Mason. (*See No. 42*). She died near Nassau, New Providence, Bahama Islands, Nov. 7, 1822, without issue. *" Her existence was touchingly beautiful and brief. Gifted by nature with a versatile, inquisitive and brilliant intellect, accomplished by education in those elegant acquisitions which throw rich and enticing hues over the passing scenes of life, animated by genius and cherished by affection, she experienced in these varied sources of hap-

*From Tablet in North Ground, Providence.

piness the benignity of Heaven, brightening her vernal years
with joy and promise. In the midst of her hopes and enjoyments, sickness made its insiduous approach, and left its blight
upon her brow. She faded from the earth like a pale autumn
flower before the coming blast of winter, leaving for the con-
templation of the young an impressive instance of mortality, and
to the heart of affection the memory of her virtues."

He married, second, Nov. 22, 1831, Caroline Matilda Clements,
of Portsmouth, N. H., who died in Warwick, R. I., July 9,
1879.

CHILDREN.

i.　ALFRED NICHOLAS, b. Sept. 16, 1832, d. Aug. 12, 1864; m.
　　May 9, 1857, Anna, dau. of Dr. Joseph and Sophia Russell
　　(Sterry) Mauran, b. May 23, 1828. Of their three children
　　the two eldest, a dau. b. Feb. 5, 1859, and a son, b. July 16,
　　1861, d. in infancy. Nicholas, the youngest, b. Sept. 23,
　　1862, is the fifth of the name in succession, and the only
　　surviving grandchild of Nicholas, third.

ii.　ANNE MARY, b. Feb. 10, 1835, d. March 22, 1837.

iii.　ANNE MARY, b. March 9, 1837, was m. June 30, 1860, to
　　Rush C. Hawkins,* b. in Pomfret, Vermont, Sept. 14, 1831,
　　son of Lorenzo Dow and Maria Louisa (Hutchinson) Haw-
　　kins, and gr. son of Dexter Hawkins, a soldier of the Revo-
　　lution who entered the Fourth R. I. Regiment at the age of
　　sixteen, and served until the end of the war, when he re-
　　moved to Vermont, where he died in 1831. Maternally, he is
　　a gr. son of Rev. Aaron Hutchinson of Hebron, Conn., who
　　graduated at Yale College in 1747, the Dean of his class.
　　He was a noted Greek and Latin scholar, and was among
　　the few Americans of that time who had a fair knowledge of
　　Hebrew. He prepared for his college course Dr. William
　　Rogers, the first student of Brown University, then the col-
　　lege of Rhode Island. Dr. Hutchinson was a distinguished
　　Congregational clergyman, and died in the fiftieth year of
　　his ministry at Pomfret, Vt., in 1800. During this long
　　period he lost but two appointments from illness, and in his
　　service was accustomed to dispense with both Bible and
　　Hymn book, reciting chapters and hymns from memory.
　　His associates said of him that had the New Testament been
　　lost, he could have reproduced the whole from memory in
　　the original Greek. From Harvard, Yale, Princeton and
　　Dartmouth he received the degree of LL. D., as well as D. D.
　　From an allusion in one of his sermons, it is supposed that he
　　was with the Green Mountain Boys in the campaign that
　　culminated in the battle of Bennington.
　　When Sumpter was fired upon, Rush C. Hawkins received
　　from the Governor of the State of New York permission to
　　organize a Regiment of Infantry which was marched into
　　service before April 24, 1861, as the Ninth New York
　　Volunteers, better known as the Hawkins' Zouaves. During
　　its term of service of thirty months it was commanded by
　　Col. Hawkins, who, at the end, was brevetted Brigadier
　　General, for gallant and meritorious conduct. When the

* A descendant of Job Hawkins, son of Richard and Jane Hawkins, who settled in
R. I. about 1640.

war commenced, Col. Hawkins was practising law in New York, but since its close has not been in active practice or other business. He has devoted his time to European travel, and has made the most important collection of books in America, relating to and illustrating the early history of printing and wood engraving. In 1883 he published a bibliographical work entitled "*The First Books and Printers of the Fifteenth Century.*" (New York, Boughton; London, Quaritch). He is also a well-known contributor to magazines and reviews.

iv. JOHN CARTER, b. March 16, 1840, m. April 15, 1859, Nancy, dau. of Crawford and Sarah S. Allen, of Providence.

v. CAROLINE MATILDA CLEMENTS, b. Oct. 28, 1841, was m. June 17, 1876, to N. Paul Bajuotti, son of a Piedmontese Judge, b. at Volvera, a small town a short distance north of Turin, Italy. He is a distinguished member of the Italian Consular Corps, and now represents the Italian Kingdom in his capacity as Consul at St. Petersburg, Russia.

vi. ROBERT GRENVILLE, b. June 17, 1846.

71. JOHN CARTER BROWN * (See No. 70), born in Providence, Aug. 28, 1797, died June 10, 1874, was the youngest son of Nicholas and Ann (Carter) Brown. He prepared for college at a school in Hartford, Conn., and graduated at Brown University in the class of 1816. He then entered into business in connection with the house of Messrs. Brown & Ives, of which his father was the senior partner, and became a member of the firm in 1832. On the death of his father in 1841, he inherited a large estate and became more fully identified with the business interests of the community, bringing to the management of the hereditary house to which he belonged, the fruits of careful training and matured judgment, and assisting both by his capital and his mercantile sagacity in maintaining for it the high character secured by its founders. But his tastes for active business were never very strong or controlling. He did not like the daily restraints it imposes, and had little relish for the excitements it involves. His fondness for observing the manners and mingling in the society of distant cities and foreign countries, led him to travel much in all parts of the United States, and he resided in Europe at different times for several years. In early life he began to take an interest in collecting rare and curious books, a pursuit on which in later years he bestowed great care and attention and in the prosecution of which he made large expenditures.

He was chosen a Trustee of Brown University in 1828, and a Fellow in 1842, and was prominently identified with the management of its affairs until the close of his life. To him his Alma Mater is indebted for many munificent gifts. He made large additions of books in English and continental literature to its library, furnished new apparatus for philosophical experiments, subscribed

* Abridged from an obituary in the Providence *Journal* of June 11, 1874, prepared by Prof. William Gammell.

liberally to its fund or for the erection of its buildings, and
materially enlarged its real estate. These benefactions, dis-
tributed through many years, were most frequent during the
Presidency of Dr. Wayland, for whom he entertained a warm
personal friendship, and in whose views of college education he
heartily sympathized. Together these gifts amounted to upwards
of $70,000. His last will and testament contained legacies of a
lot of land valued at $32,000 as the site for a new Library Build-
ing, and of the sum of $50,000 to be added to the $20,000 pre-
viously given, for the erection of the structure. His entire benefactions to the University amounted to nearly $160,000, a sum
larger than it had received from any other one of its honored
benefactors, his father alone excepted. Nor were his pecuniary
gifts for institutions of learning confined to his native city. He
frequently extended generous aid to struggling academies and
colleges in other parts of the country, especially in the new
States of the West. The leading benevolent institutions of
Rhode Island received from Mr. Brown substantial encouragement and assistance, particularly the Butler Hospital for the
Insane, and the R. I. Hospital. His provision for the latter,
including a bequest of $25,000 in his will, exceeded the sum of
$84,000.

At an early period of life he conceived an abhorrence of the
institution of domestic slavery, and while he did not approve of
violent demonstrations against it, he did not fail to give to the
anti-slavery cause his sympathy and pecuniary support. He actively enlisted in the effort to prevent the ascendancy of slavery
in the Territory of Kansas, and when the struggle was at its
height, accepted and held for a year or more the office of President of the New England Emigrant Aid Society. The large
contributions which he made for promoting its objects were
designed solely as gifts to the cause of freedom, and not as investments from which any returns were to be expected, as was,
at one time, a part of the plan of this society. During the civil
war he responded generously to every appeal in behalf of his suffering country, and at its close maintained a lively interest in
the Freedmen and in the surviving soldiers of the Republic.

But of the objects of public interest to which Mr. Brown
directed his attention, by far the most conspicuous was the collection of his splendid Library of American History. His early
purchases of books were in several departments of literature,
among which were copies of Aldine editions of the ancient
classics, and of the most famous of the Polyglot Bibles. Later,
however, his efforts were restricted almost exclusively to the
single specialty of materials of every kind for the history of the
early voyages of discovery, the methods of colonization and settlement, and the subsequent development and civilization of the
Continent of America. For more than forty years he prosecuted

this work with a zeal and liberality which made it a leading occupation, and also one of the highest enjoyments of his life.
He thus accumulated by his own selection and judgment, nearly
all the publications which are now extant in any language relating to this extensive subject, beginning with the Columbus Letters of 1493, and ending with the political pamphlets of 1800.
Those who are familiar with similar collections in this and other
countries, have pronounced it to be more complete in its special
department than any other that is known to exist. It was his
purpose to secure every work relating to North or South
America, which was published in any part of the world, between
the first voyage of Columbus and the close of the eighteenth
century.

The Collection contains all the bibliographical gems which
are most highly prized. It is particularly comprehensive in all
that relates to the English, Spanish, Portuguese, French and
Dutch colonization, and scarcely less so in materials for the history of the States and Nations to which this colonization gave
rise, or for illustrating the aboriginal races which faded away
before its progress. The works which it comprises are all of the
earliest editions, and in the languages in which they were written, and the greater part of them were substantially and often
elegantly bound under his own direction. He caused an elabor-
ate catalogue with bibliographical annotations to be prepared by
his friend, the Hon. John R. Bartlett, who was, for many years,
conversant more than any other person with the character and
growth of the collection It is executed with great care and skill,
and a few copies were printed for private distribution in four
royal octavo volumes, between the years 1865 and 1871.*

To have made a collection like this of rare and costly books
from so great a diversity of sources, is of itself a most honorable
and useful service to historical learning, and has rightly secured
for its possessor a distinguished place among the famous Historical collectors of the world. He freely placed its treasures at the
service of scholars and authors in this country and in Europe,
who wished to study the subjects to which it relates, and, in at
least three instances, he sent across the Atlantic books, which,
had they been lost, could not have been replaced.

The essential traits in the character of Mr. Brown were well
illustrated in his serene and unobtrusive daily life. His manners, though formal and reserved to strangers, were those of a
courteous and high bred gentleman of the elder generation.
His tastes were simple, and his spirit that of genuine modesty
without self-seeking or any element of arrogance. Though possessed of firm convictions he was always tolerant of dissent on

* The first two volumes have since been reprinted, copiously illustrated with portraits of
early navigators and fac-similes of title pages and rare maps. Altogether the four parts
of the catalogue contain 6,115 titles, and the total number of volumes in the Library is
probably about ten thousand. The Collection still remains at the John Carter Brown
mansion in Providence.

the part of others. He was through life unusually fond of society, and in the ancestral mansion his social entertainments were distinguished for a generous and elegant hospitality such as few have it in their power to equal. But in his daily life he was especially averse to anything like ostentation or display, and though always accustomed to the use of large wealth, he cared nothing for any kind of luxurious indulgence. He was endowed with remarkable powers of observation, and a singularly retentive memory, which seldom failed to recall the persons or the scenes he had once known. In his large library he recollected every book and knew its proper place.

Habitually cherishing grave views of human life and its responsibilites, he lived not without reference to the welfare and improvement of his fellow men. In times of perplexity or alarm either in public or private affairs, he exhibited a firmness and nerve which shrank from no sacrifice that might be demanded either of person or property. In the transaction of business and in the intercourse of life, there presided over every other quality an integrity and honor which made his written or spoken promise the basis of almost unlimited confidence. He went down to the gates of death surrounded by the objects of his fondest affections, with faculties unimpaired, and with a mind which protracted disease had scarcely clouded, leaving with those who bear his name the tenderest memories of his kindness and his devotion to their happiness.

Mr. Brown was married in Providence, June 23, 1859, by the Rev. Dr. Crocker, then rector of St. John's Church, to Sophia Augusta, born Oct. 29, 1825, youngest child of the Hon. Patrick Brown, for many years Member of the Council and Associate Justice of the General Court of the Bahama Islands, and of Harriot Thayer,* his wife. Mrs. Brown survives her husband with three children, all born in Providence, viz. :

    i. JOHN NICHOLAS, b. Dec. 17, 1861.
    ii. HAROLD, b. Dec. 24, 1863.
    iii. SOPHIA AUGUSTA, b. April 21, 1867, was m. in Newport, R. I., Oct. 7. 1885, to William Watts Sherman, of New York city. They have a daughter, Irene Muriel Augusta Sherman, b. in Paris, France, June 9, 1887.

72. CHARLOTTE RHODA IVES (*Hope*,[38] *Nicholas*,[20] *James*,[8] *James*,[4] *John*,[2] *Chad*[1]), b. Dec. 18, 1792, d. June 15, 1881, dau. of Thomas P. and Hope (Brown) Ives, was m. May 22, 1821, to William Giles Goddard, son of William and Abigail (Angell†) Goddard, and gr. son of Giles and Sarah (Updike‡) Goddard. He graduated at Brown University in 1812, and in 1815 received the degree of A. M. Some years later, the title of Doctor of Laws was conferred upon him by Bowdoin College.

*See Thayer Genealogy.
† Abigail,[5] Gen. James,[4] John,[3] James,[2] Thomas Angell[1].
‡ Sarah,[3] Lodowick,[2] Gilbert Updike[1].

While studying law at Worcester, Mass., he acted as associate editor of the *Worcester Spy*, and in 1813 became sole editor and proprietor of the *Rhode Island American*, which he conducted until 1825, when he accepted an appointment as professor of Moral Philosophy and Metaphysics in Brown University, a position which he held nine years, resigning it for the chair of *belles lettres*. In 1842, in consequence of ill health, he retired from the professorship, but was elected a member of the board of trustees and of the board of fellows, and secretary of the corporation.

Professor Goddard possessed a strong and vigorous intellect which had been cultivated with unusual care, and his literary tastes were of the most refined and discriminating character. In the suffrage controversy which resulted in the "Dorr War" in 1842, he was a consistent and unflinching exponent of the doctrines of law and order. He was a sincere and humble believer in the doctrines and precepts of the Christian religion, and a devout attendant upon the Episcopal worship. He died suddenly, Feb. 16, 1846, in the 49th year of his age. His writings, with a biographical sketch, were published in two volumes edited by his son, Francis W. Goddard, in 1870.

CHILDREN.

   i. ELIZA, b. April 8, 1822, d. Jan. 30, 1823.
112. ii. CHARLOTTE HOPE, b Dec. 1, 1823.
113. iii. WILLIAM, b. Dec. 25, 1825.
   iv. THOMAS POYNTON IVES, b. Aug. 14, 1827, m. Oct. 19, 1853, Anna Elizabeth, dau. of William and Sarah (Burrill) Fearing, of New York city. No issue.
   v. ELIZABETH ANNE, b. Nov. 24, 1829, was m. June 17, 1856, to Thomas Perkins Shepard, a merchant of Providence, who was b. in Salem, Mass., March 16, 1817, d. in Providence, May 5, 1877. He was son of Michael and Harriet Fairfax (Clarke) Shepard, and gr. son of Jeremiah and Elizabeth (Webb) Shepard No issue.
   vi. MOSES BROWN IVES, b. April 21, 1831, m. Feb. 13, 1873, Elizabeth Amory, dau. of Robert Paige and Sarah Corliss (Whipple) Swann. No issue. She is gr. dau. of Hon. John* and Maria (Bowen) Whipple, and g. gr. dau. of Dr. William and Sarah (Corliss) Bowen. Sarah Corliss was dau. of Waitstill Rhodes and her second husband, Capt. George Corlis. Capt Jeremiah Brown, the first husband of Waitstill Rhodes, d. in 1741, leaving a dau. Mary, who was married to the Hon. David Howell. (*See No.* 28.)
   vii. ROBERT IVES, a twin brother of Moses, d. July 30, 1835.
114. viii. FRANCIS WAYLAND, b. May 4, 1833.
115. ix. ROBERT HALE IVES, b. Sept. 21, 1837.

73. MOSES BROWN IVES (*See No.* 72), b. in Providence, July 21, 1794, d. in Warwick, Aug. 7, 1857, was eldest son of Thomas P. and Hope (Brown) Ives. After the death of his father he became the senior member of the house of Brown and

* Hon. John,⁶ Samuel,⁵ Joseph,⁴ John,³ Col. Joseph,² Capt. John Whipple¹.

Ives. He was distinguished, not only for his great wealth, high business qualities, and probity of character, but for all those generous qualities of head and heart, that tend to make a valuable citizen. From his early manhood he was intimately connected with Brown University, where he graduated in 1812, and of which he was for thirty-two years the Treasurer. As a means of intellectual culture and without reference to professional practice, he studied law for two years in Litchfield, Conn., and was admitted to the bar in Providence, in 1815.

Upon the decease of his father he was appointed to the presidency of the Providence Bank, and for nearly twenty-two years, discharged his official duties with singular fidelity. He was one of the founders of the Providence Athenæum, and a large contributor to its permanent endowment. He was Treasurer from its foundation to the close of his life of the Butler Hospital for the Insane, and rendered, in its behalf, most valuable service. Of the institutions of religion he was a liberal supporter, and attended worship in the church of his ancestors, the First Baptist. His career presents a most impressive example of a wealthy and accomplished merchant, occupied with the cares of the heaviest mercantile transactions, still devoting himself, with unwearied assiduity, to the active promotion of every leading enterprise and institution connected with the public good. In his will he bequeathed $50,000 to objects of public beneficence. Of this sum $40,000 was devoted to the establishment of the Rhode Island Hospital, opened in Oct. 1868. (Compiled from the papers of the day). He m. April 17, 1833, Anne Allen, dau. of Sullivan and Lydia (Allen) Dorr, b. 1810, d. March 1, 1884.

They had two children, *Thomas Poynton*, b. Jan. 7, 1834, and *Hope Brown*, b. May 18, 1839.

i. The son, Thomas P. Ives,* entered the scientific school of Brown University and received the degree of B. P. in 1855. He then studied medicine in Providence and New York, but not with the intention of practising the profession. On the death of his father in 1857, he became his successor in the house of Brown and Ives, and inherited an ample fortune. At the breaking out of the Rebellion in 1861, he offered to the United States Government his yacht, the *Hope*, and his personal services without compensation. He received a commission in the revenue service, and was actively employed for six months, when he was appointed assistant adjutant-general in the State service, with the rank of Captain, but at the same time relieved from duty to take part in General Burnside's coast expedition. Here he rendered most efficient aid from Dec., 1861, until after the fall of Newbern, N. C., when he received, Sept. 3, 1862, the appointment of acting master in the United States Navy.

His conspicuous services in Virginia were appreciated by the Government, and he was promoted in May, 1863, to the

* See Bartlett's Memoirs of Rhode Island Officers.

Robert Ahves

HELIOTYPE PRINTING CO. BOSTON. MASS

grade of acting volunteer lieutenant. The following winter he was compelled by failing health to resign his appointment, but the War Department declined to accept his resignation, and from April, 1864, to January, 1865, he acted as ordnance officer at Washington. Meantime his services were acknowledged, Nov. 7, 1864, by promotion to the grade of lieutenant commander. His health, however, had been so impaired by the arduous duties which he had performed in his devotion to his country, that he was granted leave of absence for six months, and on April 5, sailed for Europe. Relaxation from labor had a restorative effect, and he looked forward with renewed hope to a return to his native land, and future usefulness.

He was married at Vienna, Oct. 19, 1865, to Elizabeth Cabot, dau. of the Hon. John Lothrop* and Mary (Benjamin) Motley. Her father, the eminent historian, was, at that time, Minister of the United States to Austria. It was his intention to resume at once with his bride his residence in this country, but a new and fatal manifestation of pulmonary disease appeared, and he died at Havre, Nov. 17, 1865, in sight of the vessel on which he was expecting to embark. By this marriage there was no issue. His widow soon returned to Europe, where she became the wife of Sir William Vernon Harcourt, of England.

ii. *Hope Brown Ives*, sister of *Lieutenant Thomas P. Ives*, was m. Jan. 20, 1864, to Henry Grinnell Russell. No issue.

74. ROBERT HALE IVES (*See No. 72*), b. Sept. 16, 1798, d. July 6, 1875, was son of Thomas P. and Hope (Brown) Ives. He m. Oct. 3, 1827, Harriet Bowen, dau. of Thomas and Elizabeth (Bowen) Amory,† of Boston, gr. dau. of Dr. William and Sarah (Corliss) Bowen, and g. gr. dau. of Capt. George and Waitstill (Rhodes) Corlis. She was born in Boston, March 4, 1803, and died in Providence, Nov. 10, 1868.

CHILDREN.

i. Thomas Poynton, b. Aug. 24, 1828, d. Jan. 16, 1829.
116. ii. Elizabeth Amory, b. April 10, 1830.
iii. Harriet Bowen, b. Jan. 4, 1832, d. Sept. 28, 1860, unm.
iv. Robert Hale,‡ b. April 3, 1837, d. Sept. 27, 1862, unm. The early death of this brave young soldier in the late Civil War, deserves more than a passing tribute. He was a graduate of Brown University in 1857, and in 1860 became a partner in the house of his cousins, Messrs. Goddard Bros. Two years of the intervening time he spent in Europe, in travel and study. In Aug., 1862, the offer of his services as a volunteer aide to General Isaac P. Rodman was accepted, and he received from the government of Rhode Island the commission of a first lieutenant. He left Providence Sept. 1, for Washington, to join Gen. Rodman, who was in command of the third division in Gen. Burnside's

* A descendant in the fourth generation of John Motley of Belfast, Ireland, who emigrated before 1738, and settled in Portland, Maine. (*John, ⁵Thomas, ³Thomas, ²John¹*).
†The emigrant ancestor of the Amory Family in America was Jonathan Amory, son of Robert of Bunratty, Ireland. He went to the Carolinas, where he held high offices and died in 1699. His son settled in Boston, Mass. For the Amory Coat of Arms see America Heraldica, edited by E. de Vermont, New York, 1887.
‡ See Bartlett's Memoirs of Rhode Island Officers.

ninth *corps d'armée*. The movement into Maryland, then
overrun by the invasion of the rebels, commenced Sept 7,
and Lieut. Ives was at once ushered into scenes of the
greatest excitement and arduous service. His record during
the following ten days secured for him a high place in the
esteem and confidence of his general and the officers with
whom he was associated, and in this brief time he became
most favorably known throughout the division. He fell,
mortally wounded, in the battle of Antietam, Sept. 17th,
and died on the 27th, at Hagerstown, Maryland. His death
was serene and beautiful ; the fitting close of a young life
modestly and religiously, yet bravely and heroically given
up for his country in the hour of her extremity and her
greatest need. His remains were brought to Providence and
interred in the North Ground—the burial place of his
kindred. On Oct. 1, a month from his departure from
home, his funeral took place at St. Stephen's church, in
the recent erection of which he had taken an active and
liberal interest, and where he was an habitual worshipper
and a devout communicant.

75. JOHN BROWN FRANCIS (*Abby,*[40] *John,*[22] *James,*[8]
James,[4] *John,*[2] *Chad*[1]), only son of John and Abby (Brown)
Francis, b. in Philadelphia, May 31, 1791, d. at Spring Green,
Warwick, Aug. 9, 1864. His parents, soon after his birth, removed to Providence, where his father entered into business
with John Brown, the merchant, his father-in-law. Mr. Francis died when his son was five years of age, and his early training and education devolved on his maternal grandfather. He
entered Brown University in 1804 at the age of thirteen, and
graduated in 1808. After leaving college, he spent some months
in the house of Brown and Ives in order to acquire a knowledge
of mercantile business, and subsequently attended the Law
School at Litchfield, Conn. On the death of his mother in
1821, he removed to Spring Green, the country residence of the
family, a beautiful farm of about seven hundred acres, where he
resided until his death.

Inheriting an ample patrimony, and having no taste for mercantile pursuits, he early entered upon the public career which
soon placed him among the eminent men of the State. He was
in the General Assembly as Representative from the town of
Warwick from 1821 to '29, when, on account of domestic af-
fliction, he declined a re-election. In 1831 he was chosen a
member of the State Senate. He was Governor of Rhode
Island from 1833 to '38, and again entered the Senate in 1842,
as a Member of the Law and Order Party. In Jan., 1844, he
was elected to the United States Senate to fill the vacancy
caused by the resignation of the Hon. William Sprague. His
term expiring in March, 1845, he represented Warwick in the
State Senate from that year until 1856, when he retired from
all connection with public affairs.

From 1827 to '57 he was a member of The Board of Trustees
of Brown University, and Chancellor from 1851 to '54. He

Robert H. Gardiner

HELIOTYPE PRINTING CO., BOSTON, MASS.

took an active interest in popular education, was the friend and counsellor of his neighbors and fellow citizens, and was regarded by the people of the State with a mingled affection and respect which they accorded to no other public man of his time. His presence was commanding, his manners dignified though cordial, while the genial frankness and hearty warmth of his nature were irresistibly attractive. His well-stored memory, rich in anecdote and reminiscences of public men, made him one of the most agreeable of companions. He was a firm believer in the doctrines of Christianity, a liberal supporter of the ministry, and a regular attendant upon public worship, although he made no formal profession of his faith.

He m., June 18, 1822, Anne Carter, dau. of Nicholas and Ann (Carter) Brown, b. Oct. 11, 1795, d. May 1, 1828.

He m. second, May 22, 1832, Elizabeth, widow of Henry Harrison, and dau. of Thomas Willing and Dorothy (Willing) Francis, of Philadelphia, b. Jan. 27, 1796 ; d. at Spring Green, June 14, 1866.

CHILDREN (by first wife).

i. ABBY, b. Sept. 8, 1823, d. unm. Oct. 19, 1841.
ii. JOHN, b. March 17, 1825, d. Jan. 22, 1826.
117. iii. ANNE BROWN, b. April 23, 1828.

CHILDREN (by second wife).

iv. ELIZABETH, b. March 12, 1833.
v. SALLY, b. March 31, 1834.
vi. SOPHIA HARRISON, b. May 28, 1836 ; was m. Jan. 12, 1860, to George W. Adams, son of Seth and Sarah (Bigelow) Adams. She d. Sept 23, 1860.
vii. JOHN BROWN, b. Feb. 11, 1838 ; d. at Rome, Italy, Feb. 24, 1870.

76. CHARLES F. HERRESHOFF (*Sarah,*[11] *John,*[22] *James,*[8] *James,*[4] *John,*[2] *Chad*[1]), b. July 26, 1809, son of Charles F. and Sarah (Brown) Herreshoff, m. May 15. 1833, Julia Ann,* dau. of Joseph Warren and Ann (Lane) Lewis, b. March 20, 1811. Mr. Herreshoff graduated at Brown University in 1828. He lived for many years on " Point Pleasant " farm, Bristol, where all his children were born. In 1856 he removed to Bristol, his present residence.

* ANCESTRY OF JULIA ANN LEWIS, WIFE OF CHARLES FREDERICK HERRESHOFF.

George Lewis,[1] b. in East Greenwich, Kent Co., Eng., date unknown, d. at Barnstable, Mass., 1633. He m. Sarah Jenkins in Eng. and settled in Scituate, Plymouth Co., between 1633 and 1636.
James Lewis,[2] fourth son of George, b. in East Greenwich, Eng., 1633, d. at Hingham, Mass. 1726. He m. Sarah, dau. of George and Sarah Lane of Hingham, b. 1638.
John Lewis,[3] eldest son of James, b. Oct. 29, 1656, d. Nov. 8, 1715, settled in Hingham, where he m. Nov. 17, 1682, Hannah, dau. of Daniel and Susannah Lincoln, of Hingham, b. Sept. 10, 1659, d. Oct. 30, 1715.
Rev. Isaiah Lewis,[4] ninth child of John, b. in Hingham, June 10, 1703, d. in Wellfleet, Oct. 3, 1786, in the 57th year of his ministry over one church in that town. He m. June

CHILDREN.

118. i.   JAMES BROWN, b. March 18, 1834.
119 ii. CAROLINE LOUISA, b. Feb. 27, 1837.
120. iii. CHARLES FREDERICK, b. Feb. 26, 1839.
121. iv. JOHN BROWN, b. April 24, 1841.
      v.   LEWIS, b. Feb. 3, 1844
      vi. SALLY BROWN, b. Dec 1, 1845
122. vii. NATHANAEL GREENE, b March 18, 1848.
123. viii. JOHN BROWN FRANCIS, b. Feb. 7, 1850.
124. ix. JULIAN LEWIS, b. July 29, 1854.

77. SARAH B. MASON (*Alice*,[42] *John*,[22] *James*,[3] *James*,[4] *John*,[2] *Chad*[1]), b. July 25, 1804, d. Aug. 1, 1864, dau. of the Hon. James B. and Alice (Brown) Mason, was m. Aug. 23, 1825, to George Benjamin Ruggles, of Newport, R. I., b. May 19, 1804, d. Dec. 23, 1833. She was m. second, Oct. 12, 1837, to Levi Curtis Eaton,* of Framingham, Mass., son of Levi and Susannah (Howe) Eaton, b. Dec. 12, 1812, d. Aug. 25, 1852. Mr. Eaton graduated at Harvard in 1830, and soon after studied law. He practiced his profession for a time at Providence, but was compelled from ill health to abandon it. After his death, Mrs. Eaton, with her young family, lived abroad for three years, from 1852 to 1855, and gave to her children, with other advantages, the opportunity to become familiar with modern European languages.

25, 1730, Abigail, dau. of Keuelm and Abigail (Waterman) Winslow, b. June 25, 1707, d. April 13, 1776.
Capt. Winslow Lewis,[5] b. in Wellfleet, July 3, 1741, d. at sea, July, 1801. He m. Sept. 12, 1765, Mary, dau. of Willard and Bethiah (Atwood) Knowles, of Eastham, b. Oct. 20, 1746, d. in Boston, Jan. 31, 1807.
Joseph Warren Lewis,[6] tenth child of Capt. Winslow, b. Sept. 20, 1784, d. May 11, 1844, m. May 1, 1808, Ann, dau. of Levi and Elizabeth (Giles) Lane, of Boston, b. June 21, 1786, d. in Bristol. R. I., July 13, 1856.

WINSLOW.

Kenelm Winslow,[1] third son of Edward, of Droitwich, Worcestershire, Eng., b. April 29, 1599, d. in Salem, Mass., Sept. 12, 1672, settled in Plymouth Colony, where he m. June, 1631, Eleanor Adams.
Capt. Nathanael Winslow,[2] second son of Kenelm, b. in Marshfield, 1639, d. there Dec. 1, 1749, m. Aug. 3, 1664, Faith, dau. of Rev. John Miller, b. about 1645, d. Nov. 9, 1729.
Kenelm Winslow,[3] fifth child of Capt. Nathanael, b. in Marshfield, Sept. 24, 1675, d. 1757, m. 1703, Abigail, dau. of Joseph and Sarah Waterman, and gr. dau. of Robert and Elizabeth (Bonrne) Waterman, early settlers of Marshfield. Sarah, wife of Joseph Waterman, was probably dau. of Antony and Abigail (Warren) Snow, and gr. dau. of Richard Warren of Mayflower memory.

KNOWLES.

Richard Knowles,[1] who lived in Plymouth, Mass., removed about 1652 to Eastham.
John Knowles,[2] of Eastham, son of Richard, was killed in the Indian war, 1675. He m. Dec. 28, 1670, Apphia, dau. of Edward and Lydia (Hicks) Bangs, and gr. dau. of Robert Hicks, b. Oct. 15, 1651, d. ———.
John Knowles,[3] son of John, b. July 10, 1673, d. Nov. 3, 1757, m. Mary ———
Willard Knowles,[4] son of John, b. about 1712, d. March 11, 1796, m. May 10, 1733, Bethia, dau. of Joseph and Bethia (Atwood) Knowles, b. March 26, 1715.

LANE.

Levi Lane, son of Josiah and Abigail (Norwood) Lane, b. Nov. 3, 1751, at Annis Squam, Cape Ann, m. March, 1778, Elizabeth Giles, b. about 1756, d. in Boston, 1795. She was the dau. of John and Mary Maverick Giles (or Gyles), and gr. dau. of John Maverick, b. before 1700, d. ———.

* Levi,[7] Levi,[6] John,[5] Noah,[4] Jonas,[3] John,[2] Jonas Eaton[1].

Sarah B. Eaton —

CHILDREN (by first husband).

i. ALICE ELVIRA, b. June 23, 1826, d. July 19, 1833.
ii. SARAH HARRIETTE, b. June 26, 1827, d. Sept. 23, 1836.
iii. GEORGE BENJAMIN, b. Sept. 23, 1828, d. unm. Dec. 8, 1878.
A graduate of Brown University in the class of 1850.
iv. JOHN MASON, b. June 23, 1834, d. Sept. 14, 1836.

CHILDREN (by second husband).

v. HARRIETTE RUGGLES, b. Aug. 1, 1838, d. Sept. 1, 1841.
125. vi. AMASA MASON, b. May 31, 1841
126. vii. CHARLES FREDERICK, b. Dec. 11, 1842.
viii. ANNA GROSVENOR, b. July 9, 1845, d. unm. April 29, 1865.
ix. FRANK HOWE, b Aug 14, 1847, d. Sept. 14, 1852.

78. ROSA ANNE MASON (*See No.* 77), b. Nov. 10, 1817, d. April 12, 1872, was youngest dau. of the Hon. James B. and Alice (Brown) Mason. She was m. Aug. 22, 1837, to William Grosvenor, M. D., b. April 30, 1810, son of Dr. Robert and Mary (Beggs) Grosvenor, of Killingly, now Putnam Heights, Conn. The emigrant ancestor was John Grosvenor, of Roxbury, Mass., one of the proprietors of Putnam, Conn., formerly of Cheshire, Eng., who died in 1691, and was buried in Roxbury. The family coat of arms was engraved upon his tombstone. Dr. William Grosvenor is a distinguished manufacturer, and the head of the Grosvenor Dale Company, in Thompson, Ct. He studied medicine in Jefferson Medical College and Pennsylvania Hospital, and for some years was associated with his father in medical and surgical practice. He afterwards removed to Providence, where he engaged successfully in business as a wholesale dealer in drugs and dye stuffs. During the late rebellion he was a member of the Senate, and largely influential in aiding the Union cause. In 1848 he became the agent of the mills at Masonville, Conn., founded by the Mason family of four brothers, one of whom, James B. Mason, was his father-in-law. Since that time his attention has been devoted exclusively to manufactures, in which he has been eminently successful. (See Providence Plantations. J. A. and R. A. Reid, Providence, 1886).

CHILDREN (born in Providence).

127. i. WILLIAM, JR, b. Aug 4, 1838.
ii. JAMES BROWN, b. Feb. 12, 1840.
iii. AMASA MASON, b. June 12, 1841, d. Sept. 11, 1841.
iv. ALICE MASON, b Oct. 19, 1843, was m. June 26, 1867, to John J. Mason, M. D., of Thompson, Ct. She d. Jan. 14, 1886, at Enterprise, Florida, without issue.
v. ROBERT, b. Nov. 2, 1847, d July 19, 1879. He m. Oct. 20, 1875 Mary H. Wright, of Baltimore, Md.
vi. ELIZA HOWE b. Feb. 12, 1849, d. May 2, 1853.
vii. ROSA ANNE, b. at Elmhurst, N. Providence, July 3, 1855.

79. ANNA ALMY (*Sarah,*[43] *Moses,*[23] *James,*[8] *James,*[4] *John,*[2] *Chad*[1]), b. Sept. 1, 1790, d. Nov. 20, 1849, dau. of

William and Sarah (Brown) Almy, was m. to William Jenkins, who d. March 2, 1846, in his 61st year.

She was prominent in the Society of Friends, and a most excellent Christian woman, who devoted her life and means to philanthropic ends, in which her husband fully sympathized. She and her eldest daughter, Sarah, perished in the conflagration of their dwelling house, Nov. 20, 1849. A younger daughter and son escaped from the burning building by a window in the rear, and were rescued by the firemen. The mansion was, at that time, one of the largest in the city, and almost an exact duplicate of the John Carter Brown house still standing on Benefit street, corner of William.

CHILDREN.

   i.   Moses Brown, b. Dec. 29, 1824, d. Feb. 18, 1833.
   ii   Sarah, b. July 28, 1827, d. Nov. 20, 1849.
   iii.   William Almy, b. April 4, 1829, d. Sept. 11, 1830.
128. iv.   Anna Almy, b. Feb. 1, 1831.
   v.   Moses Brown, b. Feb. 7, 1835, unm.

80. ELISHA BROWN (*Welcome*,[44] *Elisha*,[24] *Joseph*,[9] *James*,[4] *John*,[2] *Chad*[1]), b. June 26, 1802, d. Oct. 21, 1886, son of Welcome and Phebe (Farnum) Brown, m. Nov. 18, 1828, Phebe II., dau. of Richard Weber and Lofie (Harrington) Fenton, b. March 27, 1804.

CHILDREN.

   i.   Cordelia II., b. Dec. 30, 1829, was m. to Frank L. Fenton.
   ii.   Jeannette L. II., b. June 21, 1833, d. April 25, 1880.
   iii.   Permelia C., b. Aug. 26, 1837, was m. Sept 11, 1867, to Rev.
       Edward P. Lee. She d. in Island Pond, Vt., Jan 3, 1875,
       leaving one son, Edward Brown Lee, born on the day of her
       death.
   iv.   Elisha Carlisle, b. May 28, 1842, m. Jan. 18, 1877, Elizabeth Tripp, of New Bedford, Mass. He is now (1888)
       Deputy Sheriff of North Attleboro, Mass.

81. JOSEPH F. BROWN (*See No.* 80), b. June 24, 1804, son of Welcome and Phebe Farnum Brown, m. Sophronia Skeele.

CHILDREN.

   i.   Martha Ann, b. April 25 1834, d. unm. Oct. 7, 1855.
   ii.   Harriet R., b. May 5, 1838.
   iii.   William C., b. March 11, 1840, m. May 13, 1862, Emeline
       Stanton.
   iv.   Harlan Page, b. Feb. 7, 1843, d. July 6, 1858.
   v.   John H., b. March 7, 1848, m Dec. 5, 1871, Helen B Somers,
       who died Jan. 5, 1877. He m. second, Aug. 27, 1878,
       Victoria E Hastings, and has a son, Henry Farnum, b.
       Feb. 27, 1882.

82. DANIEL O. BROWN (*See No.* 80), b. Oct. 10, 1816, son of Welcome and Freelove (Owen) Brown, m. Amanda Peck. Resides in Barton, Vt.

CHILDREN.

i. ALFRED, b. Jan. 28, 1847, m. July 22, 1881, Eliza Rock ; has a son, Harlan Edward, b. June 19. 1884.
ii. FREELOVE O., b. Oct. 15, 1848, m. Calef Leonard.
iii. FREDERICK, b. Dec. 23, 1850.
iv. CHARLES H., b. March 17, 1853.
v. ELLEN AMANDA, b. Dec. 23, 1855, m. Chauncey S. Skinner.
vi. DANA W., b. May 3, 1859.

83. MARY J. BROWN (*Richard,*[45] *Andrew,*[25] *Joseph,*[9] *James,*[4] *John,*[2] *Chad*[1]), b. April 6, 1821, daughter of Richard and Penelope (Farnum) Brown, was m. Dec. 25, 1844, to Andrew Winsor,* of Johnston, R. I., son of Andrew and Lydia (Winsor) Winsor. He d. March 11, 1883.

CHILDREN.

i RICHARD BROWN, b. May 24, 1848. A graduate of Brown University in the class of 1868.
ii. ANDREW, b. Feb. 8, 1852, m. June, 1883, Ella P. Baker. They have one son, Andrew, b Feb. 4, 1886.
iii. MARY JANE, b. Dec. 2, 1858, d. Sept. 3, 1882.

84. OBADIAH BROWN (*See No. 83*), b. Nov. 30, 1823, son of Richard and Penelope (Farnum) Brown, m. Sept. 18, 1849, Amey Randall, dau. of Nathaniel and Asha (Smith) Angell, b. Aug. 8, 1827. (*Nathaniel,*[6] *Enoch,*[5] *Elisha,*[4] *Hope,*[3] *John,*[2] *Thomas Angell*[1]). They have two daughters.

Obadiah Brown is a well-known farmer throughout New England, a member of the State Board of Agriculture, and State Senator. His residence is on Chalkstone avenue, N. Providence.

85. WILLIAM H. BOWEN (*Henry Bowen,*[46] *Sarah,*[26] *Obadiah,*[12] *James,*[4] *John,*[2] *Chad*[1]), b. Jan. 7, 1824, son of Henry and Harriet Amanda (Monroe) Bowen, m. Oct. 12. 1847, Ednah B. Goodhue, who d. Dec. 26, 1855. He m. second, April 30, 1858, Cordelia James. The children of the first wife, all born in Providence, are *Ednah G.*, b. Nov. 30, 1848 ; *Henry*, b. Aug. 5, 1852 ; *Joseph T.*, b. April 1, 1854. Son of second wife, *Frank*, b. Nov. 6, 1864.

86. ELIZABETH HOWELL (*J. B. Howell,*[47] *Mary,*[28] *Jeremiah,*[13] *James,*[4] *John,*[2] *Chad*[1]), b. Feb. 9, 1796, d. Dec. 2, 1866, dau. of Jeremiah B. and Martha (Brown) Howell, was m., March 4, 1818, to Benjamin Cowell, born in Wrentham, Mass., Dec. 9, 1781, d. May 6, 1860. He graduated at Brown University in 1803, and afterwards studied law in Providence : was Vestryman of St. John's Church, Collector of the Port under President Polk, and Chief Justice of the Court of Com-

*Andrew,[7] Andrew,[6] James,[5] Rev. Samuel,[4] Rev. Samuel,[3] Samuel,[2] Joshua Winsor[1].

mon Pleas. He was the author of "Spirit of '76," published in
Boston in 1850. In all his public relations he was largely re-
spected by his fellow men. Resided in Charles Field street,
Providence.

CHILDREN.

129. i   BENJAMIN, b. Dec. 28, 1818.
130. ii. SAMUEL, b. July 3, 1820.
     iii. ELIZABETH, b. Nov. 22, 1821, was m. April 9, 1872, to Edward
          P. Knowles, b. April 13, 1805, d. Oct. 16, 1881. He was
          Mayor of Providence in 1854. Mrs. Knowles resides in
          Wrentham, Mass.
     iv. MARTHA BROWN, b. Feb. 27, 1823, d. March 16, 1844.
     v   SARAH DWIGHT, b. April 30, 1824, d. Feb. 18, 1865 ; was m.
          Oct 10, 1848, to Rev. Andrew Mackie, of the Episcopal
          Church, who died ———— .   They had two children :—
          Olivia H., b. Oct. 13, 1850, was m. to Benjamin Walker ;
          Andrew, b. Aug. 29, 1852, d. Jan. 30, 1853.
131. vi. OLIVIA GEORGE, b. Sept. 1, 1828.

87. MARTHA BROWN HOWELL (See No. 86), b. Aug.
5, 1798, d. Aug. 9, 1870, dau. of Jeremiah B. and Martha
(Brown) Howell, was m. Sept. 10, 1832, to Charles Lippitt. Jr.,
b. Jan. 30, 1798, d. July 15, 1856. He was a merchant of
Providence, where they resided.

CHILDREN.

132. i.   SARAH HOWELL, b. April 12, 1834.
133. ii. MARTHA, b. July 16, 1835.
     iii. CHARLES, b. March 2, 1837, d. Aug. 22, 1838.
          JULIA   } Twins. b. Oct. 8, 1842. { d. Jan. 27, 1844.
          ANN FRANCES }   { d. Jan. 4, 1844.

88. WAITY FIELD HOWELL (See No. 86), b. Dec. 28,
1801, d. Jan. 6, 1828. dau. of Jeremiah B. and Martha (Brown)
Howell, was m. Oct. 15, 1823, to Appleton Walker, son of
Timothy and Olive (Arnold) Walker, b. May 3, 1796, d. at sea
May 15, 1833, on the return voyage from New Orleans, where
he had gone for the benefit of his health. Resided in New York
City.

CHILDREN.

     i.   GEORGE APPLETON, b. Feb. 26, 1825, d. June 20, 1825.
     ii. GEORGE APPLETON (2d), b. March 16, 1826. d. Sept. 5, 1826.
134. iii. MARTHA HOWELL, b. Dec. 25, 1827.

89. JOHN BROWN HOWELL (See No. 86,) b. Dec. 6,
1803, d. Aug. 3, 1870, son of Jeremiah B. and Martha (Brown)
Howell, m. Nov. 24, 1847, Sarah Miller, b. May 9, 1814, d.
May 27, 1848. He m. second, April 29, 1851, Elizabeth Un-
derhill, and had a dau., Elizabeth Ida, b. March 16, 1852.
Resided in Providence.

90. CHARLES FIELD HOWELL (*See No. 86,*) b. March 23, 1807, d. May 28, 1846, son of Jeremiah B. and Martha (Brown) Howell, m. Sept. 27, 1838, Maria Valentine, b. in 1811. No issue. Mrs. Valentine resides in Sparkhill, Rockland Co., N. Y.

91. SALLY BROWN HOWELL (*See No. 86*), b. May 14, 1808, d. March 1, 1861, dau. of Jeremiah B. and Martha Brown Howell, was m. May 14, 1835, to Rev. Horace Alexander Wilcox, son of Janna and Candace (Goodell) Wilcox, gr. son Janna and Diadama (French) Wilcox, and also gr. son of Edward and Dorcas (Shepard) Goodell. He was b. March 6, 1807, in Ludlow, Vt., and d. April 15, 1865, in Manhattan, Kansas. He graduated at Brown University in 1833, and at Newton Theological Seminary in 1835. His first pastorate was in Willington, Conn., where he was settled over the Baptist church, soon after his marriage. The following year he went to Raleigh, N. C., as Professor in the Wake Forest College. He next taught in an academy in Petersburg, Va., and afterwards returned to Providence, where he established a Young Ladies' School in the Arcade, but, on account of the failing health of his wife, went again to the South as agent for the American Home Missionary Society. In 1841 he removed with his family to Georgia, where he remained five years, preaching, and teaching in various academies. In 1846 he returned again to Providence, and purchased and settled on the Walnut Grove Farm, near Fruit Hill, now owned and occupied by the Providence Reform School. This venture not proving as profitable as he anticipated, he entered into partnership with Dr. Charles Morse in the manufacture of Yellow Dock Syrup, first in Providence and afterwards in New York. He went West in 1854 to explore the territory of Kansas, where, as agent for the N. E. Aid Society, he founded the city of Manhattan. In 1857 he became Secretary of the National Insurance Company, Prov., but after the death of his wife, in 1861, returned to Manhattan, where he died of heart disease, April 15, 1865.

CHILDREN.

i. CANDACE GOODELL, b. April 10, 1836, was m. Dec. 6, 1866, to Charles T. G. Tappan, who d. Dec. 31, 1881. Mrs. Tappan resides in Brooklyn, N. Y.
ii. JOHN HOWELL, b. April 10, 1838, d. Aug. 6, 1840.
135. iii EVERETT PATTISON, b. June 22, 1839.
iv. CHARLES HOWELL, b. Aug. 13, 1842, d. June 20, 1843.
136. v. JULIET LAVINIA, b. July 24, 1843.
137. vi. CHARLES FIELD, b. Jan. 8, 1845.
vii. HENRY JACKSON, b. June 4, 1847, d. Sept. 12, 1848.
138. viii. HORACE ALEXANDER, b. Dec. 20, 1848.

92. WAITSTILL DEXTER SHAW (*Mary B. Howell,*[49]
7

Mary,[28] *Jeremiah,*[13] *James,*[4] *John,*[2] *Chad*[1]), b. Oct. 17, 1809, d. April 6, 1841, dau. of Mason and Mary B. (Howell) Shaw, was m. Oct. 21, 1829, to Charles Cheney, b. Dec. 26, 1803, near Hartford, Conn., (now South Manchester) and died there June 20, 1874.

Early in life he engaged in mercantile business, and in 1837 removed to Ohio, near Cincinnati, where he settled as a farmer. During this period he became interested in the Anti-Slavery movement, and identified himself with the early workers in that cause. In 1847 he returned to Conn., and joined his brothers in the silk industry, which they had started in South Manchester, about the time of his removal to the West. The enterprise, after overcoming many obstacles, proved a success, and the house of Cheney Brothers was soon favorably known in this country and abroad. He resided, a part of the time, in Hartford, was a member of the Legislature, and distinguished for his public spirit and generous charities.

CHILDREN.

	i.	FRANK DEXTER, b. Aug. 7, 1830, d. Aug. 28, 1831.
139.	ii.	FRANK WOODBRIDGE, b. June 5, 1832.
	iii.	MARY HOWELL, b. July 13, 1834, d. May 18, 1836.
	iv.	SARAH SHAW, b. Sept. 13, 1835, d. June 20, 1836.
140.	v.	KNIGHT DEXTER, b. Oct. 9, 1837.
	vi.	ANNA WELLS, b. June 26, 1840, d. Aug. 10, 1840.

93. GAMALIEL L. DWIGHT (*Sarah Howell,*[50] *Mary,*[28] *Jeremiah,*[13] *James,*[4] *John,*[2] *Chad*[1]). b. Dec. 3, 1809, d. March 15, 1854, m. April 6, 1836, Catharine Henshaw Jones. He was a graduate of Brown University in the class of ———.

CHILDREN.

	i.	MARSHALL JONES, b. and d. June 6, 1837.
	ii.	MARSHALL JONES (2d), b. May 22, 1838, d. Nov. 1, 1846.
141.	iii.	GAMALIEL LYMAN, b. Feb. 3, 1841.
142.	iv.	CATHARINE ELIZABETH, b. May 19, 1843.

94. JAMES B. YERRINTON (*Catharine,*[53] *Jeremiah,*[31] *Dep. Gov. Elisha,*[14] *James,*[4] *John,*[2] *Chad*[1]), b. Dec. 4, 1800, d. Oct. 17, 1866, son of James and Catharine (Brown) Yerrinton, m. Jan. 17, 1825, Phebe Boyd, who d ———. He m. 2d, Mrs. Olive (Forbes) Metcalf.

James B. Yerrinton was a printer, having learned his trade in the office of Hugh H. Brown, of Providence, where he was fellow apprentice with James D. Knowles. In early life, in connection with William Goodell, he established the *Philanthropist* and *Investigator*, a paper devoted to the interests of general reformatory objects, which was published in both Boston and Providence. Subsequently, he was editor and publisher of the *Amherst Gazette*, Amherst, Mass. During the existence of the *Boston Daily Advocate* he was employed in that office as foreman. His connection with the *Liberator* commenced about 1845, and continued until its last issue, Dec. 29, 1865. He was the printer of that paper, and occasionally wrote articles for its columns. He was much esteemed by all who had his acquaintance, and numbered among his warm friends, Phillips and Garrison.

CHILDREN (by first wife).

143. i. JAMES MANNING WINCHELL, b. Oct. 24, 1825.
144. ii. CAROLINE ELIZABETH, b. April 20, 1831.
145. iii. ANNA BROWN, b.———, 1833
146. iv. PHEBE BOYD, b. Nov. 23, 1837.

CHILDREN (by second wife).

147. v. FRANK M., b June 2, 1839.
vi. WILLIAM, d. in infancy.

95. BARKER T. YERRINTON (*See No.* 94). b. April 20, 1803, d. June 26, 1875, son of James and Catharine (Brown Yerrinton), m. Jan. 14, 1833, Maria A., dau. of Capt. Preston* and Nancy (Read) Daggett, and gr. dau. of Moses and Lucy (Daggett) Read, b. Nov. 19, 1809. He was for many years book-keeper and engraver with Church and Metcalf, manufacturing jewelers of Providence.

CHILDREN.

148. i. JAMES DAGGETT, b. Oct. 13, 1833.
ii. CATHARINE BROWN, b. Feb. 7, 1835. was m. April 19, 1860, to Charles Field† Gorham, son of Jabez and Lydia (Dexter) Gorham, and gr. son of Lewis and Lydia (Comstock) Dexter, b. 1834. No issue.
149. iii. PRESTON DAGGETT, b. May 12, 1836.
150. iv. ANNE MARIA, b. Dec 14, 1837.
v. SARAH L H., b. Oct. 6, 1843, d. Jan. 26, 1858.

96. ISAAC BROWN ALLEN (*Mary,*[54] *Jeremiah,*[31] *Dep. Gov. Elisha,*[14] *James,*[4] *John,*[2] *Chad*[1]), son of Darius and Mary (Brown) Allen, b. Oct. 23, 1800, m. June 5, 1821, Maria, dau. of Daniel Snow, of Providence, b. Sept. 28, 1802. His fate is

---

* Captain Preston Daggett, born in Seekonk, Mass., in 1784, a privateer in the war of 1812, became a lieutenant, and died at the age of 36 of yellow fever. He was son of Robert Daggett (*See No.* 61), and probably a descendant of John Daggett, who came from England in 1630, and went with Thomas Mayhew to Martha's Vineyard.

† GORHAM PEDIGREE. (1) Ralph, of England. (2) Capt. John, baptized at Benefield, Northamptonshire, Eng., Jan. 28, 1621, m. 1643, Desire, eldest daughter of John and Elizabeth (Tilley) Howland, of the Mayflower. Capt. John served in King Philip's war, and died of fever in Swanzey, Mass., Feb. 5, 1676. His wife died Oct. 13, 1683. (3) Jabez Gorham, born at Barnstable, Mass., Aug. 3, 1656, m. Hannah ————. He was wounded in King Philip's war, and afterwards settled in Rhode Island. Plymouth Court granted the heirs of Capt. John, 100 acres of land at Papasquaash Neck, Bristol, for war services. (4) Benjamin, b. 1695, m. ————. (5) Benjamin, b. 1718, m. Oct. 7, 1753, Abigail, dau. of Jeremiah and Abigail (Waterman) Field, gr. dau. of Thomas and Abigail (Dexter) Field, and g. gr. dau. of Thomas and Martha (Harris) Field. (6) Jabez, b., 1760, m. Oct. 29, 1783, Catharine Tyler. (7) Jabez Gorham, b. Feb. 18, 1792, d. March 24, 1869, m. Dec. 4, 1816, Amey Thurber. He m. second, Lydia Dexter.

uncertain. He went to California in 1849, and as no tidings have come for many years to his family, they have long since ceased to think of him as living. Mrs. Allen resided in 1885 in North Attleboro, Mass., and from her letters has been gathered all that is known of her descendants.

CHILDREN.

i.   ISAAC B., b. Sept. 5, 1822, m. 1852, Nancy Blizzard, b. in England, and had a son, b. April 1853.

ii. MARIA E., b. Sept. 22, 1824, was m Aug. 31, 1845, to Lemuel Bishop, and had five children : *John H.*, b. July 11, 1846 ; *Mary E*, b. Dec. 5, 1847 ; *Charles C.*, b. April 23, 1849 ; *Sarah G*, b. Feb. 8, 1854 ; *Nellie M.*, b. Feb. 7, 1861. Of these, *John H* married and had a dau , Ella M Bishop *Mary E.* was m Dec 24, 1870, to George W Redfern, and had a son, George W., b. 1871. *Sarah G.* was m. to Frederick A. Bartlett, and had William A., b. Dec. 3, 1878, and Frederick A., b. July 18, 1881. *Nellie M.* was m. Aug 3, 1882, to Rufus Alden, and has a son, George F.

iii. SARAH A., b. Sept. 20, 1826, was m. June 15, 1845, to William E. Manchester, and had *William A.*, b. Sept. 10, 1846, and *George W.*, b. Oct. 12, 1848 *William A.* m. Amey Nicholas, and had Sarah W., b. 1868, d. 1878 ; Mary M. ; William A., b. and d. 1878, and Lucy A.

iv. LAURA T., b. Sept. 13, 1828, d. —— 1833

v.   EMMA F., b. April 6, 1830, was m July 6, 1846, to Abiel Leonard, and had *George W.*, b. Aug. 6, 1849 ; *Charles S.*, b. July 16, 1852, d. 1860 ; *Abiel A ,* b. April 8, 1856, d Aug., 1862 ; *Frederick E.*, b. March 20, 1859. She m second, —— McCormick

vi. ALFRED H., b Jan. 23, 1832, d. 1862.

vii. CHARLES L., b. March 8, 1834, d. March 16, 1835.

viii. WILLIAM B., b Sept. 24, 1835, d. Oct. 12, 1836.

ix. WILLIAM B., (2d), b Jan. 11, 1837, d. June 15, 1846.

x.   GEORGE M., b. March 8, 1838, d. Sept. 4, 1862.

97. DARIUS C. ALLEN (*See No.* 96), b. March, 1802, son of Darius and Mary (Brown) Allen, went to Newbern, N. C., about 1817, as book keeper for his uncle, Jeremiah Brown. He afterwards decided to enter the ministry and studied at Brown University, and later, at Princeton. He was ordained by Orange Presbytery, at its session in Hillsboro, N. C., May 11, 1827. (Rev. W. Plummer, D.D., was ordained at the same time). He was pastor, successively, of Presbyterian churches at Lexington, N. C., London, Ohio, and Lewistown, Ill., where he d. July, 1839. He m. in Newbern, May, 1827, Eliza Ann, dau. of James and Nancy Slover, b. Nov., 1800. His widow returned with her five children to Newbern in the Spring of 1840, and d. there Oct. 6, 1864.

CHILDREN.

i   CHARLES SLOVER, b. March 8, 1828, d. Oct. 27, 1855 ; m. 1854, Mary B., dau. of Eli and Anna E. Smallwood, b. Dec. 17, 1824, d. Dec 14, 1855, leaving a son, Charles Slover Allen, b. Nov., 1855, who is now a practising physician in New York City.

ii. HENRY MARTIN, b. in 1830, removed to California, where he d. in 1876.
iii. GEORGE, b. March 2, 1833, is a merchant in Newbern, of the firm of Mitchell, Allen & Co., North Carolina Agricultural House and Hardware Store. For many years he has been an Elder in the Presbyterian Church and Treasurer. He m. Aug., 1860, Leah Myra Jones, of Newbern. Of their twelve children, three are now living: *Hannah Shine*, b. May 25, 1863; *Mary Louise*, b. Nov. 27, 1866; *Harry Vass*, b. Dec. 6, 1877.
iv. ELIZA SLOVER, b. May, 1834, was m. Sept. 22, 1864, to John M. Davies, M. D., assistant Surgeon in the Ninth New Jersey Volunteers. Reside in Warren, Penn., and have *Mary N.*, b. Apr. 10, 1867; *John Norman*, b. March 4, 1870, and *George Allen*, b. June 12, 1876.
v. MARY J., b. Oct., 1837, was m. May, 1860, to Rev. Robert S. Feagles, of New York State, who has been pastor of several Presbyterian churches in New Jersey, and removed, with his family, in 1883 to Menoken, Dakota, near Bismarck. They have had thirteen children, of whom eleven are now living, viz.: *Eliza, Robert, Mary, Carrie, Grace, David, Frederick, Hattie, Harry, Willie, Louise*. The eldest dau. *Eliza*, was m. in 1883 to Samuel W. Smallwood, of Newbern and has two children, Margaret and Robert. *George A.*, the eldest son, d. Nov., 1887, at Bismarck, Dakota.

98. ELIZABETH E. BROWN* (*Hugh*,⁵⁷ *Jeremiah*,³¹ *Dep. Gov. Elisha*,¹⁴ *James*,⁴ *John*,² *Chad*¹), dau. of Hugh H. and Eunice E. (Taber) Brown, b. Feb. 26, 1816, was m. April 18, 1836, to Thomas W. Waterman, who d. Feb. 1, 1839. She was m. second, May 2, 1841, to Rev. Sewall Sylvester Cutting, who d. in Brooklyn, N. Y., Feb. 7, 1882. "He was born in Windsor, Vt., Jan. 19, 1813, and united with a Baptist Church in 1827. In 1835 he graduated with the highest honors at the University of Vermont. The following year he was ordained pastor of a Baptist Church in West Boylston, Mass., and from 1837 to 1845 was pastor in Southbridge, Mass., succeeding Dr. Binney. From 1845 to 1855 he was engaged in editorial labors, and was also Secretary of the American and Foreign Bible Society. He filled the chair of Professor of Rhetoric and History in the University of Rochester, N. Y., from 1855 to 1868. He next accepted the Secretaryship of the American Baptist Educational Commission, and in 1879 was elected Secretary of the American Baptist Home Mission Society, a position which he filled until his death. For talents, learning, piety and execu-

* The death of Mrs. Cutting, April 14, 1888, followed that of her sister, Mrs. Allin, in less than three weeks. United as they were in life by the tenderest ties of sisterly affection, in death they were scarcely divided. Mrs. Cutting's illness was lingering and wasting, and, after the death of Mrs. Allin, she expressed the belief that her life was rapidly drawing to its close. She was a devoted wife and mother, and an able help-meet to her husband, Dr. Cutting, in his ministerial and professional labors. A devout member of the Baptist Church from her seventeenth year, she gave much time and thought to the missionary organizations of that denomination, and was untiring in her efforts to promote their success. She died in Brooklyn at the residence of her son, in the 73d year of her age. The burial place of this family is in Southbridge, Mass., the home of Dr. and Mrs. Cutting during the earlier years of their married life.

tive abilities, he held a high place in our country, and was
known far abroad. Perhaps the most noted of his writings are
'Struggles and Triumphs of Religious Liberty,' and 'Historical
Vindication.' A competent judge has said, ' Dr Cutting was a
clear thinker, a scholarly writer, and one of the ablest men in
the American ministry.'" (Compiled from the papers of the
day.)

CHILDREN (by first husband).

i. THOMAS W., b. in Brooklyn, N. Y., Feb. 9, d. Feb. 11, 1837.
ii. THOMAS W., (2d) b. in Providence, Feb. 26, 1839, d. July 19,
    1843.

CHILD (by second husband).

151.   CHURCHILL HUNTER, b. Sept. 12, 1842.

99. MARY ALLEN BROWN* (*See No.* 98), dau. of Hugh
H. and Eunice E. (Tabor) Brown, b. March 5, 1818, d. March
26, 1888, was m. June 3, 1839, to George Allin, son of Mena-
son and Amey (Crandall) Allin, gr. son of Robert and Margaret
(Gardiner) Crandall, of Exeter, Washington Co., R. I., b. in
Warwick, R. I., March 7, 1816, d. in Brooklyn, N. Y., March
2, 1884.

" That he lived in the world almost the three score years and
ten, doing its duties daily with a patience and a precision next
to faultless— the greater portion of his entire business life holding positions of financial responsibility with absolute integrity-
suffering disappointments without repining and enjoying suc-
cesses without exaltation : holding to the right with unyielding
pertinacity, running the Christian race with alacrity to the
crowning goal - is the life record here of Deacon George Allin.
He was converted in youth, baptized by Dr. Pharcellus Church,
and united with the Second Baptist Church in Providence, R. I.
He was of a pious ancestry, a descendant, maternally, of Rev
John Crandall, of Westerly, R. I. Mr. Allin removed to New
York, where he began business in 1836, and immediately joined
the South Church of that city. On coming to Brooklyn, he,
with his wife, united with the Strong Place Church, June 1,
1849, and from that time he devoted himself to its advancement.
Next to his home and daily vocation the church was his chief

* The death of Mrs. Allin, since this work went to press, was not unexpected. She had
been ill for many months, and was impressed with the conviction that she could not
recover. With touching patience and resignation she bore the long confinement of her
sick chamber, and awaited with joy the summons that was to unite her to the husband
and friends who had gone before. When in her nineteenth year, she joined the First
Baptist Church in Providence, and after her marriage and subsequent removal to Brooklyn, was closely associated with her husband in the various interests of the Strong Place
Baptist Church. Though never in the enjoyment of robust health, she actively engaged
in charitable labors, and her work of benevolence ended only with her life. The many
natural graces of character she possessed, ennobled and sanctified by religion, endeared
her to a large circle of relatives and friends, who keenly feel the loss they have sustained
in her departure, but who sorrow not as those who are without hope. Surrounded by
much that renders life desirable, and bound by the closest ties to her family circle, she
quietly breathed her last at the residence of her son, in the 71st year of her age.

care. For this Mr. Allin refused election to every other official position, with one exception. He was a member of the Board of Managers of the Baptist Home of Brooklyn, where his labors were second only to those given to the church. He was the church treasurer for a long period, three years its clerk, President of the Board of Trustees more than thirty years, and at the time of his death, its senior deacon." (*The Examiner, March* 3, 1884.) He was a member successively of the dry goods house of Pierce, Mabbitt and Allin, and of the firm of Merrill, Fitch and Allin, wholesale jewellers in John street, New York. Of recent years he was identified with the firm of F. C. Linde, Hamilton & Co., as financial manager. He was a life member of the Long Island Historical Society.

CHILD.

152. i. GEORGE ALBERT, b. June 26, 1842.

100. JOSEPH BROWN (*See No.* 98), son of Hugh H. and Eunice E. (Tabor) Brown, b. Feb. 19, 1823, d. May 11, 1853, m. Feb. 10, 1846, Rebecca, dau. of Major Thomas Ketchum, U. S. A., and Mary Coddington, his wife. She was b. Sept. 5, 1831, and d. April 27, 1863. Resided in New York City.

CHILDREN.

153. i. MARY ELLA, b. Oct. 15, 1847.
ii. JOSEPHINE PETERS, b. July 10, 1850, d. Dec. 26, 1850.

101. ANN FRANCES BROWN (*See No.* 98), dau. of Hugh H. and Eunice E. (Tabor) Brown, b. Sept 19, 1825, was m. in Providence, Sept. 4, 1857, to Rev. Darwin Hill Cooley, b. in Clarendon, Orleans, Co., N. Y., Feb. 5, 1830. He pursued his preparatory studies in the Collegiate Institute of Brockport, graduated at the University of Rochester in 1855, and at the Rochester Theological Seminary in 1857. The same year he was ordained a minister of the gospel at Clyde, N. Y. In 1858, he removed to Wisconsin, where he served as pastor nine years and a half. His subsequent pastorates were in Cedar Rapids, Ia., Canton and Freeport, Ill. Later, he was the Financial Secretary of the University of Chicago, and, in 1885, resumed pastoral work in Council Bluffs, Ia. The degree of Doctor of Divinity was conferred on him in 1878, by the Baptist Theological Seminary at Morgan Park, Ill.

CHILDREN.

i. MARY ALLIN, b. in Stevens Point, Portage Co., Wis., July 19, 1858. She was m. Dec 27, 1887, in Council Bluffs, to Clarence J. McNitt.
ii. ELIZABETH CUTTING, b. in Stevens Point, Jan. 11, 1860. Graduated at the University of Chicago in June, 1883, and is now a teacher in Chicago.

iii. EDWARD GRANGER, b. in Appleton, Wis., Aug. 29, 1862, d.
March 4, 1863.
iv. ALBERT NORTHRUP, b. in Appleton, Wis., Nov. 27, 1863. A
graduate of Rochester University in 1887, and now a civil
engineer in the office of the Pennsylvania Central R. R. Co.,
at Jersey City.
v. FRANCIS BROWN, b. in Appleton, Wis., May 12, 1866, d. July
7, 1866.

102. SAMUEL WELCH BROWN (*Ebenezer P.*, ^{5 8} *Jere-
miah*,^{3 1} *Dep.-Gov. Elisha*,^{1 4} *James*,⁴ *John*,² *Chad*¹), eldest
son of Ebenezer P. and Sarah (Jillson) Brown, b. Jan. 19, 1824,
m. Aug. 19, 1849, Mary E., dau. of Jacob B. and Alice A.
(Martin) Thurber, b. Oct. 22, 1827. Was City Clerk of Providence from 1860 to 1879.

CHILDREN (all born in Providence).

154. i. GEORGE THURBER, b. May 7, 1850.
ii. WALTER FRANCIS, b. Jan. 10, 1853, m. April 22, 1885, Louise
T. Hower, dau. of Dr. Seth R. and Laura (Tefft) Beckwith,
of Elizabeth. N. J. A graduate of Brown University in
1873, and an artist, residing in France.
155. iii. ARTHUR LEWIS, b. Nov. 28, 1854.
iv. ALICE, b. Feb. 8, 1857.
v. MARY LOUISE, b. May 3, 1862.
vi. ELLEN PRESCOTT, b. Sept. 20, 1864.
vii. FRANCES JILLSON, b. July 18, 1869.

103. ABBY ISABEL BROWN (*John S.*,^{5 9} *Jeremiah*,^{3 1} *Dep.
Gov. Elisha*,^{1 4} *James*,⁴ *John*,² *Chad*¹), eldest dau. of John S.
and Ann (Rounds) Brown, b. in Providence, Feb. 8, 1834, was
m. in Brooklyn, N. Y., July 13, 1872, to John Williams Bulkley,
son of Ebenezer and Diana (Williams) Bulkley, b. in Fairfield,
Conn., Nov. 3, 1802, a descendant of Dr. Peter Bulkeley, of
Odell, Bedfordshire, England, one of the founders of Concord,
Mass., in 1636. (*John W.*,⁷ *Ebenezer*,⁶ *Ebenezer*,⁵ *Joseph*,⁴
Joseph,³ *Thomas*,² *Peter*¹). No issue. *J. W. B. d. June 17, 1888.*

A graduate of the Girls' Department of the Providence
High School in 1849, and a teacher in the public schools of
Providence from 1851-'61. From 1861-'62 an assistant
in Mrs. Williames' Private School in West 39th street, New
York city ; from 1862-'70 a teacher in the Public Schools
of Brooklyn, N. Y., the larger part of the time as Principal of
Female Grammar Department ; from 1870-'72, engaged in the
Packer Collegiate Institute, as Head of First Academic Depart-
ment, Second Grade.

JOHN W. BULKLEY is widely known as an educator and School
Superintendent. His early instruction was gained in the schools
of his native town, where his devotion to study gave promise of
high culture and usefulness. Through the influence of his
pastor, Rev. Dr. Waterman, of Bridgeport, Ct., he decided to
enter the Christian ministry, and pursued his preparatory studies

at Clinton, N. Y., unde the care of Prof. Monteith, of Hamilton College, intending to commence his college course with the Sophomore class. Ill health, however, compelled him to abandon his chosen vocation, and, returning to Fairfield, he entered upon what proved to be his life work, the calling of a Teacher, for which it soon became apparent that he possessed eminent qualifications. A sea voyage taken shortly after the commencement of his educational career, so restored his vigor that he was enabled, without interruption, to devote himself to his arduous labors. He addressed himself earnestly to an examination of the various systems of instruction, opened a correspondence with some of the most distinguished educators of the country, and began the collection of a teachers' library. He soon attained, by his untiring zeal and intelligent action, a place in the front rank of his profession.

In 1832, he removed to Troy, N. Y., where he conducted successfully a private school until 1838, when he accepted an appointment as Principal of a new Grammer School in Albany, N. Y. While residing in Connecticut, Mr. Bulkley commenced the work of reform in the schools of that State, and excited much interest there. He continued his labors in his new field, was a member of an Educational Convention in 1836 and '37, and was one of the leading spirits in those early efforts, which, after repeated failures, contending with apathy and ignorance, resulted, at length, in 1845, in the organization of the New York State Teachers' Association, of which he was chosen the first President. This association gave birth to the first Teachers' Journal in the United States. Of the *New York Teacher*, he was one of the editors from the commencement, and for some years Chairman of the Board of Editors, contributing largely to its usefulness. In view of his character as an educator, his success as a teacher, and his earnest devotion to the common cause of educational reform, Hamilton College conferred on him the honorary degree of A. M. Mr. Bulkley was one of the pioneers in the introduction of music into the public schools, and a co-laborer with the other early advocates of that cause.

In 1851 he received the appointment of Principal of one of the largest of the Williamsburgh public schools, now known as No. 19 in Brooklyn, and brought to the administration of its affairs enlightened views and a sound policy. His success as a teacher culminated in the organization of this school, where he remained nearly five years. He entered heartily into schemes of reform in his new relations, and was made Principal of the Saturday Normal School, which he had been the chief instrument in organizing.

On the consolidation of Brooklyn, Williamsburgh and Bushwick, Mr. Bulkley was chosen City Superintendent of Schools, and entered upon his duties in March, 1855. To this office he was annually re-elected until 1873, and then accepted the less onerous position of Associate Superintendent. He continued in active service until 1885, when he resigned, and severed his connection with the Board of Education, after thirty years of continuous labor. The excellence of the Brooklyn system of Public Schools is attributed largely to his wise direction and zealous, untiring efforts for their welfare. In every national movement for the encouragement of sound learning and the diffusion of education, he has borne a conspicuous part. He was a member and officer for many years of the American Institute of Instruction, and was a prominent leader in the organization of the National Educational Association in 1857, serving as Secretary from 1858-'59, and as one of the Vice-Presidents from 1863-'66. At the Washington, D. C., meeting in 1859, he was elected President, presiding the next year, 1860, in Buffalo. He was also connected with the American Association for the Advancement of Education, the State Association of Superintendents, the National Association of Superintendents, and, in all these bodies, from year to year, acted upon important committees, often preparing reports involving great labor and research.

Mr. Bulkley's religious connections are with the Presbyterian Church, in which he has for many years been an Elder.

104. EVA W. BROWN (*See No.* 103), dau. of John S. and Ann (Rounds) Brown, b. June 18, 1848, was m. June 1, 1876, to Cornelius Clarke Sisson, son of Barnet and Susan Arnold (Brown) Sisson, b. Aug. 25, 1850. They have one child, Clarence Brown, b. April 6, 1877. Reside in Providence.

105. CHARLES D. COOKE (*Amey,*[63] *Isaac,*[33] *Dep.-Gov. Elisha,*[14] *James,*[4] *John*[2] *Chad*[1]), son of Capt. Benoni and Amey (Brown) Cooke, b. Sept. 19, 1813, m. Aug. 16, 1836, Mary Anna, dau. of Gov.* Samuel Ward King and his wife, Catharine L. Angell. She was b. May 1, 1816, d. in New York city of typhoid fever, Nov. 28, 1884. Buried at Laurel Hill, Philadelphia. Mr. C. D. Cooke is a successful merchant in New York (commission dry goods), who, in the frequently recurring financial crises of the times, has never failed to meet his obligations. Mrs. Cooke was a descendant, maternally, of the first Thomas Angell, of Providence. (*Catharine,*[7] *Olney,*[6] *Daniel,*[5] *Stephen,*[4] *John,*[3] *John,*[2] *Thomas*[1].)

CHILDREN.

i. ISAAC BROWN, b. in Johnston, R. I., May 24, 1837, d. Sept. 30, 1854, unm.
ii. CHARLES ALBERT, b. in Baltimore, Md., Sept. 12, 1841. Is unm. and resides in New York.
156. iii HENRY CLARENCE, b. in Baltimore, Sept. 6, 1843. Resides in New York. Charles A. and Henry C. Cooke form the firm of Cooke Brothers, oil manufacturers. Works, Elizabeth, N. J. Office, New York city.

* Governor of Rhode Island from 1840-'43. Resided in Johnston.

106. NATHANIEL W. BROWN (*Isaac*,[64] *Isaac*,[33] *Dep.- Gov. Elisha*,[14] *James*,[4] *John*,[2] *Chad*[1]), son of Isaac and Lydia (Williams) Brown, was b. Feb. 22, 1811.

" Conspicuous in the list of Rhode Island officers who were engaged in the service of their country during the great Rebellion of the South, is the name of Col. Nathaniel Williams Brown. He was born in Dighton, Mass., at the house of his maternal grandfather, for whom he was named. His early progress in his studies was so marked, that at the age of eleven he was ready for a preparatory course, intending to enter college. A severe attack of inflammation of the eyes changed his plans, and at the age of fourteen he entered upon a mercantile life in the counting-room of his father. In 1833, he commenced business for himself in the wool trade. He recovered the use of his eyes, but the severe strain upon his nervous system, increased by an attack of brain fever in 1830, rendered him peculiarly liable to acute nervous and inflammatory disease, and unusually susceptible to the influences of passing events. Later in life these tendencies were less marked. In common with other business men, he suffered from the commercial crises of 1837 and 1857. In the latter year he withdrew from the Dunnell Manufacturing Company, of which he was a member, and, his health being impaired, remained until 1861 in retirement in his pleasant home at Dighton.

" On the breaking out of the rebellion, his military experience acquired in the First Light Infantry Company, of Providence, commended him to the notice of the State authorities, and he was summoned to Providence, where he accepted the command of Company D, in the First Rhode Island Regiment. At the battle of Bull Run his coolness and courage brought him into prominent notice. His well drilled company was specially exposed, and suffered a greater loss in killed and wounded than any other in the regiment. In September, 1861, he was commissioned Colonel of the Third Regiment, R. I. Vols. Their destination was Port Royal, S. C., where they arrived in time to participate in the bombardment of the rebel forts which surrendered November 7, and Col. Brown was appointed to the command of the Post. His admirable executive abilities, aided by the willing co-operation of his subordinate officers, soon gave the regiment an enviable reputation, and it was considered second to none in the service.

" In the Summer of 1862 he returned to his home for a much needed rest, but resumed his command in September, in improved health and spirits, and was at once appointed Chief of Artillery. His last service was rendered in connection with an unsuccessful expedition organized by Gen. Mitchell in October, for the purpose of reconnoitering the rebel force in the interior, and destroying a portion of the Charleston and Savannah railroad. During this engagement Col. Brown was especially con-

spicuous for his gallant and noble bearing. On his return to
Hilton Head he was attacked by fever, which soon proved fatal,
and on Oct. 30, 1862, he quietly breathed his last, far from
home and kindred, but supported by an unwavering trust in
Divine mercy, and a clear and undisturbed faith in the love of
God through Jesus Christ. His remains were interred at Hilton Head, but afterwards removed to Providence, where they
repose in the North Burial Ground. 'Greater love hath no
man than this, that a man lay down his life for his friends.'"
(See "Memoirs of Rhode Island Officers," by John R. Bartlett,
Providence, 1867.)

He m. June 5, 1834, Sophia, b. Sept. 21, 1813, dau. of Ebenezer and Sophia (Smith) Frothingham, of Boston, Mass., gr.
dau. of Capt. Simon and Freelove (Fenner) Smith of Providence, and g. gr. dau. of Hon. Arthur and Mary (Olney)
Fenner. Mary Olney was dau. of Capt. James and Hallelujah
(Brown) Olney, gr. dau. of Daniel and Alice (Hearnden) Brown,
and g. gr. dau. of Chad Brown. Thus Sophia (Frothingham)
Brown is a descendant in the seventh generation of Chad
Brown.

CHILDREN.

i.   SOPHIA FROTHINGHAM, b. Oct. 4, 1836.
ii. NATHANIEL WILLIAMS, b. Sept. 1, 1838, d. Jan. 10, 1844.
iii. FREDERIC LOTHROP, b. July 20, 1840, m. Oct. 6, 1870, Mary
     Louisa, dau. of William P. and Mary E. Eddy, of Dighton,
     Mass She d. July 6, 1885, leaving one child, *Bessie Froth-
     ingham*, b. Dec. 1, 1877.
iv. AMEY, b. July 16, 1842, was m. Nov. 16, 1864, to Harrison
     Bliss, Jr., of Worcester, Mass., who d. May 12, 1868.
     They had one son, *Theodore Harrison*, b. Nov. 9, 1867.
v.   LANGDON, b. April 4, 1850, d. June 30, 1870.
vi. NATHANIEL WILLIAMS, b May 9, 1853, d. June 14, 1856.
     There were five others who died in infancy.

107. AMEY D. BROWN (*See No.* 106), dau. of Isaac and
Lydia (Williams) Brown, b. Feb. 22, 1814, was m. Dec. 29, 1834,
to Jacob Dunnell, of Pawtucket, R. I., b. Dec. 29, 1811, d.
May 21, 1886. She d. Sept. 9, 1868 He was son of Jacob
and Mary (Lyman) Dunnell, and gr. son of Judge Daniel and
Polly (Wanton) Lyman.*

CHILDREN.

i.   MARY LYMAN, b. Oct. 29, 1835, d. Feb. 3, 1841.
157. ii   SOPHIA BROWN, b. June 14, 1837.
158. iii. JACOB, b. Feb. 6, 1839.
iv.   EDWARD WANTON, b. May 8, 1841, d. July 29, 1841.
v.   AMEY, b. June 17, 1844, d. Oct. 23, 1844.
vi.   ADELA, b. July 5, 1845, d. Nov. 28, 1853.

* The emigrant ancestor of the Lymans in America was Richard Lyman, who came in
1631 from High Ongar, Essex Co., England, to Hartford, Conn. (See " Lyman Genealogy" and " America Heraldica.")

159. vii. ALICE MAUD MARY, b. Sept. 15, 1846, m. Sept. 15, 1873, Amasa M. Eaton. (See No. 125).
viii. MARGARET, b. May 3, 1848, d. Aug. 28, 1849.
ix. WILLIAM WANTON, b. Sept. 13, 1850, m. June 20, 1882, Susan Williams, dau. of Joseph G. and Lydia Williams (Presbury) Grinnell, and gr. dau. of Rev. Samuel and Myra (Williams) Presbury. Myra Williams was a descendant in the sixth generation of Richard Williams, of Taunton, Mass. (*Myra*,⁶ *Benjamin*,⁵ *Benjamin*,⁴ *Seth*,³ *Samuel*,² *Richard*¹.)

108. SUSAN T. BECKWITH (*Alice D.*,⁶⁵ *Isaac*,³³ *Dep. Gov. Elisha*,¹⁴ *James*,⁴ *John*,² *Chad*¹), dau. of Truman and Alice D. (Brown) Beckwith, b. June 13, 1815, was m. Jan. 9, 1838, to Rev. Arthur Savage Train, D. D., the only child of Rev. Charles and Elizabeth (Harrington) Train, b. Sept. 1, 1812, d. Jan. 2, 1872. After graduating at Brown University in 1833, he remained there for a year as tutor. He studied theology under Dr. Francis Wayland and his father, Rev. Charles Train, of Framingham, and became pastor of the First Baptist Church in Haverhill, Mass., in 1836, where he continued until 1859. He then accepted the Chair of Sacred Rhetoric and Pastoral Duties in Newton Theological Institution, resigning, in 1866, to take charge of the Baptist Church at Framingham, Mass., of which his father had for many years been pastor. Six years later, he died in its service, much lamented. Mrs. Train d. Feb. 5, 1851, in her 36th year. They had three daus., *Alice Brown*, b. June 23. 1839 ; *Elizabeth Harrington*, b. May 9, 1843 ; *Annie Russell*, b. Feb. 4, 1845, who was m. July 29, 1873, to James A. Hale.

109. AMOS A. BECKWITH (*See No.* 108), son of Truman and Alice D. (Brown) Beckwith, b. Dec. 4, 1822, m. Nov. 15, 1848, Clara, dau. of Warren Lippitt. She d. June 15, 1879, aged 51 years.

CHILDREN.

i. DANIEL, b. Sept. 13, 1849.
ii. ALICE DEXTER, b. June 13, 1852 ; was m. Sept. 18, 1873, to Ernest C. Oppenheim, and d. July 3, 1884, leaving a son, *Beckwith*, b June 24, 1874, and a dau., *Clara Lippitt*, b. Jan. 20, 1877.
iii. ROBERT LIPPITT, b. Aug. 14, 1855, m. Oct. 2, 1879, Carrie, dau. of William and Theresa (Brown) Joslin. They have four children : *Amos*, b. Aug. 22, 1880 ; *Henry T.* (2d), b. March 26, 1882 ; *William*, b. June 6, 1884 ; *Alice Brown*, b. Nov. 6, 1885.
iv. TRUMAN, b. Aug. 20, 1859, m. Feb. 2, 1887, Harriette Lincoln, dau. of Henry L. and Sarah (Armstrong) Parsons. They have a son, *Truman Beckwith, Jr.*, b. Oct. 10, 1887.
v. HELEN STUART, b. June 8, d. Sept. 14, 1861.
vi. WARREN LIPPITT, b. Sept. 13, 1867.

110. ELISHA BROWNE (*Esek*,⁶⁹ *Elisha*,³⁵ *Chad*,¹⁵ *Obadiah*,⁵ *John*,² *Chad*¹), son of Esek and Mary (Sayles) Browne.

m. Rhoby, dau. of Nathaniel and Betsey (Huntington) Bowdish, and gr. dau. of Elijah Huntington, of Ashford, Conn. She d. in Chepachet in 1871 in her 81st year. He was a man of undoubted integrity and respected by all who knew him. Though in feeble health, he was enabled by his industry to leave his family in comfortable cir_umstances. At the time of his death, in 1826, he was a large land owner in Westfield, Orleans Co., Vt. He lived and died in Chepachet, R. I. (See Huntington Family Memoir, 1863.)

CHILDREN.

160. i.   GEORGE HUNTINGTON, b. Jan. 6, 1818.
ii. EMELINE ARMSTRONG, d. young.

111. CELINDA BROWN, (See No. 110), dau. of Esek and Mary (Sayles) Browne, b. in Glocester, R. I., April 4, 1799, was m. in 1818 to Anthony Sanders, b. in Glocester, May 16, 1796, son of Oliver and Mary (Pollock) Sanders, and gr. son of Stephen and Sarah (Paine) Sanders. He removed soon after his marriage to Williamstown, Mass., where he d. July 24, 1853. His widow d. at Fulton, N. Y., Nov. 30, 1859, while on a Thanksgiving visit to her daughter, Mrs. Mary J. Lord. Her remains were taken to Williamstown for burial. They had 14 children, 11 of whom grew to maturity. The two eldest were b. in Glocester, the remainder in Williamstown.

CHILDREN.

i.   ELIZA ANN, b. March 18, 1819, was m. March 18, 1859, to William Danforth, of Williamstown, son of Coon and Clara Danforth, who d. Dec. 16, 1885. No issue.
ii.   MARY, b. March 12, 1820, d. Oct. 12, 1822.
161. iii. MARSHALL DANFORTH, b. July 3, 1823.
iv.   MILTON, b. April 12, 1825, d. Nov. 12, 1826.
162. v.   MARY JANE, b Oct. 21, 1826.
vi.   FRANCES CELINDA, b. Nov. 24, 1828, was m. Aug. 14, 1858, to Dr. Samuel Duncan, of Williamstown, son of Samuel and Sarah Duncan, and had two children, *Eleanor*, b. Feb. 3, 1864, and *Richard*, b. July 20, 1865. Dr. Duncan was in the United States Service during the Civil War of 1861, as surgeon. He d. Feb. 3, 1882.
vii. LUCY ADALINE, b. Nov. 20, 1830, was m. Nov. 29, 1855, to Erastus N. Bates, now of Riverside, Cook Co., Ill. He is a graduate of Williams College, a lawyer by profession, and was State Treasurer of Illinois for four years. In the late war of the rebellion he enlisted as Major of the 80th Regt. of Ill. Vols., in Gen. Straight's command, was captured, and confined in Libby and other prisons of the South for over fifteen months. He was one of the officers sent to Charleston, S. C., to be placed under fire of the Union troops, but was subsequently exchanged, returned to his home, and was years in recruiting from his hardships. He was promoted to the rank of Brigadier General.
Lucy A. Bates d. at Springfield, Ill., Feb. 13, 1872. They had three sons, *George*, *Bertie* and *Walter*.

SEVENTH GENERATION.   103

viii. BETSEY ABBY, b. Dec. 26, 1832, d. Feb. 10, 1835.
ix. OLIVER BROWN, b. July 12, 1834, was m. May 28, 1865, to
    Julia A. Edson, at Centralia, Ill., and has two daughters.
    They now reside in Chicago, Ill., where he is Secretary of the
    Provident Savings Insurance Co.
x. GEORGE ANTHONY, b. July 4, 1836, m. Nov. 16, 1865, at
    Fulton, N. Y., Antoinette C., dau. of Hon. M. Lindley Lee,
    M. D., and his wife Anna (Core) Lee. A graduate of
    Williams College, a lawyer by profession, and was Assistant
    State Treasurer of Illinois for six years   Resides at Spring-
    field, Ill., and is of the firm of Sanders and Bowers,
    Attorneys   They have had five children   (1) *Unnamed*, b.
    Nov. 25, d. Nov. 28, 1866. (2) *Walter Lee*, b. June 13, 1868.
    (3) *Alice Bates*, b. June 27, 1870, d. Feb. 19, 1876. (4)
    Frances Antoinette, b. June 30, 1873, d. Feb. 22, 1876. (5)
    Effie Stork, b. Dec. 2, 1874.
xi. WILLIAM HENRY, b. Nov. 4, 1838, m. in autumn of 1868,
    Hattie Green, of New York city. He is a farmer, and lives
    at Blue Earth City, Faribault Co., Minn. They have three
    children living.
xii. JAMES BRAINARD, b. Sept. 13, 1840, m. March 25, 1869, Mary
    Tompkins, of Centralia, Ill. He served one year in the war
    of 1861 as musician in the 33d Regt. Ill. Vols., and is now a
    hardware merchant of Centralia. They have three daugh-
    ters : *Jessie T.*, b. Jan. 25, 1870 ; *Lucy Josephine*, b. Jan. 26,
    1872 ; *Mabel Augusta*, b. Nov. 5, 1874.
xiii. HELEN JOSEPHINE, b. March 13, 1843, was m. Nov., 1872,
    at Springfield, Ill., to Julius Butler Ranney, son of Oliver
    Ranney, of Bethlehem, Conn., and his wife Lynda Adams, of
    Genoa, N. Y. He is a fruit grower and farmer of Mulberry
    Corners, Geauga Co., Ohio. They have two children :
    Antoinette Augusta, b. Aug. 12, 1874, and *Oliver Anthony*,
    b. Nov. 14, 1883.
xiv. CATHARINE AUGUSTA, b. May 2. 1846, was m. at Springfield,
    Ill., Dec. 15, 1870, to William Talcott, of Jersey City, N. J.,
    a graduate of Williams College, and a lawyer by profes-
    sion. She d. at Denver, Colorado, of consumption, March
    8, 1878. No issue.

EIGHTH GENERATION.

112. CHARLOTTE HOPE GODDARD (*Charlotte R. Ives,[12] Hope,[38] Nicholas,[20] James,[8] James,[4] John,[2] Chad[1]*), dau. of William G. and Charlotte R. (Ives) Goddard, b. Dec. 1, 1823, was m. June 14, 1848, to William Binney, of Philadelphia, son of Horace and Mary (Woodrow) Binney. She d. April 26, 1866, leaving four children. (1) *Hope Ives*, b. May 10, 1849, m. Samuel Powell, Jr., of Philadelphia. (2) *Mary Woodrow*, b. Dec. 14, 1856, m. Sidney F. Tyler, President of the Fourth Street National Bank, Philadelphia, son of George F. Tyler. She d. Dec. 19, 1884. They had two children, a son and a daughter. (3) *William*, b. July 31, 1858, m. Harriet Da Costa Rhodes. (4) *Horace*, b. May 18, 1860.

113. WILLIAM GODDARD (*See No.* 112), eldest son of William G. and Charlotte R. (Ives) Goddard, b. Dec. 25, 1825, m. Feb. 19, 1867, Mary Edith, dau. of Hon. Thomas Allen and Mary J. (Fuller) Jenckes, and gr. dau. of Thomas and Abigail (Allen) Jenckes.

William Goddard graduated at Brown University in 1846. After studying law and traveling extensively, he engaged in mercantile and manufacturing pursuits. During the late civil war he espoused the cause of the Union, and, as Major of the First Rhode Island Regiment, was highly complimented by Colonel Burnside in his official report to General Scott. He was subsequently appointed a member of the staff of General Burnside, and for gallant and meritorious conduct at the battle of Fredericksburg, was brevetted Colonel. He is now the senior partner of the firm of Goddard Brothers, Providence, successors to the house of Brown and Ives.

They have one child, *Edith Hope*, b. Jan. 4, 1868.

114. FRANCIS W. GODDARD (*See No.* 112), son of William G. and Charlotte R. (Ives) Goddard, b. May 4, 1833, m. May, 1862, Elizabeth Cass, dau. of Henry and Matilda (Cass) Ledyard, of Newport, R. I., and gr. dau. of Hon. Lewis and Elizabeth (Spencer) Cass, of Detroit, Mich.

Elizabeth Spencer was a descendant in the seventh generation of Dr. Edward Bulkeley, rector of All Saints Church, Odell, Bedfordshire, Eng., in 1558. The have two children : *Charlotte Ives*, b. March 1, 1863, and *Henry Ledyard*, b. Nov., 1866.

Charlotte Ives was m. Oct. 12, 1887, to Amos Lockwood, son of John W. and Sarah (Lockwood) Danielson. Reside in Providence.

115. ROBERT H. I. GODDARD* (*See No.* 112), b. Sept. 21,

---

* Brevet Lieutenant-Colonel Robert H. I. Goddard served upon the staff of General Burnside as aide-de-camp.

1837, m. Jan. 26, 1871, Rebekah Burnet, dau. of William and Elizabeth (Bennet) Groesbeck, of Cincinnati, Ohio. They have had three children : *William Groesbeck*, b. Nov. 21, 1871, d. April 25, 1882 ; *Madeline Ives*, b. June 30, 1874 ; *Robert Hale Ives*, b. Feb. 12, 1880.

116. ELIZABETH A. IVES (*Robert H. Ives,*[74] *Hope,*[38] *Nicholas,*[20] *James,*[8] *James,*[4] *John,*[2] *Chad*[1]). dau. of Robert H. and Harriet B. (Amory) Ives, b. April 10, 1830, was m. Sept. 22, 1851, to Professor William Gammell, eldest son of Rev. William and Mary (Slocomb) Gammell, b. in Medfield, Mass., Feb. 10, 1812. The family removed to Newport, R. I., in 1822. William Gammell graduated at Brown University in 1831, and, in the following year, was made tutor of the Latin language in that institution In 1835, he was appointed Professor of Rhetoric and English Literature, and in 1850 was transferred to the Professorship of History and Political Economy, a post which he occupied until his resignation in 1864. He is known as an author, and writer for magazines and reviews, and has, since 1882, been President of the Rhode Island Historical Society.

CHILDREN.

i. ROBERT IVES, b. Dec. 30, 1852, m. Feb. 28, 1878, Eliza Anthony, youngest dau. of Francis Edwin and Eliza (Anthony) Hoppin, b. Jan. 20, 1858 They have had three children : *Hope*, b. March 12, 1879, d. Oct. 15, 1880 ; *Virginia*, b. Oct. 16, 1880 ; *Robert*, b. Jan. 9, 1883, d. Feb. 8, 1883.

ii. ELIZABETH HOPE, b. Nov. 7, 1854, was m. May 19, 1880, to John Whipple Slater, son of William Smith and Harriet Morris (Whipple) Slater.

iii. WILLIAM, Jr., b. May 20, 1857, m. Feb. 20, 1884, Bessie Gardiner, twin dau of Tully Dorrance and Louisa (Holmes) Bowen, b. Dec. 19, 1859. They have a son, *William*, b. March 8, 1885.

iv. ARTHUR AMORY, b. March 13, 1862, d. in Providence, March 23, 1887. A graduate of Brown University in the class of 1886.

v. HARRIET IVES, b. May 16, 1864.

vi. HELEN LOUISE, b. April 24, 1868.

117. ANNE B. FRANCIS (*John B. Francis,*[75] *Abby,*[40] *John,*[22] *James,*[8] *James,*[4] *John,*[2] *Chad*[1]). dau. of John B. and Anne C. (Brown) Francis, b. April 23, 1828, was m. July 12, 1848, to Marshall Woods, of Providence, son of Rev. Alva Woods, D. D., and Almira (Marshall) Woods, his wife, born in Boston, Mass., Nov. 28, 1824.

CHILDREN.

i. ABBY FRANCIS, b. May 27, 1849, was m. Oct. 15, 1873, to Samuel Appleton Brown Abbott, of Boston, son of Judge Josiah and Caroline (Livermore) Abbott. They have four children : *Helen Francis*, b. July, 20, 1874 ; *Madeline Liver-

8

more, b. Nov. 2, 1876; *Anne Francis*, b. Sept. 8, 1878; *Caroline Livermore*, b. April 25, 1880.

ii. JOHN CARTER BROWN, b. June 12, 1851. A graduate of Brown University in the class of 1872.

118. JAMES B. HERRESHOFF (*C. F. Herreshoff*.[16] *Sarah*,[41] *John*,[22] *James*,[8] *James*,[4] *John*,[2] *Chad*[1]), son of Charles F. and Julia Ann (Lewis) Herreshoff was b. March 18, 1834. From 1852–1855 he studied in Brown University, taking a special course, chiefly in chemistry. He m. May 14, 1875, Jane, dau. of William and Margaret Jane (Morrow) Brown, of Ireland, b. Aug. 21, 1855. They have five children. (1) *Jane Brown*, b. in Brooklyn, N. Y., July 13, 1876. (2) *James Brown*, b. in London, Eng., March 18, 1878. (3) *Charles Frederick*, b. in Nice, France, May 28, 1880. (4) *William Stuart*, b. in Hampton Wick, Eng., April 21, 1883. (5) *Anna Frances*, b. in Bristol, R. I., July 5, 1886. Reside in Bristol.

119. CAROLINE L. HERRESHOFF (*See No.* 118), b. Feb. 27, 1837, was m. Aug. 16, 1866, to Lieut. E. Stanton Chesebro,' of New York city, son of Albert G. and Phebe Etes (Cobb) Chesebro,' b. in New York, Aug. 17, 1841, d. in Bristol, R. I., Oct. 22, 1875.

They had one child, *Albert Stanton Chesebro*,' b. in Bristol, Jan. 11, 1868.

120. CHARLES F. HERRESHOFF (*See No.* 118), b. Feb. 26, 1839, m. March 19, 1863, Mary, dau. of Charles and Mary (Bateman) Potter, of Portsmouth, R. I., b. March 3, 1843, d. in Bristol, March 24, 1866. He m. second, Dec. 3, 1868, Alice, dau. of Isaac Cook and Alice (Bateman) Almy, of Tiverton, R. I., b. Aug. 15, 1838.

He has one daughter by the first wife, *Julia Ann*, b. in Bristol, Aug. 20, 1864.

121. JOHN B. HERRESHOFF (*See No.* 118), b. April 24, 1841, m. Oct. 6, 1870, Sarah Lucas, dau. of John and Catharine (Bumstead) Kilton, of Boston, Mass., b. Nov. 21, 1836. He is President and Treasurer of the Herreshoff Manufacturing Company, established in Bristol, R. I., in 1863. For ten years schooners and sloops only were built, but, since 1873 steamers have supplanted sailing vessels. The high rate of speed attained by some of the well-known Herreshoff yachts, has achieved for the company a national reputation.

They have a dau., *Katharine Kilton*, b. in Bristol, July 31, 1871.

122. NATHANAEL G. HERRESHOFF (*See No.* 118), b. March 18, 1848, m. Dec. 26, 1883, Clara Anna, dau. of Algernon

Sidney and Clara Anna (Diman) De Wolf, of Bristol, R. I., b. Sept. 5, 1853. For several years he was connected with the Corliss Steam Engine Company, of Providence, and was afterwards a student at the Mass. Institute of Technology, in the class of 1869. He is now the Superintendent of the Herreshoff Manufacturing Company.

They have three children, all born in Bristol : (1) *Agnes Muller*, b. Oct. 19, 1884. (2) *Algernon Sidney De Wolf*, b. Nov. 22, 1886. (3) *Nathanael G.*, Jr., b. Feb. 5, 1888.

123. J. B F. HERRESHOFF (*See No.* 118), b. Feb 7, 1850, m Feb 9, 1876, Grace Eugenia dau. of John and Louisa (Chamberlin) Dyer, of Providence, b. March 20, 1851, d. Dec. 2, 1880. He m. second, Oct. 25, 1882, Emilie Duval, dau. of Dr. Richard Henry and Sarah (Lothrop) Lee, of Philadelphia, Penn., b. March 24, 1863. He entered Brown University in 1867, and soon developing a marked aptness in chemistry, concentrated his attention upon that science. In Nov., 1868, he was appointed Assistant Professor in the laboratory under Prof. Appleton, where he remained two years. Since 1876, he has been Superintendent of the Laurel Hill Chemical Works on Newtown Creek, L. I. This establishment is the largest of the kind in the country, and, in the production of sulphuric acid, surpasses any manufactory in the world.

He has three children : (1) One child by the first wife, *Louise Chamberlin*, b. in Providence, Nov. 29, 1876. (2) *Francis Lee*, b. in Brooklyn, N. Y., Oct. 2, 1883. (3) *Frederic*, b. in Brooklyn, March 7, 1888.

124. JULIAN L. HERRESHOFF (*See No.* 118), b. July 29, 1854. m. Sept. 11, 1879, Ellen Frances, dau. of James Madison and Frances E. (Mowry) Taft, of Pawtucket, R. I., b. Jan. 3, 1852. For the last two years he has been pursuing a classical course at the University of Berlin, Germany. They have one child, *Grace*, b. in Bristol, March 31, 1881.

125. AMASA M EATON (*Sarah B. Eaton,*[77] *Alice,*[42] *John,*[22] *James,*[8] *James,*[4] *John,*[2] *Chad*[1]), son of Levi C. and Sarah B. (Mason) Eaton, b. May 31, 1841, m. Sept. 15, 1873, Alice Maud Mary, dau. of Jacob and Amey (Brown) Dunnell, of Pawtucket, R. I. (*Amey,*[107] *Isaac,*[64] *Isaac,*[33] *Dep.-Gov. Elisha,*[14] *James,*[4] *John,*[2] *Chad*[1]), b. Sept. 15, 1846. He graduated at Brown University in 1861 (A. M.), and at Harvard Law School in 1878 (LL. B.). A member of the First Rhode Island Regiment, under Col. Burnside, he was in the military service of the United States for three months in the Spring and Summer of 1861. This regiment, composed of the choicest material, achieved a national reputation, and in the fiery ordeal of the con-

flict at Bull Run, was highly commended for bravery and fortitude in the day of battle. Mr. Eaton has frequently represented
his native town, North Providence, in the General Assembly ;
has served as member of the Common Council and as Alderman
from the Tenth Ward. Since 1878, he has practised the profession of law in Providence.

They have six children, four sons and two daughters : (1)
Amasa Mason, b. Sept. 24, 1874. (2) *William Dunnell*, b.
Feb. 26, 1877. (3) *Sarah Brown*, b. June 30, 1878. (4)
Charles Curtis, b. Jan. 16, 1880. (5) *Lewis Diman*, b. Sept.
13, 1881. (6) *Amey Brown*, b. Jan. 1, 1885.

126. CHARLES F. EATON (*See No.* 125), son of Levi C.
and Sarah B. (Mason) Eaton, b. Dec. 11, 1842, m. April 24,
1867, Helen Justice, dau. of Edwin and Mary A. (Peterson)
Mitchell, of Philadelphia, Penn. After a residence of several
years abroad, he returned with his family to this country in 1886.
They now reside in Santa Barbara, California.

They have three children : (1) *Mary Elizabeth*, b. Jan. 20,
1869. (2) *Charles Frederick*, b. April 22, 1873. (3) *Lewis
Francis*, b. at Nice, France, Dec. 15, 1877.

127. WILLIAM GROSVENOR, JR. (*Rosa A. Mason*,[18]
Alice,[42] *John*,[22] *James*,[8] *James*,[4] *John*,[2] *Chad*[1]), son of William
and Rosa Anne (Mason) Grosvenor, b. Aug. 4, 1838, m. Oct. 4,
1882, Rose Dinwood Phinney, of Newport, R. I.

They have two children, b. in Providence : *Alice Mason*, b.
Aug. 6, 1883, and *Caroline Rose*, b. Feb. 9, 1885. He graduated at Brown University in 1860, and was trained to business
in his father's office. He is one of the members of the Gros-
venor-Dale Company, and its treasurer and general agent.

128. ANNA A. JENKINS (*Anna Almy*,[79] *Sarah*,[43]
Moses,[23] *James*,[8] *James*,[4] *John*,[2] *Chad*[1]), dau. of William
and Anna (Almy) Jenkins, b. Feb. 1, 1831, was m. to Thomas
F. Hoppin, who d. in 1873. She was m. second, Nov. 5, 1874, to
Henry A. Babbitt, of Pomfret Centre, Conn.

Her two daughters, children of the first husband, are *Anna
Jenkins*, b. May 16, 1853, and *Alice*, b. Jan. 14, 1857. *Anna
J.* was m. to Frederick W. Chapin, and has Anna Alice, b. Dec.
16, 1881. *Alice* was m. to Austen G. Fox, and has had two
children: Austen Hoppin, b. Nov. 4, 1877, and Henry, b. May
24, 1883, d. Dec. 30, 1884.

129. BENJAMIN COWELL (*Elizabeth B. Howell*,[86] *J. B.
Howell*,[47] *Mary*,[28] *Jeremiah*,[13] *James*,[4] *John*,[2] *Chad*[1]), son of
Benjamin and Elizabeth B. (Howell) Cowell, b. Dec. 28, 1818,
d. Oct. 14, 1873, at his residence in Peoria, Ill. He was one of

the "Argonauts" of California in 1849, and subsequently settled in Peoria. Ill., in 1858, where he entered into business as a merchant. He m. Oct. 1, 1845, Amey W. Harris.

CHILDREN.

i. JOSEPH HARRIS, b. April 4, 1847, in the homestead on Charles Field street, Providence. He fitted for college in Peoria, and in 1864, served one hundred days in the 139th Illinois Volunteers. The following year he entered Brown University, and graduated in 1869 with the degree of B. A. He then studied medicine at Michigan University, receiving the degree of M. D. in 1871. The same year he was elected Professor of Pathology in the Homœopathic College at Lansing, Mich., and held the position for two terms, when he removed to East Saginaw, Mich., where he is now a practising physician and surgeon. He m. May 23, 1878, Clarissa, dau. of Mark L. Child. They have three children: *Mary Child*, b. June 17, 1880 ; *Elizabeth Howell*, b. Aug. 20, 1883 ; *Amey Cowell*, b June 16, 1886.

ii. ELIZABETH HOWELL, b. Oct. 18, 1848.

iii. BENJAMIN, b. May 9, 1853, m. Feb. 5, 1880, Mary Anne Goss, and has *Ruth*, b. July 23, 1881, and *Mark Wentworth*, b. July 30, 1883.

iv. HARRY, twin brother of Benjamin, d. Sept. 1, 1853.

v. AMEY ADALINE, b. Dec. 30, 1861.

130. SAMUEL COWELL (*See No.* 129), son of Benjamin and Elizabeth B. (Howell), was b. July 3, 1820. He graduated at Brown University in 1840, and at the General Theological Seminary of New York, where he studied for the Episcopal ministry, in 1844. The same year he was ordained Deacon by Bishop Henshaw, of Rhode Island, and Oct. 10, 1845, was ordained to the priesthood by Bishop Alonzo Potter, of Penn. He has had charge of several parishes in New Jersey and Maine, and from 1858-1884 was settled in Lockport, Ill. He was Chaplain of the State Penitentiary at Joliet, Ill., under Gov. Bissell, and subsequently had charge of a parish at Wilmot, Wisconsin. At present, he resides in Wrentham, Mass.

He m. Sept. 16, 1846, Anne, dau. of Henry and Anne Sweitzer, b. April 26, 1823, d. June 16, 1848. He m. second, Oct. 5, 1852, Margaret, dau. of John and Margaret Marshel, b. Oct 27, 1829, d. May 24, 1884. He m. third, Aletha, dau. of Reynold and Sarah Ann Arnold, b. Feb. 11, 1845.

He has had six children : (1) *Henry Sweitzer*, the only child by the first wife, b. June 16, 1848, d. Aug. 19, 1848. (2) *Elizabeth Howell*, b. Feb. 19, 1854, d. Aug. 5, 1871. (3) *Walter Marshall*, b. Sept. 28, 1856. (4) *Herbert*, b. Oct. 7, 1858, m. Abby Harris, and resides in Joliet, Ill. (5) *Anne Sweitzer*, b. Nov. 24, 1860. (6) *James Henry*, b. March 2, 1863.

131. OLIVIA G. COWELL (*See No.* 129), dau. of Benjamin and E. B. (Howell) Cowell, b. Sept. 1, 1828, was m. July 20,

1847, to Charles Hitchcock, artist, eldest son of Judge Hitchcock, of New Haven, b. in 1823, d. Dec. 10, 1858. She d. Feb. 18, 1865.

They had three children: *Charles*, b. May 12, 1848 ; *George Herbert*, b. Sept. 29, 1850 : *Amelia Swift*, b. Aug. 7, 1852. The eldest son, *Charles Hitchcock*, graduated at Brown University in 1869 (B. A.), and has been for some years a practising physician in New York city. He m. Nov. 27, 1872, Fannie Lapsey, and had Ethel, b. June 27, 1877 : Margaret, b. April 13, d. April 14, 1879 ; Charles, b. Aug. 25, 1881 : Howard Lapsey, b. Sept. 3, 1883 : Olive, b. 1886. *George H. Hitchcock*, m. July, 1881, Henrietta Richardson. He is an artist, and resides in Holland.* *Amelia S. Hitchcock* was m. June 24, 1884, to Herbert Maynard, of Dedham, Mass., b. June 27, 1854. They have a son, b. April 18, 1885, and a second son, Howell Hitchcock, b. Sept. 24, 1887.

132. SARAH H. LIPPITT (*Martha B. Howell,*[87] *J. B. Howell,*[47] *Mary.*[28] *Jeremiah,*[13] *James,*[4] *John,*[2] *Chad*[1]), eldest dau. of Charles and Martha B. (Howell) Lippitt, b. April 12, 1834, was m. Oct. 21, 1857, to Asa Arnold, a descendant in the eighth generation of Roger Williams, through his paternal grandparents, Benjamin and Jemima (Potter) Arnold, who were both of Joseph Williams, youngest son of Roger. She d. Oct. 1, 1873.

They had two children : *Isabelle*, b. July 7, 1858, and *Charles Lippitt*, b. Jan. 5, 1861, d. June 24, 1870. *Isabelle Arnold* was m. in Providence, April 30, 1878, to Johann Christian Graepel, b. May 10, 1848, of Hamburgh, Germany, and had Sarah Theresa, b. May 17, 1879 : Johann Julius, b. Oct. 12, 1882, d Jan. 29, 1883 : Christian Adolph, b. April 9, 1885. Resides in Hamburgh, Germany.

133. MARTHA LIPPITT (*See No.* 132), dau. of Charles and Martha B. (Howell) Lippitt, b. July 16, 1835, was m. Oct. 27, 1858, to Eben K. Glezen, who d. Sept. 5, 1868. They had one son, *Frank Lippitt*, b. May 13, 1862. She d. in Providence, Dec. 16, 1887.

134. MARTHA H. WALKER (*Waity F. Howell,*[88] *J. B. Howell,*[47] *Mary.*[28] *Jeremiah,*[13] *James,*[4] *John,*[2] *Chad*[1]), dau. of Appleton and Waity F. (Howell) Walker, b. Dec. 25, 1827, was m. June 12, 1856, to Robert Sterry Burrough, a merchant of Providence, b. Dec. 13, 1814, d. Oct. 7, 1877. He was son of Robert Sterry and Esther Grant (Armington) Burrough, gr. son of John and Sarah (Pearce) Burrough, and g. gr. son of William and Sarah (Power) Burrough. Sarah Power was dau. of Nich-

---

* See Scribner's Magazine, Aug. 1887, "The Picturesque Quality of Holland."

olas and Mercy Tillinghast Power, sister of Hope (Power) Brown, and half sister of Mary (Power) Cooke, mother of Gov. Nicholas Cooke. Mrs. Burrough resides in the Charles Field street mansion, built in 1810 by her maternal g. gr. mother, Wait (Field) Smith.

They had a dau., *Martha Walker*, b. Dec. 10, 1867.

135. EVERETT P. WILCOX (*Sally B. Howell,* [91] *J. B. Howell,* [47] *Mary,* [28] *Jeremiah,* [13] *James,* [4] *John,* [2] *Chad* [1]), son of Rev. Horace A. and Sally B. (Howell) Wilcox, b. June 22, 1839, m. July 31, 1872. Maria M. Owens, who d. without issue, Aug. 16, 1875. He m. second, June 23, 1880, Lucy E. Mills.

They have had two children : *Susan E.*, b. Sept. 29, 1881, d. Aug. 17, 1883, and *Reina Elizabeth*, b. Dec. 14, 1886. Reside in Brooklyn, N. Y.

136. JULIET L. WILCOX (*See No.* 135,) b. July 24, 1843, was m. Dec. 6, 1866, to James P. Reynolds, who d. Jan. 11, 1880.

They had five children : (1) *James W.*, b. Oct. 18, 1867. (2) *Sarah K.*, b. Oct. 18, 1869. (3) *Annie E.*, b. Oct. 24, 1872. (4) *Candace W.*, b. Feb. 7, 1875. (5) *Everett P.*, b. April 29, 1877. Reside in Walton, Eaton Co., Ill. *??*

137. CHARLES F. WILCOX (*See No.* 135), b. Jan. 8, 1845, m. April 2, 1868, Lucy Wilson, b. Aug. 2, 1841, dau. of George Wade and Lucy (Wilson) Smith, gr. dau. of Asaph and Susan (Wade) Smith and g. gr. dau. of Oliver Smith. Also g. gr. dau. of Oliver Wade, James Wilson and William Ross. Mr. Wilcox is an architect by profession, and resides in Providence.

They have four children : (1) *Sarah Brown*, b. March 23, 1869. (2) *Alice Wilson*, b. June 25, 1871. (3) *Edith Field*, b. Nov. 3, 1872. (4) *Howell George*, b. Jan. 7, 1877.

138. HORACE A. WILCOX (*See No.* 135), b. Dec. 30, 1848, removed in 1868 to Melbourne, Australia, where he m. July 30, 1873, Louisa E. Owen, who d. July 27, 1874. He m. second, Aug. 16, 1877, Emma Nodin, who d. Oct. 23, 1884. He m. third, Aug. 5, 1886, Alice Marion Maplestone, half-sister of Emma Nodin. He has three children : (1) *Nellie Henrietta Owen*, only child by first wife, b. June 29, 1874. (2) *Charles Gilbert*, b. Feb. 15, 1883. (3) *Emma Nodin*, b. Oct. 8, 1884.

139. FRANK W. CHENEY (*Waitstill D. Shaw,* [92] *Mary B. Howell,* [49] *Mary,* [28] *Jeremiah,* [13] *James,* [4] *John,* [2] *Chad* [1]), son of Charles and Waitstill D. (Shaw) Cheney, was b. June 5, 1832. He graduated at Brown University in 1854, and soon after entered into business in Hartford, Conn. In the Civil

War of 1861, he was Lieut.-Colonel of the 16th Conn. Vols.,
and after being severely wounded at Antietam, retired from the
service in Dec., 1862. Subsequently, he travelled extensively in
Europe. China and Japan, studying the silk interests of those
countries, and on his return became a member of the firm of
Cheney Brothers, and its treasurer. This well-known house in
the silk manufacture, was founded in 1836 in South Manchester,
Conn., by his uncles and his father. As a model manufacturing
establishment, it has received the highest encomiums both in
this country and abroad. He m. Nov. 3, 1863, Mary, dau. of
Rev. Horace Bushnell, D. D., and his wife, Mary (Apthorp)
Bushnell, of Hartford, Conn. and gr. dan. of Ensign and Dotha
(Bishop) Bushnell. They have twelve children : (1) *Emily*,
b. Oct. 15, 1864. (2) *Charles*, b. June 7, 1866. (3) *Horace
Bushnell*, b. May 19, 1868. (4) *John Davenport* and (5) *Howe-
ell*, twins, b. Jan. 1, 1870. (6) *Seth Leslie*, b. Jan. 12, 1874.
(7) *Ward*, b. May 26, 1875. (8) *Austin*, b. Dec. 13, 1876.
(9) *Frank Dexter*, b. Oct. 16, 1878. (10) *Marjory* and (11)
Dorothy, twins, b. July 12, 1880. (12) *Ruth*, b. Nov. 23,
1884.

140. KNIGHT D. CHENEY (*See No.* 139), b. Oct. 9,
1837, m. at Exeter, N. H., June 4, 1862, Ednah Dow Smith.
He is of the firm of Cheney Brothers, and resides at South Manchester.

They have eleven children: (1) *Ellen Waitstill*, b. Oct. 16,
1863. (2) *Elizabeth*, b. Sept. 18, 1865. (3) *Harriet Bowen*,
b. Feb. 4, 1867. (4) *Helen*, b. March 7, 1868. (5) *Knight
Dexter*, b. June 1, 1870. (6) *Ednah Parker*, b. Feb. 3, 1873.
(7) *Theodora*, b. Sept. 12, 1874. (8) *Clifford Dudley*, b. Jan.
3, 1877. (9) *Philip*, b. May 8, 1878. (10) *Thomas Langdon*,
b. Nov. 20, 1879. (11) *Russell*, b. Oct. 16, 1881.

141. GAMALIEL L. DWIGHT (*G. L. Dwight*,[93] *Sarah
Howell*,[50] *Mary*,[28] *Jeremiah*,[13] *James*,[4] *John*,[2] *Chad*[1]). son
of G. L. and Catharine H. (Jones) Dwight, b. Feb. 3, 1841, m.
Jan. 16, 1871, Anne Ives, dau. of Edward and Candace Craw-
ford (Dorr) Carrington. He d. in Nassau, Bahama Islands,
Jan. 19, 1875.
They had one child, *Margaretha Lyman*, b. Nov. 8, 1871.
His widow m. second, Col. William Ames, and resides in Provi-
dence.

142. CATHARINE E. DWIGHT (*See No.* 141), dau. of G.
L. and Catharine H. (Jones) Dwight, b. May 19, 1843, was m.
July 2, 1864, to E. Arthur Rockwood, and resides in Buffalo,
N. Y.

They have had five children : (1) *Arthur Jones*, b. March 26, 1865. (2) *William Patten*, b. Oct. 13, 1867, d. Jan. 1, 1870. (3) *Charles Frederick*, b. Sept. 23, 1871. (4) *Edward Vermilye*, b. May 30, 1874. (5) *Catharine Dwight*, b. July 3, 1877.

143. JAMES M. W. YERRINTON (*James B. Yerrinton,*[94] *Catharine,*[53] *Jeremiah,*[31] *Dep.-Gov. Elisha,*[14] *James,*[4] *John,*[2] *Chad*[1]), son of James B. and Phebe (Boyd) Yerrinton, b Oct. 24, 1825, m. May 21, 1850, Susan Elizabeth, dau. of Benjamin and Sophia (Wyman) Mayhew. She is a descendant in the ninth generation of Thomas Mayhew, a merchant of Southampton, England, b. 1592, d. 1682, who, in 1641, procured a patent of Sir Ferdinand Gorges, agent of the Earl of Stirling, for Martha's Vineyard, Nantucket, and the Elizabeth Isles. (*Benjamin,*[8] *Francis,*[7] *Ephraim,*[6] *Benjamin,*[5] *Benjamin,*[4] *John,*[3] *Thomas,*[2] *Thomas*[1]).

They have had six children: (1) *Eleanor E.*, b. March 2, 1851, was m. Oct. 31, 1881, to James P. Duncan, and has Eleanor, b. Nov. 4, 1882. (2) *Anne I.*, b. April 26, 1853. (3) *James F.*, b Oct. 27, 1854, d. April 30, 1858. (4) *Wendell P.*, b. Feb. 7, 1857, m. Sept. 6, 1883, Sarah Marshall, who d. July 19, 1887, leaving a dau., Catharine Ivanetta, b. May 2, 1885. (5) *Arthur Brown*, b. Oct. 21, 1863, d. Sept. 18, 1864. (6) *Carrie Mayhew*, b. Oct. 3, 1866.

144. CAROLINE E. YERRINTON (*See No. 143*), dau. of James B. and Phebe (Boyd) Yerrinton, b. April 20, 1831, was m. March 24, 1850, to Daniel S. Remington, of Providence.

They have had five children : (1) *Samuel W.*, b. 1851, d. April 26, 1877. (2) *James Winchell*, b. Sept. 15, 1852. (3) *George Walter*, b. April 6, 1855, d. Aug. 19, 1886. He m. Sept. 21, 1876, Almie H. Chapman, and had Annie Isabel, b. July, 11, 1877 ; Walter Augusta, b. July 29, 1879 ; Clinton Chapman, b. Jan. 30, 1881. (4) *Carribel C.*, b. July 30, 1858, was m. Jan. 4, 1883, to John A. Howard, and has Louise R., b. Jan. 28, 1884. (5) *Olivia S.*, b. June 29, 1871.

145. ANNA YERRINTON (*See No. 143*), dau. of James B. and Phebe (Boyd) Yerrinton, b. 1833, was m. Dec., 1854, to David White, who d. April 21, 1873. She d. Aug. 30, 1873.

They had two children : (1) *Carrie Della*, b. June 6, 1856, was m. June 1, 1882, to Alfred J. Sidwell. (2) *Anna Bell*, b. Dec., 1857, d. Nov., 1865. Resided in Hadley, Mass.

146. PHEBE YERRINTON (*See. No. 143*), dau. of James B. and Phebe (Boyd) Yerrinton, b. Nov. 23, 1837, was m. July 9, 1857, to Albert F. Arnold, of Providence. She d. in Salem,

Mass, May 1, 1870. They had three children, all born in Providence: (1) *Adela J.*, b. April 10, 1858, was m. June 10, 1880, to Edward G. Pratt, and has Adela Yerrinton, born in Newport, R. I., Dec. 30, 1882. (2) *Mary Elizabeth*, b. Aug. 23, 1859, was m June 20, 1883, to Elisha P. Reeve. (3) *Anna Francis*, b. July 21, 1864, d.——, 1866.

147. FRANK YERRINTON (*See No.* 143), son of James B. and Olive F. Yerrinton, b. June 2, 1839, m. Ellen M. Waterman, in Fairlee, Vt., who d. Nov. 10, 1875. Their three children, b. in Boston, were *Nellie*, b. 1868 ; *Frank M.*, b. Jan. 14, d. Jan. 30, 1870 ; *Alice W.*, b. Aug. 1, 1872, d. Dec. 17, 1873.

148. JAMES D. YERRINGTON* (*B. T. Yerrinton,*[94] *Catharine,*[53] *Jeremiah,*[31] *Dep.-Gov. Elisha,*[14] *James,*[4] *John,*[2] *Chad*[1]), son of Barker T. and Maria (Daggett) Yerrinton, b. Oct. 13, 1833, m. Nov. 24, 1859, in Chelsea, Mass., Annie Catharine Mayhew, sister of S. E. Mayhew. (*See No.* 143.)

They have had three children : (1) A dau. b. Oct., 1860, lived but a day. (2) *Mayhew*, b. Jan. 1, 1863. (3) *Frederick Barker*, b. Oct. 31, 1871. He is of the firm of J. D. Yerrington & Co., dealers in precious stones, New York city, and resides in Cresskill, Bergen Co., New Jersey.

149. PRESTON D. YERRINGTON (*See No.* 148), son of Barker T. and Maria (Daggett) Yerrinton, b. May 12, 1836, m. Sept. 12, 1867, Mrs. Mary P. (Carpenter) Hawley, dau. of Samuel A. and Susan A. (Smith) Carpenter, of Angelica, N. Y. She d. July 9, 1871. They had one child, *Preston*, b. Sept. 6, 1868, in Alton, Ill. After the death of his mother, he was entrusted to the care of relatives in Providence, where he now resides. Preston D. Yerrington was for many years a railroad station agent in Indiana and Illinois, and is now (1888) with J. D. Yerrington and Co., of New York city.

150. ANNIE M. YERRINTON (*See No.* 148), dau. of Barker T. and Maria (Daggett) Yerrinton, b. Dec. 14, 1837, was m. Feb. 4, 1869, to William P. Griffin, son of Thomas Jefferson and Julia Ann (Fuller) Griffin. They have one child, Henry Irving, b. June 18, 1870. In the autumn of 1887 they removed from Pawtucket, R. I., to Knoxville, Tennessee.

151. CHURCHILL H. CUTTING (*Elizabeth,*[88] *Hugh H.,*[57] *Jeremiah,*[31] *Dep.-Gov. Elisha,*[14] *James,*[4] *John,*[2] *Chad*[1]), only child of Rev. S. S. and Elizabeth (Brown) Cutting, b. Sept. 12, 1842, m. May 15, 1864, Mary Augusta, dau. of Carlos Dutton, of Rochester, N. Y. Their two children are *Grace Dutton*, b. Sept. 4, 1866, and *Elizabeth Brown*, b. Nov. 1, 1871. A merchant in New York city, and resides in Brooklyn.

---

* The two sons of Barker T. Yerrinton, when they became of age, restored the g to the family name, writing it Yerrington.

152. GEORGE A. ALLIN (Mary,[99] Hugh H.,[57] Jeremiah,[31] Dep.-Gov. Elisha,[14] James,[4] John,[2] Chad[1]), only child of George and Mary A. (Brown) Allin, b. June 26, 1842, m. June 25, 1874, Heloise M., dau. of Electus B. and H. Marie (Breed) Litchfield. They have had four children : (1) George Litchfield, b. Aug. 29, 1875. (2) Lawrence Blanchard, b. Nov. 11, 1878. (3) Heloise Maria, b. March 1, 1883, d. April 2, 1886. (4) Kate Duryea, b. April 10, 1886.

Mr. Allin is Secretary of the West Brooklyn Land and Improvement Company. Office in New York city.

153. MARY ELLA BROWN (Joseph,[100] Hugh H.,[57] Jeremiah,[31] Dep.-Gov. Elisha,[14] James,[4] John,[2] Chad[1]), dau. of Joseph and Rebecca (Ketchum) Brown, b. April 15, 1847, was m. June 12, 1866, to James Roosevelt Hitchcock, b. at Tompkinsville, Staten Island, March 23, 1841, son of Daniel Roosevelt and Mary (Howard) Hitchcock, and gr. son of Major George Howard, U. S. A. "Col. J. R. Hitchcock* commenced his military career in Jan., 1861, when he enlisted in Company F, Seventy-first Regiment. He served with his company in the three months' campaign of that year at Washington and Bull Run. Subsequently he was elected, successively, Captain, Major, Lieutenant-Colonel and Colonel of the Ninth Regiment, N. G. S. N. Y. During his term of service as Major, the great Orange riot took place in July, 1871, and Col. Hitchcock distinguished himself by his coolness and bravery as commander of the left wing. When the railroad riot of July, 1877, occurred, the first regiment called on for duty was the gallant Ninth, which responded in a few hours, and without overcoats or blankets, and with only ammunition in the way of stores, Col. Hitchcock took his men to West Albany. Good service was performed there and encomiums were showered upon the regiment and its intrepid colonel. The illness which resulted fatally, caused by undue exposure to the heat of the sun, was contracted at this time, and he died in New York city, on the 12th of April, 1878, at the age of 37. An efficient and beloved officer, his early death was greatly lamented. He was buried with military honors, and his remains were interred in the family plot at Stapleton, Staten Island." They had two children, Alice, b. June 22, 1867, and Wilbur Kirby, b. Dec. 31, 1871.

154. GEORGE T. BROWN (Samuel W.,[102] Ebenezer P.,[58] Jeremiah,[31] Dep.-Gov. Elisha,[14] James,[4] John,[2] Chad[1]), son of Samuel W. and Mary E. (Thurber) Brown, b. May 7, 1850, m. Oct. 15, 1874, Lydia James, dau. of James and Lydia (Paine) McGary, of Masonboro', N. C., b. Jan. 21, 1850.

They have had four children, all born in Providence. (1)

* Abridged from the papers of the day.

Elizabeth Thurber, b. Aug. 2, 1875, d. March 2, 1888. (2)
Samuel Walter, b. July 8, 1877. (3) *Lydia James*, b. Jan. 22,
1882, d. March 5, 1888. (4) *Emily Selinger*, b. Sept. 6, 1883.

155. ARTHUR L. BROWN (*See No.* 154), son of Samuel
W. and Mary E. (Thurber) Brown, b. Nov. 28, 1854, m. Feb.
12, 1885, Cora Elizabeth, dau. of Hiram B. and Margaret M.
(Hatfield) Aylsworth, b. March 14, 1860, a descendant in the
tenth generation of Chad Brown, and in the eighth of Arthur
and Mary (Brown) Aylsworth (*Hiram B.,*[7] *Eli,*[6] *Arthur,*[5]
James,[4] *Philip,*[3] *Arthur,*[2] *Arthur*[1]). (*See No.* 7.)
They have two children : *Aylsworth*, b. Feb. 14, 1886, and
Beatrice, b. Aug. 11, 1887. Arthur L. Brown graduated at
Brown University in 1876, and subsequently studied law. He
is of the firm of Miller and Brown, attorneys, Providence.

156. HENRY C. COOKE (*C. D. Cooke,*[105] *Amey,*[83] *Isaac,*[33]
Dep.-Gov. Elisha,[14] *James,*[4] *John,*[2] *Chad*[1]), son of Charles D.
and Mary A. (King) Cooke, b. Sept. 6, 1843, m. in New York
city Sept. 6, 1864, Harriet Ruth,* only dau. of William and
Harriot (Driver) Waters, b. in Andover, Mass., March 18, 1841.
They have had two children, b. in New York : *Henry Dexter*,
b. Dec. 27, 1865, d. July 1, 1868; *Maud Aline*, b. May 23, 1869.

157. SOPHIA B. DUNNELL (*Amey,*[107] *Isaac,*[64] *Isaac,*[33]
Dep.-Gov. Elisha,[14] *James,*[4] *John,*[2] *Chad*[1]), dau. of Jacob and
Amey D. (Brown) Dunnell, b. June 14, 1837, was m. April 5,
1865, to John T. Denny, b. June 7, 1835, son of Thomas and
Sarah (Tappan) Denny, of New York city. They have had
three children : (1) *Amey Dunnell*, b. Nov. 12, 1866, was m.
Dec. 2, 1884, to Chalmers Dale, a merchant of New York city,
son of Gerald F. and Elizabeth (Sparhawk) Dale, of Philadelphia. They have one child, Francis Colgate, b. Dec. 18,
1885. (2) *Thomas Denny, Jr.*, b. Sept. 27, 1869. (3) *Maude
Dunnell*, b. July 23, 1872.

158. JACOB DUNNELL (*See No.* 157), son of Jacob and
Amey D. (Brown) Dunnell, b. Feb. 6, 1839, m. Sept. 25, 1861,
Jeannie Tucker, dau. of Samuel Chace and Jane (Bull) Blodget.
He d. April 9, 1874. They had five children : (1) *Jacob*, b.
Oct. 2, 1862, d. in infancy. (2) *Jacob Wanton*, b. Nov. 16,
1864. (3) *Amey Dexter*, b. July 25, 1866. (4) *Henry*, b. June
23, 1869. (5) *Jeannie Power*, b. Sept. 25, 1871.

159. ALICE MAUD MARY DUNNELL (*See No.* 157), dau.
of Jacob and Amey D. (Brown) Dunnell, b. Sept. 15, 1846, was
m. Sept. 15, 1873, to Amasa M. Eaton (*See No.* 125).

* Mrs. Cooke is the compiler of a Genealogy, entitled "The Driver Family."

160. GEORGE H. BROWNE (*Elisha,*[80] *Esek,*[69] *Elisha,*[24] *Chad,*[15] *Obadiah,*[5] *John,*[2] *Chad*[1]), son of Elisha and Roby (Bowdish) Brown, was b. in Chepachet, R. I., Jan. 6, 1818. Maternally, he was in the fifth generation from Captain David Bowdish, of Glocester, R. I., who came from Wales, and was a master mariner, and later a farmer (*Roby,*[4] *Nathaniel,*[3] *Nathaniel,*[2] *David*[1]). He was a descendant of the Huntingtons, of Conn., through his grandmother, Betsey (Huntington) Bowdish. The following sketch of his life is compiled from various sources :

His father, Elisha Browne, died when his son was eight years of age, leaving the homestead in Chepachet, and a large landed property in Northern Vermont. His early education was obtained in his native village, where his classical tastes soon became apparent. After studying for a time at Brownington Academy in Northern Vermont, he entered Brown University in 1836, and graduated in 1840. He industriously worked his way through college, supporting himself largely by his own exertions. He studied law in the office of Samuel Y. Atwell, was admitted to the bar in 1843, and began to practice in Chepachet, where he soon established a successful law office. For several years he represented the town of Glocester in the General Assembly, and took a prominent position as leader of the Democratic Party. In 1860, he was chosen from the western district of Rhode Island to represent the State in the thirty-seventh Congress. On the 18th of Sept., 1862, he was commissioned as Colonel of the Twelfth Regiment of Rhode Island Volunteers for nine months. This regiment was destined to severe service. It took part in the battle of Fredericksburg in December, 1862, and occupied one of the most exposed positions on the field, losing one hundred and nine in killed and wounded, with ninety-five missing. In February, 1863, the Twelfth moved to Newport News, and from thence accompanied General Burnside to the department of the Ohio, encamping April 1st, at Lexington, Kentucky. The remainder of the campaign was spent chiefly in Kentucky. In July the regiment was ordered to Providence, and mustered out of service. Of the one thousand and seventy-three men on the rolls at departure, seven hundred and seventy-eight returned to their homes.* Col. Browne resumed his seat in Congress, and served the remainder of his term. Failing of re-election, he continued the practice of his profession, and kept an office in both Chepachet and Providence, his associate in the city being Col. Nicholas Van Slyck. In 1872 and 1873 he was elected State Senator from Glocester, and in 1874, by a Legislature composed mainly of his political opponents, was chosen to the Chief Justiceship of the Supreme Court of the State, a memorable tribute to his integrity, learning and ability. This honor he

---

* See Memoirs of Rhode Island Officers, by John R. Bartlett.

declined, preferring to continue in the practice of the law. The latter part of his life he discontinued his country office, and made Providence his home.

George H. Browne died at his residence, Sept. 26, 1885, as the bells were striking the midnight hour. He was stricken with paralysis Sept. 19, and lingered but a week, most of the time in an unconscious condition. His funeral was held in the First Congregational Church, and his remains conveyed to Swan Point Cemetery.

Many eloquent and appreciative tributes were paid to his memory by the members of the Rhode Island Bar, and the Twelfth Veteran Association. In the "minutes" of the latter occurs this paragraph : " As commanding officer of the regiment he was highly esteemed by his command, both officers and privates, for his stalwart manliness, his unselfish and untiring devotion to the personal welfare of his men, and his bravery and heroism on the field of battle."

He m. Aug. Aug. 8, 1844, Harriet Newell Danforth, of Williamstown, Mass., b. April 4, 1818, a descendant of Nicholas Danforth, of Framingham, England, who emigrated in 1634 to Cambridge, Mass. She d. April 30, 1859. They had three children: (1) *Keyes Danforth,* b. Dec. 14, 1846, m. in Ogden City, Utah, July 30, 1876, Bertha Burt, and had Chad Burt, b. in Ogden City, April 25, 1877, d. in Providence, Oct. 31, 1882 ; Harriet Danforth, b. Jan. 11, 1879 ; George H., b. Oct. 2, 1881, and Edward Keyes, b. April 27, 1884. (2) *Chad Elisha,* b. Oct. 21, 1848, d. Oct. 6, 1850. (3) *Mary Bushnell,* b. Oct. 27, 1850, was m Sept. 1, 1870, to Jacob Maus Schermerhorn, of Homer, N. Y. Reside in Syracuse, N. Y. No issue. He m. second, Sept. 1, 1864, Mrs. Mary L. (Baker) Lidgerwood, dau. of the late Judge C. M. Baker, of Geneva, Wisconsin. Their only child, *Edward Baker,* b. June 8, 1865, d. Dec. 4, 1881. He was a bright and promising lad of studious habits, and his early death, just as he was entering upon manhood, was a great grief to his parents.

161. MARSHALL D. SANDERS (*Celinda,*[111] *Esek,*[69] *Elisha,*[35] *Chad,*[15] *Obadiah,*[5] *John,*[2] *Chad*[1]), son of Anthony and Celinda (Brown) Sanders, b. July 3, 1823, m. Sept. 4, 1851, Georgianna, dau. of Rev. Joseph and Ruby (Hyde) Knight, of Peru, Mass., b. June 15, 1825, d. Nov. 2, 1868, at Batticotta, Ceylon. He m. second, April 6, 1870, Caroline Zerviah, dau. of Dr. Walter and Lucy Leffingwell Lord (Salisbury) Webb, of Adams, N. Y., b. Feb. 18, 1840. He d. Aug. 29, 1871, at Batticotta, a suburb of Jaffna.

BIOGRAPAHICAL SKETCH OF REV. MARSHALL D. SANDERS.

" He pursued his preparatory studies at the Academy in Williamstown, entered Williams College in 1842, and graduated in

1846. After two years spent in teaching, he entered Auburn Theological Seminary, graduating in 1851. He was ordained at Williamstown, July 17, 1851, and on the 31st of the next October, sailed with his wife from Boston as a missionary of the A. B. C. F. M. for Ceylon, arriving at Madras, India, Feb. 21, 1852. From thence he proceeded to Ceylon, where he was stationed successively at Batticotta, Chavagacherry, Tillipally, and again at Batticotta. In 1859 a Training and Theological School was opened at Batticotta, which was placed under his personal charge. In the autumn of 1864, he was granted a leave of absence from the mission, and, with his family, sailed for America, where he arrived July 25, 1865. After a visit of two years, he and his wife returned to Ceylon, leaving their five sons with friends in this country. Mrs. Sanders died at Batticotta of pleurisy, Nov. 2, 1868, in the forty-third year of her age. The following year he returned again to America, for the purpose of raising funds for founding a college at Jaffna.

"While in this country he married the second time, and, with his wife, sailed for Ceylon from New York, May 10, 1871, arriving at their destination the fourth of the next July. Eight weeks later, he died suddenly of apoplexy, Tuesday, Aug. 29, 1871." (Contributed by Dr. J. A. Sanders.)

THE MISSIONARY ACTIVITY, by Frank K. Sanders.

"The work of Rev. M. D. Sanders as a missionary was typically successful. Generations of mission effort, and especially the careers of such men as Dr. Duff, St. Francis Xavier and Dr. Miller, have shown that the core of missionary effectiveness is personal influence and example. This intense personality belonged to him as well. He was not remarkable for linguistic ability, nor for oratorical power, though good in both respects. His power consisted in getting close to men's hearts and impressing upon them a conviction of the excellence, the urgency and the truth of his divine message.

"Possessing a genial and sympathetic nature, and expressing himself earnestly and clearly, he was well fitted to be a real pastor to the natives of Jaffna. He was revered by Christian and heathen alike to such a degree, that his son, returning to Ceylon many years after his death, found his name a ready passport to the affection and esteem of the hardest of heathen, who had known the father.

"His New England parentage and training had fostered a practical efficiency, which made him a natural leader. He founded, and until his death managed, the Jaffna Religious Tract Society, which to this day is doing an important work. He organized the Mission and Normal Training School, and was for some years its Principal, being thus instrumental in preparing for their work a large number of teachers, catechists and pastors. With all these duties he found time for wide evangelistic work throughout his district, for overseeing and guiding the catechists and colporteurs, and for other details of active missionary service.

"He knew how to express so clearly the needs and opportunities of the interests committed to him, that he rarely failed to command the interest and support of those to whom he appealed. When, therefore, there was felt an imperative need for a Christian College at Jaffna, both natives and missionaries, with one accord, turned to him to be its representative to the friends of missionary enterprise in America, and its first president. He labored with zeal and success in raising an endowment, but was not permitted to finish his commission. He was "called up higher," soon after his return to Ceylon. His life-work was brief compared to that of some, but of concentrated effort and abundant success, it was full."

CHILDREN (by the first wife, all born in Ceylon).

JOSEPH ANTHONY, b. July 7, 1852, m. Jan. 31, 1888, Cascenda, dau. of Hiram and Jennie (Parteh) Calkins, of New York city, b. July 4, 1862. He graduated at Amherst College in 1878, and at the Medical Department of the University of the city of New York in 1881. Is a practising physician in New York city.

ii CHARLES SYLVESTER, b. April 18, 1854, m. Dec. 24, 1881, at Aintab, Turkey, Illie Grace,* dau. of Rev. John Shepherd and Mary Field (Williamson) Bingham, b. at Higginsville, N. Y., Oct. 22, 1859, d. at Aintab, Jan. 15, 1888. They had one child, *Maud Mary*, b. April 4, 1884. He graduated at Amherst College in 1875, and at Hartford Theological Seminary in 1879. Has been for some years a missionary of the American Board of Commissioners for Foreign Missions, stationed at Aintab, Asiatic Turkey.

iii. WILLIAM HENRY, b. March 2, 1856, m. Sept. 12, 1882, at Bailundu, Southwest Africa, Mary J. Mawhir. No issue. He graduated at Williams College in 1877, and at Hartford Theological Seminary in 1880. Is a medical missionary of the A. B. C. F. M. of the West Central African Mission, stationed at Bihé.

iv. MARSHALL DANFORTH, JR., b. Sept. 29, 1858, d. at Lakeville, Conn., Oct. 31, 1877.

v. FRANK KNIGHT, b. June 5, 1861, graduated at Ripon College, Wisconsin, in 1882, and subsequently taught, for a time, in the college founded by his father in Jaffna. He is now (1888) residing at New Haven, Conn., taking a special course in Yale College, as preparation for the profession of a teacher.

CHILD (by the second wife).

vi. WALTER EDWARD, b. Feb. 19, 1872, in New York city. He is now (1888) at Auburndale, Mass., fitting for college.

* Mrs. Sanders died of pneumonia, the result, apparently, of a severe cold caught on a chilly day, when she was returning with her husband from Aleppo, where they had thought of taking up their permanent home. Mr. and Mrs. Fuller, of Aintab, thus wrote of her: "She was one of the most widely loved and useful of our whole mission; was active and earnest to the last, and her loss will be keenly felt by the native women. It was touching to see their grief at the funeral." (See *Missionary Herald*, April, 1888.)

162. MARY J. SANDERS (*See No.* 161), dau. of Anthony and Celinda (Brown) Sanders, b. Oct. 21, 1826, was m. Aug. 20, 1846, to Rev. Edward Lord, son of Chester and Betsey Lord, both of Danby, N. Y. He is a graduate of Williams College and of Auburn Theological Seminary, and was Chaplain in the 110th Regiment, N. Y. Volunteers. For fourteen years he was pastor of a Presbyterian church in Fulton, N. Y., and afterwards preached at Adams, N. Y. Later, he was settled at Metuchin, N. J., but, on account of failing health, retired from the ministry, and now resides at Patchogue, L. I.

CHILDREN.

i. CHESTER SANDERS. b. March 18, 1850, m. Oct. 18, 1871, Kate M., dau. of Naum and Mary (Segur) Bates, of Adams, N. Y. Resides in Brooklyn, and is connected with the *New York Sun* as associate editor. They have had four children. (1) *Chester*, b. Dec. 2, 1876, d. in infancy. (2) *Edward Roy*, b. May. 1878. d. in infancy. (3) *Kenneth*, b. Dec. 2, 1879. (4) *Richard*, b. June 24, 1881.

ii. ANNA CELINDA, b. Jan. 13, 1854, was m. June 5, 1881, to Dr. Charles Phelps Williams Merritt, son of James McKnight and Elizabeth (Smith) Merritt, of Stelton, N. J. (now of Brooklyn, N. Y.) Dr. Merritt is a medical missionary of the A. B. C. F. M. of the North China Mission, stationed at Paoting-fu. They have had three children : (1) *Edward Lord*, b. May 18, 1883. (2) *Royal McKnight*, b. Aug. 28, 1884. (3) *Charles Chester*, b. Aug. 4, 1886, at Kalgan, China, d. Sept. 8, 1887.

iii. CHARLES EDWARD, b. May 21, 1860. Is a reporter on the *New York Times*.

iv. BLANCH ELIZABETH, b. Jan. 21, d. Feb. 15, 1865.

A PARTIAL HISTORY OF JAMES, JEREMIAH AND DANIEL BROWN, THE THREE YOUNGEST SONS OF CHAD AND ELIZABETH BROWN, AND A PORTION OF THEIR DESCENDANTS.

JAMES BROWN,
SECOND SON OF CHAD.

The information here given of James Brown, second son of Chad and Elizabeth, and a portion of his descendants, is derived from Austin's Genealogical Dictionary and the Russell Genealogy. The time and place of his birth are not known. He married Elizabeth, daughter of Robert Carr, and lived in Newport, R. I., where he was admitted Freeman in 1671. He was by trade a cooper. Dec. 31, 1672, he and his wife Elizabeth sold the home lot of his father, Chad Browne, deceased, to Daniel Abbott, of Providence, reserving a portion twenty feet square within the orchard, where his parents were buried. He died about 1683, as on May 5th of that year it is recorded that " Elizabeth Brown of Newport, widow and executrix of James Brown, sold land in East Greenwich, to Clement Weaver, for £12." They had three sons : *John,*[3] *James*[3] and *Esek.*[3]

CHILDREN (Third Generation).

i. JOHN BROWN,[3] b. 1671, died in Newport, Oct. 20, 1731. He held the title of Captain from 1709, and was frequently Deputy between 1706 and '26. May 4, 1709, he was appointed on a Special Council to assist the Governor in managing the affairs of the intended Canadian expedition. In 1721 he served on a committee to rebuild or repair Fort Ann. It was voted by the Assembly in June, 1730, " to deliver to Captain John Brown, at the fort, the great guns and appurtenances now on board the brigantine *Two Brothers.*" He married Elizabeth, dau. of Gov. John and Mary (Clarke) Cranston. After Capt. Brown's death, his widow became the second wife of Rev. James Honeyman, Rector of Trinity Church, Newport. John and Elizabeth Brown had seven children : (1) *John*, b. Dec. 26, 1696. (2) *Jeremiah*, b. Sept. 30, 1693, d Oct. 30, 1723. (3) *James* (4) *William*. (5) *Robert*. (6) *Peleg*, b. 1709, d. Feb 21, 1756 ; m Feb 20, 1746, Sarah, dau. of John and Sarah Freebody, b. 1721, d. Sept. 27, 1806. They had Samuel, b. 1746, d March 22, 1825, unmarried, a wealthy and prominent merchant of Boston, and Elizabeth, b. 1748, d. April 6, 1753. (7) *Elizabeth*, third wife of John Gridley. He was killed by an explosion of gunpowder, Sept. 1744. (Of this family the line only of John, the eldest son, who m. Jane Lucas, will be continued)

ii. JAMES BROWN,[3] of Newport and later of Scituate, R. I., b.——, d. in 1756. As he was admitted Freeman, May 6, 1701, his birth must have been before 1680. His first wife, Ann, who may have been daughter of James and Hope (Power) Clarke, was the mother of his five children. He m. second, April 27, 1740, Catharine, b. March 19, 1702, dau. of Job and Phebe (Sayles) Greene, and g. gr. dau. of Roger Williams. No issue. The Colonial Records contain frequent mention of his name. In 1704, he was appointed to assist in supervising the printing of the Laws. With the exception of one year, he was Deputy from 1706-1715, and Assistant from 1715-1723. He was Justice of the Peace in 1708, and Major for the Island from 1711-1713. At that time there were two Majors—one for the Island, and one for the Main.* It was the highest military title of the period. After 1711, the name of James Brown was always written with the prefix, Major. With two others, he was appointed June 2, 1711, to buy a vessel for the intended expedition of the Colony against Canada, and the following year, he and the Governor were empowered to employ workmen to enlarge the Colony House.

James and Ann Brown had four sons and one daughter : (1) *James*, b. 1700. (2) *John*. (3) *Clarke*. (4) *Hope*, who was m. March 20, 1719, to Nathaniel Coddington, b. Jan. 18, 1692, son of Nathaniel and gr. son of Gov. William Coddington. They had ten children. (5) Thomas, m. April 3, 1746, Almey, dau. of John Greene,[4] of Potowomot. (*Thomas*,[3] *Thomas*,[2] of *Stone Castle*, *John*,[1] the *Surgeon*). They had five children. (i) Fleet, b. July 17, 1747, m. April 19, 1767, Elizabeth Coope. He m. second, April 6, 1780, Mary, dau. of John Hopkins. (ii) Judith, b. June 3, 1748. (iii) Job, b. April 29, 1751. (iv) Deborah, b. Jan. 11, 1754. (v) Thomas, b. Oct. 18, 1765.

In the will of Major James, proved Nov. 27, 1756, mention is made of land which he owned in South Amboy, N. J., and in Northfield, Mass.

iii. ESEK BROWN,[3] b. March 8, 1679, d. Dec. 10, 1772, removed in 1715 from Newport to Swanzey, Mass. He m. Nov. 29, 1705, Mercy, dau. of Caleb and Deborah Carr, and gr. dau. of Caleb and Mercy Carr. She was b. Oct. 7, 1683, and d. Dec., 1776. They had eleven children, born between 1707 and 1723, viz : *Mary, Elizabeth, Deborah, Esek, Roby, Deborah, Mary, James, Benjamin, Jeremiah, Daniel.*

FOURTH GENERATION.

(1.) JOHN BROWN,[4] (*John*,[3] *James*,[2] *Chad*[1]), b. Dec. 26, 1696, d. Jan. 2, 1764, m. Jane, dau. of Augustus and Bathsheba Lucas, of Newport. She was b. at St. Malo, in the north of

*Governor Joseph Jenckes was Major for the Main.

France, Oct. 16, 1697, and d. at Newport, Oct. 13, 1775. Her portrait, painted in miniature about 1730, in the costume of the period, was copied for illustration in the Russell Genealogy, and forms one of its most attractive pages. Bathsheba Lucas, wife of Augustus, was dau. of Rev. Joseph Elliott, of Guilford, Conn., son of John, the Apostle to the Indians, who married Sarah, dau. of Gov. William Brenton, of Newport. John and Jane (Lucas) Brown had 13 children.

CHILDREN (Fifth Generation).

i. MARY, b. Oct. 28, 1718, d. Feb. 2, 1721.
ii. JOHN, b. Aug. 21, 1721, d. Oct. 2. 1763 ; m. May 6, 1744, Sarah Emmott, who d. May 12, 1767. Their two children, John and James, died in infancy. He m. second, Sept. 27, 1747, Ann Chapman, and had Sarah and Abigail, who d. young, and Jane, b. Oct. 20, 1752, was m. March 5, 1779, to Stephen Deblois (second wife), and had Stephen, Elizabeth, Rebecca, John, Jane.
iii. JANE, b. Jan. 23, 1724, d. April 18, 1765 ; was m. Sept 9, 1741, to Thomas Vernon. (See R. I. Hist. Tracts, No. 13, Diary of Thomas Vernon.)
iv. MARY, b. April 20, 1726, was m. Sept. 14, 1752, to Richard Beale ; d. 1792, in Yorkshire, England.
v. ELIZABETH, b. Jan. 22, 1728, was m. April 27, 1749, to Edward Cole.
vi. JEREMIAH, b. Nov. 8, 1729, d. Aug. 12, 1764 ; m. Aug. 22, 1753, Mary, dau. of Rev. James Honeyman.
vii. ABIGAIL, b. April 4, 1732, d. Sept. 9, 1744.
viii. ANN, b. Aug. 19, 1733, d. July 26, 1786 ; was m. Sept. 27, 1753, to Charles Handy, and had 13 children. A daughter, Ann Handy, b. March 6, 1763, d. Sept. 8, 1807, was m, Aug. 29, 1873, to Thomas Russell, son of Thomas, gr. son of Joseph, and g. gr. son of John Russell, Jr. Of their five children, Ann and Mary d. young. The eldest son, Thomas H. Russell, b. Dec. 27, 1791, d. at Matanzas, Cuba, July 22, 1819. He m. June, 1813, Anna P. Bosworth, of Bristol, R. I., and had one son, William Henry Thomas, b. Feb. 8, 1817, d. in Detroit, Michigan. Charles H. Russell, the second son, b. in Newport, Sept. 13, 1796, d. in New York city, Jan. 21, 1884. He. m. April 3, 1818, Ann, dau. of Capt. William and Ann (Olney) Rodman, b. in Providence, May 23, 1797, d. in New York, Aug. 18, 1842. They had four daughters: Eliza Rodman, Anna Rodman, Cora and Fanny Geraldine. He m. second, Oct. 29, 1850, Caroline, dau. of Samuel S. Howland, b. Nov. 21, 1821, d. in New York, March 7, 1863. Of their seven children, five attained maturity : Charles Howland, b. Dec. 14, 1851 ; Samuel Howland, b. May 19, 1853 ; Caroline Alice, b. Oct. 23, 1854; Joanna Hone, b. Aug. 30, 1856; Mary Grace, b. March 17, 1860.

Charles H. Russell was a merchant of Providence in early life. In 1825 he removed to New York, where he was in active business many years, and held an honored position in the community. The house of Charles H. Russell & Co. was known prominently at home and abroad. During the late Civil War, he contributed largely of his time and means to the service of the Government, was a member of the Union Defence Committee of New York, and a prompt supporter

of the administration and measures of President Lincoln.
He resided in New York in the winter, and at "Oaklawn,"
Newport, in the summer.

William H. Russell, brother of Charles H., b. June 16, 1799,
died in Paris, France, Dec. 14, 1872. He m. May 6, 1823, Mary
Alice Crapo, and had two daughters, the eldest of whom,
Mary Caroline, b. Feb. 4, 1824, was m. to Theodosius
A. Fowler. William H. Russell m. second, Dec. 8, 1836,
Anna Kane. Their eldest child, Helen Nicholson, b. in
New York Sept. 15, 1837, was m. in Paris, March 5, 1868,
to Maxime Outrey. A son, William H., b. in New York,
Jan. 4, 1841, educated at Columbia College, served as Captain
on the staff of Major-General Hooker, and died in
Paris, Feb. 26, 1877. William H. Russell, Sr., was an associate
and partner with his brother, Charles H., and extensively
engaged in the business of foreign importations in
New York.

    ix. Robert, b. April 9, 1735, d. Aug. 1794; m. Jan. 6, 1763,
        Elizabeth Cooke.
    x. Augustus, b. July 2, 1736, d. in the West Indies, Feb. 1780.
    xi. James, b. Dec. 1, 1737, d. in Holland, Dec, 1758.
    xii. Francis, b. Oct. 28, 1739, d. in Maryland, July 13, 1799.
    xiii. Hart, b. Aug. 22, 1741, was m. July 7, 1765, to Isaac Cannon

JEREMIAH BROWN,

Third Son of Chad.

The information concerning Jeremiah Brown, third son of
Chad and Elizabeth, is meagre, and is derived wholly from
Austin's Genealogical Dictionary of Rhode Island. He removed
to Newport, R. I., where he died in 1690, between Sept. 16 and
Oct. 30th. Nothing is known of his first wife but her name—
Mary. He m. 2d, about 1680, Mary Cook, widow of Thomas,
who survived him. It is certain that he had one son, James, by
trade a cooper, who in 1693, sold to William Gibson, of Kings
Town, for £12, certain land in Providence given by last will of
his father, Jeremiah. Possibly, Samuel, Daniel and William
Brown, of Kings Town, were his sons, but of this there is no
proof. He was living in Kings Town in 1687, as he was taxed
there on Sept. 6, 2s. 2d. He probably returned to Newport.
He was Freeman in 1671, served on the Grand Jury in 1686,
and in 1690, Sept. 16, with two others, was appointed by the
Assembly to proportion the rate of tax for Kings Town's part of
money for French and Indian War.

DANIEL BROWN,

Fifth Son of Chad.

More is known of Daniel Brown, youngest son of Chad and
Elizabeth, than of his two older brothers, James and Jeremiah.
The greater part of this information is derived from Austin's
Genealogical Dictionary of Rhode Island. He lived in Providence,
and died, while temporarily at Newport, Sept. 29, 1710.
He m. Dec. 25, 1669, Alice, dau. of Benjamin and Elizabeth

(White) Hearnden, b. 1652, d. after 1718. They had eight children : *Judah*, *Jabez*, *Sarah*, *Jeremiah*, *Hallelujah*, *Hosanna*, *Jonathan and Daniel*. He was a farmer, living "in the neck," on fifty acres of land, which, on Dec. 10, 1706, he deeded conditionally to his two eldest sons, Judah and Jabez. To his son Daniel, he deeded "for love, etc., Feb. 18, 1710, a forty foot lot, a little north of Great Bridge, from the town over to Weybosset." His will, proved Nov. 10, 1710, gave administration to the widow, Alice. The inventory of his personal estate amounted to about £78.

His posterity is undoubtedly numerous, as seven of his children married, and his grandchildren numbered thirty-two. The information available is too fragmentary to admit of a connected account of his descendants, but it has been drawn from many sources, and, being deemed reliable, is here given, notwithstanding its incompleteness.

CHILDREN (Third Generation).

i. JUDAH BROWN[3] (*Daniel,*[2] *Chad*[1]), d. Jan. 18, 1734. He lived in Providence and Scituate, R. I., and m. Hannah——, who d. after 1745. They had six children : *Joseph*, *Deborah*, *Abigail*, *David*, *Hannah*, *Elisha and Phebe*.

ii. JABEZ BROWN[3] (*Daniel,*[2] *Chad*[1]), d. Sept. 9, 1724. He was of Providence, and m. Anne——, who died Feb. 25, 1727. They had two sons, *William* and *Jeremiah*.

iii. SARAH BROWN[3] (*Daniel,*[2] *Chad*[1]), b. Oct. 10, 1677, d. after 1744, was m. April 4, 1700, to Thomas Angell,[3] son of John[2] and Ruth (Field) Angell, and grandson of Thomas and Alice Angell. She was b. March 25, 1672, and d. Sept. 14, 1744. They had seven children : *Martha*, *Isaiah*, *Jeremiah*, *Jonathan*, *Sarah*, *Nehemiah* and *Thomas*, whose history may be partly traced in the Angell Genealogy. Mention will here be made of two only, *Martha*[4] and *Jeremiah*.[4] *Martha Angell*,[4] b. March 23, 1704, m. Jonathan Knight, of Cranston, and had a dau., Elizabeth,[5] who became the wife of Col. Joseph Knight. Their son, George Knight,[6] of Scituate, b. Sept 13, 1771, m. Mercy Stone, dau. of Hugh, and had a son, Rev. Daniel Richmond Knight,[7] b. Aug. 15, 1805, d. in Exeter, April 27, 1877. He m. Susan Colvin, and had a dau., Jane Frances Knight,[8] b. in Scituate, Dec. 31, 1838, who was m. May 1, 1860, to Charles W. Hopkins, son of Pardon and Lydian (Lillibridge) Hopkins, b. Aug. 8, 1839, author of the "Home Lots of the Early Settlers of the Providence Plantations." They have a dau., Anne Miller Hopkins,[6] b Jan. 2, 1865.

Jeremiah Angell,[4] m. Mary Matthewson, and had a son Andrew, who m. Tabitha Harris. Their son Charles[6] m. Olive Aldrich. The latter were the parents of Andrew Angell,[7] who married Amey Aldrich, and had a son, James Burrill Angell,[8] born in Scituate, R. I., Jan. 7, 1829, married Nov. 26, 1855, Sarah Swoope, dau. of Alexis Caswell, D. D., LL. D., President of Brown University, and his wife, Esther Lois Thompson. They have three children : *Alexis Caswell,*[9] b. April 26, 1857 ; *Lois Thompson,*[9] b. Feb. 15, 1863, and *James Rowland,*[9] b. May 8, 1869. The eldest, *Alexis Caswell Angell,*[9] m. June 5, 1880, Frances Cary, dau. of Hon. Thomas M. Cooley, and has Sarah Caswell, b. Feb. 2, 1883, and Thomas Cooley, b. Feb. 21, 1885. James B. Angell graduated at Brown University in 1849, with the honors of his class. Two years later, he went to Europe for study and travel, and on his return in 1853, was appointed Professor of Modern Languages and Literature in the University from which he graduated. In 1860 he succeeded the recently elected Senator, Henry B. Anthony, as editor of the *Providence Daily Journal,* and remained in that position until 1866, when he was called to the Presidency of the University of Vermont. In 1867 the degree of LL. D. was conferred upon him by his *Alma Mater.* He has been President of the University of Michigan since 1871. In the Spring of 1880 he was appointed Envoy Extraordinary and Minister Plenipotentiary to China, and was also Chairman of a Commission to negotiate treaties with that nation. Two treaties were procured, one relating to commerce, and another to Chinese immigration. He resigned his place as Minister at Peking in Oct., 1881. In Oct., 1887, he was appointed by President Cleveland member of a Commission to meet Commissioners from Great Britain, to consider questions connected with the United States' right of fishing in the waters adjacent to Canada and Newfoundland. The Commission signed a treaty Feb. 15, 1888, which is now before the Senate.

In addition to his labors as College President and Diplomat, Dr. Angell is a well-known contributor to periodical literature.

iv. JEREMIAH BROWN[3] (*Daniel,*[2] *Chad*[1]), a brickmaker and innkeeper, m. Dec. 8, 1715, Sarah Tucker. He was living in Smithfield, R. I., in 1736, where, on Dec. 8, he and his wife, Sarah, sold to David Hearnden 121½ acres for a consideration of £900.

v. HALLELUJAH BROWN[3] (*Daniel,*[2] *Chad*[1]), d. 1771, was m. Aug. 31, 1702, to James Olney,[3] b. Nov. 9, 1670, d. Oct. 6, 1744, son of Epenetus[2] and Mary[2] (Whipple) Olney, gr. son of Thomas Olney[1] and also gr. son of John Whipple[1]. They had eight children : *James, Mary, Joseph, James, Jonathan, Jeremiah, Lydia, Mercy.* Of these, the line only of *Mary,* the second child, will be continued. She was b. Sept. 30, 1704, d. March 18, 1750 ; was m. June 2, 1723, to Hon. Arthur Fenner[3] (*Major Thomas,*[2] *Capt. Arthur*[1]) b. Oct. 17, 1699, d. Feb. 2, 1788. This is her record.* "She was one of the smart and

* See Genealogy of the Fenner Family, No. 2, by Rev. J. P. Root, of Providence.

active women of her time; was a merchant, and owned more
navigation than any other woman in town ; acquired the estate,
kept a store and shop, and maintained the family in affluence.
Her husband for many years was sickly, and unable to do business." They had twelve children, born between 1723 and 1748,
of whom six lived to maturity, and married, leaving families.
James, the fourth child, b. Feb. 9, 1730, m. Freelove Whipple.
Mary, the seventh child, b. May 15, 1737, m. E. Rumreil. John,
the eighth child, b. Oct. 2, 1739, m. Phebe Brown[5] (*Obadiah,*[4]
James,[8] *John,*[2] *Chad*[1]). (See No. 12). Freelove, the
tenth child, b. July 13, 1743, m. Simon Smith, a descendant,
probably, of Christopher Smith, and was the mother of
Sophia Smith, who m. Ebenezer Frothingham, of Boston. Their
dau. Sophia Frothingham, b. Sept. 21, 1813, m. Nathaniel W.
Brown,[106] (*Isaac,*[64] *Isaac,*[33] *Dep.-Gov. Elisha,*[14] *James,*[4] *John,*[2]
Chad[1]). (See No. 106).

Arthur, the eleventh child, b. Dec. 10, 1745, m. Amey Comstock. He was the popular Gov. Arthur Fenner, of Rhode
Island, who was elected in 1790 and served until his death, Oct.
15, 1805. His son, James Fenner, b. in Providence, Jan. 22,
1771, a graduate of Brown University in 1789, was elected Governor in 1807, and held the office four years. He was re-elected
Governor in 1824, serving until 1831, and again, from 1842 to
1844 – a conclusive evidence of the estimation in which he was
held by the people of the State. In his earlier years, Gov.
James Fenner was frequently in the General Assembly, and was
United States Senator from Dec., 1805, until the Spring of 1807.
He d. in Providence, April 17, 1846, and was buried with the
highest civic and military honors.

Lydia, the twelfth child, b. March 1, 1748, was m. to Hon.
Theodore Foster, Town Clerk of Providence, and United States
Senator from 1790 to 1803.

vi. HOSANNA BROWN[3] (*Daniel,*[2] *Chad*[1]), m. Mary,[3] dau.
of John and Sarah Hawkins, and gr. dau. of William and Margaret Hawkins. They had two children, *Mary,*[4] who m. David
Burlingame, and *Othniel,*[4] who m. ——, and was the father of
Colonel Chad Brown,[5] of Glocester, R. I. Hosanna Brown was
Freeman in 1708, and early removed to Glocester, where he settled on land on the east side of the Chepachet river. His
cousins, Andrew and Chad Brown, purchased land in the same
vicinity some years later, and also became residents of Glocester.

Colonel Chad Brown[5] was deputy of Glocester in 1776, and
in 1777 was chosen Field Officer (Col.) for the State, from the
county of Providence. In 1780, he was chairman of the committee to raise soldiers from Glocester, to co-operate with the
French in repelling the British from Rhode Island. Col. Chad
m. June 19, 1749, Zerviah Evans. They died within two days

of each other, and were buried near Harmony Village, R. I.
A double head-stone bears this inscription :

Col. Chad Brown,	Mrs. Zerviah Brown,
died Sept. 19, 1814,	wife of Col. Chad Brown,
in his 85th	died Sept. 17, 1814,
year.	in her 90th year.

They had six children, all b. in Glocester : (1) *Ezekiel*[6]
(Ensign), b. Oct. 11, 1749, m. Ruth, b. May 18, 1751, dau. of
John and Mary (Smith) Winsor, (*John*,[3] *Joshua*,[2] *Samuel
Winsor*[1]). Mary Smith was in the fifth generation from John
Smith, Miller (*Solomon*,[4] *Benjamin*,[3] *John*,[2] *John*[1]). *Ezekiel*
and his father, Col. Chad, voted in 1788 against the adoption of
the Federal Constitution. He received from his father, April
5, 1780, a deed of fifty acres of land in Glocester, which he and
his wife Ruth sold, Nov. 7, 1783, to Simon Smith. In the
census of Rhode Island in 1774, he had a family of three persons,
one a female under sixteen years of age. He removed to Dudley,
Mass., where he bought land and settled near his brother-in-law,
John Eddy, who m. Deborah Winsor. *Ezekiel* and Ruth Brown
had two sons, John,[7] and Chad.[7] John[7] m. and had three sons,
John,[8] Chad,[8] and Ezekiel,[8] who came to New York, where they
established themselves in the wholesale grocery business in
Broad street. John[7] had also a dau., Ruth,[8] who m. Frederick
Goodell, and another dau., Sarah,[8] who m. —— Baker, and had
Zephaniah[9] and Jacob,[9] both preachers in the Universalist
Church. Zephaniah Baker[9] was afterwards Librarian of the
Public Library in Worcester, Mass. (2) *Esek*,[6] b. Nov. 1, 1754.
It is known that he had a son, Ezekiel,[7] who had a son,
Benjamin.[8] This family removed to Ohio. (3) *Thankful*,[6] b.
Jan. 13, 1757. (4) *Othniel*,[6] b. April 20, 1759. (5) David,[6]
b. Sept. 4, 1761. (6) *Zerviah*,[6] b. Feb. 22, 1765. But *two*
daughters are enumerated in the above record. Miss M. T.
Bruner, who, on June 5, 1878, wrote to the Town Clerk of
Glocester, R. I., from Oakland, Alameda Co., California, for
information concerning Col. Chad Brown, mentioned that they
had four sons and *three* daughters.

vii. JONATHAN[3] (*Daniel*,[2] *Chad*[1]). Nothing has been recorded of this son of Daniel, except that in 1713, May 21, he
sold Nicholas Sheldon 75 acres of land. Three years later the
deed was confirmed by his brothers, Judah and Daniel.

viii. DANIEL[3] (*Daniel*,[2] *Chad*[1]), m. Mary, dau. of Jonathan and Mehitable (Holbrook) Sprague. He was a cooper and
lived in Providence. They had six children b. between 1715
and 1725, viz : *Susanna, Daniel, Phineas, Penelope, John* and
Phebe. Of these, *Phineas* m. Phebe ——, and had at least two
children, Marcy and Dexter, both of whom died young.

APPENDIX.

GENEALOGY

OF

A PORTION OF

THE BROWN FAMILY;

PRINCIPALLY FROM THE MOSES BROWN PAPERS AND
FROM OTHER AUTHENTIC SOURCES.

PROVIDENCE
PRESS OF H. H. BROWN.
1851.

NOTE.

[The following is a reprint of the Brown Genealogy of 1851, upon which The Chad Browne Memorial is based, and to which reference has been made in the Preface. It furnishes an interesting example of the earlier genealogical work, and, though familiar to some of the older members of the family, is unknown outside of a very limited circle. A few trifling errors have been corrected, and inscriptions from the North Burial Ground, which have been reproduced in preceding pages, are here omitted With these exceptions, the pamphlet is printed as originally written. The researches of the last few years have brought to light many forgotten facts, and supplied information which was inaccessible to the preceding generation. This will account for apparent discrepancies between the Brown Genealogy and The Chad Browne Memorial.]

GENEALOGY.

NOTE.—All dates here mentioned previous to 1752, are in Old Style, to which 11 days should be added, in order to agree with the New Style. The following abbreviations are made : b. for born ; m. married ; d. died ; unm. unmarried ; æt. aged ; dau. daughter.

THE name of BROWN, so numerous everywhere, was duly represented among the first settlers of Providence. Out of one hundred and one original proprietors, there were four of the name, Chad, John, Daniel and Henry Brown Of these, we have of John and Daniel no account ; they may, perhaps, have been related to Chad, their names being the same as those of two of his sons, but it is certain that Henry Brown was of a different family. He was the ancestor of the Browns who formerly lived on Providence Neck, so called, including Richard Brown, who died in 1812, aged 100 years and 12 days, and others. The spelling of the name, it may be remarked, has, like many others, been varied. At the first settlement of the country and for some years after, it was in most cases spelt with a final E (BROWNE) ; but that has since been dropped by nearly all who bear the name, including those embraced in this account. The following is a brief sketch of Chad Brown, and of a small portion of his numerous descendants.

CHAD BROWN came from Salem to Providence in 1637, (the year after Roger Williams,) with his wife Elizabeth and his son John, and was an Elder of the Baptist church in Providence ; whether the first pastor of the church, as Moses Brown says, or the first after Roger Williams, has been a disputed point. He held various appointments in the community, and was a man of excellent character, as described by Hague, in his Hist. Discourse First Baptist church, as follows : "Contemporary with Roger Williams, he possessed a cooler temperament, and was happily adapted to sustain the interests of religion just where that great man failed. Not being affected by the arguments of the Seekers, he maintained his standing firmly in a church which he believed to be founded on the rock of eternal truth, even "the word of God, which abideth forever." We know only enough of his character to excite the wish to know more, but from that little it is clear that he was highly esteemed as a man of sound judgment, and of a Christian spirit. Often referred to as the arbitrator of existing differences, in a state of society where individual influence was needed as a substitute for well digested laws, he won that commendation which the Saviour pronounced when he said, "blessed are the peace-makers, for they shall be called the children of God."

In 1640 we find that Robert Cole, Chad Brown, William Harris and John Warner were the committee of Providence Colony who reported to them their first written form of government, which was adopted and continued in force until the arrival of the first charter, and to this report or agreement, which is given in Staples' Annals of Providence, Chad Brown's name is the first signed, followed by about forty others ; and in 1643 he and three others were a committee of the Providence people who wrote a letter to the Governor of Massachusetts, endeavoring, though ineffectually at that time, to settle the controversy that existed between that colony and the Warwick settlers. He died about A. D. 1665, and was buried at first where the Town House now stands, which was on his home lot, but his remains were afterwards removed to the North burial ground, where a stone marks his grave.

He left five sons, viz :

John,
James, } Removed to Rhode Island.
Jeremiah, }
Judah,   do   do   d. May 10, 1663.
Daniel m. Alice Herenden, Dec. 25, 1669.

JOHN BROWN, the oldest of these, accompanied his father when he came to Providence, having been at that time, as Moses Brown says, about eight years of age. He was chosen a member of the Town Council in 1665, and is stated by Backus, in his Church History, to have been afterwards an Elder in the Baptist church. He resided at the North end of Providence, northward of the house of Elisha Brown, whom we shall hereafter mention, and married Mary, daughter of Rev. Obadiah Holmes, second pastor of the First Baptist church, Newport. Their children were,

John m. Isabel Mathewson, June 9, 1696.
    Children—Mary, Lydia, Isabel, Nathan, Obadiah.
James, b. 1666, d. Oct. 28, 1732.
Obadiah,
Martha,
Deborah.

Of these, the second,

JAMES BROWN, lived at the North end, where his father lived, was a pastor of the Baptist church, and married Mary, daughter of Andrew, and grand-daughter of William Harris, one of the first six who came to Providence in 1636. Some account of his life and character, as well as of his grand-father Chad, may be gathered from Hague's Hist. Discourse, Benedict's History of the Baptists, Annals of Providence, &c. He died Oct. 28, 1732, after a pious life of about 66 years, and his wife Mary deceased August 18, 1736, also in the 66th year of her age.

Their children were—

1. John, b. Oct. 8, 1695 ; d. unmarried, æt. about 21.
2. James, b. March 22, 1698.
3. Joseph, b. May 5, 1701 ; m. Martha Field ; lived in N. Providence ; d. May 8, 1778.
4. Martha, b. Oct. 12, 1703 ; m. Elisha Greene ; d. July 27, 1725, leaving a son, James.
5. Andrew, b. Sept. 20, 1706.
6. Mary, b. April 29, 1708 : d. Feb. 20, 1729.
7. Anna, b. 171-

8. Obadiah, b. Oct. 2, 1712.
9. Jeremiah, b. Nov. 25, 1715.
10. Elisha, b. May 25, 1717.

We shall continue the account of a portion of the above, those whose descendants we have ascertained for a short period, or to the present time, denoting each by number and name corresponding to the above list.

2. JAMES, b. March 22, 1698, owned and occupied the house which formerly stood where Malletts's building in South Main street (Nos. 10 to 16) now is, and was moved to Tockwotten when that building was erected. He m. Hope, dau. of Nicholas and Mercy Power, and grand-dau. of Elder Pardon Tillinghast, a pastor of the First Baptist church, and d. April 27, 1739. She d. June 8, 1792, æt. 90. Their children were—

James, b. Feb. 12, 1724 ; d. unm. at York, Va. in 1750.
Nicholas, b. July 28, 1729.
Mary, b. 1731 ; married Dr. Vanderlight ; d. May, 1795.
Joseph, b. Dec. 3, 1733.
John, b. Jan. 27, 1736.
Moses, b. Sept. 12, 1738

Comprising, as will be perceived, the celebrated Nicholas, Joseph, John and Moses Brown, familiarly designated as "the four brothers," in their day. "For the times in which they lived, they were all uncommon men, remarkable for broad views, and for the active and efficient prosecution of public aims." They early engaged in mercantile business, in which they were eminently successful, the younger of them, Moses, however, soon retiring to his residence in this vicinity, where much the greater portion of his long life was passed.

NICHOLAS, the eldest of the four, b. July 28, 1729, m. 1st, Rhoda, dau. of Daniel Jenckes, and 2d, Avis, dau. of Barnabas Binney, and d. May 29, 1791, leaving two children by his first wife ; 1st, Nicholas, his only surviving son, long distinguished for his virtues and his public and private charities, b. April 4, 1769, m. first, Anne Carter, Nov. 3, 1791, and 2d, Mary Bowen Stelle, who d. without issue Dec. 12, 1836. He d. Sept. 27, 1841, leaving two sons, Nicholas (who is married and has children) and John Carter Brown. A dau. Anne. m. Hon. J. B. Francis, and died in 1828. 2. Hope, only surviving dau., b. Feb. 22, 1773, m. Thomas P. Ives. March 16, 1792, and has children surviving, Charlotte R. m. Wm. G. Goddard, Moses B. and Robert H. Ives.

JOSEPH, b. Dec. 3, 1733, m. Elizabeth, dau. of Nicholas and Anne Power, Sept. 30, 1759, and d. Dec. 3, 1785. Children, Mary. m. Rev. Stephen Gano, d. December 8, 1800, (leaving one dau. Eliza, m. Joseph Rogers,) Obadiah, d. unm. Feb. 14, 1815 ; Elizabeth, M. Richard Ward, d. Mar. 1, 1845, æt. 75 ; Joseph, b. 1771, d. æt. 3 years ; another son of the same name d. 1791, æt. 16.

JOHN, b. Jan. 27, 1736, m. Sarah, dau. of Daniel and Dorcas Smith, d. Sept. 20, 1803, leaving children, James, b. Sept. 22, 1761, d. unm. Dec. 12, 1834 ; Abby, m. John Francis, d. Mar. 5, 1821 ; Alice, m. Hon. James B. Mason, d. Nov. 7, 1822 ; Sarah, m. Frederick Herreshoff, d. 1846.

MOSES was b. Sept. 12, 1738, O. S. and d. Sept. 6, 1836, N. S. wanting 17 days to complete his 98th year. He married 1st, Anna Brown, his cousin dau. of Obadiah Brown ; 2d, Mary Olney ; 3d, Avis Lockwood. By his first wife he had two children : (1) Obadiah, m. Dorcas Hadwen, d. without issue, Oct. 15, 1822, æt. 51. (2) Sarah married the late William Almy, (who with her brother composed the firm of Almy & Brown), and left one dau., Anna, m. the late Wm. Jenkins. She, with her dau. Sarah, perished in the flames, when her house was destroyed by fire, Nov. 20, 1849. Two children survive, Anna and Moses B. Jenkins.

5. ANDREW, b. Sept. 20, 1706, removed to Gloucester, R. I. He is stated by Backus to have been "a Justice of Peace in the State, and long an exemplary Christian in the Baptist Church in Gloucester, where he died in peace, 1782." He left one son, Elisha, and three daus. from whom have descended a numerous offspring.

7. ANNA, b. 171—, m. Samuel Comstock, and d. Nov. 16, 1776. One of her sons, Benjamin, was the father of Jesse, Joseph, William, Samuel and Benjamin Comstock, the first three of whom for many years commanded packets between this port and New York. Of these sons, William alone survives. Ann B., a dau., m. Samuel Thurber, jun. Sally B. m. Samuel Comstock.

8. OBADIAH, b. Oct. 12, 1712, lived in the house No. 51 N. Main street, where T. Whitaker & Son's store now is. On one of the chimnies is the date 1726. This was formerly on the large old chimney, and when that was removed some years since, the figures were replaced on one of the smaller ones that were erected in its stead. The house is one of the few specimens remaining in the city, of the architecture of that period. He m. Mary, dau. of Toleration Harris, and d. June 17, 1762, leaving four daus. :

Phebe, b. April 21, 1738, m. John Fenner.
Sarah, b. Sept. 24, 1742, m. Jabez Bowen ; d. Mar., 1800.
Anna, b Nov. 28, 1744, m. Moses Brown ; died 1773.
Mary, b. Nov. 25, 1753, m. Thomas Arnold.

9. JEREMIAH, b. Nov. 25, 1715, m. Waitstill Rhodes, and was lost at sea in the winter of 1740–'41, leaving one dau., Mary, who m. Hon. David Howell, and d. July 6, 1801, leaving one son, Jeremiah B. and three daus.

10. ELISHA, b. May 25, 1717, m. first, Martha, dau. of John and Deborah Smith, a descendant of John Smith the miller, one of the first settlers of Providence, from whom the grist mill property has descended, through John Brown, the eldest son of Elisha, to the Howell family. 2d, he m. Hannah, widow of Elijah Cushing, and dau. of James Barker, of Newport. He was a man of great ability and enterprise, and possessed at one time a large property, but was afterwards unfortunate in business and lost most of it. He was also a great politician, a member of the General Assembly for a number of years, and finally Deputy Governor (as it was then called) of the Colony of Rhode Island, from 1765 to '67. His house stands on North Main, a little to the northward of Olney street, with the inscription E B 1749 remaining upon the stone in front of it. The latter part of his life he lived at Wenscutt, in North Providence, and d. April 20, 1802. His children were, by his first wife six sons, and by both wives three daughters, Deborah, Martha and Martha again, who d. young. The sons were—

John, b. Jan. 28, 1742.
James, b. April 27, 1744.
Jeremiah, b. Dec. 28, 1746.
Elisha, b. June 1, 1749.
Isaac, b. May 23, 1751.
Smith, b. April 12, 1756.

Of these, JOHN m. Wait, dau. of Charles Field, and d. May 24, 1775, leaving one dau. Martha, who m. Jeremiah B. Howell, her second cousin. He d. Feb. 6, 1822, she d. Feb. 14, 1851. Their children were—Eliza, m. Benj. Cowell ; Martha m. Charles Lippitt ; Sarah B m. Horace A. Wilcox; Wait F. m. Appleton Walker, (both dec'd) ; John and Charles ; the latter d. May 28, 1846.

JAMES, m. Freelove Brown, July 19, 1764 ; d. at St. Crox Jan. 6, 1766, leaving one son, James, who married, but left no children, and his line is extinct.

JEREMIAH, m. first, Mary Cushing, by whom he had—

1. Abigail, b. June 2, 1766, m. Nathaniel Smith, who d. April 8, 1814 ; she died Oct. 24. 1839, leaving two children, Nathaniel and Abby, of whom only the former survives.
2. Catharine, b. April 11, 1768, m. James Yerrinton. She died Aug. 28, 1831 ; he d. 1843. Their children were—James B. m. first Phebe Boyd ; second, Mrs. —— Metcalf. Catharine m. Eliakim Briggs ; Barker T. m. Maria Daggett ; and Sarah m. William Webster. Catharine and Sarah are deceased.
3. Mary, b. May 19, 1770, m. Darius Allen. She survived her husband many years and died in 1817. Their children were—Mary, Abby, Darius C., Isaac and Jeremiah N. The last two only are living.
4. Cushing b. Jan. 5, 1777, d. 1834.
5. Jeremiah, b. Nov. 10, 1778, removed to Newbern, N. C.; m. Mary S. Blackledge in 1812, died Sept. 30, 1847, having had twelve sons and two daughters, of whom seven sons and the daus. survive.

Jeremiah Brown (father of the above) married for his second wife, Susannah, widow of Thomas Bowen, and dau. of John Welch, of Boston. She died Dec. 1821, æt. 64. Children—

1. Hugh Hall, b. May 16,1792 ; m. Eunice E. Taber, May 23, 1815. Children—Elizabeth E. b. Feb. 26, 1816 ; m. first, April, 1836, Thomas W. Waterman, who d. Feb. 1, 1839 ; and second, May 2, 1841, Rev. Sewall S. Cutting. Mary A., b. Mar. 5, 1818 ; m. George Allin, June 3, 1839. James, b. Aug. 14, 1820 ; m. Virtue Chappell, Nov. 1841, d. Jan. 16, 1845. Joseph, b. Feb. 19, 1823, m. Rececca Ketchum, Feb. 10, 1846. Ann Frances, b. Sept. 19, 1825. Charles C. b. June 22, 1829 ; d. July 16, 1846.
2. Obadiah, b. 1793 ; d. in infancy.
3. Ebenezer P. b. April, 1797, married Sarah Jillson, 1822. He died June 16, 1839 ; she died July 1, 1851. Children—Samuel W. and Ebenezer.
4. John S. b. October 4, 1799 ; m. Ann Rounds, 1829. Children—Ferdinand, Isabella, Ann Eliza and Evelyn.

ELISHA, m. Elizabeth Bowen, of Rehoboth, April 24, 1774 ; she d. 181—; he d. March, 1827. Children—

1. Lydia, b. Jan. 2, 1775 ; m. Colville Dana, who was lost at sea, Dec. 1804, æt. 35; she d. Sept. 5, 1847. Children—Ann Eliza, m. Rev. James Burlingame, d. —— ; Jonathan d. some years since, unm.; Lucy, m. Rev. James Burlingame ; Deborah, m. Samuel Boyd ; Sarah, m. Amasa Stone, and Abby, m. Nelson Sweetland.
2. Deborah, b. Dec. 27, 1776 ; d. April 26, 1800.
3. Elizabeth, b. Sept. 24, 1779 ; m. John Kinnicutt ; both deceased for many years. Children—Sarah, m. Ezra Hubbard ; and John, the latter deceased.
4. Lucy, b. Nov. 1, 1781 d. Jan. 25, 1784.
5, 6. Elisha and John, twins, b. Jan. 20, 1784. Elisha d. at Batavia, Oct. 6, 1802. John married, and died in 1822, leaving four children.
7. Lucy, b. May 24, 1785 ; d. May 15, 1787.
8. Alonzo, b. Dec. 24, 1787.
9. James, b. Oct. 4, 1790 ; d. May 12, 1791.

ISAAC, m. Amey, dau. of Christopher Dexter, of North Providence, and was lost at sea, Nov. 20, 1793. She d. March 28, 1844, æt. 93 years, 8 months and 18 days. Of their family of nine children, all d. young but three.

1. Amey, m. Benoni Cooke ; d. Dec. 9, 1822, æt. 38. Surviving children—Charles D. and Benoni Cooke, jun.

2. Isaac, b. Oct. 4, 1787, m. Lydia Williams, of Dighton, Mass., April 1, 1810. She d. May 26. 1848. He m. 2d, Jan. 30, 1850, Caroline, dau. of Otis Bartlett, of Smithfield, R. I. Children—Nathaniel Williams, m. June 5, 1834, Sophia Frothingham, of Boston. Children—Sophia, Frederick Lothrop, Amey Dunnell and Langdon.

Alice, m. Moses B. Lockwood, May 9, 1842.

Amey Dexter, m. Jacob Dunnell, Dec. 29, 1834. Children—Sophia, Jacob, Edward Wanton, Adela and Alice Maud Mary.

Mary, m. Rev. J. P. Tustin, March 29, 1848.

Adeline.

Isaac.

3. Alice, m. Truman Beckwith ; d. Aug. 19, 1837, æt. 47, leaving children—Susan T., Henry T., Abby G. and Amos N. The former d. Feb. 5, 1851.

SMITH, resided the latter part of his life at Pembroke, Mass., where he d. 20th 11th mo. 1826. He m. Lydia Goold, of Pembroke, dau. of Samuel and Elizabeth Goold, 12th 10th mo. 1785. Children—

1. Samuel, b. 12th 2d mo. 1787 ; m. Maria Hussey, of Nantucket, 6th 3d mo. 1816 ; their children are—Ann, b. 28th 9th mo. 1818, m. Joseph S. Barnard, 6th of 2d mo. 1844. Children—George Albert and Edward Goold Barnard. Sarah Joy, b. 24th 11th mo. 1820 ; Lydia Goold, b. 27th 8th mo. 1822, m. Nath'l K. Randall, 1st 1st mo. 1843, has one child, Charles Franklin Randall. Joseph Goold, b. 19th 6th mo. 1825. Elizabeth, b 25th 8th mo 1827. George Smith, b. 6th 10th mo. 1829. William Austin, b. 11th 10th mo 1832. Moses, b. 30th 3d mo. 1835.

2. Anna, b. 4th 10th mo. 1788 ; d. 16th 6th mo. 1813.

3. Goold, b. 7th 3d mo. 1791 ; m. Mary, dau. of Nath'l Starbuck, 8th 11th mo. 1842. Their adopted children are, Ann Eliza, b. 20th 2d mo. 1844 ; Mary S. b. 17th 6th mo. 1850.

4. William B. b 21st 3d mo. 1793 ; m. Beulah Purington. 8th 11th mo. 1827. Children—William G. b. 18th 7th mo. 1830 ; Charles Purinton b. 19th 6mo. 1833.

5. Elizabeth, b. 10th 5th mo 1795 ; m. James Oliver, 3d 5th mo. 1821 ; d. 20th 11th mo. 1823. Children—Lydia Maria, b 18th 3d mo. 1822, d. 29th 11th mo. 1828. Elizabeth B., b. 7th 10th mo. 1823 ; m. Pliny E. Chase 28th 6th mo. 1843. Children—James A., Eliza Brown and Edward Oliver Chase.

6. Lydia, born 14th 1st mo. 1798.

INSCRIPTIONS.

At the North Burial Ground, Providence.

IN MEMORY OF

CHAD BROWN,

Elder of the Baptist Church in
this Town.
He was one of the original Proprietors of
the Providence Purchase,
Having been exiled from Massachusetts,
for conscience sake.
He had five sons,
JOHN, JAMES, JEREMIAH, CHAD and DANIEL,
Who have left a numerous Posterity.
He died about A. D. 1665.

THIS MONUMENT
Was erected by the Town of Providence.

Here lieth interred
ye Body of
JAMES BROWN.
Died Octr. ye 28th, 1732. In ye 66th year
of his age.

Here Lies Inter'd ye Body of
MARY BROWN,
Widow and Relict of James Brown,
Dec'd August ye 18, 1736,
In ye 66th year of her age.

Old Age being come her race here ends
When God ye Fatal Dart he sends.

NOTE.—This monument to the memory of Chad Brown, in Nicholas Brown's yard, is believed to be the only memorial of any of the first settlers of Providence, except the monument erected by Richard Waterman, Esq. to his ancestors, in the lot north of his house on Benefit-street. It will be observed that the fourth son's name is here given as Chad, instead of Judah ; but this is the only place out of several where we have seen the names, in which it is so stated. Another remarkable circumstance besides this monument is, that in the Nicholas Brown lot are the graves of eight generations, save one, from Chad Brown to a child of the present Nicholas Brown. Gov. Elisha Brown and others of the family are buried near by, the Governor without any head-stone, as he became a Friend in the latter part of his life.

Here lies inter'd ye Body of
Mr. J A M E S B R O W N, Jun
Dec'd April ye 27th, 1739,
in ye 41st year of his age.

My time is come, next may be—Thine ;
Prepare for it whilst thou hast time.
No Time we have but what is lent,
Then dust we are when that is spent.

———

H O P E B R O W N,
Widow of
JAMES BROWN, Esq.
Died June 8, 1792,
Aged ninety years and six months.
The mother of
NICHOLAS, JOSEPH, JOHN and MOSES BROWN.

———

Here lies ye body of
M A R T H A,
Ye wife of Elisha Green,
Who died July ye 27, 1725, aged 21 years,
9 months and 15 days.

———

Here lieth
M A R Y,
Ye daughter of James and Mary Brown,
Died Feb. ye 20, 1729,
aged 20 years, 9 mos.

———

IN MEMORY OF
M R S. M A R T H A B R O W N,
Wife of ELISHA BROWN, Esq.
Who departed this Life,
September the 1st, A. D. 1760,
Aged 41 Years, 4 Months and 29 days.

———

IN MEMORY OF
M R. J O H N B R O W N,
Son of Elisha Brown, Esq.
Who died May 24th, 1775,
In the 34th year of his age.

THOMAS ANGELL.

According to tradition he was the son of Henry Angell, of Liverpool, born about 1618. When a lad of twelve he went to London, and the same year accompanied Roger Williams to New England. They emigrated in the ship *Lyon* from Bristol, Dec. 1, 1630, arrived in Boston Feb. 5, 1631, and were in Salem as early as the next April. He is spoken of as a "young lad living in the family of Roger Williams." He was with Roger Williams in Seekonk, and was one of his five companions, when, in search of a new site, in the early summer of 1636, they pursued their way by boat from the landing at State Rock, to the shore of the Moshassuck River, where they commenced the settlement of Providence.

He received a grant of land, signed the first compact, and the agreement for a form of government in 1640. From 1652-55 he served as Commissioner, Juryman, Constable, and in the latter year, was admitted Freeman. In 1676, after the close of King Philip's war, he was on the Indian Committee to regulate the terms under which the services of the captives were to be sold. He died in 1694, and his widow Alice, in 1695.

They had eight children : *John, Amphillis, Mary, Deborah, Alice, James, Hope* and *Margaret.* To his son *James,*[2] who m. Sept. 3, 1678, Abigail, dau. of the Rev. Gregory Dexter, he gave in his will his "dwelling house next unto the street, with lot where house standeth, another lot adjoining," etc. This was his Home Lot, and also the Home Lot of Francis Weston, acquired by purchase. The land remained in the family until 1774, when John Angell,[3] son of *James,*[2] sold the portion of it now occupied by the First Baptist Church, to William Russell, who transferred it the same year to the First Baptist Society. (See "Home Lots of the Early Settlers," by C. W. Hopkins, Providence, 1886.) The descendants of Thomas Angell and Chad Browne are closely allied by frequent intermarriages. (*See Nos.* 11, 14, 22, 27, 29, 44, 69, 72, 84, 105 *and page* 126.) The Angell Genealogy, by Avery F. Angell, was published in Providence, in 1872.

WILLIAM, THOMAS, JOANNA AND ELIZABETH ARNOLD.

Information regarding the Arnold Family is derived mainly from the "Genealogy of the Family of Arnold in Europe and America, with Brief Notices by John Ward Dean, Henry T. Drowne and Edwin Hubbard." It is a pamphlet of sixteen pages, and is a reprint from the New England Hist. and Genealogical Register for Oct., 1879. "The family of Arnold is of great antiquity, having its origin among the ancient princes of Wales. According to a pedigree in the College of Arms, they trace from Ynir, King of Gwentland, of the twelfth century, who married Nesta, daughter of Jestin ap Gurgan, King of Glamorgan. Ynir was paternally descended from Ynir, the second son of Cadwaladir, King of the Britons, who built Abergavenny and its castle in Monmouth Co., in the southwestern part of England." The town is near the Welsh border at the confluence of the Usk and Gavenny, in the centre of a coal and iron district, 143 miles from London. Portions of the castle walls still remain. The first of the family who adopted a surname was Roger Arnold, of Monmouthshire, twelfth in descent from Ynir. Thomas Arnold, of Cheselbourne, Dorsetshire, of the sixteenth generation, was the father of the emigrants, William and Thomas Arnold, who were half brothers.

WILLIAM, b. June 24, 1587, son of the first wife, Alice, who was daughter of John Gully, married Christian, dau. of Thomas Peak, and with his wife and four children, *Elizabeth, Benedict, Joanna* and *Stephen,* emigrated to New England in 1635. He was in Hingham, Mass., for a time, and came the following year to Providence. He received grants of land from Roger Williams, and his initials, W. A., are second in the Initial Deed. In 1639 he removed to Pawtuxet, where he resided until his death, which occurred about 1676, the precise date not being known. Though not always in accord with Roger Williams, he was held in high esteem, and filled various offices of trust. His eldest son, *Benedict Arnold*, born in Leamington, Warwickshire, England, Dec. 21, 1615, was the first Governor of Rhode Island, under the Royal Charter, granted in 1643.

THOMAS ARNOLD, half brother of William, baptized April 18, 1599, married his first wife in England. He came to America in 1635, and settled at Watertown, Mass., but afterwards removed to Providence, where he purchased lands at the north end of the town. He was admitted Freeman in 1658, was Deputy from 1666–'72, and was in the Town Council in 1672. His death occurred in Sept., 1674. Of the three children by his first wife, *Susannah*, the youngest, was the only one who survived infancy. She was married April 7, 1654, to John Farnum. The second wife of Thomas Arnold was Phebe, daughter of George and Susanna Parkhurst, of Watertown. They had six children, four of whom became heads of families, viz.: *Richard*, *John*, *Eleazar* and *Elizabeth*. *Richard* married Mary Angell, daughter of the first Thomas, and had a great grandson, Thomas, who married Mary Brown (*See No.* 27). *Elizabeth* was married Nov. 22, 1678, to Samuel Comstock[3] (*Samuel,*[2] *William,*[1] *of England*). One of her grandsons, Samuel Comstock, *married Anna Brown, daughter of Elder James* (*See No.* 11).

JOANNA ARNOLD, sister of William, baptized Nov. 30, 1577, married William Hopkins, and had (1) *Frances*, who married William Mann, an early settler in Providence; (2) *Thomas*, great grandfather of Gov. Stephen Hopkins (*See No.* 17); (3) *Elizabeth*.

ELIZABETH ARNOLD, sister of Thomas, and half sister of William and Joanna, born in 1596, was married Feb., 1617, to John Sayles, Jr. They are supposed to have been the parents of *John Sayles, the Emigrant*, who married Mary Williams, daughter of Roger (*See No.* 16).

There have been frequent intermarriages between the Arnolds and Browns and their descendants. This is illustrated to some extent in the Arnold Genealogical Tree, drawn by the late George C. Arnold, of Providence, of which a reduced *fac-simile*, thirty inches by twenty-four, was executed in 1877 by the Graphic Company of New York. (*See Nos.* 2, 10, 13, 15, 55, 71, 72, 74, 88, 104, 132.)

STEPHEN BECKWITH.

In Hall's Historical Records of Norwalk, Conn., there is occasional mention of Stephen Beckwith, presumably the ancestor of Truman Beckwith. (*See No.* 65). There is no complete list of the original settlers, but in a Table of "Estates of lands and accommodations" in 1655, the name of Stephen Beckwith is third. He is included in "Hinman's Catalogue of the First Puritan Settlers of Connecticut" at an earlier date—1649. In a later table of "Estates of Lands," etc., and in "The Estates of Commonage," 1687, his name is repeated. The last mention of him in Hall's Records occurs in a List of Voters at Norwalk Town Meetings, Dec. 4, 1694.

·REV. EDWARD BULKELEY, D. D.

This family,* which is descended from remote antiquity, derived its surname from a ridge of mountains in the County Palatine of Chester, Eng. In the time of King John, 1199–1216, it was spelled Buclough, signifying larger mountain. The name was afterwards modified to Bucclogh, and was finally corrupted into Bulkeley, the form adhered to by the present generations in England and America, except that, in some families in this country, the first (E) has been eliminated. Edward Bulkeley,[5] born in Odell,

---

* For the Bulkeley Coat of Arms, see America Heraldica. Motto, *Nec temere*, *Nec timide*, neither rashly nor timidly.

Bedfordshire, was a descendant of Peter,[3] second son of Robert,[2] Lord of Bucclogh, in the reign of Edward III. (*Edward*,[9] *Thomas*,[8] *William*,[7] *Humphrey*,[6] *Hugh*,[5] *John*,[4] *Peter*,[3] *Robert*,[2] *William*[1]). He married Olive Irlby, of Lincolnshire, and was made Rector of All Saints' Church in Odell in 1558. An eminent minister of the gospel, he became a non-comformist, but was undisturbed in the exercise of his clerical functions.

His son, *Peter Bulkeley*,[10] born Jan. 31, 1583, was admitted, at the age of sixteen, a member of St. John's College, Cambridge, of which he was afterwards chosen fellow, and from which he received the Degree of Bachelor of Divinity. He succeeded his father in the ministry, and inherited from him a large estate. Dr. Williams, Bishop of Lincoln, connived at his noncomformity as he had done at that of his father, but, after preaching twenty-one years, he was at length silenced by command of Archbishop Laud. The prospect of ministerial usefulness in his own country being at an end, he sold his estates, and in 1635 emigrated to New England.[*]

He remained for some months in Cambridge, and in July, 1636, "carried a good number of planters up with him farther into the woods, where they gathered the 12th church in the colony, and called the town, 'Concord.'" (*See Mather's Magnalia, b.* 3, 96–98). The next year he was constituted teacher of the church, and Rev. John Jones,[†] son of William, of Abergavenny, Monmouthshire, was ordained pastor. He expended a large estate in Concord by giving farms to his servants, whom he employed in husbandry. His labors in the church were continued with little interruption until his death, March 9, 1659. Dr. Peter Bulkely was distinguished for theological knowledge, general literature and eminent piety. He wrote Latin with ease and elegance, and some of his Latin verses are still extant. As an author, he was best known by his treatise, "The Gospel Covenant," the 2d edition of which was published in London in 1651. He was an early benefactor of Harvard College, to which he contributed a large part of his own library. Three of his younger sons, *John, Gershom* and *Peter,* were graduates of that institution.

His family was a numerous one ; by his first marriage to Jane, dau. of Thomas Allen, of Goldington, there were nine sons and two daughters He married, second, Grace, dau. of Sir Richard Chetwood, who survived him, and died in New London, Conn, 1669. They had three sons and one daughter. *Thomas Bulkeley*,[11] b. April 11, 1617, second son of Peter,[10] m. Sarah, dau. of Rev. John Jones, of Concord, and removed to Fairfield, Conn., where he was a large land holder. The generations intervening between him and John W. Bulkley,[17]‡ of Brooklyn, N. Y., are Joseph,[12] b. 1644, m. Martha Beers ; Joseph,[13] b., 1682, m. Esther Hill ; Ebenezer,[14] b., 1731, m. Hannah Maltbie ; Ebenezer,[15] b., 1766, m. Diana Williams, of Saybrook, Conn. (See *The Bulkeley Family,* compiled by Rev. F. W. Chapman, Hartford, 1875.)

SARAH BULKELEY.

Sarah Bulkeley,[10] daughter of Dr. Edward, and sister of Peter Bulkeley, married Oliver St. John, Bart. Their daughter, *Elizabeth St. John*[11] was married Aug. 6, 1829, to Rev. Samuel Whiting, and accompanied him in 1636 to New England where he became first pastor of the church in Lynn, Mass. Their daughter, Elizabeth Whiting,[12] was married to Rev. Jeremiah Hobart. Of their children, Dorothy Hobart,[13] the third daughter, born in Topsfield, Mass., Aug. 21, 1679, married for her second husband, Hon. Hezekiah Brainard, of Haddam, and had nine children. One of their sons, Rev. David Brainard,[14] was missionary to the Indians. A daughter, Martha Brainard,[15] b. Sept. 1, 1716, became the first wife of Maj.-Gen.

[*] See N. E. Hist. and Genealogical Reg., April, 1887.
[†] See New York Biographical Record, April, 1875.
[‡] See No. 103.

Joseph Spencer, of the Revolutionary Army. They were the parents of Elizabeth Spencer,[16] wife of Gov. Lewis Cass, of Michigan. Their daughter, Matilda Cass,[17] married Henry Ledyard. of Newport R. I., and had a dau., Elizabeth C. Ledyard,[18] wife of Francis W. Goddard, of Providence. (See No. 114.)

The family of St. John in England is of noble origin. Oliver St. John, Baron of Beauchamp, upon the coming of his third cousin, Queen Elizabeth, to the throne, was created Lord St. John of Bletshoe. His great grandson, Oliver St. John, whose mother was Sarah Bulkeley, was Chief Justice of England during the Commonwealth, and Minister to the Netherlands. He is said to have been own cousin of Oliver Cromwell. (For the account of the descent of Elizabeth (St. John) Whiting from ten Sovereigns of Europe, see Drake's Hist. of Boston, p. 363, and New England Hist. and Genealogical Reg. for 1861, p. 217).

JOHN CRANDALL.

JOHN CRANDALL was a Baptist Elder of Westerly, R. I., to which place he removed from Newport. He was admitted Freeman in 1655, and was Commissioner from 1658-'63. His name frequently appears in connection with public affairs in Rhode Island. In July, 1651, he, with John Clarke and Obadiah Holmes, representatives of the church in Newport, made their memorable visit to William Witter, in Lynn, Mass. While Mr. Clarke was preaching, they were arrested by the authorities on several charges, and the next day imprisoned in Boston. After undergoing the form of a trial he was sentenced to pay £5 or be publicly whipped, but was released upon promising to appear at the next court.

On account of the Indian war he returned to Newport, where he died in 1676. The name of his first wife is not known. She was buried Aug. 2, 1670. Of their seven children, Samuel, the youngest, b. 1663, d. May 19, 1736, married Sarah —— and lived in Little Compton, R. I. Their oldest child, Samuel, born Oct. 30, 1686, was probably the father of Samuel Crandall, who married Margaret ——, and had Joseph, b. Nov. 24, 1731, Thomas, b. Jan. 10, 1734, Mary, Simon, Rebecca, Ezekiel and Hannah. Of these, Thomas, who married in Little Compton, March 20, 1760, Mary Stoddard* and lived in Newport "on the Point," was a soldier in the Revolutionary army. During the occupation of Newport by the British, his wife abandoned their home, and, with her family of young children, sought refuge at her father's in Tiverton, where they remained until the war was over. On their return, nothing remained of their possessions but the well and the cellar walls. Ezekiel Crandall, brother of Thomas, remained in Newport, but was compelled to share his house with British officers, from whom he and his wife suffered many indignities.

Abby Crandall, youngest child of Thomas and Mary (Stoddard) Crandall, married Richard Rounds, son of Martin and Wealthy (Briggs) Rounds, of Rehoboth, Mass., and died in Providence, Jan. 19, 1826, in the forty fifth year of her age, leaving eight children, the eldest of whom, Ann, born in Providence, June 14, 1807, was married to John S. Brown. (See No. 59.)

George Allin, who married Mary A., daughter of Hugh H. Brown, was a descendant of John Crandall through his mother, Amey (Crandall) Allin, daughter of Judge Robert and Margaret (Gardiner) Crandall, and granddaughter of Robert Crandall of Exeter, R. I., a Revolutionary soldier, who, returning to his home at the close of the war, died on his way at Wickford. (See No. 99.)

* The name Stoddard is derived from the office of Standard Bearer, and was anciently written De-La-Standard. The emigrant ancestor was Anthony Stoddard, who came to Boston in 1639.
For Coat of Arms, see America Heraldica.

GREGORY DEXTER.

Gregory Dexter was born in Olney, Northampton Co., England, in 1610. He was a printer and stationer in London, where he was also connected with the Baptist ministry. He was in Providence about 1638, and had a lot assigned to him. In July 27, 1640, he and thirty-eight others affixed their signatures to an agreement for a form of government. Roger Williams' "Key to the Indian Language" was printed at his establishment in London, in 1643. An original copy of this book is in the Library of Brown University Gregory Dexter was influential in both the civil and religious affairs of the Colony. He was Commissioner, Town Clerk, President of Providence and Warwick ; was admitted Freeman in 1655, and served as Deputy from 1664–66. He was an able and successful preacher, and was ordained as the fourth pastor of the First Baptist church in 1654. The banks of the Moshassuck river witnessed many baptismal scenes as results of his ministry. Roger Williams alludes to him as "a man of education and a noble calling and versed in militaires." His services as an accomplished printer were frequently in requisition in Boston, "to set in order the printing office there." His Home Lot, a short distance east of the junction of North Main and Benefit Streets, bounded on the north by Dexter's Lane, now Olney Street, was the most northerly of the fifty-two lots of the first division. In 1663, he acquired by purchase the Home Lot of Matthew Waller, which adjoined his own, on the south. His first habitation, a log house, destroyed by the Indians in 1676, was replaced by a second, built in better style. This was demolished, about 1800, to give way to the structure which now occupies the site. He died in 1700 at the age of ninety. His wife Abigail Fullerton, survived him, dying after 1706. They had four children, *Stephen*, b. Nov. 1, 1647 ; *James*, b. May 6, 1650 ; *John*, b. Nov. 6, 1652, and *Abigail*, b. Sept. 24, 1655, who was married, Sept. 3, 1678, to James Angell, son of the first Thomas. (*For intermarriages see Nos.* 14, 29, 30, 33, 48.)

WILLIAM EDDYE.

Rev. William Eddye, A. M., Vicar of the Church of St. Dunstan, Cranbrook, Kent Co., England a native of Bristol, married Mary Fosten, daughter of John, and second, widow Elizabeth Taylor. Of his eleven children, *John*, *Abigail* and *Samuel* (of the first wife) emigrated to New England. The latter, styled *Samuel the Pilgrim*, b. May, 1608, married Elizabeth ——, and came in the ship *Handmaid* to Plymouth, Mass., arriving Oct. 29, 1630. His descendants, as early as the third generation, were in Glocester and Providence, R. I. (*For intermarriages see Nos.* 11, 16, 50, 57, 106). The Eddy Genealogy, by Robert H. Eddy, of Boston, was published in 1883, and a second edition in 1884. Robert H. Eddy was a well-known patent solicitor, who died in May, 1887. In his will he left $5,000 for a suitable tablet in memory of his ancestor, Rev. William Eddye, at Cranbrook, England.

ARTHUR FENNER.

Arthur, William and John Fenner, were probably sons of Thomas Fenner, an Indian trader, who died in Branford, Conn., May 15, 1647. Capt. Arthur Fenner, the eldest, born in 1622, was, by tradition, a lieutenant in Cromwell's army. He was not only a soldier, but also an expert engineer and surveyor, and prominently identified with the history of the Providence Plantation for the greater portion of fifty years. He lived in Cranston, where he built a house which was burned before Jan. 14, 1676, by the Indians. The remains of the second house, erected probably on the same site, have long been known as "Fenner Castle." The first wife of Arthur Fenner was Mehitable, dau. of Richard and Bethia Waterman.

Descendants of two of their children, *Major Thomas Fenner*, and *Freelove* who married Gideon Crawford, intermarried with the Browns. (*See Nos.* 12, 18, 26, 37, 106.) The Genealogy of the Fenner Family, in two parts, was compiled by the late Rev. J. P. Root, of Providence.

JOHN AND WILLIAM FIELD.

John Field, of Providence, signed the first compact of 1637, and the agreement of 1640 ; the latter document has also the signature of William Field. The Home Lot of John, on the Towne street, adjoined that of William on the south. William's house stood nearly on the site of the Providence Bank, a building erected by Joseph Brown in 1774 and occupied by him as a residence. In the time of King Philip's war the William Field house was garrisoned, and escaped the conflagration of March, 1676, remaining until 1772, when it was purchased by Joseph Brown. John and William Field were large land owners in Rhode Island, and the latter gave his name to Field's Point, the homestead of later generations, where eight hundred acres were included in his possessions. William Field married Deborah ———, and died in 1665 without issue. *Thomas Field*, his nephew, who may have been son of John, became his heir.

The history of the early Fields is somewhat obscure. It is believed, though positive proof is lacking, that John and William Field were brothers, sons of William, and grandsons of Sir John Field, the astronomer of Ardsley, a village between Wakefield and Bradford, in the West Riding of Yorkshire. Hubertus de la Feld, the progenitor of the English Fields, who is said to have accompanied William the Conqueror to England, traced his family back to the Chateau de la Feld, near Colmar, a town southwest of Strasburgh in Alsatia, where the counts of that name had been seated for centuries. The cathedral of Strasburgh received many benefactions at their hands, and, in the chantries they founded, several of the family were interred. The arms of the Yorkshire Fields, "Sable a chevron between three garbs argent," were confirmed to Sir John in 1558, and an additional crest granted in recognition of his services to science. "A dexter arm issuing out of clouds, proper, pessways, habited Gules, holding in the hand, also proper, a sphere Or."

John Field, of Providence (name of wife not known), died in 1686, leaving four children : *Hannah*, the eldest, married James Matthewson, and had a daughter, Isabel, wife of John Brown[3]. *Ruth*, the youngest child, married Jan. 7, 1669, John Angell,[2] son of Thomas[1]. Their daughter, Mercy, b. 1675, married Benjamin Smith. (*See Nos.* 3 *and* 22). *Thomas Field*, nephew and heir of William, married Martha Harris, daughter of the first Thomas. She inherited by will the Home Lot of her father, which was separated from that of John Field, on the south, by the Home Lot of Joshua Winsor. Of their six children, the descendants of their son, William Field, were, in two instances, allied to the Browns by marriage. He was born June 8, 1682, died Nov. 1, 1729 : married Mary ———, and had eight children, the eldest of whom, Martha Field, married Joseph Brown (*See No.* 9). Charles Field, the youngest, born Feb. 6, 1614, married Wait Dexter[4] (*Stephen*,[3] *Stephen*,[2] *Gregory*[1]). Their daughter, Wait Field, married John Brown, eldest son of Dep. Gov. Elisha (*See No.* 29). The Field Genealogy, a pamphlet of 65 pages, was printed in Providence in 1878, compiled by Mrs. Harriet A. Brownell.

PHILIP FRANCIS.*

Philip Francis[1] was Mayor of Plymouth, England, in 1644. His son, Rev. John Francis,[2] D. D., was Dean of Leighlin, Ireland. His grandson, Rev. John Francis,[3] D. D., Dean of Lismore, Ireland, and Rector of St. Mary's Church, Dublin, married ——— Tench of Dublin, and had three

* Communicated by the family.

sons, *Tench*, *Richard*, an eminent lawyer, and *Philip*, who entered the church, and was the father of Sir Philip Francis, the reputed author of "Junius." Of these, *Tench Francis* emigrated to Maryland, where he married Elizabeth, daughter of Foster Turbutt, of Kent Co. He removed to Philadelphia, and was Attorney-General of the Province of Pennsylvania. He died Aug. 14, 1758, leaving a son, Tench Francis, merchant, born 1730, died May 1, 1800, who married, Feb. 8, 1762, Anne, daughter of Charles and Anne (Shippen) Willing, born July 16, 1733, died Jan. 2, 1812. The latter were the parents of John Francis, who married Abby, daughter of John Brown, merchant, of Providence. (*See No.* 40.)

Charles Willing, merchant, son of Thomas and Anne (Harrison) Willing, born in Bristol, Eng., May 18, 1710, emigrated to Philadelphia in 1729, and became Mayor of the city. He died Nov. 30, 1754, of ship fever, contracted while in the discharge of his official duties. Anne Harrison was grand-daughter, paternally, of Gen. Harrison, the Regicide, and maternally, of Simon Mayne, also one of the regicides.

WILLIAM GODDARD.

The Goddard family in America is said to have descended from William Goddard, second son of Edward and Priscilla (D'Oyley) Goddard, of Inglesham, Wiltshire, Eng., who emigrated to New England in 1666, after the great fire in London by which he was a sufferer, and settled in Watertown, Mass.[*]

The ancestor of Edward Goddard was Walter Goddardville, who, in the time of Henry III., had lands in North Wilts, was made castellar of Devizes Castle in 1231, and died in 1273. The Norman termination—*ville*—which he added to his Saxon name Goddard, was dropped by his descendants. The mother of William Goddard was from the ancient family of D'Oyley in Oxfordshire, who came to England with the Conqueror, were barons of Hokenorton, and built Oxford Castle and Osenay Abbey. William Goddard married Elizabeth, daughter of Benjamin or William Miles, of London, and was ancestor of Giles Goddard, postmaster and physician of New London, Conn., who married Sarah, daughter of Lodowick and Abigail (Newton) Updike, grand-daughter of Thomas and Joan (Smith) Newton, and also grand-daughter of Gilbert and Katharine (Smith) op Dyck. Joan and Katharine Smith were daughters of Richard Smith, of Glocestershire, Eng., the first white settler in the Narragansett country, who purchased a tract of the Indians, erected a trading house, and gave free entertainment to travellers as early as 1641. Gilbert or Gysbert op Dyck, a physician who settled at Loyd's Neck, L. I., and afterwards removed to Kings Town, R. I., was son of Lodowick and Gertrude (Van Vesek) op ten Dyck, born in Wesel, Germany, in 1605. This line has been traced through eight generations to Henrick op ten Dyck,[†] burgomaster in Wesel from 1333-1368. Wesel is a city of Rhenish Prussia, on the right bank of the Rhine, near the confluence of the Lippe, in the district of Dusseldorf.

William Goddard, son of Dr. Giles, born in 1740, after learning the printer's trade in New York, removed to Providence, where he established the first printing press in that town,[‡] and commenced the publication of the *Gazette* and *Country Journal*. Not meeting with sufficient encouragement, he went, successively, to New York, Philadelphia and Baltimore, where he engaged in newspaper enterprises. In the latter city, he founded the *Maryland Journal and Baltimore Advertiser*, the first issue of which appeared Aug. 20, 1773 and was published under that name until about the close of the century, when, in consequence of a change of proprietors, it assumed the title of *The Baltimore American*. The Anniversary num-

[*] See New England Hist. and Genealogical Reg., July, 1874.
[†] The Opdyck Genealogy, now in course of preparation, is soon to be privately printed in New York. This surname, in Rhode Island, is written Updike.
[‡] Oct. 20, 1762.

ber of Aug. 20, 1883, of *The Baltimore American and Commercial Advertiser*, devotes several columns to the life of William Goddard, which is
illustrated by a fine wood-cut, from a portrait in possession of one of his
grandsons in Providence.

William Goddard is regarded as the founder of our postal service,
which was adopted in 1775, when he was appointed Surveyor of the Post-
roads and Comptroller of the Post Office, under Dr. Benjamin Franklin, the
first Postmaster General. He returned to Rhode Island in 1792, was
elected to the Legislature in 1795, and died in Providence Dec., 1817, at the
age of seventy-seven years. He married Abigail,[5] daughter of Brig. Gen.
James,[4] and Mary (Mawney) Angell, (*John*,[3] *James*,[2] *Thomas*[1]). Their son,
William Giles Goddard, born Jan. 2, 1794, died, Feb. 16, 1846, married
Charlotte R., daughter of Thomas P. and Hope (Brown) Ives. (*See No.* 72).

JOHN GREENE, OF WARWICK.

The Greenes are an ancient family of Northamptonshire, England, whose
exact records date from the beginning of the 13th century. John Greene,[4]
the emigrant (*Richard*,[3] *Richard*,[2] *Robert*[1]), a surgeon in Salisbury, b.
1597, at Bowridge Hall, Gillingham, Dorsetshire, married, Nov. 4, 1619,
Joan Tattersall. With his family of four sons and two daughters, he
and his wife came to New England in the Spring of 1635, and were, for a
time, at Boston, and afterwards at Salem. Incurring the displeasure of
the Massachusetts authorities for "speaking contemptuously of Magistrates," he removed in 1637 to Providence, where he became one of the
thirteen original proprietors (the fifth named in the Initial Deed), and one
of the twelve members of the First Baptist Church. His Home Lot was
partly bounded, on the north, by the present Star street.

In Nov. 1642, he bought of Miantonomi, the Indian Chief, a tract of
land (Spring Green Farm), which remained in the family until 1782, when
it was purchased by John Brown, the merchant, and is now occupied by
the heirs of his daughter Abby, who married John Francis. The house,
erected on this land by his son, *John Greene, Jr.*, afterwards Deputy-
Governor, is still standing in good preservation.

In 1643, John Greene, Sr., with ten others, bought land of the Indians
(Shawomet), to which they gave the name of Warwick. In behalf of the
colonists he visited England in 1644, accompanied by Samuel Gorton and
Randall Holden. He was a leading citizen of Warwick, and influential in
the affairs of the Colony of Rhode Island. The seal which he used was
engraved with the arms of the Northamptonshire Greenes.*

He married, second, widow Alice Daniels, and, third, Philippa ——, who
survived him thirty years. There was no issue by either of these mar-
riages. Five of his children became heads of families, and the descendants
of his forty grandchildren are numerous in the line of both sons and
daughters. *James Greene*, fourth son of John, Sr., b. 1626, married
Deliverance, daughter of Robert and Isabel Potter. Their son James, b.
June 1, 1658, married, Jan. 29, 1689, Mary, daughter of Capt. John and
Margaret Fones. The latter were the parents of Rev. Elisha Greene, born
Aug. 5, 1698, who married Martha Brown, daughter of Elder James. (*See
No.* 4)

THOMAS AND WILLIAM HARRIS.

It is conjectured, in the absence of positive proof, that Thomas and William Harris, brothers, were born in Haverford West, Pembrokeshire, South
Wales. They sailed, in company with Roger Williams, in the ship *Lyon*,
from Bristol, England, Dec. 1, 1630, and landed at Nantasket, Feb. 5, 1631.
Thomas Harris signed the compacts of 1637 and 1640, was admitted Freeman in 1655, and served frequently as Commissioner, Juryman, Deputy,

* For Coat of Arms, see America Heraldica.

and as member of the Town Council. In his capacity of surveyor he laid
out lands, and was a member of the committee appointed, in 1665, to run
the seven mile line. It would seem that he had the courage of his convictions, for, on a visit to Boston in 1658, when he publicly denounced the
" pride and oppression " of the people, and warned them of that " dread-
ful, terrible day of the Lord God which was coming upon them," he was
arrested, imprisoned, and twice punished with stripes. (*See Bishop's "New
England Judged."*)

His Home lot, on the Towne street, adjoining that of Joshua Winsor on the
south, became, in 1691, the property of Thomas Field, who married *Martha Harris,*[2] youngest daughter of Thomas. He married Elizabeth — ,
and died June 7, 1686, leaving a son *Thomas,*[2] and two daughters. *Mary*[2] and
Martha,[2] *Thomas Harris,*[2] married Elnathan, daughter of Richard and
Mary (Clark) Tew, and had a son William, born May 11, 1673, who married Abigail——. Their daughter, Dorcas Harris, born May 16, 1704, married Daniel Smith. The latter were the parents of Sarah Smith, wife of
John Brown, merchant. (*See Nos. 9, 22 and 29.*)

WILLIAM HARRIS, born in 1610, was one of the five companions of
Roger Williams in the canoe, when they left Seekonk to found the new
settlement of Providence. In 1638 he received a grant of land from Roger
Williams (the seventh named in the Initial Deed), was one of the twelve
original members of the First Baptist Church in 1639, and signed the
agreement of 1640. His Home Lot, on the Towne Street, midway between what are now Bowen and Cushing streets became the property of
Daniel Brown, who sold it, in 1705, to Daniel Williams. Serious disagree-
ment soon arose between William Harris and Roger Williams in regard
to the Pawtuxet Purchase and the treatment of the Quakers, whose cause
Harris espoused. The controversy in regard to the Pawtuxet Purchase,
which was marked by the most bitter invective on both sides, extended
over a period of many years, and was finally settled after the death of
Harris, in accordance with the views to which he had so tenaciously clung.

He possessed strong intellectual ability, a powerful will, and extensive
and accurate knowledge of the law. As agent of the Pawtuxet proprietors he visited England three times, in 1663, 1675 and 1679. In December
of the latter year, he again embarked for England, in the same interests, on
the ship *Unity,* Capt. Condy. A month later, the vessel was captured by
an Algerine corsair, and he, with others, was sold into bondage in Algiers.
After more than a year's slavery he was ransomed by the payment of
£1,200, to which sum Connecticut, in whose service he had engaged, contributed nearly £300. On his release he traveled through Spain and
France to London, arriving in March, 1681. Worn out by the hardships he
had experienced, he died three days afterward, at the house of his friend,
John Stokes, in Wentworth street, near Spitalfields, London. His widow,
Susannah, survived him but a short time.

Of their five children, *Andrew,* the eldest, born in 1635, married, Dec. 8,
1670, Mary, daughter of Richard and Mary (Clarke) Tew. Their eldest
child, Mary, became the wife of Elder James Brown. *Toleration Harris,*
youngest child of William and Susannah, married Sarah Foster, and had a
daughter, Mary, who married her cousin Obadiah Brown son of Elder
James. (*See Nos. 4 and 12*).

OBADIAH HOLMES.

Obadiah Holmes was born in Preston, Lancashire, Eng., in 1607, of parents who, to use his own words, " were faithful in their generation and of
good report among men, and brought up their children tenderly and honor-
ably." Three of their sons were educated at the University of Oxford. It
is known that he had a brother Robert, and sisters who lived in the parish
of Manchester. He married Katharine ——, about 1636, and soon after

emigrated to New England. He was in Salem, Mass., in 1639, where he had two acres granted, being one of the "glassmen," or manufacturers of glass. His daughter *Martha*, and sons, *Obadiah* and *Samuel*, were baptized in Salem between 1640 and 1644. He removed to Rehoboth, Mass., in 1646, and from thence, about 1650, went to Newport, R. I. This last removal was in consequence of a change in his religious views, he having left the Congregational Church and joined the Baptists. With eight others, after many conflicts, he separated from the church of the Rev. Samuel Newman, in Rehoboth. They were all re-baptized and formed a new organization, of which Mr. Holmes was chosen pastor. In Rhode Island he purchased and settled upon a tract of land formerly belonging to the Hutchinsons, in the eastern part of the township of Newport, now Middletown.

The farm consisted originally of four hundred acres, and included the third beach. It is not now in possession of his descendants, having been sold in recent years, and in a neglected and unimproved state is rented to tenants, who occupy the plain farm house which stands upon the site of the building he erected, and upon the original cellar walls. A portion of the old mansion was removed to one side, where it is in use as a carriage house. The mile long ditch built by Obadiah Holmes to drain the land, can still be plainly traced. This farm reached its highest state of cultivation in the time of John Holmes,[3] grandson of Obadiah, and son of Jonathan. He was the last male of the Holmes family on the Island, and died at an advanced age in Newport. His sister, Martha Holmes,[3] was m. May 3, 1692, to Philip Tillinghast[2] (Pardon[1]). Their daughter, Anne Tillinghast,[3] became the wife of her first cousin, Nicholas Power,[3] son of Nicholas[2] and Mercy (Tillinghast) Power. The latter were the parents of Elizabeth Power,[4] wife of Joseph Brown. (*See No.* 21).

In 1651 occurred the event which has given immortality to the name of Obadiah Holmes, as the first martyr to religious liberty in the Colony.* In July of that year, he, in company with John Crandall and John Clarke, arrived in Lynn, Mass., on a visit to William Witter, an aged member of the church in Newport. The following Sunday, as Mr. Clarke was preaching to a small assembly in the house, he was arrested with his companions, and the next day all were sent to prison in Boston. Mr. Clarke was tried for the crime of preaching the gospel and administering the sacrament while under sentence of excommunication, of disclaiming against the sprinkling of infants, and similar charges. July 31, sentence was passed. Mr. Holmes was fined £30, Mr. Clarke, £20, and Mr. Crandall £5. In default of the fine they were to be publicly whipped. Elder Clarke's fine was paid by his friends, and Elder Crandall was released on bail, but Elder Holmes preferred to submit to punishment, rather than to acknowledge that he was in the wrong. He was kept in prison until September, when he received the infliction of thirty stripes. The sentence was executed with such severity that those who, in after years, saw the scars upon his back, (which he was wont to call the marks of the Lord Jesus) expressed a wonder that he should survive. In a manuscript of Gov. Joseph Jenckes it is recorded "that in many days, if not some weeks, he could take no rest but as he lay upon his knees and elbows." He was advised to make his escape by night, and says : "I departed, and the next day after, while I was on my journey, the constables came to search at the house where I lodged, so I escaped their hands, and was by the good hand of my Heavenly Father brought home again to my wife and eight children. The brethren of our town and Providence having taken pains to meet me four miles in the woods, where we rejoiced together in the Lord."

In 1652 he was chosen Pastor of the First Baptist church in Newport, succeeding the Rev. John Clarke in the ministry, and so continued till his death, which occurred on the 15th of Oct., 1682, in the 76th year of his age. He was buried in his own field on the Middletown farm, and a small

* See Backus' and Benedict's Histories of the Baptist denomination.

stone erected to his memory. This inclosure, which was used by several,
generations as a burial place, is still intact. His wife did not long survive
him and was buried by his side, where a stone, with the inscription of her
name, but not the date of her death, marks the spot. Her character has
been handed down by tradition as one of the most amiable of women, and
one who had secured, in an eminent degree, the affection of her husband,
as appears by his address to her, still extant in manuscript. Many of his
writings have been preserved, among which are the thirty-five articles of
his religious belief, and various addresses to his wife, his children, the
church and the world. Obadiah Holmes was admitted Freeman in 1656,
was Commissioner from 1656-'58, and was frequently a member of the
General Assembly.

Of his eight children, four sons and four daughters, six became heads
of families, and his grand-children numbered forty. His eldest son,
Obadiah, removed to Cohansey, N. J., where he was for twelve years a
Judge of the Court in Salem county. The Holmes Posterity multiplied so
rapidly, that their number was estimated, in 1790, at not less than five
thousand. His name was held in such reverence that there were few families among his descendants in which an Obadiah was wanting, and in Rhode
Island, at the present time, most of the possessors of that name trace their
lineage to this one ancestor. His surname was originally *Hullme*, and his
will, dated April 9, 1681, now in possession of Henry Bull, Esq., of Newport, bears that signature.

In the reading-room of the Long Island Historical Society, Brooklyn,
stands a pendulum clock in good running order, with this inscription: "This
Clock was Presented by John H. Baker, Esq, of Brooklyn, in May, 1869, to
the Long Island Historical Society. The Clock has been running for over
200 years. It was brought to this country from London in 1639, by the Rev.
Obadiah Holmes, at whose death it passed to his oldest (living) son, Jonathan, then to Jonathan's son, Joseph, who left it to his son, John Holmes,
who was the great-grandfather of the donor."

Mary Holmes, eldest child of Obadiah and Katharine, became the wife of
John Brown,[2] (*See No. 2.*) (For a more extended account of Obadiah
Holmes, consult Benedict's History of the Baptists.)

THOMAS OLNEY.

Thomas Olney, born in 1600, was a native of St. Albans, Hertford Co.,
Eng. He married Mary Small, born in 1605. With his wife and two children he came in the ship *Planter* to New England in 1635, and settled in
Salem, where he was admitted Freeman in 1637, and received a grant of
land. Being warned to depart from Massachusetts in 1638, he followed
Roger Williams to Providence, where he became one of the thirteen original proprietors, and one of the founders of the First Baptist Church. He
signed the agreement of 1640, was frequently Assistant, Commissioner,
Deputy, member of the Town Council, and, in 1669, was elected Town Treasurer. His Home Lot on the Towne Streete adjoined that of Thomas Angell
on the north, and was nearly midway between the present Meeting and
Angell streets. He was by trade a shoemaker, and also a surveyor. His
death occurred in 1682, as his will was proved Oct. 17th of that year.

Of his seven children, *Thomas*,[2] *Epenetus*,[2] *Mary*,[2] and *Lydia*[2] became
heads of families, and his descendants, both in the male and female line,
are numerous.

Thomas Olney,[2] the eldest son, was ordained Pastor of the First Baptist
church in 1668. *Epenetus Olney*,[2] a tavernkeeper in Providence, married
March 9, 1666, Mary Whipple,[2] daughter of John[1] and Sarah. Their son,
Captain James Olney,[2] married Hallelujah Brown,[3] a grand-daughter of
Chad. Another son, Epenetus Olney,[3] married Mary Williams,[3] grand-
daughter of Roger. *Lydia Olney*,[2] youngest child of Thomas[1] and Mary,
married Joseph Williams[2] son of Roger. (*See Nos. 12, 16, 23, 35, 36, 105.*)

NICHOLAS POWER.

Nicholas Power was, by tradition, from Ireland, or of Irish descent. He was in Providence as early as 1646, when he signed the agreement, and received a grant of land. His Home Lot was directly south of the present Power street. He subsequently acquired by purchase the home lots adjoining his own, both on the north and south. He was constable in 1649, admitted Freeman in 1655, was juryman the same year, and Surveyor of Highways in 1656. He died Aug. 25, 1657, intestate, and ten years later, "the children coming near the age of possessing," the Town Council made his will, and disposed of his estate. To his widow Jane, was granted the dwelling house, home lot, and other lands, during her life. He left two children, *Nicholas,*[2] and *Hope.*[2] *Nicholas*[2] married, Feb. 3, 1672, Rebecca, daughter of Zachariah and Joanna (Arnold) Rhodes. He was accidentally shot at the Great Swamp Fight in Narrangansett, Dec. 19, 1675, leaving two children, Hope,[3] who died young, and Nicholas,[3] who married, second, Mercy, daughter of Pardon and Lydia (Taber) Tillinghast. Their daughter, Hope Power,[4] born Jan. 4, 1701, became the wife of James Brown, son of Elder James. Another daughter, Sarah Power,[4] married William Burrough. A son, Nicholas Power,[4] married Anne Tillinghast, and had a daughter, Elizabeth[5] who married her cousin, Joseph Brown. (*See Nos.* 8, 21, 134.)

ZACHARIAH RHODES.

Zachariah Rhodes was born in 1603, in the southern part of England. He was a settler in Rehoboth, Mass., where his estate was rated in 1643 at £50. July 3, 1644, he, with twenty-nine others, signed the Seekonk Compact. He afterwards removed to Pawtuxet, R. I., where he became a large landholder. His name occurs frequently in the public records as Freeman, Commissioner, Constable, Juryman, Deputy, and as a member of various committees. He was Town Treasurer in 1665, and was also in the Town Council. He married Joanna, daughter of William and Christian (Peake) Arnold, and had eight children. Of these, four sons and two daughters married, and left numerous descendants. His death occurred in the Spring of 1666, when he was drowned "off Pawtuxet shoare." His wife survived him many years, and died after 1692.

Malachi Rhodes, second son of Zachariah, married Mary Carder, and had a daughter, Mary, who became the wife of Richard Brown,[2] son of Henry[1]. Their son, William Brown,[3] b. June 3, 1705, married Susannah Dexter, and had a daughter, Freelove,[4] who was married to James Brown, son of Dep.-Gov. Elisha. (*See No.* 80.)

Rebekah Rhodes, third daughter of Zachariah, was early left a widow by the death of her husband, Nicholas Power[2]. She married, second, Daniel Williams,[2] son of Roger, and had seven children. Of these, a son, Roger,[3] born May, 1680, had a daughter, Rebekah Williams,[4] who married David Thayer. The latter were the parents of Williams Thayer,[5] who married Sarah Adams, and had a daughter, Harriott,[6] who became the wife of the Hon. Patrick Brown, of Nassau, New Providence. By the marriage of their daughter, Sophia Augusta, to John Carter Brown, a descendant in the sixth generation of Rebekah Rhodes and her first husband, Nicholas Power,[2] the two lines of the posterity of Rebekah Rhodes were united. (*See No.* 71.)

John Rhodes, fourth son of Zachariah, born in 1658, married Waite,[3] daughter of Resolved and Mercy (Williams[2]) Waterman, and had a son, William Rhodes,[4] born July 14, 1695, who married Dec. 18, 1721, Mary, dau. of Nehemiah and Rachel (Mann) Sheldon. Their eldest child, Waitstill Rhodes,[5] born Feb. 8, 1722, married Jeremiah Brown, son of Elder James, and, second, George Corlis. (*See Nos.* 13 *and* 74.)

RICHARD SCOTT.

Richard Scott, born in 1607, is supposed to have descended from the Scotts of Kent Co., England. This family trace their origin to William Baliol le Scot, a younger brother of John Baliol, King of Scotland. To avoid the persecution of Edward I., he dropped the surname Baliol, and assumed the name of William Scott. The old Norman Church at Brad-bourne, Kent, contains many monuments of the Scotts of Scott's Hall. (See Hasted's History of Kent.) The immediate ancestors of Richard were seated in the parish of Glemsford, Suffolk Co., about the middle of the 16th century. It has been stated that he was the eldest son and heir of Richard and Margaret (Haney) Scott, and grandson of Edward Scott. He came to New England in the ship *Griffin* in 1634, in company with William Hutchinson and his wife, the famous Anne Hutchinson, and her sister, Katharine Marbury, whom he afterwards married. The Marburys were an ancient family in Lincolnshire. Katharine, born in 1617, was daughter of Rev. Francis and Bridget (Dryden) Marbury. Her father was Preacher and Parson of St. Martin's in the Vintry, London. Her mother was sister of Sir Erasmus Dryden, Bart., grandfather of the poet Dryden.

Richard Scott first settled in Ipswich, Mass., but soon removed to Providence, where he signed the compacts of 1637 and 1640, and was admitted Freeman in 1655. In 1650 he was taxed £3, 6s., 8d.* His Home Lot on the Towne Streete adjoined that of William Field, on the north. The present George Street was laid out through a portion of this land. At a later period he bought the home lots of Widow Reeve and Joshua Vern, now separated by Church Street. His residence was at this locality, as was also that of William and Mary Dyer. It is said that from her home at this place, Mary Dyer went forth, in 1660, to her martyrdom on Boston Common.† He owned a large estate in Smithfield, R. I., a portion of which remained in possession of his heirs until about 1825, when Jeremiah Scott sold it to the Lonsdale Company. The manufacturing village of Lonsdale is built upon this land. To his daughter *Mary*, and her husband Christopher Holder, he gave Patience Island, in Narragansett Bay.

Richard Scott‡ and his wife were among the first to join the Society of Friends in New England. Persecution immediately arose, and, in 1658, Katharine Scott, while on a visit to her imprisoned brethren in Boston, was herself arrested, and thrown into confinement, for protesting against the unjust course of the authorities. These were her words : " That it was evident they were going to act the works of darkness, or else they would have brought them forth publicly, and have declared their offences that all may hear and fear." For this utterance, by order of the court, she received " ten cruel stripes with a three-fold corded knotted whip." The immediate occasion of this expression of her views, was the cutting off, in Boston, of the right ear of her future son-in-law, Christopher Holder, for the crime of being a Quaker. The following year, her daughter *Patience*, eleven years of age, having gone to Boston as a witness against the persecutions of the Quakers, was sent to prison. Shortly after, her elder daughter *Mary*, when on a visit to Christopher Holder, also in prison, was arrested and kept in confinement for a month. The testimony in regard to Katharine Scott is thus recorded : " A mother of many children, one that had lived with her husband, of an unblamable conversation, and a grave, sober, ancient woman, and of good breeding as to the outward, as men account." (*See Bishop's New England Judged.*) She returned to England on a visit in 1660, and died May 2, 1687, in Newport, R. I., at the age of 70 years.

* The heaviest tax was £5, paid by Benedict Arnold, who was afterwards Governor.
† " She was put to death at the town of Boston with the like cruel hand as the Martyrs were in Queen Mary's time, upon the 31 day of the 3d mo. 1660." (See The Friends' records of Portsmouth, R. I.)
‡ According to Gov. Hopkins, Richard Scott was the first Quaker, resident in Providence.

Richard Scott died either in 1679 or 1680. He was a man of influence in the colony and a large land owner. Of their six children, one son and three daughters married, and had numerous descendants. John Scott,[2] the eldest child, married Rebecca, who may have been daughter of Sylvanus, and grand daughter of Peregrine White, who was born on board the *Mayflower*. Catharine Scott[4] (*Sylvanus*,[3] *John*,[2] *Richard*[1]), m. Capt. Nathaniel Jenckes, son of Gov. Joseph and Martha (Brown) Jenckes. (See No. 6.) Rhoda Jenckes (*Joanna*,[4] *Sylvanus*,[3] *John*,[2] *Richard Scott*[1]), became the wife of the first Nicholas Brown. (*See No.* 20.) See N. E. Historical and Genealogical Register 1868 and '69.

JOHN SHELDON.

John Sheldon, of Providence, born in 1630, married, 1660, Joan Vincent. The Christian name of her father is unknown. Her mother was Fridgswith Carpenter, of Amesbury, Wiltshire, Eng., sister of William Carpenter, an early settler in Providence and Pawtuxet. It is probable that Joan Vincent and her brother William, were sent over to the care of their uncle in America, the mother remaining in England. Of the five children of John and Joan (Vincent) Sheldon, *Nehemiah*, the youngest, born in 1672, married Rachel, born April 15, 1679, daughter of Thomas and Mary (Wheaton) Mann. It is assumed that Mary Sheldon, wife of William Rhodes, was daughter of *Nehemiah* (*See No.* 13). Thomas Mann, of Rehoboth, Mass., was a participant in the desperate conflict known as "Pierce's Fight," March 26, 1676, in which he was severely wounded. Mary, his second wife, was daughter of Robert and Alice (Bowen) Wheaton.

JOHN SMITH, THE MILLER.

The birthplace and parentage of John Smith are unknown. He was born in 1595, and married, probably in England, Alice ——, whose family name has not been preserved. He was an early settler in Dorchester, Mass., where, Sept. 3, 1635, "for divers dangerous opinions which he holdeth and hath divulged," sentence of banishment was passed upon him. In the early summer of 1636 he, in company with Roger Williams and four others, left Seekonk, where they had commenced to build and to plant, and, embarking in a canoe, sought a new site on the shore of the Moshassuck River. They selected a spot a little below and to the westward of the present St. John's Church, and there determined to form a new settlement, which Roger Williams, in grateful commemoration of their escape from the land of persecution, named Providence. Many years after, Nov. 16, 1677, it was declared by Roger Williams, "I consented to John Smith, Miller, at Dorchester (banished also) to go with me. The Home Lot assigned him adjoined that of Widow Reeve on the north, near the present site of St. John's Church. The earliest mill grant in Rhode Island was made March 1, 1646, to John Smith, when it was agreed at a monthly court meeting "that he should have the valley where his house stands, in case he set up a mill, as also excepting sufficient highways." He was to pay the cost of the wooden stampers that had been imported from England by the colonists, amounting to about £100. The offer was accepted, and the mill built at the lower falls of the Moshassuck, thus fixing the business centre of the town at that locality, where it long remained. The town agreed to permit no other grist mill to be built. In 1647, he had laid out to him "ten acres where mill now standeth, six acres of meadow land and six acres at Wainscote." Part of this land was granted him as purchaser, and part for building the mill.

The precise time of his death is not known. In 1649 the mill grant, on certain conditions, was confirmed to Alice Smith, widow, and John Smith, her son, administrators on estate of John Smith, Miller, late deceased. The land grant is mentioned as 150 acres. Sept. 2, 1650, widow Smith was taxed £2 10s. Nothing further is known of her history. They had two children,

John Smith,[2] and *Elizabeth,*[2] who married Shadrack Manton, son of Edward.

John Smith[2] continued the mill, was Ensign, Juryman and Deputy. From 1672-'76 he filled the office of Town Clerk. In the latter year, his house, opposite the mill on the west side of the Moshassuck, was burnt by the Indians in King Philip's war. The town records, partially burned, were saved from total destruction by being thrown into the mill pond, from which they were subsequently rescued. He married Sarah Whipple, daughter of the first John, and had seven sons and three daughters. (*See Nos.* 3, 11.) His death occurred in 1682, and two of his young sons died not long after.* Five sons and the daughters married, and the grandchildren numbered 65.

John Smith,[3] Miller, was the last of that title. His son, John Smith,[4] the Fuller, died before him, May 24, 1719, leaving an infant child, Martha, who became the wife of Elisha Brown, youngest son of Elder James. (*See No.* 14.) John Smith[3] died April 20, 1737. His mother, Sarah Whipple, born in 1642, was probably married about 1660, and, as he was her eldest child, it is reasonable to suppose that his age exceeded seventy-five years. Of his seven children, five were living at the time of his death. In his will, made Feb. 10, 1724 (codicil Aug. 2, 1734), he entrusted to the care of his wife Hannah, the "two small children, Hannah and Prince." His older children had long since been married. His grand daughter, Martha Smith, eighteen years of age, was married a month previous to his death. It is, therefore, believed that Hannah was a second wife, but of this no proof is known to exist, and no conjecture has been made as to the name of the first wife. Hannah survived her husband twenty years, and in her will, proved Sept. 29, 1757, gave her estate "to son Prince and daughter Hannah," making no mention of the older children.

Benjamin Smith,[3] son of *John,*[2] born about 1672, married Mercy Angell,[3] (*John,*[2] *Thomas*[1]), and settled on a farm in the southwestern part of Smithfield. Of their twelve children, three only are here mentioned. Daniel,[4] born June 27, 1697, married Dorcas Harris. On the Smith map, Daniel Smith is put down as the owner of Lot No. 2 on Charles Street, 40 ft. x 79, adjoining on the south the "D. Hill House," from which it was separated by a gangway, twenty feet wide. It is possible that his residence may have been here. *Mary Smith,*[4] born Aug. 3, 1704, married Daniel Whipple, and had a daughter Mercy, who married Israel Sayles. Abigail,[4] born June 10, 1714, married Jonathan Arnold. (*See Nos.* 22, 16, *and* 27.)

The grist mill property descended from father to eldest son for four generations. John Smith,[3] Miller, ran the mill from 1682-1731, a period of nearly fifty years. On Aug. 6th of the latter year, he deeded to his son Philip Smith,[4] Miller, with other property, his corn mill, fulling mill, etc. Philip continued the occupation of his father but a short time, as he died in 1734, leaving the mill property to his son Charles,[5] who carried on the business for twenty years longer, until his death in 1754. He left no legitimate child, and his inheritance was afterwards recovered by his first cousin, Martha (Smith) Brown, wife of Elisha Brown, at a Superior Court held at Providence, March, 1754. (*See No.* 14.) This estate comprised the greater part of what was then known as Charlestown, formerly the Home Seat of John Smith, Miller.

Martha (Smith) Brown died Sept. 1, 1760, leaving six sons, all minors. In her will, dated July 1, 1760, occur the following items: "*Imprimis,* I Give and devise unto my said Husband, Mr. Elisha Brown, the Issues and Proffits of one full half of all my Mills, Stream and Dam thereunto belonging, During the full Term of his Natural Life. Tho' perhaps the Law would cast the whole upon him by my death." After giving to her younger sons small house lots designated by numbers, which can still be identified by means of the Smith Map, she thus concludes: "I Give and

---

*Elisha Smith, b. April 14, 1686, who m. Experience Mowry, was the sixth son. (See No. 15.)

Devise unto my Son John Brown, his heirs and assigns forever, all the Residuum of said Estate Devolved on me by the Death of my Said Cousin Charles Smith, that remained unsold, and not therein disposed of, to be by him entered upon as soon as he attains the full age of Twenty-one years, at which age my Will is that all my other Sons should enter on their respective Rights hereby given them, and not before."

John Brown, eldest son of Martha, died in 1775, leaving an only child Martha, who inherited his property. The mill was kept in operation until about 1827, when, on account of the construction of the Blackstone Canal, the part of the building containing the grinding machinery was taken down. The town of Providence had several times claimed an interest in this estate, on the ground that the original grant was conditioned upon a continuance of the grist mill by the proprietors, for the benefit of the inhabitants of the town. This claim, the owner, Mrs. Martha B. Howell, disputed. In 1829, suit was brought against her by the town for the recovery of the property. Deep interest and much anxiety was awakened on the part of owners, by purchase, of parts of the Smith property upon Smith's Hill and vicinity, who feared that their titles might become invalid. But, after trial by eminent counsel, the court decided that the town had no claim to the property. The present owner of the mill site is Mrs. Martha H. Burrough, daughter of Waity (Howell) Walker, and grand-daughter of Martha (Brown) Howell. (*See No.* 134.)

Beside John Smith, Miller, there were four other early settlers, who bore the same name, viz.: *John Smith, Mason ; John Smith, of Newport ; John Smith, of Prudence Island ; John Smith, of Warwick.* The Smith Family was still further represented by *Christopher Smith, Edward Smith,* and *Richard Smith. (See Nos.* 52, 29, 33, 72.)

RICHARD TEW.

Richard Tew, son and heir of Henry, of Maidford, Northampton Co., Eng., emigrated to New England in 1640, with his wife, Mary Clarke, daughter of William, and settled at Newport, now Middletown. He was admitted Freeman in 1655, and served frequently as Commissioner, Assistant, Deputy and as a member of various committees. He became a Quaker, and according to tradition, died about 1673, in London, whither he had gone to look after some property. Of their four children, two only are here mentioned, *Elnathan*[2] and *Mary*[2]. *Elnathan*,[2] born Oct. 15, 1644, married Thomas Harris, son of the first Thomas, and had a son, William Harris,[3] born May 11, 1673, who married Abigail ———. Their daughter, Dorcas Harris,[4] became the wife of Daniel Smith. The latter were the parents of Sarah Smith,[5] wife of John Brown, merchant. *Mary Tew*,[2] born Aug. 12, 1647, married Andrew Harris, son of the first William, and had a daughter Mary, wife of Elder James Brown. (*See Nos.* 22 and 8.)

JOHN THURBER.

In 1671, John Thurber and his wife Priscilla, with six of their eight children, emigrated to New England from the parish of Stanton, Lincolnshire, Eng., and settled in Rehoboth, Mass., at a place called New Meadow Neck, now a part of the town of Barrington, R. I. The names of the children who accompanied their parents were *Abigail, John, Thomas, Edward, Charity and Elizabeth.* The next year, *James* and *Mary,* who had remained in England, joined the family.

James Thurber, b. Aug. 26, 1660, d. March 26. 1736, m. Elizabeth Bliss. Their son Samuel,[3] b. in Rehoboth, Aug. 27, 1700, d. in Providence, Dec. 20, 1785, m. Rachel Wheeler. The latter were the parents of Samuel,[4] b. in Rehoboth, Oct. 27, 1724, d. July 18, 1807, who m. Hopestill ———, and had a son Samuel,[5] b. Feb. 15, 1757, m. Mehetable, dau. of Christopher and Priscilla Dexter, b. Feb. 25, 1759, d. Dec. 9, 1829. She was sister of

Amey Dexter, wife of Capt. Isaac Brown. (*See No.* 33.) Samuel, son of Samuel and Mehetable, b. Jan. 21, 1785, d. July 2, 1821, m. Ann Comstock, grand-daughter of Elder James Brown. (*See No.* 11.)

PARDON TILLINGHAST.

Pardon Tillinghast, born in 1622, was a native of Seven Cliffs, Sussex Co., Eng. According to tradition, he had been a soldier in Cromwell's army. The first record of him in Providence dates from Jan. 19, 1646, when he was received as a quarter shares man, and granted 25 acres of land. He was admitted Freeman in 1658, was Deputy from 1672-1700, Overseer of the Poor in 1687, and a member of the Town Council from 1688-1707, during which period he served almost continually. The most prominent merchant of his time, he was also Pastor of the First Baptist church for many years, declining all remuneration for his services. About 1700, he erected, at his own expense, a house of worship located near the northwest corner of North Main and Smith streets, which, in 1711, he deeded to the church with the lot on which it stood. Previous to this time, the people had assembled in private houses or in the open air.

The Home Lot of Thomas Painter, on Constitution Hill, had become the property of the town, and was assigned to Pardon Tillinghast. He afterwards purchased the Home Lot originally laid out to Hugh Bewit, north of the present Transit street, where he built his residence. In his will, dated Dec. 15, 1715, he bequeathed to his youngest son Joseph, "my present dwelling house and house lot, after his mother's decease."

He was twice married and had twelve children, eleven of whom married into well known Rhode Island families and left numerous descendants. His grand-children numbered 79. The name of his first wife was —— Butterworth. Of their three children, *Sarah, John* and *Mary,* the eldest, *Sarah,* born in 1654, died young. He married second, April 16, 1664, Lydia, daughter of Philip and Lydia (Masters) Tabor, and grand-daughter of John and Jane Masters, of Cambridge, Mass. Philip Tabor, born in England in 1605, settled in Watertown, Mass., as early as 1634. After living in Yarmouth, Martha's Vineyard and New London, he became a resident of Portsmouth, R. I., where he was admitted Freeman in 1656, and served as commissioner from 1660-'63. Later, he removed, first, to Newport, and then to Providence, where his testimony and that of his second wife, Jane Tabor, in regard to a case of drowning, was recorded June 10, 1669. He finally settled in Tiverton, where he died after 1672.

Pardon and Lydia Tillinghast had nine children: (1) *Lydia.* (2) *Philip,* b. Feb. 16, 1668, married —— Keech, and had five children, the youngest of whom, Mercy, born in 1706, became the wife of Col. Peter Mawney.* Their daughter, Mary Mawney, married Gen. James Angell, and was the mother of Abigail (Angell) Goddard. (*See No.* 72.) (3) *Philip,* b. Oct., 1669, m. Martha, daughter of Jonathan and Sarah (Borden) Holmes, and grand-daughter of Rev. Obadiah Holmes. Of their fifteen children, Anne, the twelfth, born April 13, 1713, married her cousin, Nicholas Power, third son of Nicholas and Mercy (Tillinghast) Power. Their daughter, Elizabeth Power, married her cousin, James Brown, son of James and Hope (Power) Brown. (*See No.* 8.) (4) *Benjamin.* (5) *Abigail.* (6) *Joseph.* (7) *Mercy,* b. 1680, married Nicholas Power, son of Nicholas and Rebecca (Rhodes) Power. Of their eight children, Hope, b. Jan. 4, 1701, was the eldest. Allusion has been made to her as the wife of James Brown. Sarah Power, the fifth child, married William Burrough. (*See No.* 134.) (8) *Hannah* married John Hale. (9) *Elizabeth* married her cousin, Philip Tabor, son of Thomas.

Pardon Tillinghast died Jan. 29, 1718, at the age of 96, and was buried on his Home Lot. This burial ground, west of Benefit street, and a little

* Corruption of Le Moine.

north of Transit, was used by the family for several generations, and is the only one of its kind that has been preserved in its original condition.

RICHARD WATERMAN.

Richard Waterman, born about 1590, emigrated from England in 1629, and settled in Salem, Mass. In 1638 he removed to Providence, where he received a grant of land, and was the eleventh named in the Initial Deed. He was one of the original members of the First Baptist Church, and one of the signers to the agreement of 1640. In 1643, he and ten others purchased land in Warwick of Miantonomi, and suffered, in common with his associates, many indignities from the interference of Massachusetts. He was the owner of two adjoining Home Lots on the Towne Streete—one by grant, and the other by purchase in 1651, from Hugh Bewit, of the Ezekiel Holliman Home Lot. The western front of his own lot now forms a portion of the grounds of the First Baptist Church. He was admitted Freeman in 1655, and afterwards served as Commissioner, Juryman and Warden. He died in October, 1673, and was buried on that part of his estate which now forms the southeast corner of Benefit and Waterman streets. A granite monument, erected in 1840 by a descendant in the sixth generation, marks the spot.

The family name of his wife, Bethia, is not known. They had four children : (1) *Mehetable*, married Arthur Fenner. (*See Nos.* 12, 26, 37, 106.) (2) *Wait*, married Henry Brown. (*See Nos.* 2, 30.) (3) *Nathaniel.* (*See No.* 3.) (4) *Resolved*, married in 1659, Mercy Williams, daughter of Roger. Their youngest child, Wait Waterman, born about 1668, married John Rhodes. The latter were the parents of William Rhodes, born July 14, 1695, who married Mary Sheldon. (*See Nos.* 9, 13, 24, 25, 30.)

JOHN WHIPPLE.

John Whipple, born in England about 1617, was in Dorchester as early as 1632, in service to Israel Stoughton. In 1637, he received a grant of land at Dorchester Neck. Some two years later he married Sarah ——, who was born in Dorchester about 1624. In 1658 he sold his homestead and land, and, the following year, removed with his family to Providence, where he was received as a purchaser. In 1667 he was in possession of the Home Lot of John Greene, Sr., south of the present Star street. At an earlier date he purchased the Home Lot of Frances Weeks, where he erected the old " Whipple Tavern," on Constitution Hill, midway between Benefit street and the junction of North Main and Mill streets. As he was by trade a carpenter, it is supposed that he was the builder of this house. His license to keep an ordinary dated from 1674. He took the oath of allegiance in 1666, and served several years as Deputy. He was one of those " who staid and went not away," in King Philip's war, and so had a share in the disposition of Indian captives, whose services were sold for a term of years.

He died May 16, 1685, and his wife survived him but a short time. They were, at first, buried on his own land, but their remains were afterwards removed to the North Burial Ground, where stones, with inscriptions to the memory of " Capt. John Whipple," and " Mrs. Sarah Whipple," mark their resting place. They had eleven children, eight sons and three daughters, who all became heads of families. The grand-children numbered seventy three. The posterity of John Whipple and Chad Browne are united by numerous intermarriages. *Sarah Whipple*, second child of John, born in 1642, married John Smith,* Miller. (*See Nos.* 14, 22.) *Samuel Whipple*, born in 1644, third child of John, married Mary Harris, daughter of the first Thomas. Their grandson, Daniel Whipple, son of Thomas, married his second cousin, Mary Smith, a grand-daughter of Sarah (Whipple) Smith, and daughter of Benjamin Smith. Mercy Whipple, daughter of

Daniel and Mary, married about 1748, Israel Sayles. (*See No.* 16.) *Mary Whipple*, fifth child of John, born in 1648, married Epenetus Olney,[2] son of the first Thomas. Their son Epenetus,[3] married Mary Williams, daughter of Daniel, and grand-daughter of Roger. Paris Olney and Mercy Winsor, great grand-children of Epenetus,[3] married, and were the parents of Mary Ann Olney, who married Clark Sayles,* (*See No.* 16.) *Abigail Whipple*, ninth child of John, married Stephen Dexter, and, second, William Hopkins, son of the first Thomas. Her great grand-daughter, Sarah Hopkins, a descendant of Martha (Brown) Jenckes, was married in 1761, to Commodore Abraham Whipple. (*See No.* 17.) *Joseph Whipple*, tenth child of John, born in 1662, married Alice Smith, daughter of the first Edward, and grand-daughter of Thomas Angell[1]. Their daughter, Susannah, born April 14, 1693, married Stephen Dexter, a grandson of Sarah (Whipple) Smith. (*See Nos.* 29 *and* 25.)† Some years since a Whipple Genealogy was published in Providence.

ROGER WILLIAMS.

No authentic account has been preserved of the birthplace and parentage of Roger Williams. According to tradition, he was born in Wales, about the beginning of the seventeenth century. In the parish church of Gwinear, Cornwall, Eng., is recorded the baptism of Roger, second son of William Williams, Gent., July 24, 1600. Conclusive evidence connecting this account with the founder of Rhode Island, is wanting. In Elton's Life of Williams, it is stated that he was the son of William Williams, born in 1606, in Conwyl Cayo a small town in Caermarthenshire, Wales. But no proof has been adduced to support this theory, which is founded upon a record in the archives of Oxford University. He was a *protégé* of Sir Edward Coke, who sent him, in 1621, to Sutton's Hospital (afterwards the Charterhouse). He entered Pembroke College, Cambridge, in 1625, and in 1627 took the Degree of Bachelor of Arts. For a short time he was a clergyman of the Church of England, but soon abandoned it, and, with his wife, Mary, emigrated at the close of the year 1630, to New England, arriving in Boston, Feb. 5, 1631. Gov. Winthrop speaks of him as "a young minister, godly and zealous, having precious gifts."

After a brief pastorate in Salem, in which he incurred the hostility of the authorities by his religious opinions, he went to Plymouth, where he preached as assistant pastor two years. Returning to Salem in 1635, he resumed his ministerial labors, and became, after the death of the Rev. Mr. Skelton, the pastor of the church. His teachings not being in harmony with the views of the Massachusetts settlers, he was summoned to Boston for trial, and, on Oct. 9, 1635, sentence was pronounced by the General Court as follows :

"*Whereas*, Mr. Roger Williams, one of the elders of the church of Salem, hath broached and divulged divers new and dangerous opinions against the authority of magistrates; as also writ letters of defamation both of the magistrates and churches here, and that before any conviction, and yet maintaineth the same without any retraction, it is therefore ordered that the said Williams shall depart out of this jurisdiction within six weeks now next ensuing, which, if he neglect to perform, it shall be lawful for the Governor and two of the magistrates to send him to some place out of this jurisdiction, not to return any more without release from the Court."

He received permission to remain until the following Spring, but, in the meantime, as he continued to promulgate his opinions, the Court resolved to send him to England. Anticipating their messenger, he left his home, and "was sorely tossed for one fourteen weeks in a bitter winter season,

---

*These intermarriages are clearly shown in "The Sayles' Pedigree," a chart drawn by Charles F. Wilcox, of Providence. It was not intended for publication.
†Line not traced in No. 25.

not knowing what bed or bread did mean." He purchased of Massasoit lands on the eastern shore of the Seekonk river, and had planted his corn for the season, when, being informed by Gov. Winslow that he was within the bounds of Plymouth Colony, he, with five companions, William Harris, John Smith, the Miller, Joshua Verin, Thomas Angell and Francis Wickes, set out on new explorations. Embarking in a canoe, they landed at Slate Rock to exchange greetings with the Indians, and then pursued their way to the site of the new settlement on the Moshassuck River, which, in grateful remembrance of "God's merciful Providence unto him in his distress," Roger Williams named Providence. "I desired it might be a shelter for persons distressed for conscience," he said. The lands which he acquired by purchase of Canonicus and Miantonomi, Sachems of the Narragansetts, he generously divided equally among twelve of his associates, "Reserving only unto himself," as he afterwards testified, "one Single Share Equal unto any of the Rest of that number." The Memorandum or "Initial Deed" from Roger Williams of these lands to his "loving friends," executed in 1638, was afterwards confirmed by him in 1661. Succeeding settlers were admitted into the fellowship, and by the payment of thirty shillings each, formed a common fund of £30, which Roger Williams received, not as an equivalent for the land, but as a "loving gratuity," it being "far less than what he had expended.

Subsequent events in the life of the Founder of Rhode Island, which are, in a great measure, the history of the Colony, may be traced in the Memoirs of his Life, which have been written by James D. Knowles (Boston, 1833); William Gammell (Boston, 1846); Romeo Elton (London, 1852). See also "As to Roger Williams and his 'Banishment' from the Mass. Colony," by Henry M. Dexter, D. D., 1876; Foot Prints of Roger Williams, by R. A. Guild, Providence, 1886; Oration by the Hon. Thomas Durfee, LL. D., Chief Justice of the Supreme Court of Rhode Island, delivered at the Municipal Celebration of the City of Providence, June 23, 1886.*

The precise date of the death of Roger Williams is not known. It occurred early in the year 1683, and he was buried "with all the solemnity the colony was able to show," in the orchard on his Home Lot, the present site of the Dorr Mansion, on Benefit street. His house was erected near the spring where he landed, on the hill side below the orchard, now Howland street. His wife Mary, whose maiden name is believed to have been Warnard, is supposed to have survived him. They had six children : *Mary* b Aug., 1633, in Plymouth ; *Freeborn*, b. Oct. 1635, in Salem ; *Providence*, b. Sept., 1638, in Providence ; *Mercy*, b. July 5, 1640 ; *Daniel*, b. Feb., 1642 ; *Joseph*, b. Dec. 12, 1643. Of these, the eldest son died unmarried in his forty-eighth year. The others married into the Sayles, Hart, Waterman, Winsor, Rhodes and Olney families, and the grand-children numbered 31. *Mary Williams[2]* married about 1650, John Sayles, and had six children, of whom the second child, John Sayles,[3] born Aug. 17, 1654, married Elizabeth ——. They were the parents of Richard Sayles,[4] who married Mercy Phillips, and had six children, all sons. Israel Sayles,[5] the third son, of Sayles Hill, Smithfield, married about 1748, Mercy Whipple, and had twelve children. Of these, Ahab,[6] married Lillis Steere, and Mary[6] married Esek Brown. (*See Nos.* 16 *and* 69.)

Mercy Williams[2] married about 1659, Resolved Waterman, son of the first Richard. She married second, Jan. 2, 1677, Samuel Winsor,[2] son of the first Joshua. Of the five children by the first marriage, Wait Waterman,[3] the youngest, born about 1668, married John Rhodes. Their daughter, Waitstill Rhodes,[4] married Jeremiah Brown, and second, George Corlis. (*See Nos.* 13, 72, 74.) By the second marriage of Mercy Williams, there were three children, of whom Samuel Winsor,[3] the eldest, born Nov. 18, 1677, married Mercy Harding, and had nine children. Their daughter, Martha Winsor,[4] married Robert Colwell. A younger daughter, Hannah

Winsor,[1] married James Olney. Paris Olney, grandson of Hannah, and also grandson of Martha (Brown) Jenckes, married Mercy Winsor, a descendant of both Mercy and Daniel Williams. Mary Ann Olney,[6] daughter of Paris, married Clark Sayles, son of Ahab, and a great grandson of Martha (Williams) Colwell, through her grand-daughter, Lillis Steere.[*] (See No. 16.)

Joshua Winsor,[3] son of Mercy Williams, born May 25, 1682, married Mary Barker, and second, Deborah Harding. John Winsor,[4] son of the second wife, married Mary Smith,[5] (Solomon,[4] Benjamin,[3] John,[2] John,[1] the Miller), and second, Phebe Dexter, widow of William. Of his twenty children, Ruth,[5] the fifth child, born May 8, 1751, married Ezekiel Brown, son of Col. Chad. (See page 129.) Daniel Williams,[2] married Dec. 7, 1676, Rebecca Power, widow of Nicholas, and had seven children. Mary Williams,[3] the eldest, married Epenetus Olney,[3] (Epenetus,[2] Thomas[1]). Of their nine children, Martha,[4] and Freeborn,[4] were the two youngest. Martha Olney[4] married Stephen Angell,[4] (John,[3] John,[2] Thomas[1]), and had a great grand-daughter, Catharine Angell,[5] wife of Gov. Samuel W. King. (See No. 105.) Freeborn Olney[4] married her second cousin, Joshua Winsor,[4] son of Joshua[3] and Mary (Barker) Winsor. Mercy Winsor,[6] wife of Paris Olney, was their grand-daughter. Roger Williams,[3] (Daniel,[2] Roger[1]), married May 1, 1729, Elizabeth Walling, and had two children, both daughters, the youngest of whom, Rebecca,[4] born April 20, 1735, became the wife of David Thayer. (See No. 71.)

JOSHUA WINSOR.

This surname, said to have been derived from the winding shore of the Thames river at Windsor, Eng., has been abbreviated from Windleshore or Windshore to Winsor. Joshua Winsor was among the first settlers in Providence, where he signed the compacts of 1637 and 1640. His Home Lot, which adjoined that of John Field on the south, became, in 1691, the property of Gideon Crawford, from whom Crawford street obtained its name. Nothing is known of the wife of Joshua Winsor, aside from the record of her death in Feb. 1655. They had five children, one son and four daughters. Samuel,[2] the eldest child, born in 1644, married Jan. 2, 1667, Mercy Waterman, widow of Resolved, and daughter of Roger Williams, and had three children : Samuel,[3] Hannah[3] and Joshua[3]. Of these, Samuel,[3] born Nov. 18, 1677, married Mercy, daughter of Abraham and Deborah Harding, and had a family of seven daughters and two sons. He was ordained Pastor of the First Baptist Church in 1733, and preached until his death in 1758. The following year, his son Samuel,[4] the youngest child, born Nov. 1, 1722, succeeded to the pastorate. (See No. 83). Joseph,[4] the eldest son, born Oct. 4, 1713, removed to Glocester, R. I., where, in 1763, he was ordained pastor of the Baptist church, and so continued until his death in 1802, in the eighty-ninth of his age. He was buried on his farm, on Winsor Hill. He had five sons and six daughters, all of whom married, and left numerous descendants. Judge Samuel Winsor,[5] the youngest son, inherited his father's homestead, and resided there until his death. (See No. 10.)[†] The Winsor Genealogy, a small pamphlet by Olney Winsor, was printed in 1837.

[*]See the chart. "The Sayles' Pedigree."
[†]The line not traced.

CORRECTIONS, OMISSIONS AND ADDITIONAL

INFORMATION.

In the Running Titles, "The Chad Brown Memorial," supply the final (e) in Browne.

PAGE.

26. First paragraph. The present owners are Lewis F. Hubbard, and Sarah E. Hull, of Canterbury, Conn.

28. Frederick Clark Sayles was m. 1861 (not 1851). Omit the birth of the first child, which is an error, copied from the Providence Records.

64. Rice's City is in Kent County, R. I.

64. ELINOR BROWN, dau. of John and Betsey (Daggett) Brown, m. Erastus R. Mowry, and had three children. (1) *Daniel D.*, b. Jan. 5, 1840, m. in Sidney, Australia, Nov. 14, 1863, Mary James, b. in S. Jan. 9, 1843, and has Charles A., b. in S., Feb. 20, 1865, and William G., b. at sea, April 2, 1868. (2) *Charles F.*, b. Sept. 19, 1846, d. ——. (3) *Arthur P.*, b. June 8, 1855, m. May 30, 1877, Alice Eugenia Tray, and has a son, Frederick E., b. April 25, 1878.

65. Frances W. Bird graduated at Brown University in 1831.

66. Moses B. Lockwood graduated at Brown University in 1857.

70. In the fifth line from the top the number attached to *Elisha*, should be 35 (not 24).

72. Substitute Brown University for College of Rhode Island.

79. Thomas P. I. Goddard graduated at Brown University in 1846.

79. Thomas P. Shepard graduated at Brown University in 1836.

87. Supply the initial letter B. in name of Elizabeth Howell (No. 86).

87. The first Andrew Winsor in the closing line of the page, was of the seventh generation.

88. Rev. Andrew Mackie graduated at Brown University in 1845.

90. G. L. Dwight graduated at Brown University in 1828.

101. William W. Dunnell graduated at Brown University in 1873.

101. Read Amos N. Beckwith (not Amos A). The mother of Clara Lippitt was Eliza (Seamans) Lippitt.

101. Daniel Beckwith graduated at Brown University in 1870.

104. Robert H. I. Goddard graduated at Brown University in 1858.

105. Robert I. Gammell graduated at Brown University in 1872.

107. Transpose the sentence at the top of the page, and read thus: He was a student at the Mass. Institute of Technology in the class of 1869, and, for several years afterwards, was connected with the Corliss Steam Engine Company of Providence.

111. Walton, Eaton Co., is in Michigan, not Illinois. (No. 136.)

113. Change the name Augusts to Augustus.

113. Supply the initial B. in Anna and Phebe Yerrinton. (Nos. 145 and 146.)

PAGE.
114. *Henry Irving*, of the ninth generation, should have beeen printed in italics.
126. Anne M. Hopkins is of the ninth generation, not the sixth.
138. In the first line, read St. Croix
144. John W. Bulkley is of the sixteenth generation, not the seventeenth.
144. Martha Brainard was of the fourteenth generation, not the fifteenth; therefore Elizabeth C. (Ledyard) Goddard is of the seventeenth generation, not the eighteenth
148. Read Lloyd's Neck, not Loyd's.
152. The Olney Genealogy, by James H. Olney, Providence, is in course of publication.

Inscription on a well worn gray stone, in Old Trinity Church-yard, north side, Broadway, New York :

In

Memory of

PHILIP NICHOLAS BROWN,

a native of Providence,

in the State of Rhode Island.

Aged 28 years.

(*Remaining lines illegible.*)

INDEX.

INDEX NO. 2.—NAMES OF DESCENDANTS OTHER THAN BROWN.

MISCELLANEOUS.

INDEX No. 4.—LOCALITIES OUTSIDE OF RHODE ISLAND.

INDEX No. 5.—INDEX TO FAMILY NOTES.

www.ingramcontent.com/pod-product-compliance
Lightning Source LLC
Chambersburg PA
CBHW030134030726
47498CB00007B/2699